"A beautifully written evocation of young girls coming-of-age, and plunging into womanhood and war, which gradually intensifies into a gothic unease that would make Daphne du Maurier proud. Excellent—I could not put it down."

—Helen Simonson,
author of *The Summer Before the War*

"Reading Elizabeth Brooks's new novel *The Woman in the Sable Coat* feels like stepping into an alternate version of *I Capture the Castle*, if it were written by Patricia Highsmith and filmed by Alfred Hitchcock. A mesmerizing, psychologically complex story about two women who meet at an impromptu dinner party in the 1930s English countryside—an encounter that sets off a decade of secrets and betrayals—only to discover their dreams of romance might be the greatest self-betrayal of all. From quaint village life and a war-time RAF airbase, to the snowy wilds of Canada and a storm-tossed ocean liner, *The Woman in the Sable Coat* spins a literary tale full of penetrating detail, enigmatic characters, and delicious plot twists. Not since *Atonement* have I read a book so unexpected in its telling, or its power."

—Natalie Jenner,
author of *The Jane Austen Society*

THE
WOMAN
IN THE
SABLE
COAT

THE
WOMAN
IN THE
SABLE
COAT

a novel

Elizabeth
Brooks

TIN HOUSE / PORTLAND, OREGON

Copyright © 2024 Elizabeth Brooks

First US Edition 2024
Printed in the United States of America

Manufacturing by Kingery Printing Company
Interior design by Beth Steidle

Library of Congress Cataloging-in-Publication Data

Names: Brooks, Elizabeth, 1979– author.
Title: The woman in the sable coat : a novel / Elizabeth Brooks.
Description: First US edition. | Portland, Oregon : Tin House, 2024. |
Identifiers: LCCN 2023043086 | ISBN 9781959030355 (paperback) |
ISBN 9781959030508 (ebook)
Subjects: LCGFT: Novels.
Classification: LCC PR6102.R6628 W66 2024 |
DDC 823/.92—dc23/eng/20230922
LC record available at https://lccn.loc.gov/2023043086

Tin House
2617 NW Thurman Street, Portland, OR 97210
www.tinhouse.com

DISTRIBUTED BY W. W. NORTON & COMPANY

1 2 3 4 5 6 7 8 9 0

For Stephen, with love from Mum.

THE
WOMAN
IN THE
SABLE
COAT

Nina

March 14, 1946

THE WIND IS POURING DOWN FROM THE NORTH AND IT tastes of snow. It's too cold to sit and too rough to stroll, so there aren't many passengers braving the open deck. There's only Nina, in her usual chair by the rails, and the large, well-dressed man swaying towards her with a cup and saucer.

Nina has noticed this man before, because he prefers to eat at unoccupied tables—as does she. Yesterday evening he caught her eye across the crowded dining-room and lifted his water glass, as if to say, "Cheers, from one loner to another!" Only it wasn't such a jovial gesture as that sounds, because he did it without smiling. She pretended not to understand and turned to the window, although the view had disappeared by then: there was only the churning darkness of sea and sky, and the restaurant in reflection.

The planks of the deck are slick with sleet and spray, and when the man reaches her, he leans back against the rail and spreads his feet wide

1

for balance. He points to the cup and shouts over the bluster, "You look peaky, ma'am; I brought you some tea." His accent is American.

Of course, it's possible he's simply being kind. The old Nina would have taken his kindness for granted—she'd have thanked him warmly, invited him to sit beside her, made some banal comment about the weather.

He's waiting for a reaction. There's nothing to do but to take the cup and saucer and rest them on her lap. It's obviously foolish to assume she'll be left alone, just because she wears her wedding ring on her right hand and dresses in black. What does the man see, when he looks at her? A widow with so much romantic grief in her soul that she can sit through wind, rain, and snow, hour after hour, day after day, watching the ocean? A widow with so much wealth she can afford to ruin a full-length sable coat in the process?

Nina takes a sip of sweet, tepid tea and says, "Thanks," by way of dismissal. Poor man. If he's only being nice, he deserves better, but how can she know? She's not a mind-reader.

The ship lurches and tea slops over her fingers, into the saucer. The man offers a handkerchief from his pocket, but she waves it away with a polite smile. The smile is a mistake, because it prompts him to say, "Okay! Good!" and drop into the chair beside her.

"Not much of a sailor, huh?"

Nina burrows her chin into her collar, reluctant to make chit-chat. "I don't know about that. It depends."

It's only half a year since she crossed the Atlantic in the opposite direction, thinking she'd seen the last of England. It feels like another lifetime, but it's six months, almost to the day. She and her husband travelled on this very liner—the SS *St. Ursula*—when it still felt like a troop-ship, crammed to the gunwales with demob-happy soldiers and their new European wives. The weather had been glorious throughout the crossing, and the sable coat had stayed at the bottom of her trunk. In the daytime everyone had sprawled and smoked in these very chairs, their eyes lightly closed against the sun. At night they'd danced on deck with a live band, under skies dusty with stars, and she hadn't felt seasick at all—not once.

The hull and funnels of the SS *St. Ursula* are still painted wartime grey, but, other than that, the ship has completed its transformation from troop-carrier to liner. This time around, meals are served on porcelain rather than enamelled tin, and the art deco panels in the lounge have been stripped of their protective leather covers. There's the odd military uniform about, but most of the passengers seem older and more businesslike than they were last August, and the sense of a delirious common purpose is gone. People write letters, or read books, or sip coffees behind newspapers, and their reasons for leaving the New World, and heading for the old, war-torn one, are private.

The American sits squarely and grips his knees. Nina's eyes dart to his hands, which are bare like hers, although it's certainly the weather for gloves. His fingers are plump and pale.

Why is he drawn to her? Is it her stillness? They are both oddly still. When a flurry of snow whirls over the ship, flecking their coats and stinging their faces, neither of them stirs. Most people would shiver and fidget and make a move to go inside.

"Pardon me, ma'am, but I've been watching you pretty closely ever since we set off."

Unease kisses the back of her neck lightly, briefly. She begins to ask, "Why?" but can't. How silly. He doesn't know the first thing about her; he's just some old lech.

"May I ask a question?" He waits for permission, but carries on regardless when it doesn't come. "Why is it you always choose to sit as far as possible from the nearest lifebelt?"

Nina lifts her eyebrows and glances along the railings, where the red-and-white-striped rings are neatly roped, at intervals of several yards.

"How observant! I don't know—maybe I've a subliminal desire to drown immediately, if I fall overboard, as opposed to bobbing about and dying of exposure?" Nina glances at him. "Or maybe it's just that they obscure the view?"

The man frowns. He appears to have missed the second half of her answer, along with her sense of humour.

"Do you mean to say that you wouldn't wish to be saved? In your heart of hearts, you'd rather drown than be pulled out?"

Nina laughs. Still, it's a question. Over the last few days she has often imagined what it would be like to drop over the side, and feel the shock of the icy water, and watch the towering ship diminish and disappear. Not longing for it, exactly, but enjoying the frisson. It would be so very, very possible. She can reach the rails from here, with her foot, and there are only four of them to climb.

"How can you shrug?" he asks. "Come on! Nobody's that cool about their own death—only saints and out-and-out sinners."

Nina is silent. She presses her fingers round the teacup, but there isn't a whisper of warmth to be had anymore.

"So, which are you?" he presses. "Saint or sinner?"

It's her turn to frown. She will not be goaded into speaking.

"The latter? Am I right?"

No answer.

"I don't mean to be personal, ma'am, but you got a look on your face like you went and murdered someone."

Silence. The man remains as motionless as ever, but Nina has to press her teeth together to stop them from chattering. Snowflakes drift onto the surface of her tea and float for a few seconds before melting.

"I call that pretty personal," she manages, eventually. Horrible man: let him think what he wants. She glances at his hands again. They're the colour and texture of a mackerel's belly.

Nina is fixated by hands, especially men's hands. Perhaps it's pardonable, in the circumstances, but she wishes she could stop. The waiters wear white gloves at dinner, but she studies them nonetheless, recognising the maître d' by his long fingers, and the head sommelier by the fluid way he twists the bottle's neck as he draws its cork. Some of her fellow passengers have been introduced formally, over drinks, but she can't remember their names. She remembers the women's faces all right, but their husbands go by secret nicknames: Hairy Knuckles, Pianist Hands, Jagged Nails, Monsieur Signet Ring...

Ever since she left Canada her mind has been full of such stupidities (*What would it be like to fall overboard? Do a strangler's hands look different from a normal person's?*), rather than the vital, practical things she needs to consider (*Where will I live, back in England? How will I make ends meet?*). When she boarded at Halifax, she swore she'd use the crossing to untangle her aims and intentions, but she's managed nothing of the sort. It's funny: she used to have a knack for blocking out inconvenient thoughts, but she seems to have lost it along the way.

The American could strangle her now, easy as pie. What would it be like if he stood up and wrapped his hands around her neck? Her skin is warm inside her fur collar, and the chill of his touch would be the first thing to make her shudder, followed by the pressure of his thumbs in the hollow of her throat.

—*Stop it, Nina. You're being idiotic.*

—*And yet these things happen.*

In fact, the man does get up, and does stand in front of her, blocking her view of the horizon. He bends towards her, coming far closer than any stranger has the right, and his gaze crawls over her face without apology. It might not be impossible to push past him, or even to scream—somebody might hear and come to her aid—but Nina freezes. She thinks, "At least I won't have to think and feel anymore, when I'm dead."

The wind gusts. Dirty steam swirls downwards from the funnels, forming a momentary cloud behind the man's head. He reaches into his breast pocket and removes a folded paper, which he presses into her hand.

"You are being watched," he says. "Every minute, every second, you are being watched. Read this—read it with your inmost heart—and we'll talk again before Liverpool."

He retrieves the cup and saucer from the bench and staggers back along the deck, the way he came. Nina stares at the Atlantic wilderness, while the wind whips at the paper. The snow is moving across the vista in great shadowy swathes, and wherever it goes it makes the ocean—which had seemed dark and opaque before—even darker, more opaque.

Minutes pass before Nina looks down. She has no idea what to expect. A letter in his own hand, perhaps? A declaration of some kind—sentimental, or obscene, or accusing?

It's not a letter, but a printed pamphlet.

SINNER, REPENT!

Nina's mouth moves in the ghost of a laugh. Stick-men plummet down the margins of the sheet, into a zigzag hell at the bottom. Flames, she realises. For a moment she thought they were waves.

In between the tumbling figures, a spiky typeface reads:

But for the fearful, and unbelieving, and abominable, and murderers, and fornicators, and sorcerers, and idolaters, and all liars, their part shall be in the lake that burneth with fire and brimstone; which is the second death.

REVELATION 21:8

There's more text on page two, more wrath and damnation, but she only skims it.

"Well! Thank you!" she shouts down the deck, though her voice is reedy in the gale, and the man has gone. "Thanks a million!"

Surely she's not going to cry on his account, and yet she does. It's the kind of angry sobbing she'd make if she'd bashed her shins on a sharp corner, or stubbed her toe. She hopes to goodness he's not spying on her through some little porthole, watching her shoulders shake, congratulating himself on having touched a sinful heart.

Nina rubs her eyes and nose on her coat-sleeve. She wants that man to know she's untouched by his insight. All right, so she's one of the liars and abominables, and whatever else. She doesn't need a prophet to tell her that. It's his brutality that's wounded her. The cup of tepid tea had looked like an act of compassion, but all he'd wanted was to save a soul and add it to his tally.

Nina looks down at the pamphlet again. There's no mention of paradise, only hell, and perhaps that's fair enough. Not that she can't imagine paradise—she can, and vividly—but there's no realistic way in.

When Nina pictures heaven she thinks of her friend Rose Allen, and their childhood summers. She remembers that hot August night—were they ten? eleven?—when they'd been allowed to drag their bedding into Nina's tree-house and camp till morning. They'd whispered and giggled for hours, huddling under the same blanket, frightened by the rustle of leaves, amazed by the stars. It was nearly dawn when they fell quiet; she remembers turning her head to look at the emerging shapes of trees and houses, and feeling Rose's feet warm against her own.

Since there's no way back to that time and place, there's no way into heaven.

Stiffly, Nina gets up and leans over the rails. Far below, the grey-brown waters froth and rush, and she pulls her coat tight at the neck. The pamphlet flutters and snaps in her other hand.

Four metal rails, painted white. Nina places one foot on the lowest rung and takes her weight off the other. The top rail was pressing into her ribcage, before; now it's pressing against her waist.

Her conversation with the man of God was strange, but honest. She might not have given much away, but she didn't tell him any lies.

Nina has done her best to dodge conversations, for the duration of the voyage, but it's impossible to avoid them altogether. Yesterday evening, Mrs. Bell from the next-door cabin—herself a widow—stopped Nina in the corridor as they made their way to bed. They'd shared the bare bones of a dialogue on a couple of previous occasions, but after-dinner port must have loosened the old lady's tongue. She gripped Nina's arm and said, "Poor child, to lose a husband when you've hardly begun to be a wife. But then, there are so many young widows these days; it breaks my heart. Thank heavens your father will be waiting for you at Liverpool—he must be longing to welcome you home!"

"And I'm longing to see him."

"Yes. Oh, my poor dear, you must mourn your husband's death so dreadfully. It's twenty-seven years since I lost Mr. Bell, and I miss him every day, but for you the wound is raw."

Nina freed her arm. "Yes. Yes, it is."

She revisits this exchange in her mind, as she climbs to the next rung. It was all so simple and well intentioned on Mrs. Bell's part, yet none of her own replies were true. Quite the opposite, in fact. Even the way she'd smiled at the mention of her father, and cast her eyes down at the mention of her husband—even these were dishonest.

The topmost rail is digging into Nina's hip bones now, and the pamphlet flaps like crazy in the wind. She is tempted to let it go, but she doesn't. It belongs to her, in some strange way; she's kept so few souvenirs of the past.

Nina stuffs the paper into her coat pocket and places her foot on the second to last rail.

1

Nina

August 24, 1934

NINA WANTS TO GO TO THE TREEHOUSE FOR A SECRET TALK, but Rose is unwilling. "We can talk just as well sitting on a rug on the grass, like civilised people," she points out, "and anyway, if I remember rightly, it's hardly a 'house,' it's a broken packing-case lid wedged into the branches of a cherry tree."

If I remember rightly. Nina doesn't know how to express her indignation in words, so she does it by turning her back and scaling the tree in question. Rose shades her eyes from the sun, watching her friend's vigorous ascent. "You see?" she says. "You've gone and got green muck on your shorts." She positions herself on the picnic rug and opens one of her magazines.

The treehouse has been their private realm, forever. Three summers ago they camped in it overnight; two summers ago they painted it green. Last summer they'd furnished it with cushions and a basket for apples, and rigged up a canopy for when it rained.

Last summer they were thirteen-year-olds with a shared passion for atlases, den building, and horses, and when Rose went home to Buxton they'd sworn to write even more often than usual. This summer nothing is certain, except that they're fourteen, and Rose's married brother still lives in the house opposite, and Rose has come to stay with him as usual. The conversational gambits they've made so far (*Did you arrive by train? Are you keeping well? Do you read* Marjorie's Chums?) would have sounded preposterous to both of them, twelve months ago. Nina doesn't take any magazines, and has never heard of *Every Girl's Paper*, or *Screen Star*, or *Marjorie's Chums*.

The treehouse wobbles as Nina sits down and stretches her bare legs to the full. She wants to say, "You promised to write at least once a week, if I remember rightly," but she can't, having failed to keep up the correspondence herself. Instead she says, "You're in Dad's way, down there."

Nina's father is mowing the grass, and every time he clickety-clacks past the cherry tree, he gives them a mock-gallant bow, or touches the brim of his sun hat.

"I'll move when he reaches this bit."

Nina looks down on her friend's blonde head, her primrose-yellow dress, and her folded, stockinged legs. Surely it's too hot for stockings? She runs her palms up and down her own shins, bristling the sun-bleached hairs, and making them smooth again. There's a whopper of a bruise on her left knee, and several long scratches that look like strings of rubies, from when she lost a tennis ball in the brambles.

Biscuit emerges from the side door and crosses the grass, tongue lolling, tail waving. When he sniffs at Rose's legs she cries, "Careful!" and pushes him away. After a moment she says, "Sit, Biscuit, there's a good dog," and presses on his haunches to make him obey.

Nina can see Cottenden church tower from up here, and the humpback bridge, and most of Canal Road, until it curves away to join the main road. Their house—hers and Dad's—is No. 7, and it looks much the same as all the other numbers from this angle: they all have the same mock-Tudor gables, the same pinkish bricks, the same preference for ornamental cherry trees. When you're at normal eye level the houses seem more distinctive, somehow: you notice the gnomes in Mr. and Mrs. Atherton's garden, and the bicycle inside Miss Riley's front gate, and the Lawsons' rabbit hutch, and their chicken coop with its half-dozen white bantams.

Rose is reading aloud from *Marjorie's Chums*, something about fixing your hair in finger-curls like Norma Shearer. Nina can't hear properly over the mower.

Living in a Cheshire village seems like a very dull fate today. The dullest fate imaginable. Last summer the two of them sat in the tree-house with their grubby knees touching, poring over Nina's dad's atlas, and Rose had said, "As the crow flies, Cottenden is four miles from Chester and twenty miles from Liverpool." Nina had crunched a pear drop pensively before adding, "And it's one hundred and seventy miles from London, and . . ." (flicking to page 21, "Europe: political") "one and a half thousand miles from Leningrad and . . ." (pages 14 and 15, "The Atlantic Ocean") "about three and a half thousand miles from New York City. Three and a half thousand miles!"

It wasn't that they'd foreseen the slightest chance of leaving Cottenden last August—not for London, anyway, or Leningrad, or New York—but at least they'd had their friendship, and the world had spread itself out for their imaginative pleasure. In the summer of '33, and in all the summers before it, for as long as Nina can remember, the earth had pivoted around the treehouse at 7 Canal Road.

Rose shuffles closer to the tree as Dad completes another stripe of the lawn, and Biscuit flops lazily onto his side. Nina picks at the scabs on her shins and thinks how much she hates characterless blue skies, and this empty time of day, just after lunch, when there are hours and hours to endure before tea. She yawns so hard that her eyes shut, and when they open again there's a man coming round the bend in the road.

He's not from Cottenden. Nina pushes the leaves aside, to take a better look. He's walking down the middle of the road, as if there's no likelihood of any vans or cars, and everything about him says not-Cottenden, not-Cheshire, perhaps not even England. She can't decide why. It has something to do with his height and breadth, and the swing of his arms, and the sunburn that flushes his cheeks, and the jaunty way he shoulders his enormous backpack. None of these things on their own would mark him out, yet somehow, taken together . . . Nina tries to guess his age, but it's impossible to tell with adults. He's definitely younger than Dad, who is thirty-nine.

While Mr. Woodrow mows around the foot of the tree, Rose stands up, gathering the rug into her arms and managing to stay glued to her magazine. "Gosh, listen to this, Nina!" she calls over the noise. "This could be you!"

Nina doesn't want to hear snippets from *Marjorie's Chums*—not within Dad's earshot, anyway. She is watching the strange man and hoping, with a bored sort of hope, that he'll notice her too. He does glance about as he strides down the lane, a slight smile lighting his eyes, but he never turns in her direction. She rustles the branches with her foot, but he remains oblivious, and in another moment he's gone past the house and out of sight.

"Listen, Nina! There's a letter on the 'Ask Marjorie' page, and honestly, it could have been written by you."

"Well, I promise it wasn't." Nina sighs and rolls onto her side, propping her head on her hand. At least Dad has finished and disappeared into the shed.

"No, but listen!" Rose pauses theatrically and clears her throat. "*Dear Marjorie, I would be grateful for your advice, please. I am a fifteen-year-old girl, and I have grown up without a mother, because she passed away when I was born. I do have a father and two older brothers, but I worry about the absence of a feminine role model in my life and feel that I am lacking in confidence and general 'know-how' as a result of having no mother. I don't have any aunts, or grown-up women friends, and although I have friends my own age, it is not the same as having a maternal figure to turn to. Ordinary feminine skills like wearing the right clothes, choosing and applying cosmetics, talking to boys, etc., seem mysterious and rather daunting to me, whereas none of the other girls in my class feels like this at all. If my mother were still alive, I feel sure everything would be different . . .* Nina! It could be you!"

"Except that I'm fourteen and an only child."

"Apart from that."

"And my mother didn't die when I was born. She died when I was two."

"All right, apart from *that*."

These are the only objections Nina can articulate, so she rolls onto her back again and wonders how long it will be before Rose goes home. This is Day One, and her shortest stay ever was a fortnight. Sometimes, in previous years, the two of them have travelled back together on the train and Nina has spent a few days in Buxton, but she won't be doing that this time. No, thank you very much!

Nina thinks, *I'm having hateful thoughts about Rose*, and the novelty of it makes her feel sick and wobbly, as if she's standing at a very great height, trying not to look down. It's horrible but addictive.

"Are you listening? Do you want me to read you Marjorie's advice?"

"No."

No, I want you to go to hell.

Nina squints through the shadowy layers of leaves, to the shards of sun and blue sky. Something touches her elbow, and when she turns her head she's surprised to see Rose's face on a level with her own. She hasn't climbed all the way up, but she has risked

13

her shoes, stockings, and dress to balance on the stump near the base of the tree.

"Nina?"

Rose crooks her little finger and holds it out. Nina hesitates, reluctant to let go of her righteous anger, before joining in their secret handshake (hook little fingers; shake hands; clasp wrists; bump fists). In a rush of relief and nostalgia, she almost accompanies the handshake by saying, *I wouldn't actually want you to go to hell,* but she bites her tongue in time.

"I wasn't trying to be mean," says Rose. "I'm sorry if it came out like that; I'm only concerned for you. Look, I brought you this. Lyn was having a clear-out of her make-up drawer and she gave me her old lipsticks."

Lyn is Rose's sister-in-law from across the way. Nina studies the tube that has been pressed into her hand. The casing is black with a silvery rim, and it's labelled at one end: *Secret Orchid.*

"Why are you concerned for me?" she asks, unscrewing the lipstick. Lyn has used most of it; there's only a short stub left over. It's red and ripe, like something you might long to crush between your teeth if you were thirsty. Like a strawberry.

"I think you know why."

"No, I don't!"

"Well then . . . because you're like the girl in that letter. In fact, you're worse off than her, because at least she knows she's missing something."

"Yes, but *what* am I missing? Other than a mother, which I can't do much about."

The treehouse wobbles as Rose adjusts her grip. Her voice drops to a whisper. The dear old Rose—the Rose of the secret handshake— is gone again, and the new version is back.

"What would you do if you were . . . you know . . . attracted to a boy? If you wanted him to kiss you? Or, never mind kissing, if you just wanted him to *see* you? Would you have the first clue what to do?"

Nina thinks of the tall, broad man striding down Canal Road, which makes no sense, because although she idly desired to be noticed by him, she felt—and feels—no desire to be kissed by those subtly smiling lips. The idea is enough to make her queasy, but he stays in her mind all the same. He had a short, untidy beard, as if he hadn't bothered to shave for a week or two, and his hair was reddish gold.

Rose continues: "It's about getting them to look at you in that way . . . you know. Oh Nina, you *must* know what I mean?"

"Of course I do, I'm not a complete ignoramus." Nina draws a greasy line across her thigh with the lipstick, then turns it into a mouth by adding two dots for eyes. She is saved from further discussion by a shout, which makes them both jump.

"Hey!"

It's him. It's the man with the backpack. He must have retraced his steps, and now he's leaning his folded arms on the garden gate while he catches his breath. His arms are huge—muscular—and they make the wrought-iron gate look spindly. Nina thinks "Hey!" is a rather rude way to attract attention, or rather, it ought to be, but somehow the man makes it sound civil. He sounds as if he really means, "Hello!"

Biscuit barks doubtfully, and Nina clambers down from the treehouse. Both girls are gripped by stage-fright, but Dad reappears round the side of the house in the nick of time.

"Afternoon!" Dad's been tinkering with the mower, and his hands are green and oily. He wipes them on a handkerchief as he crosses the lawn, and pauses a few feet from the gate. The stranger smiles and straightens. His skin is glistening, and his clothes are dusty, as if he's been walking for a long time.

"Pardon me, sir, is this Cottenden village?"

"It is!"

Rose pinches Nina just above the elbow, and whispers in her ear, *"American!"*

The man goes on: "Phew, well that's something. I'm looking for a place called Hawthorn House, but I don't have the full address? I only know it's in Cottenden."

"Hawthorn House . . ." Dad reddens, then makes matters worse by wiping his face on the rag and streaking his cheek with oil. Nina loves her father all the more for being shy, but she also wishes he wasn't.

"Yeah, it belongs to an old friend of mine—Guy Nicholson. I figured I'd surprise him with a visit. Him and his wife, I should say."

"Hawthorn House . . . I'm not sure . . . Isn't that the new build, just off Manor Farm Lane?"

"Could be. You know the Nicholsons? Guy and Kate?"

"I'm afraid not, but I've been past their place." Dad hesitates. "Lovely spot to build a house. Lovely views of the Welsh hills."

Dad begins giving directions, but there are too many third turnings on the left, and second turnings on the right, and "take a shortcut over the field with two oaks, not the field with one oak tree and a pond." In the end he gives up, and waves the girls over.

"You two can take this gentleman to Manor Farm Lane, can't you?"

Nina nods and Rose says, "Sure!" although she doesn't even live in Cottenden and is hardly likely to know the way.

The man gazes at them mildly. "I don't want to put anyone out."

"Oh, not at all," says Dad, and Rose echoes, "Not at all."

Dad goes on, "Why don't you take that lazy hound of yours, Nina? He hasn't had much of a walk today."

"Okay."

"Take care, though, crossing that main road."

Nina frowns at being babied. Biscuit's curly ears quiver at the word *walk*, and he circles Dad's legs, panting and grinning. The stranger leans over the gate and rubs the dog's head with his knuckles, saying, "Hey there, mutt."

When the man looks up again, Dad holds out his hand. "Henry Woodrow, by the by. This is my daughter, Nina, and her friend Rose."

"Joey Roussin." The man gives Dad's hand a brisk jiggle. He pronounces his surname in the French way, with the *R* at the back of his throat.

Dad comes across as wary and slight, next to the stranger. Nina wishes he'd ask Joey Roussin about his accent, but of course he won't, for fear his curiosity will be interpreted as some subtle form of ill will. Instead, he says, "Can I offer you a glass of water before you set off?"

Rose darts into the kitchen before Joey has even said yes, and reappears clutching one of the cut-glass tumblers that Dad keeps for best. It's full to the brim, and the water splashes over the sides however carefully she walks. Her lips are freshly reddened, and she's smiling in a different way from usual, as if she's decided to show fewer teeth and more dimples.

Nina remembers the lipstick scribble on her thigh. As soon as Joey tips his head back to drink, she rubs at it fiercely, but she can't get rid of it before he's finished; she can only make it look like a slight, strange wound.

. . .

THE WALK IS A CALAMITY for Rose's white shoes, especially the short cut across the field, which is rutted with dry mud. She pretends that she couldn't care less, but Nina sees how she compresses her lips and tiptoes over the worst bits. When they reach an especially wide spattering of cow muck, Rose takes hold of Joey's arm in order to leap across.

Nina keeps Biscuit on the lead, in case he decides to go barrelling through the hedge to chase the cows in the next field. He's in the mood to sniff and cock his leg at every tussock, and Nina ends up walking behind the other two, although they're relying on her for directions. She half listens to their conversation (desperately casual questions on Rose's part; idle answers on Joey's), interrupting now and then with a "Straight on over the stile!" or "Left here!"

At some stage—Nina doesn't notice when or why—Joey takes to calling Rose "Madeleine Carroll." "Why, thank you, Miss Carroll," he says, when she holds the gate for him.

"Do you know what?" Rose confesses, as if the coincidence is almost too much to bear, "I'm going to the Odeon with my brother and sister-in-law this evening to *see* a Madeleine Carroll picture!"

"Yeah?"

"Yes. It's called *The World Moves On*. It's American, of course—all the best pictures are, aren't they? I'd love to go to Hollywood."

"Uh-huh. Well, I've no doubt you'll make it there one day."

Nina steps into the next cowpat deliberately. There is a certain grim pleasure in breaking the crust, and staining her school shoes a greener shade of brown.

"What part of the States are you from?" Rose wonders.

Joey looks down from his great height and laughs. He seems to laugh with every other breath, and mostly it sounds genial, but occasionally, when he narrows his eyes, it sounds mocking.

"I'm not from the States," he says. "I'm from Canada."

"Canada!"

"Rossett Falls, to be precise. It's a small town outside Winnipeg."

"Oh!" Rose's eyes are wide again. "Winnipeg is a city in . . . Quebec?"

"Manitoba," Nina mutters, though she's not as certain as she sounds. (*Page 148? "Canada and Alaska"?*) Joey rewards her with a nod and a wink, and Nina has to frown in order not to smile.

For the rest of the walk, Nina and Biscuit continue to hang back, but she doesn't mind so much now. Rose can't see Joey, as long as she stays by his side—not unless she strains her eyes sideways or gawps at him openly—whereas Nina can study his back view at her leisure.

Joey Roussin is what Nina's form teacher would call an "absolute sight." His boots, along with the lower half of his trousers, are caked in dirt; his plaid shirt is darkly stained around the armpits and down the back, and he stinks as if he hasn't washed in days. The nape of his neck is beetroot red, and his golden curls shine with sweat. He ought to be repulsive.

Perhaps it's his exoticism that saves him? Or partly that? Nina pictures Canada as best she can: turquoise lakes, snowy peaks, forests of fir trees, brown bears, leaping salmon, solitude, vastness. The picture is familiar and strange, at the same time. It reminds her of imaginary adventures on sleepless nights, when she runs away from home, all by herself, and sleeps beneath a wilderness of stars, and lives off her wits like an animal.

. . .

NINA DOESN'T NEED TO SAY, "Here we are," because there's a painted sign beside a low sandstone wall, which reads *Hawthorn House*. Beyond it there's a paved driveway, and a garden, and the house itself.

Joey stops when he reaches the sign, swings the backpack off, and plants it on the ground. The girls stop too, and Biscuit winds his lead round Nina's legs.

There's a woman on the far side of the garden, facing away from them, ankle-deep in grass as she hangs a basket of washing. Her movements are slow and heavy, and every time she finishes pegging something out—even something as slight as a handkerchief—she pauses to flex her back.

In the driveway, a man is leaning over the open bonnet of a car with a toolkit at his feet. Joey says, "Guy Nicholson," quietly, as if he is talking to himself, but it must be loud enough for the man to hear because he straightens abruptly, wrench in hand, and turns towards the sound. For a long moment he seems merely confused, his eyes glancing guardedly from Nina, to Rose, to Biscuit, but then his features widen and he advances on them—practically runs at them—and the wrench falls, clanging, onto the driveway.

"Roussin!"

The girls stand back as the men collide. Joey makes a noise, more like a roar than a laugh, as he catches his friend mid-flight. "You didn't expect to see me!"

"How could I possibly expect to see you? I didn't know you were in England!"

They part, at last, but even then they keep their hands on one another's shoulders, and Joey gives his friend a gentle shake.

"You look well, Nicholson. I guess married life suits you."

"Yes, but I'm not a patch on you. Look at you, Roussin! Just . . . look at you!"

It's true that the healthiest man in Cheshire would look puny beside Joey Roussin, in his grimy, sunburned splendour, and yet it's Guy Nicholson who draws Nina's eye. She studies his compact build, and lightly tanned skin, and brown eyes (it's easy to stare, since he takes no notice of her, or Rose, or Biscuit), and finds him more difficult to read than Joey. Even though he is beside himself with joy, his face holds some secret in reserve—an ingrained flaw that might be sadness, or meanness, or disappointment, or some other form of darkness altogether.

Biscuit whines and sits down.

"Poor old Biscuit," says Rose, slipping out of her cardigan and tying the sleeves round her waist, "is everyone ignoring you? What a patient boy you are." When she moves her arms around, the air smells of perfume—real perfume, such as real women dab on their necks and wrists.

"Ladies—and Biscuit—I do beg your pardon," says Joey, ushering them forwards. His right hand feels hot through the sleeve of Nina's jersey, so his left one must feel even hotter on Rose's bare skin. "Guy, if it hadn't been for these two, I never would have found Hawthorn House. May I present, all the way from the other side of Cottenden, Miss Madeleine Carroll and . . . ah . . . who shall we say?"

Nina tenses while he chooses a name for her. She thinks of the poster in her bedroom: some actress in a flimsy gown, bent and crushed beneath the kiss of some actor in a cowboy hat. She hadn't stuck it on the wall for their sakes, but for the careering horse and wagon in the foreground, and because she liked the movie's title: *Meet Me at Echo Canyon*.

"Miss Greta Garbo," Joey concludes, and Nina knows the comparison is flattering by the way Rose's smile tightens.

Guy smooths his hair awkwardly, with a glance at Joey, but then the penny drops. "Oh, I see, neither of you are really called . . . I see . . . You'll have to forgive my friend, I'm afraid this is what passes for a sense of humour in Canada."

He shakes their hands in turn, saying, "Guy Nicholson, how d'you do?" both times. Rose remembers to give her actual name, which Nina forgets to do.

"I'm Rose Allen, and I actually do want to be an actress, so when Joey called me Madeleine Carroll he wasn't entirely wrong, in a funny sort of way!"

The idiocy of this assertion irritates Nina even more than the news—and it is news—that Rose wishes to be an actress. Last summer they'd made detailed plans to open a pet shop together and save up to travel the world.

Nina feels heartened when the two men burst out laughing, but then Rose laughs too, and she's not so sure. She pretends to fiddle with Biscuit's lead, so that she doesn't have to look at Rose's red lips and white teeth. Nina wishes she wasn't wearing a jersey, because she can feel the sweat dripping down her back; and she wishes she wasn't in shorts, because her thighs keep sticking together, and everyone must be able to hear them unstick when she moves her legs. *Greta Garbo*, she thinks, as if the name is a talisman.

"And *your* real name?" Guy is saying.

"Oh—Nina. Nina Woodrow."

"Are you intending to be an actress too?"

"Definitely not!"

"Wise girl." Guy looks at her kindly, as if she really is wise, and she feels buoyed again. *One point to me*, she thinks, with a rapid glance at Rose. She's starting to get the same breathless nausea that afflicts her on School Sports Day, when she knows the long jump is hers for the taking, and she wants it so badly, and she thinks she'll die—or, more embarrassingly, cry—if she doesn't win.

The woman has drifted away from the washing-line and joined their circle. She's nothing like as vivid as the rest of them; she's just a pregnant stomach, a shapeless body, a neutral face. It turns out she's Kate Nicholson—Guy's wife—and not only does she look more boring than the two men, she also speaks in a much more boring way. For example, she greets Joey politely rather than rapturously, and when the girls are introduced by their new actress names she smiles slightly, barely even pretending to be amused, and says, "What are you really called?" On the upside, she invites everyone to sit in the garden while she fetches five glasses and a jug of lemonade from the house, and a bowl of water for Biscuit.

There's only one garden chair, and naturally it's ceded to the pregnant wife. The others settle in the shaggy grass while Guy passes the lemonade round, and they sip and wince at its tartness. It's easy to forget the wife is there, since she contributes very little to the conversation, and her face is not on a level with everyone else's. Occasionally she moves her thick ankles, the chair wobbles, and Nina thinks, *Oh yes, she's here too*, before turning away and forgetting again.

Nina doesn't say much either, to be fair. What she wants to say—that this hot afternoon, which threatened to be so stodgy, is turning into something potent—is an idea she can barely formulate in her own mind, let alone out loud. Small talk feels even more pointless than usual.

Hawthorn House is different from the Edwardian semis in Canal Road. It's not especially grand, but it feels airy and generous, with its billowing bow windows, cloud-white walls, and sprawling, odd-shaped garden. Where the sunlight pools under the garden trees, there are whirling clouds of midges, but Nina doesn't think, *Ugh!* as she normally would; she thinks, *Beautiful*. The tall chimneys of the Red Lion pub are visible at the bottom of the dip, beyond the hawthorn hedge, but it's the only building in sight. The Welsh hills, which Nina has seen so often that she's stopped seeing them at all, are freshly present in the distance: blue and dreamy, like the mountains you journey towards in a fairy tale, on a quest to discover some lost and precious object.

The girls sit upright and sip slowly, but the men sprawl, their throats rolling up and down as they gulp their lemonade. Guy complains that it needs more sugar, but Joey says, "Fiddlesticks! Lemonade isn't lemonade if your eyes aren't popping out of their sockets."

Guy lies on his side, resting on one elbow. He's close enough that Nina could reach out and stroke his springy hair, if she wanted to. She worries that she might; that the afternoon is strange and sultry enough to make her do anything. She clenches her fists and sits on them.

Rose is not lost for words. When she isn't rattling on about life in Buxton, and her plans to take Hollywood by storm, she pouts and sips, leaving lipstick stains on the glass—and the men watch her. Their gaze is idle, but it's still a gaze, and it makes Nina wish she'd had the gumption to smear Secret Orchid on her mouth instead of her leg.

"My parents have a Baby Austin like yours, only yours is newer and smarter. Daddy let me have a go once—just on a quiet lane, you know—and he said I wasn't bad at all. Oh, I love going for drives, I can't wait to have my own car!"

"My dad . . ." Nina only speaks to make them look at her, and her voice emerges loud and gruff. She hasn't anything particular to say, so she clears her throat. If she were on her own, she might give in to temptation and say something like, "My dad used to own a Rolls-Royce," but Rose would be bound to betray her, so she tells the truth instead.

"My dad can't drive. We don't have a car."

It's not the throwaway line she means it to be. It sounds aggressive, like the statement of some eccentric moral principle. Joey says, "Uh-huh?" and there's a silence, which Mrs. Nicholson ends by saying, "Oh, look up there! An aeroplane!"

They shield their eyes and watch the yellow biplane as it drones across the blue.

"Imagine it . . ." Guy's wife runs her hand over her bump. "Rattling about, miles above the ground, inside a flimsy little machine like that. Crazy!"

"I'd do it in a heartbeat," says Joey promptly. "You would, wouldn't you, Guy?"

"You bet!"

"Me too!" cry the girls, but Rose says it a fraction of a second sooner, which makes Nina sound like a copycat. *Oh, but I really mean it*, she longs to explain. *I mean it more than she does!*

Nina feels close to laughter or tears; there's a danger of one or the other if she opens her mouth again. The heat is making her ears buzz, and she downs her second lemonade quickly, in case she's about to faint. The others keep talking, but she can't concentrate. Her mind keeps moving in a dazed circle, from Guy's bewitching hair, to Joey's sunburned neck, to her own mucky shoes, to Biscuit's hectic panting and the breathy sound of Rose's hateful new laugh.

It's only when the conversation tenses that Nina starts to listen properly. Joey is saying, "Hey, I wouldn't dream of putting you out. I'll camp in the garden overnight, no problem. I've got everything I need."

Mrs. Nicholson says, "What will you eat?"

Guy says, "Roussin! Why on earth would you sleep in the garden? You're our honoured guest for as long as you like. Tell him he's welcome, Kate!"

"Of course he's welcome."

Kate and Guy manage to imbue the same words with contradictory meanings, and Guy looks daggers at his wife.

"You *are* welcome, Joey," Kate relents. "It's only that I'm not sure how we'll manage for dinner. I was going to serve leftovers this evening, and shop tomorrow, and it's a question of how far they'll stretch . . ."

Guy tuts and waves his hand. "We've got eggs, haven't we? We'll make omelettes."

"We're out of eggs. You had the last one for breakfast."

Nina swears to herself she'll never be like Kate Nicholson: pregnant, weary, earthbound in body and spirit. How awful, to worry about leftovers and eggs on such an afternoon. If Nina was in her place she'd come up with some wildly imaginative solution; she'd say, *Let's drive all the way down to London and dine at the Ritz*, and the men would marvel at her pizzazz.

The real Nina says, "Why don't you all come for dinner with me and my dad?"

If she'd given it a moment's thought, she'd never have said it, and her heart gives a startled bound, as if the suggestion has come from someone else. Rose whips her head round to stare, and even while she's panicking, Nina thinks, *Advantage, Miss Nina Woodrow.*

"Really!" she insists. "Dad will be delighted. There's nothing he likes more than a dinner party, and getting to meet new people."

If Rose dares to snort . . . But Rose opens her eyes wide and doesn't make a sound.

Guy begins to demur. "It's awfully kind of you . . ."

"But at such short notice," Kate chips in. "We couldn't possibly . . ."

"And having never even met your father . . ."

But Joey rolls onto his back with a contented sigh, placing his hands behind his head. "Problem solved! I knew Miss Garbo was a woman of hidden depths the moment I laid eyes on her. As for the shopping, Kate, you leave that to me. I'll take Guy's car into town tomorrow and fill the trunk with caviar and champagne. You won't have to lift a finger the whole time I'm here."

Kate says, "Nina, really . . . Are you sure about this evening? Won't your father think it odd?"

"No, not in the least." She is astonished by her own composure. "Shall we say eight o'clock?"

Joey demonstrates his satisfaction by blowing a kiss at the sky, and Guy looks straight into her eyes and smiles. Nina reddens and flashes a look at Rose.

Game, set, match.

· · ·

EVEN WHEN THEY'RE SAFELY OUT of earshot, the girls don't speak. Biscuit keeps trying to burrow under hedges, and Nina is busy hauling on his lead, which helps lessen the awkwardness. It's only when they've crossed the field with the oak trees, and passed through the stile, that Rose breaks the silence.

"I didn't have your dad down as a socialite."

"He won't mind."

"What will you wear?"

Nina shrugs. "I'll find something. You know, you're not the only person in the world to own clothes."

"Yes, but nice clothes . . ."

Biscuit sees a grey cat, and Nina is sick of holding him back, so she tightens her grip and says, "Come on, Biscuit, let's run!" The dog tears away, and she yelps and sprints in his wake with her arm at full stretch. The quicksilver cat slips under a garden gate, but they keep running, until Biscuit gets bored.

Rose picks her way along the lane behind them, watchful of the dust and her white shoes. Nina waits, arms folded, making it as obvious as possible that she's struggling to hide a smirk.

. . .

AS IT TURNS OUT, DAD does mind. Deep down Nina understands why, and she's sorry, but she pretends to be indignant.

"It's just a simple dinner party," she insists, while he's still gaping at her news, and before he's had a chance to speak. "It's what people do."

Rose has gone, thank goodness. Nina leaves the bright garden for the shady kitchen, and coils Biscuit's lead into the drawer. Her father follows.

"How do you mean, *It's what people do*? What is? Casually giving out dinner invitations, at short notice, to absolute strangers?"

"Yes! Yes! This is the sort of thing that normal people do!" Nina is desperate to exude nonchalance, but her mood is edged with hysteria, and she's struggling to hide it. She wants to be carried on and on by the instinctual lightness that made her issue the invitation in the first place. Dad mustn't keep doubting the rightness of it, or she might doubt it too.

"I never should have let you go with that man," he says, as if the idea strikes him with horror, in hindsight. As if something much worse than a dinner-party invitation had transpired.

"Dad . . ."

"Jessie has gone home!"

Jessie Brown is the Woodrows' "daily." She comes to their house four hours a day, six days a week, to wash, clean, shop, and cook. On the rare occasions that Mr. Woodrow does invite guests, she will do the honours in the kitchen.

"We don't need Jessie!"

"Oh really? And how will we feed them? *What* will we feed them?"

Nina hasn't given it a moment's thought, but she answers as easily as if she has: "There's that cold roast chicken in the larder, and plenty of potatoes, and you said yourself the garden is overflowing with lettuce. I can make a mayonnaise."

"And for pudding?"

"For pudding . . . raspberries. We're out of cream but I can pop over to the Allens', I bet they'll lend us some."

Rose's brother is a dairyman at the farm beyond the canal, and the Allens are always well stocked.

Dad doesn't argue, but he doesn't forgive her either. As she heads for the stairs he says, "I suppose we'll manage this once, but don't go making a habit of it!" and when she ignores him and carries on walking, he barks, "Nina!" in a way that she knows to dread. She pauses halfway up the stairs, unable to look round, and the silence drags on and on until she mutters, "Sorry."

At least he hasn't vetoed the whole thing. Imagine that. Imagine having to return to Hawthorn House to say, *My apologies, the whole thing's off. I was wrong: my father dislikes new people, after all.*

. . .

ALONE IN THE DIM, ECHOEY bathroom, Nina feels sure of herself again. She sits in six inches of tepid water, studying her body afresh, as if it is a newly unearthed artefact, and she must clean it to find out what it really is, and whether it has a purpose, and how much it might be worth.

According to Rose, the ideal female figure is tall and sharp-boned ("like Katharine Hepburn," she'd said, meaning, "like me"). Nina reflects on her own sturdy, shortish stature and decides that the diktats of Rose and *Marjorie's Chums* don't bother her as much as they probably should. She cups her calves in her hands, and then the backs of her thighs, liking their firm roundness. She does the same—tentatively—with her breasts, and with the sides of her face. *I'm lovely*, she thinks as she starts to wash, and considering it's not the first time she's been told (Dad often says, "Goodbye, my lovely," when she's heading off to school, or up to bed), she is surprised and pleased by the revelation. Dunking a sponge and squeezing it over her neck may be the most ordinary gesture in the world, but today it strikes her as something graceful and artistic. She is moved by the way her arms rise like a ballet dancer's, and the shivery sensation on her skin, and the trickling sound the water makes, as it courses over her shoulders and into the tub.

Nina swashes the water round her bent legs, rinsing the dust from her shins and ankles. When she closes her eyes to picture Joey Roussin and Guy Nicholson, she finds it hard to remember what they look like as individuals, let alone to choose between them. In the end she plumps for Guy, and when she's fixed his face in her mind as best she can (dark hair, wide mouth, secretive eyes), she parts her lips and presses them against her left kneecap—gently at first, and then pushing harder, the way they kiss in films.

. . .

ROSE IS RIGHT, THOUGH, ABOUT Nina having nothing nice to wear. After the bath she empties her wardrobe and chest of drawers, heaping everything on the floor, but they're mostly tops, shorts, and slacks. As far as dresses are concerned, there's the velvet, wintry thing she last wore when she was twelve, and a much-mended, much-washed gingham sundress, and her new school gym-slip, but she'd rather die than appear at dinner in that.

It's the sort of situation that would make Rose—the new version of Rose—panic, so Nina does her best to find it archly amusing. "Oh dear!" she says, addressing the various horses, dogs, and film stars that gaze out from her bedroom walls. She turns to the wardrobe mirror and studies her reflection thoughtfully. If she unfastens the top two—top three—buttons on her dressing-gown, and ties a scarf around her waist, the effect verges on glamorous, but only in the privacy of her own imagination. In the real world, it's still a bobbly woollen dressing-gown, and a hand-knitted scarf that's seen better days.

Nina picks up the framed photograph from her dressing-table and sits down on the edge of the bed.

"Oh Mum, this actually is a disaster."

People who knew her mother say she was always smartly turned out, and you can tell that's true from the well-cut dress in the photograph, the long string of beads, and the soft, wavy bob. It's a studio portrait, so nobody is smiling—neither Mum, nor Dad, nor baby Nina—but sometimes she thinks she glimpses humour at the corners of her mother's eyes and lips. Sometimes not. The photograph is too familiar to read. Whenever Nina picks it up, she tries to pretend she's seeing it for the first time, in the hope that it will take her by surprise, but it never does.

Dad isn't himself in the photograph: he looks skinny, clean-shaven, and cross, as opposed to moderately slim, moustached, and diffident. As for Nina, her 1921 self lolls gormlessly on her mother's lap in a shapeless smock and bare legs—a forgivable state of dress for a one-year-old, perhaps, but not the fourteen-year-old host of a dinner party.

Nina imagines herself in her mother's gown—thirteen years out of date, but chic and original, and a whole sight better than faded gingham or school uniform. She'd wear it if she could, but she can't, since Dad got rid of all her mother's things in the first throes of his grief.

The first throes of his grief. That phrase doesn't suit her self-contained father at all, and yet in Nina's mind it's his. Someone must have applied it to him once, in her hearing, and it stuck. Occasionally she stops to wonder what it means; what people actually look like when they're in "throes." She pictures him screaming and thrashing about on the lawn, lit by a lurid pyre of books, beads, clothes, perfume bottles, and trinkets.

Of course, there wasn't anything as dramatic as a bonfire. She knows that really. Dad donated Mum's possessions to the church bazaar. Kind Mrs. Dempsey, who ran the Women's Institute stall, was the one who'd rescued the family photograph and returned it to him. Apparently he'd said, "I can't bear to keep it. Put it on the white elephant stall—someone might buy it for the frame," but Mrs. Dempsey had replied, "No, you must keep it. As Nina grows up, she'll want to know what her mother looked like."

There's a tap on the bedroom door, and Nina hastily fastens up her dressing-gown.

"What is it?"

"Can I come in?"

"I suppose."

Dad glances at the tumble of clothes on the floor, but makes no comment as he comes in and sits down beside her. If she'd still been small, she'd have clambered onto his lap and encircled his neck with her arms.

"I was just wondering what to wear," she says.

Her voice sounds funny, though she doesn't mean it to. Dad takes the photograph from her hands and lays it on the bedside table, before putting his arm around her shoulders and giving her a squeeze.

"I'm sorry I was cross," he says.

Nina bites her lip, but she can't seem to stop her mouth from contorting and the tears spilling onto her cheeks.

"Sweetheart, don't cry!" In his anxiety he tries to look into her face, but she turns away. Anyway, she's not upset because he was cross, she's upset because she hasn't got anything nice to wear, and because she was an idiot to invite those people to dinner, and because today has been so strange, because Rose isn't her friend anymore. A part of her wants him to know this—wants him to know that she's too old to care about being ticked off—but then he'd ask what were her real reasons for crying, and she'd never be able to explain. Dad strokes her shoulder and makes soothing noises, and after a while she stops being standoffish and sags against his chest.

"That's it," he says. "Let it all out. Have a good cry."

When the worst is over, but her breathing is still jerky, she blows her nose and says, "I wish I had something nice to wear."

Dad isn't one to notice clothes, as long as they're tidy, so she expects him to reply, *Won't your gingham dress do?* or *Can't you just wear some slacks and a clean blouse?* It's greatly to his credit that he actually says, "Wouldn't Rose lend you something, just for this evening?" which wouldn't be a bad idea at all, if relations with Rose hadn't taken such a peculiar turn. He even adds, "I'm sorry, I should have realised you were short of clothes. I'll ask Mrs. Atherton to take you into Chester next week and sort you out with some new bits and pieces."

"Thanks, Dad."

He kisses the top of her head and musses her damp hair, and she gives a final, shaky sigh. She feels light again—lighter than ever—like a balloon tugging at its string, eager to float away.

Rose's yellow dress was very pretty, with its white belt and pearly buttons. Perhaps there'll be no harm in mentioning it, since she's popping over to the Allens' anyway to borrow some cream? The old Rose wasn't interested in fashionable dresses, but if she had been, she'd have said, "Of *course*! Take it!"

. . .

THERE'S A GAP IN THE fence between the Woodrows' back garden and the Allens', which the girls have always used as a short cut. In the honeyed light of late afternoon, Nina sidles through and makes her way up the Allens' lawn, brushing past the dry washing on the line. In previous summers, she wouldn't have bothered knocking, but now it seems odd not to.

It's Rose who opens the kitchen door.

"Oh!" Her eyes are a little pink and swollen, but everything else is perfectly in place, and her tone is one of polite surprise. "Hello again!"

"Rose, I just want to say that I'm sorry we quarrelled."

"Did we?" Rose tucks a lock of hair behind her ear. She has bathed too, and changed into a sky-blue dress, and her skin gives off the scent of flowers. Nina used coal tar soap in the bath, as usual, and smells merely clean.

"Well, maybe 'quarrelled' is too strong. Whatever it was that came between us this afternoon."

"Did something come between us this afternoon?"

Rose's voice is as flat as her smile, and Nina is flummoxed. She looks away, and addresses the potted bay tree to the left of the door.

"I would have invited you over for dinner too, but I didn't think there'd be enough chicken for six. It's a bit of a stretch, as it is."

"Oh goodness, don't apologise, I couldn't have come anyway. Michael and Lyn are taking me to the cinema tonight, and we're going on to a restaurant afterwards. I ought to be getting ready—was there something you wanted?"

Nina would like to say no, so as not to cheapen her apology, but the empty jug in her hand is a giveaway, and the thought of the prim-rose-yellow dress spurs her on. It doesn't matter if it's slightly creased and dusty—even if it's a bit sweaty under the arms—it's still a million times nicer than anything of her own. Her hesitation is as good as a yes. Rose takes the jug and says, "Let me guess . . . Milk? Cream?"

Nina frowns at the bay tree before forcing herself to raise her eyes and smile. "Cream, if you can spare some? We'll pay you back tomorrow. Oh yes, and there was one other thing . . ."

Rose is assessing the gingham sundress.

"You know you can see your legs through that dress, with the sun behind you?"

"It's just an old . . . I threw it on to come to yours. Obviously I'm not wearing it this evening."

"What are you going to wear?"

"I don't know. I wondered whether you might lend me something."

Rose smiles faintly. Nina can't stand much more of these courteous hostilities. In the old days it was always clear whether they were having a quarrel, and why, and what to do about it. Just as she's working herself up to say something dramatic (*For heaven's sake, what's wrong with you?*), Rose murmurs, "Come on up to my room, but we'll have to be quiet because Lyn's having a nap." Then she steps aside, and gestures for Nina to enter the house.

. . .

LAST SUMMER, AND ALL THE summers before, Rose was notorious for her untidiness. When she visited Cottenden she never used to unpack her suitcase properly, or fold her clothes, and Nina used to tell her off about the way she treated books. (*For heaven's sake, use a bookmark! My dad would throw a fit if he saw what you'd done to the spine.*)

This year Rose has put her clothes away and stored her suitcase under the bed, and although the dressing-table is cluttered, it's a different sort of clutter. There are no bird's feathers sharpened into quills, or collections of stones, or notes from Nina in private code. It's all lipsticks and pots of cold cream, and a postcard portrait of Clark Gable slotted into the frame of the mirror.

Rose sits on her dressing-table stool, offering neither encouragement nor discouragement as Nina approaches the wardrobe. She nudges open the door and looks without touching. There's a mint-green dress with white zigzags, a pale-pink dress patterned with dark-pink rosebuds, three pastel-coloured skirts, and several pastel-coloured blouses. Rose says, "The yellow dress is in the wash, in case you were wondering."

Nina is at a loss. Perhaps she should leave with her pride intact and make the best of what she's got at home? Her navy slacks are newish and smartish, and they'd look all right with her school blouse. She tugs at her lower lip and turns to the window. There's a dress on the Allens' washing-line: black silk, with lacy sleeves and a sweetheart neckline, and a red polka-dot pattern.

"Oh! Is that yours too?"

If Nina notices Rose's hesitation, she thinks nothing of it.

"Do you like it?"

"I love it! It's so . . ."

There's a tap on the door and Lyn calls through, "Rose? Your brother's home. Can you be ready to leave in half an hour?"

"Okay."

Lyn and Michael's bedroom is across the landing, at the front of the house. They're both there now, preparing for their evening out; their murmured conversation is audible through the walls. Rose says, "You'd better clear off, I need to get ready," as she steers Nina out of her room. Normally, Nina would protest against the rush, but her head's too full of the polka-dot dress. Can she? Can't she?

"Rose, what about the dress?"

"Help yourself, just unpeg it from the line on your way. It might need an iron."

It's not obvious why Rose's voice has dropped, but Nina is content to follow her lead, and whispers, "Thank you, thank you, thank you!" all the way downstairs.

Rose submits to a hug and a kiss before pushing her friend away, into the garden, and closing the door.

. . .

NINA IS TERRIFIED OF SCORCHING the dress, but it is rather crumpled, so she covers it with a damp towel and skims it very lightly with the iron. Dad says, "What are you up to?" as he's passing through the sitting-room, but it's only his vague way of saying hello. "I'm ironing you a shirt for tonight," she replies, which isn't exactly a lie, because she's going to do that next.

When the ironing's done, the mayonnaise mixed, the potatoes scrubbed, and the dining table laid, Nina goes upstairs to get changed.

The hooks and eyes up the back are a struggle, but she manages without any awful tearing sounds, and once the dress is on, the bodice adjusted, and the skirt smoothed down, she is afraid to look at herself. She walks to the wardrobe mirror with her eyes lowered, counts to three, takes a deep breath, and raises her eyes.

Perhaps she is right to be afraid, because the effect is uncanny. There is a new person in the mirror, with a new shape, a new complexion, and a new understanding in her eyes. The gingham dress puffed out from the waist, but this one glides over her hips, as if it knows her and likes her. She turns, trying to see herself from the back. The red polka dots are, in fact, cherries, and each one has been printed with a tiny white dot, which gives the impression of shiny plumpness.

Nina remembers the finger-curls in *Marjorie's Chums*, and makes a half-hearted attempt at a fancy hairdo, but it looks better loose, with a bobby pin behind each ear.

What else? The big toenail on her left foot is jagged, so she trims it with scissors from her pencil case. The only stockings she owns are woolly school ones, and none of her shoes seem right, so she decides not to wear any. Rose would be horrified (bare legs and feet!), but it's a hot evening, and the marvellous, marvellous dress can carry it off. She removes her watch, since the leather strap is so tatty, and puts on the gold necklace that Dad gave her at her Confirmation.

Secret Orchid is still in the pocket of her shorts, so she draws the curvy caricature of a mouth on top of her own—like Rose's, but even more extreme. The effect makes her blood rush for a pulse or two; it makes her look unnatural, like a clown, and she hates it, but she's also slow to wipe it off. She can't bring herself to get rid of it entirely, but dabs it down and softens the contours, until her lips look . . . sort of . . . naturally vivid.

The mirror is mesmerising, but it's only when she walks away from it that she knows, for certain, she's beaten Rose in this hostile contest that neither of them will ever acknowledge. There's something about the way she moves that's different. Better. Rose either slinks, or struts, or hunches as if she's thinking about being watched, but Nina walks like a cat, with a sureness she's never noticed before, and can't explain.

On her way downstairs she peeps through Dad's bedroom door. He's dressed and ready, but on his knees by the bed, saying his prayers. It's just as well; he mustn't see her till the guests arrive, when it will be too late to make her change. She goes down to the kitchen. The time is ten to eight, according to the clock above the oven.

What is happening? Nina wonders as she crosses the grass with Biscuit at her heels. *What is this joyful thing I've just discovered?* Her body seems to know things her mind has no idea of, about who she really is, and what she might do. She can't put any of it into words; she can only press her bare feet into the grass and feel the flow of silk like fresh water over her skin.

She grips the lowest branch of the cherry tree, and balances with one foot on the stump, which gives her enough height to see over the hedge. The view from the treehouse would be better, but she daren't climb up for the sake of Rose's dress.

Is that the Nicholsons' car, now? Oh God, it is! It's the Austin 7 that Guy was tinkering with, earlier on. It's a fair bet that the men wanted to walk, on such a glorious evening, but the pregnant wife made them drive.

What was her name, again? The wife? Nina can't remember, but not to worry. It's not important.

2

Kate

August 24, 1934

DAMN, DAMN, DAMN—AND, TO MAKE MATTERS WORSE, IT'S my own stupid fault! It wouldn't be so galling if I'd had it foisted on me, but I was the one who grumbled about running out of eggs and having nothing to give Joey for dinner. If I'd kept my trap shut, the men could have gone to the Red Lion for a cheese sandwich and some beers, and I could have had a few hours on my own, in the garden, with a book. Instead of which, the boyish one—Nina—is suggesting dinner at eight, and my well-bred outer voice is replying, "Well, that would be splendid, if you're sure your father won't mind," while my inner voice is going, "Damn and blast and bugger it!"

I think the girls have taken their Madeleine Carroll/Greta Garbo labels to heart, rather: you can tell by their manner, as they walk away, that they feel self-conscious. Blonde, chatty Rose sways her hips and fidgets with her dress, while Nina rushes along, fussing over the dog. I'm the only one watching, which would disappoint them sorely, if they knew. The men are lying with their hands behind their heads, gazing at the sky and talking about (what else?) their schooldays.

Why do they always fall back on their schooldays? They're on about that Latin master, Mr. Cain, who—in a masterstroke of wit that was no doubt Joey's—went by the nickname Cain the Cane. Don't they ever get bored of him? What is there to say, that hasn't been said before?

I shouldn't mock. My siblings and I are the same when we get together; we can turn nothing—absolutely nothing—into a fevered discussion. Sometimes it's like that with me and Guy too: usually late at night, when neither of us can sleep. We face each other in the dark and talk about the other people at his accountancy firm, or what we might name our baby (if we hadn't already settled on Phillip or Julia), or little incidents from years ago, when we were children together. We always whisper, even now that we have a house to ourselves and no near neighbours.

The garden chair groans as I shift my weight, trying and failing to find a comfortable way to sit.

"Are you all right there, darling?" asks Guy.

Joey rolls onto his front and says, "How are things, Kate? You look blooming, you know. I should have said so already."

I do not look blooming. My eldest sister, Deborah, looked blooming when she was pregnant—with her apple cheeks and neat little bump—but it's not like that for me. I've turned into a fat, slow, morose, dull-skinned insomniac with perpetual heartburn. Deb says I'd feel better about everything if I talked and sang to the baby, but I can never think of anything to tell it, except "I apologise for being so grumpy," and "Don't take it personally," and "I will do my best to love you." I murmur these things when I'm alone in the garden, and only if I'm certain Guy can't hear. I've not been able to bring myself to sing.

"Thanks, Joey."

"When's the baby due?"

"September."

"September, eh? No need to ask whether you two enjoyed your first Christmas as a married couple."

Guy shoves his friend's shoulder, and I force myself to smile, so I won't be written off as prim.

God, I love this garden and its view. I may—I do—have misgivings about Hawthorn House itself, but not the garden. When I think what this evening might have been, with the cooling air on my face, the birdsong, and the swish of a turning page, it's enough to make me cry. No, that's too picturesque: it's enough to make me say something mean, or throw my book at Joey Roussin.

The Collected Works of Oscar Wilde would make a pretty hefty missile. I'm halfway through *The Picture of Dorian Gray*, at the moment. Unfortunately, I can't read it in the bath, as the volume is too big and too beautifully bound, but I could have read it out here, this evening, and stared up at the darkening hills between each paragraph.

"Kate? Can you guess the one and only way in which your superb lemonade might be improved?"

Joey addresses the question to me, but Guy answers, "With the addition of gin?"

"Aha!" says Joey, approvingly.

Neither of them moves.

I'm not going to move either.

"Don't you think it's odd of that girl's father to let her traipse across the village with a strange man?" I muse. "You could have been anyone, Joey—a murderer, or a rapist."

The men exchange a glance.

Guy says, "She did have a friend with her, and a dog."

"More to the point, I don't look like a murderer or a rapist. I look like the genial fellow that I am. You think so really, don't you, Kate?"

Joey reaches out to touch me, but I twitch my feet out of the way and stand up.

. . .

WHEN I LOOK DOWN FROM our bedroom window, I don't feel pleasure for the sake of the view, or the warmth, or the light, but because Joey and Guy are lounging down there, waiting for me to fetch the gin, and I'm not going to oblige. Ha! They think that's why I've come inside, but it's not! That's how mean-minded I am, lest there be any remaining doubt.

On the other hand, it's lonely indoors, and I miss their company. Solitude in the garden is enchanting, whilst solitude inside Hawthorn House is . . . not. It's not. I wish I could say this to Guy, in so many words, but I daren't. He's over the moon with our brand-new home.

I sit down at the dressing-table and open *Oscar Wilde*, but I can't settle. It's funny—whenever I read *Dorian Gray* in my garden chair, the prose strikes me as decadent and lush, but whenever I read it indoors it strikes me as dark and eerie. After a couple of pages I close the book and start making up my face. I put a blob of Pond's vanishing cream on my nose, before remembering I want a bath first, so I skim it off again and return it to the pot.

At least getting dressed for tonight won't be a headache. There are only a couple of outfits that fit me at the moment (both Deb's cast-offs), and the green maternity dress is the closest one to stylish, so that's that. Not that it will make *me* look stylish—any more than fastening a blue whale into a frock would make it look nicer than it did before, or put it in the mood for a dinner party—but I'm past caring. My sole ambition for this evening is to get home in good time.

When I screw the lid back on the vanishing cream, it makes a sound like fingernails clawing at the window. This, I should explain, is not the fault of Pond's, but of Hawthorn House. Every innocent little noise gets amplified and warped inside these four walls. Drop a book, or shut a door too hard, and it sounds like a gun going off. Step too heavily on certain stairs or floorboards, and you might reasonably assume that Count Dracula is near at hand, swinging open his coffin lid.

It's our fault—Guy's and mine—for going ahead with the purchase. We can't plead ignorance. We knew why the price was low. Nobody—almost nobody—wants to buy a house with a horror story attached. "Oh, but it would be idiotic to turn our noses up at such a chance," we reassured one another. "What with the garden, and those big, sunny rooms, and the views . . ."

I make my way to the bathroom (large! modern! every convenience!) and set the taps running. In my opinion, it doesn't help that we only know half the horror story; I think we ought to set our curiosity to rest by finding out exactly what happened. Guy disagrees; he thinks our best course is to forget the little we do know. "Try not to dwell on it," he says with a maddening shrug, but what sort of advice is that? He might as well stand in the garden and counsel the weeds to stop growing.

Maybe that's something I could do tonight, at dinner, when the conversation flags? I could ask Nina's father for the Tale of Hawthorn House, in all its gory detail.

I sprinkle Epsom salts over the steaming water and notice—oh, bother—I've left *Lives of the Romantic Poets* in the sitting-room. (Unlike *Dorian Gray*, it has a torn frontispiece, so I don't feel bad about reading it in the bath.)

Lumbering down the stairs, holding tight to the banister, I think what a mistake it was to decorate the house in such pallid tones. Guy left me to choose the colours, so that was entirely my fault. I was inspired by some vague idea of purification—clean page, untrodden snow, etc., etc.—but the effect is chilly, even on a day like today. Not *cool* or *fresh*, but *chilly*.

Here's my book. Oh, and there's the gin.

The house chooses this moment to pull one of its favourite tricks: falling deeply, illogically silent, as if there's nobody but me—and it—for miles. I hate it when it does that. It's worse than the noises.

I wait, tensed, for a good minute, and then: *All right, you couple of lazy swine!* I say, inside my head. *I'll bring you the gin!*

When I was a child, I used to talk to myself, out loud, all the time. It was the thing my brother and sisters ragged me for. Janey had her thumb-sucking, Deb her hair-chewing, Ron his fear of the dark, I my semi-audible muttering. The others outgrew their quirks years ago, but it took Hawthorn House to deprive me of mine.

Guy and Joey shout, "Hooray!" when they see me, and "Kate, you're a sport!" and they laugh when I roll my eyes. It feels good to step into the sun, and I'd like to stay, but they don't really want me. Anyway, the bath is running.

. . .

SOMEHOW OR OTHER WE MANAGE not to be late, despite making two circuits of the village green, three U-turns, and very nearly colliding with a double-decker bus as we cross the main road. (*Very nearly* is a bit over the top, insists Guy, but I disagree.)

Nina opens the door. After she's said, "Hello," and "Come in," she dries up, so it's just as well her father comes down the stairs when he does. I've brought a jar of my rhubarb jam, which goes down well (with him, anyway) and gives us something to talk about for at least ten seconds.

Mr. Woodrow looks at me suspiciously when I blurt, "What a beautiful house!" I suppose he thinks 7 Canal Road run of the mill compared to our place, and suspects me of sarcasm, but I'm perfectly sincere. The Woodrows' sitting-room is exactly what a sitting-room should be—full of lamps, warm colours, slightly shabby cushions, a chess table, an upright piano, and a curious Gothic desk decorated with Chinese dragons and chock-full of hidey-holes and odd-shaped drawers. The french windows are open, and there's a rosebush outside, thick with white flowers, which makes me remember the opening paragraph in *Dorian Gray*. I do have an unfortunate habit of prattling when I'm nervous, and all of a sudden I break out with the line in question: "*The studio was filled with the rich odour of roses, and when the light summer wind stirred amidst the trees of the garden, there came* . . . something, something, something . . . *the more delicate perfume of* something. I've forgotten. Sorry. I think it's *lilac*."

Everyone, apart from Nina, is looking at me now, and their expressions range from startled-sceptical (Guy), to startled-amused (Joey), to merely startled (Mr. Woodrow). Nina is absently running her fingertips over her lower lip, and I'm not sure she'd notice me if I broke into song and danced a hornpipe on the sofa.

I'm never my best at parties, but I didn't expect to be this edgy. I put it down, in part, to Mr. Woodrow's manner. At first glance I had him down as gentle—which he is—but he's also one of those unsettling people who *truly* look at you when you shake hands for the first time, and *truly* listen when you speak. I also feel worried about Joey, who has the potential to say something chummy/rude (he says *chummy*, I say *rude*) even when he's sober—which he's very much not.

Guy's been knocking back the gin all afternoon too, but he holds his drink well. If anything, it makes him unduly quiet.

The party is struggling to move on from my Wildean declamation, so I say, "Please forgive me, Mr. Woodrow. The rosebush put me in mind of a book I'd been reading, with a description of a charming room—that's all it was. I'm not eccentric, I just talk too much when I'm nervous."

His unease seems to melt. "Don't apologise! Don't be nervous, either, and do please call me Henry, Mrs. Nicholson."

"Kate."

". . . Kate. Do sit down, all of you."

Guy takes his place next to me on the sofa, Joey drops into an armchair, Nina perches on a stool with her back to the piano. The dog wanders in and has a good sniff at us all, before flopping down on the hearthrug. We talk for a while about small things: the weather, the royal family, the potholes on Canal Road. Henry says something about the difficulty of finding good servants nowadays, but Guy says, "Kate and I manage without any help," and the conversation dries up.

Nina looks radiant, in a way that children sometimes do and adults don't, though no doubt she'd take that as an insult if I said it to her face. (I would dearly like to be called a child again, but I'm twenty-five—two years older than my husband—and soon to be a mother, so the likelihood is small and shrinking.) I get a sad-happy feeling at the sight of her sitting there, framed by the flowering garden—tensed, shy, and lost in a dream. I'd say it was nostalgia for my own teenaged years, but that seems presumptuous. I wasn't pretty like Nina, and I never wore a dress half so well.

"Your shoes, Nina?" murmurs her father, returning from the kitchen with a tray of sherry glasses, but she shoots him such a pleading look that he lets it go, and a thought touches me, suddenly, like a shaft of sunlight. It's too swift and strange to put into words, but I'll try, anyway. It goes something like: *Nina is a daughter! I might have a daughter! This thing I'm lugging around like a boulder in my belly might be—will be—an actual person, with a physical presence, and private ideas of her own. One day we might have a guarded tiff, in front of strangers, about bare feet versus shoes.* It's seems so extraordinary that I'm tempted to speak, but I don't.

I wonder what's become of Nina's mother. She's dead, I'm sure. Henry doesn't look like the divorcing kind; he's got "widower" written all over him. I watch the careful way he pours four glasses of sherry, and a half-measure for Nina, and hope to goodness Joey doesn't say anything (*Hey, Henry, where're you hiding the lovely Mrs. Woodrow?*). It's exactly the sort of thing he might do with half a bottle of gin inside him.

I'm about to compliment Nina on her striking dress, but her father is handing me my glass, and then Joey pipes up:

"Henry, I almost forgot! I brought you a bottle of rye from home."

Well, thank goodness he's finally remembered. He's been clutching that bottle since we arrived, and it was starting to get ridiculous. It looked as if he'd brought his own provisions.

"Oh, Mr. Roussin, how kind."

"Call me Joey, please."

". . . Joey, but it's too generous. You certainly didn't bring it all the way from Canada for me."

"No, that's true. I brought it for Guy here, but he doesn't need it. He's already pickled in gin, through and through, like a . . . like a herring."

Guy might at least defend himself—but no. He says, "Herring aren't pickled in gin, you ass."

"Open it!" Joey insists. "C'mon, Henry, have a taste. You'll love it! It'll put the hairs on your chest." He prises the whisky bottle from his host's hands, proffering it around, and Guy downs his sherry in one, so as to make room in the glass.

"Guy!" I hiss.

Henry clears his throat.

Nina watches avidly, but when I catch her eye she looks demurely at her knees.

What should I do? There's a folded copy of *The Times* on the hearth and I can just make out the headline. Oh God, I want to go home.

"How about all this to-do in Germany?" I ask brightly. "What do you think of this new president fellow?"

Henry corrects me, but with such a look of gratitude that I can't mind.

"I believe the title is *Führer*, rather than *president*," he says. "As I understand it, on Hindenburg's death the roles of president and chancellor were merged, and the new title—this Hitler fellow's title—is *Führer*, or, to be really precise, *Führer und Reichskanzler*."

"Oh . . ." In different circumstances, Henry's pedantry might amuse me, but Joey and Guy are snorting into their whiskies like naughty boys at the back of class, which makes me feel about fifty years older than I am.

"Well," I plough on. "What do you make of him, anyway? He seems a bossy piece of work, from what I've read."

My beloved husband tops up his rye and says he's not given it much thought. Joey says, "Hitler? The guy with the droll moustache?" which sets them spluttering again. Presumably, the fact that Henry wears a moustache has some bearing on their hilarity, although his is perfectly nice and not in the least Führer-esque.

"I don't know." Henry applies himself to my question. "You may be right. We'll see. It's early days."

He doesn't show that his guests have upset him, except by turning away and pretending to occupy himself with the decanter. If only he were a child, rather than a middle-aged man, I could put my arm around him and tell him to take no notice of those half-baked boozers. Isn't it stupid, sometimes, what etiquette will and will not permit? By the same token, there's not much I can do about Guy and Joey, except glare.

"I forgot to pick any parsley." Nina stands up abruptly, places her untouched glass on the corner of the desk, and slips away through the french windows. Somehow, whatever the reason, this evening has significance for her—because she's young, because it's summer, because she's got a new dress—and they're spoiling it. Honestly, I could kill them both. Guy, at least, notices her departure and his cocksure smile fades.

I wonder whether Nina is aware of how she looks, moving through the twilight garden, her face and arms ghostly white among the shadows? She's a poem in human form, walking in beauty like the night (*pace* Byron). I hadn't noticed the dewy scent of the grass before, but I notice it now, as if she's crushing out its sweetness with the soles of her feet.

"I need some fresh air," says Guy, in a humbler tone. Joey agrees—"Yeah, me too"—recharges their glasses to the brim, and follows his friend into the garden. I stay put, of necessity. The sofa is deep and soft, and getting up will involve me in ungainly antics. Either that, or I'll need a hand, and I'm too shy to ask Henry to help.

We watch the men loitering and drinking on the lawn, and Nina standing with her hand flat against the trunk of the cherry tree, forgetful of the parsley. They don't speak to her, and she neither speaks nor looks at them, but somehow, in this brief moment, they're a trio. Is it the failing light that makes the scene so eerie? I don't know. It makes me wish I were a painter.

"That dress . . ." says her father with feeling.

"It suits her," I assure him. "She looks lovely. It must be hard to watch your child turn into a grown-up, though. Preferable to any realistic alternative, but still hard."

I'm beginning to suspect Henry of never smiling, so when he does, it's oddly touching.

"Children have an awkward habit of changing, just as you're getting used to them," he says, and I nod. I'm exchanging parental platitudes like an old hand, when really I know nothing. I haven't even read the *Essential Advice for New Mothers* book that Deb lent me—not properly. No doubt it's useful, but I can't stand Dr. What's-his-name's tone of voice. He sounds so frigid compared to Oscar Wilde.

I accept a top-up of sherry and think how pleasant it is in this room, with the lamplight, and the old-fashioned seascapes on the wall, and the book of Arthurian legends on the chess table. Despite Henry's last observation, I think it must be nice to live here in quiet harmony, a father and daughter together. I bet they never bicker at the tops of their voices, or mire themselves in sullen silences, or ago-nise about what the other one is thinking. I bet they talk about art and books all the time.

"Your home reminds me of mine, when I was growing up," I say, "except that there were lots of us—three girls and one boy—not to mention Guy."

"Ah, so you've known Guy from childhood?"

"Yes, we were next-door neighbours, growing up in Carlisle. He didn't have any siblings, and his parents were not very... Well, we took pity on him, rather. He must have spent half his life round at ours."

"And then the two of you grew up, and fell in love, and left Carlisle?"

"We grew up, and shortly after we married, Guy got a job at an accountancy firm in Chester, so we moved here—to Cottenden—to Hawthorn House."

Henry leans back against the Gothic desk, and folds his arms. He looks as though he's going to make a deep pronouncement, but all he says is, "Yes, I see."

I sip the dark-brown sherry and crave a long, ice-cold drink. Oh, if only the baby would stop thrashing about! It gives me heartburn, and I have to splay my free hand across my bump to hide its ripples and bounces.

"How long have you lived in Cottenden?" I ask, as soon as I can catch breath.

Outside, the men are moving closer to Nina, who is still standing by the cherry tree. Their figures are dim in the twilight. I catch the rumble of their voices, although not their words.

"All my life."

"Aha, then you'll know about our haunted house?"

"Your...?" Henry looks flustered; he thinks I'm being eccentric again. "I'm afraid I... Surely it was built very recently, wasn't it, Hawthorn House? I remember the fuss, a couple of years ago, when the builders were in. The Red Lion pub raised a stink about access being blocked along the lane."

Does Henry not know about our murder, then? He must know, if he's lived here all his life. I'm counting on it.

"It's not *new*, as such. It was a dilapidated farmhouse for years; the man who sold it to us did it up, and added an extension. The old building's still there, underneath."

"Is that right?"

The baby wriggles wildly, and I have to close my eyes for a second.

"Yes, and the woman who made our curtains said someone was murdered there, not so very many years ago. She said Hawthorn House was haunted by the 'Dark Lady' and that we were 'brave' to live there."

I know some men (e.g., my brother-in-law Mike, Deb's husband) who would have laughed a condescending laugh and said, "Poppy-cock!" but Henry doesn't do that. He frowns hard at the carpet and says, "A murder? In Cottenden?"

"Someone left flowers for her in the spring—at least, I suppose they were for her. A bunch of purple hyacinths, by the gate."

Henry's face clears. "Yes, I think . . . Yes, I do remember. I believe it was during the war, or shortly afterwards; a young woman, stran-gled by her lover. I'd forgotten it had anything to do with your house." His voice drops, apologetically. "There was so very much death, around then. Perhaps that sounds . . ."

"No, no. I understand."

He adds, "They weren't Cottenden people—neither the mur-derer nor his victim. If I remember rightly, they were Londoners, passing through."

I haven't lived here long enough to class myself as a "Cottenden person," so I can't draw much comfort from this.

"Do you know what happened? I suppose they were driving along, having a blazing row, and the man—what?—he turned down the quiet lane and pulled up outside the deserted old ruin and . . ."

"Something along those lines. There was no great mystery to it."

"He was caught?"

Henry nods.

"And hanged?"

He nods again.

"And the poor woman . . ."

Henry holds up a warning hand as Nina enters, full of smiles, twirling a single sprig of parsley.

I fall silent. I understand him perfectly. My sister Janey used to be thin-skinned when she was in her early teens; nobody dared mention the word *death*, let alone *murder*, in her earshot, in case it sent her off in a spin. She used to berate me for reading crime stories and leaving them lying around.

"Dad, we must eat; it's getting terribly late."

"Quite right, darling. Let's go through."

Guy and Joey appear behind Nina. The three of them have matching smiles, and I wonder what they've been discussing, but I don't know how to ask. If I say, *What's the joke?* I'll sound crabby and left-out.

Nina leads Guy and Joey into the dining-room. Henry gazes down at me, beached on the sofa cushions, and says, "Are you . . . ? Can you . . . ?"

His hands are dry and sinewy, and they don't waver in my grasp. I let go the moment I'm upright, and if there's any embarrassment I disguise it with laughter—or try to. Henry won't join in.

"May I say . . ." he hesitates. "May I say, I think you're awfully patient. It's a quality I admire."

Damn it, now I'm blushing. It's kind of him, but not necessary in the least. I hope I don't come across as martyred.

. . .

ALL THIS TIME THE DINING-ROOM windows have been ajar and the lamps switched on. No one else notices the insect invasion, or maybe they're not bothered that there are moths and mayflies and goodness knows what, fluttering on the leafy wallpaper and creeping across the ceiling. I take my seat, conscious of a hundred tiny bodies pulsating above my head.

Perhaps it's my head that's pulsating. I want to lie down in a cold, dark place, where there's no need to talk. An underground cave would suit me well, yawningly black and silent, except for the drip of water down the walls.

Henry carves the chicken and I say, "This looks lovely!" but I feel a fool when nobody reacts. There are secret glances passing about between Joey, Guy, and Nina, and I have a funny, fleeting daydream in which Henry and I are married, and the other three are our children, and I tell them to stop being rude if they expect to have any pudding.

Somehow it's hotter in here than it was in the sitting-room, despite the open windows, and I'm not the only one to feel it. Guy has loosened his tie and pushed up his sleeves. Joey has ditched his tie altogether and unfastened his collar. Everyone's clothes, except Nina's, look damp and wilted.

"What a summer!" I remark, brilliantly. "We could do with some rain, though."

Yet again, there's no response, unless you count a meagre smile from Henry. Nina passes the potatoes, and as I'm helping myself the baby squirms, trampling my stomach, squashing my spine, bruising my lungs. I try everything that discretion will allow to get comfortable—sitting straighter, slumping my shoulders, arching my back, twisting sideways in my chair—but nothing works. I can't eat, because there's not enough room inside me. Eventually someone will notice, and I'll have to explain, but for now, I keep my knife and fork busy, cutting potatoes into smaller and smaller pieces, and moving lettuce leaves around the plate.

"This is delicious," I say. (Why won't I learn?)

"Thank you," Henry replies. "I hope you gentlemen are enjoying it too?"

I note, anxiously, that Henry addresses his question to the water-jug rather than the "gentlemen." (He and I and Nina have moved on to water; Joey and Guy are still on whisky.)

Joey lifts a drumstick to his mouth and peels the skin away with his teeth. He's staring at Nina. "Delicious . . ." he says, lingering over the word and turning it into something filthy. I'm not entirely sure how he does it; I don't think Guy could do it if he tried. Joey chews and swallows through a lazy smile.

Guy murmurs, "Joey . . ." but as reprimands go, it's weak.

"They've been sitting in the blazing sun all afternoon, drinking gin," I say loudly. "Not that that's any excuse."

"Excuse for what?" Joey hiccups and laughs simultaneously. "Darling Kate, love of my life, excuse for what?" He reaches across the table for my hand, but I lay it in my lap.

Joey thinks Henry hasn't a clue—that he's an old dear who wouldn't recognise an innuendo if it hit him in the face—but I'm not so sure. I study the straight-backed way Henry sits, with his jacket on and his tie properly tied, sipping water, helping himself to mayonnaise, stabbing a polite-sized chunk of chicken with his fork.

"When are we going to meet Mrs. Henry Woodrow?" asks Joey, belching softly. "Where is she? She's not dead, is she? Or, I know, maybe Nina didn't have a mother, she just emerged from a scallop shell like the goddess thingummy."

Nina stopped eating and smiling some time ago. She shoots Guy a furtive glance, and he says, "Joey!" more sharply than before, which isn't to say *sharply*. I would intervene, but the baby is battering my insides with great gusto and I'm reluctant to open my mouth in case the sherry comes back up. We're already the dinner-party guests from hell; all we need is for me to be sick on my plate.

"The goddess Aphrodite," says Henry. "I'm sorry to disappoint, but Nina did have a mother, who died in a car accident twelve years ago. Tell me, Mr. Roussin, are you a family man yourself?"

Joey spurts a mouthful of whisky back into his glass.

"Hell, no! I had a woman for a couple of years—had a kid too—but it didn't work out. Family life isn't for me—not yet, not ever."

I close my eyes and think, *Do something, Guy*, but my husband is not receptive to telepathy today. There's a tickle at the back of my neck, and it may only be a strand of hair, but I picture insects raining from the ceiling. Gingerly, I itch my scalp and wriggle my shoulders. The table has gone quiet, except for the sound of Joey's chomping. I can't bear to look directly at Henry, but I watch from the corner of my eye as he lays down his knife and fork and dabs the corners of his mouth with his napkin.

"Forgive me, Mr. Roussin," he says mildly, "but when you say you 'had a woman,' do you mean to say you were married?"

Joey shrugs and carries on eating. "I guess. Not *married* married, in a church and all, but Patty and I were an item all right."

Nina looks frightened. What must she think? "Joey, Patty, and the Kid" is a very familiar—a very Joey-ish—story to me, and I've allowed it to lose its edge over time.

"I see," Henry continues. "And when you say you 'had a kid,' are we to understand you actually fathered a child with this woman?"

"Uh-huh." Joey rubs his greasy fingers on the napkin and starts to laugh. "Oh yes, Mr. Woodrow, sir, that's exactly what I did with this woman. You've hit the nail on the head. Patty and me, we f . . . we f . . ." Joey is laughing so hard he can't get the word out. Or maybe it's the other way round; maybe it's the fact he can't get the word out that's making him laugh. "We *fathered* away together, like you wouldn't believe."

"Nina, go to your room." Henry's voice is as level as ever, but his stillness is the hushed sort that precedes a storm. I begin to feel dizzy, and find I'm holding my breath without meaning to.

Nina gets up and stands behind her empty chair, clutching the wooden back. The chair looks like an antique, and a delicate one at that, and when she leans her weight on it, it creaks. You can see by the way her knuckles fluctuate from white to pink that she is tightening and loosening her hold. I wonder why she doesn't do as she's told, and leave? If I were her, I wouldn't wait to be asked twice.

Joey drains another glass of rye. "Aw, come on Henry, old chap! Don't be sore about it. Patty and I had our fun, and then agreed to go our separate ways. She's fine—she and the kid are both fine—she married some other guy and they all went off to live in Alberta, or some place west."

Henry adjusts his knife and fork so that they are lying across his plate in the "finished" position. Quietly, he gets to his feet and disappears into the kitchen, leaving the rest of us in silence. Another moment goes by before Joey shrugs, reaches across the table, and lifts an untouched chicken wing off Henry's plate. I can't stand the sound of his chewing, and I can't stand the casual way he tops up Guy's glass, and above all I can't stand the way my husband gives me a little shrug as if to say, *What can I do? Joey will be Joey.* Nina is staring at her plate, her lips slightly parted, her fingers squeezing the back of the chair. A moth blunders about inside the lampshade, its dark shape coming and going against the lighted linen.

Nobody, apart from me, seems to hear the tinkle of breaking glass from the kitchen. I look round the table, but they're all nestled in their own little worlds. My napkin falls to the floor as I heave myself up from my chair.

Henry is standing by the kitchen sink, studying the blood that's welling on his left palm. There's a shattered glass at his feet.

"Oh, goodness!" I exclaim. "How did that happen?"

He glances at me impatiently, whips a handkerchief from his pocket, and winds it round at double speed.

"Let me take a look."

He ducks out of reach. "No, thank you."

I frown and poke at one of the larger shards with my foot, recognising the stem of a sherry glass. Most of the other bits are tiny, like granules of sugar.

"You're angry," I say. "Quite right, too. You were so kind to invite us, and we've ruined your evening."

"*You* haven't ruined it." Henry slides his injured hand into his jacket pocket. I don't think he's noticed the smear of blood on his shirtfront, or the three droplets on the tiled floor.

"All right, *they* have. My husband and Joey. You wouldn't have hurt your hand if it wasn't for their appalling rudeness."

"Your husband and his friend are not responsible for my clumsiness with the sherry glass."

"I don't believe it was clumsiness."

"It was."

"I'm pretty sure it wasn't."

His expression wavers between annoyance and amusement, but in the end he laughs, and I let out the sigh that's been gathering in my chest all evening. He takes his hand from his pocket and allows me to bandage it properly, with my own clean handkerchief.

We were already talking quietly, but Henry lowers his voice another notch. "You know, there's something I ought to tell you, or rather, something I ought to clarify . . ."

He takes a deep breath, as if bracing himself to speak, but before he can go on, a new, shrill voice starts up in the dining-room, startling us both. The speaker is female, but she's certainly not Nina. "Well, would you . . . Rose was right! She said she'd spotted you just now, through the window, but I didn't believe her. The cheek of it, you little minx! Right off my washing-line in broad daylight! I was going to wear that dress tonight—I washed it specially—and I've been that upset, wondering where it had got to. Where's your father, I should like to know? Where is he?"

I follow Henry to the doorway. The stranger is dressed to kill, in red, and the dining-room smells of her musky perfume.

"Mrs. Allen?" Henry is weak with bemusement.

At the sight of him, Mrs. Allen renews her tirade, but it's impossible to make sense of her accusations, because Nina is talking over them with childlike grief: "No! It wasn't like that! Rose said I could! She said I could! She told me it was hers!" and the louder the woman gets, the louder Nina gets, until the back of the antique chair gives way and the top strut snaps off in her hands.

Guy watches blearily, through half-closed eyes. Joey seems thoroughly entertained, and continues to eat.

I touch Henry's arm and lean close to his ear. "We'll get out of your way."

Amidst all the noise and confusion he turns and looks at me. We're like two people on passing trains, staring out of our respective windows, coming suddenly face to face. For a second—less than a second—I am his whole view, and he is mine, and then we're drawn apart again, in opposite directions.

Oh, honestly Kate, listen to yourself. Whatever it is (if anything), it's over before it's begun. There's no need to make some great romance out of it.

. . .

IT'S A GOOD JOB THERE'S hardly any traffic on the roads, because Guy's steering is erratic, to say the least. Joey is no help, guffawing away in the passenger seat, making Guy helpless with laughter, offering swigs of whisky all round.

"I thought that bottle was a present for Mr. Woodrow?" My eyes are closed and my head is bouncing against the back window as we veer from hedge to hedge. It's not that I want to talk, but Joey keeps reaching round and pressing me to have a taste of "Manitoba's finest," and it's difficult to shut myself away inside my own mind. I contemplate my bed with a yearning so fervent, it's practically religious.

"I don't think rye whisky is Henry's thing," Joey replies. "He's more of a sweet sherry man, wouldn't you say, Guy, *old chap*?"

I open my eyes to see Joey giving his friend a jovial dig in the arm, which sends the car onto the verge, bumping in and out of a shallow ditch. Joey pronounces *Henry* as "Hen-rare" and *old chap* as "old chep," although Henry's English was no posher than Guy's or mine.

When I shut my eyes again I see Nina, close to tears and red in the face. Goodness knows what that business with the dress was all about, but something about her anguish moved me—I don't know why. She had seemed so luminous, earlier on.

I know when we've arrived home, because the wheel arch scrapes the gatepost and we bang into something that shatters, and Guy says, "Damn it, Kate, what'd you want to put a bloody great flowerpot there for?" He stops and yanks the handbrake, and they burst out laughing as if this is the funniest evening of their lives.

. . .

I LIE DOWN IN ALL my finery, and for the first time since we moved in I don't care if the house is haunted, just as long as it's dark, and there's a leafy breeze ruffling the curtains. I'm almost sure Guy won't come up—Joey's unearthed a bottle of port from the cupboard under the stairs—but he does. He brings me a glass of water and a cigarette, and says, "Darling, are you okay up here, all on your own?" I ask him to take my shoes off, and he manages, even though they're the ones with the fiddly buckles.

He sits beside me on the bed, and offers me a light, but I don't feel like smoking. We hold hands in silence and he strokes my knuckles with his thumb. I can smell the whisky on his breath.

"I'm sorry it went a bit wrong this evening," he says.

The baby kicks, so I take Guy's hand and place it palm-down on my belly. It's meant to be in lieu of words—it's meant to signify, *Never mind, I still love you*—but I've forgotten about Guy's distaste for touching the bump. I can't make out his expression, but I can feel the stiffness in his arm, and the uneasy twitch in his fingers. After a few seconds—after he's done his bit—he removes his hand and sits apart from me, with his elbows on his knees.

"Don't be cross with Joey," he says. "It's not his fault. You know what he's like—he's a free spirit—he can't cope with stuffy types."

"Free spirit! Guy, he was downright rude. You both were."

The mattress wobbles as he straightens his back.

"Oh, come on, Kate. You don't see eye to eye with Henry Woodrow types, any more than I do."

"Why does Henry Woodrow have to be written off as a 'type'? He was a polite, normal person. Just because he doesn't have a string of illegitimate children, or a drink problem—just because he keeps his tie on at dinner—it doesn't mean he has a smaller soul than Joey."

"Joey doesn't have a *string* of illegitimate—"

"Don't be obtuse. You know what I mean."

"You know what *I* mean, too. I bet Henry Woodrow has a private income; bet he sits around all day writing letters to *The Times* about 'The Trouble with Servants.'"

Joey bellows up the stairs. "Guy! C'mon, where are you? Bring Kate. This port won't drink itself."

Guy gets up and crosses the room. I'm getting used to the dark, and I can see the whites of my husband's eyes as he looks back at me.

"Hey, Guy! We need cheese! D'you have any cheese?"

Guy sighs. He keeps twisting the door-knob and releasing it with a snap. I'm reminded of Nina, gripping the back of her chair, lost in her mysterious thoughts.

"Go," I say. "Please, go. I'd rather be on my own."

Once he's gone, I press the cool glass against my temples and drink the water in long, swift gulps.

. . .

WHEN I WAKE, THE DARKNESS has softened to grey, but it's still too early for birdsong. The breeze has dropped and there's no noise from downstairs. I sweep my arm across the bed, but Guy isn't there.

A pain woke me. Was that it? Or a nightmare? A nightmare woke me. There was a puppet prancing about like a maniac, and suddenly all its strings were cut, with a single slice from a pair of shears.

Something has happened. The taut threads that held the baby have snapped; the weights and balances inside my belly have fallen loose. Cautiously, I move my legs apart. They, and the dress, and the bed-sheets, are soaking wet and warm.

The pain comes again. I'm caught in a giant's fist—*fee-fi-fo-fum*—and he's grinding my bones to make his bread. I shout, "Mum!" but my shout comes out as a whisper.

The baby isn't due for three weeks.

I lie very still.

I want my mother and father. I want my sister Deborah. I want Mum to swish the curtains apart on our sunlit street and tell me it's all a dream. Of course I didn't marry Guy! (Guy Nicholson? Quiet little Guy, from next door? What a funny idea!) I didn't move away from home. I'm too young to be a wife, and to have a baby.

The spasm comes again and what I want . . . what I want . . . Oh my God, what I want is to brace myself against a pair of sinewy hands; a pair of hands that won't waver inside my grasp, or pull away when I push too hard, or wince when I dig in with my nails.

I want a pair of hands that will save me, and hold me, and never let me go.

3

Nina

September 30, 1938

THE GIRLS LOUNGE ON ROSE'S BEDROOM WINDOWSILL, warming their backs in the sun. They've done a lot of talking this week, but now they are silent, in an easy-going, eyes-closed way. There's something about smoking together that feels like peace.

Nina was the first to discover cigarettes, but it doesn't seem to matter that she beat Rose to it. When she arrived in Buxton at the end of last week, and unearthed the packet of Player's Navy Cut from the bottom of her suitcase, there were none of the usual difficulties. Rose did not say, *I'm not sure I want to be the kind of woman who smokes*, and Nina did not say, *It takes a certain skill; you probably won't take to it*. The one was as eager to sample a new bad habit as the other was to share.

Nina blows a long, thin stream of smoke and smiles. It all started four years ago, that summer when Rose seemed, suddenly, to know everything, and they fell out over Lyn's black-and-cherry dress. After that, the competition looked likely to go back and forth forever: Rose was the first to get a permanent wave, but Nina was the first to drink in a pub without her father's knowledge; Rose was the first to leave school and get a job; Nina was the first to kiss a boy. So it had gone on until this year, when they turned eighteen and called a tacit truce to their tacit war. There's no obvious reason for the change, unless it's the fact that they aren't children anymore.

"Can I say something awful?" Rose asks.

Nina opens her eyes.

"Fire away."

Rose smokes glamorously, with a languid sweep of her arm and her head tilted back against the wall. This time last year she would have done so with a defensive air, and Nina would have loathed her for it, but now they both find it funny.

Rose lowers her voice. "I hope there *is* a war."

"Me too," Nina agrees, without a pause.

"I suppose that makes us terrible human beings, doesn't it?"

"Pretty bloody terrible."

Nina shifts her legs so that she's sitting sideways to the glass with a better view of her friend. The sash is open a few inches at the top, in a forlorn attempt to stop Rose's bedroom from smelling of cigarettes, since her parents are of the view that nice girls don't smoke. Mr. Allen himself keeps a pipe clenched between his teeth, morning, noon, and night—Nina pictures him puffing away in his sleep—but he answers their indignation with a smile and says, "Ah, I'm neither nice, nor a girl, so I'm excused."

Nina runs her eyes along the steep curve of Hillier Street, with its cobbled pavements and crooked chimney-pots. A young man moved into the terraced house across the way, a few days ago, and his bedroom is opposite Rose's. He spies on them when he thinks they're distracted, and blushes fiercely when they wave back, but he's not around this evening. Disappointing.

Nina will have to leave Buxton tomorrow. She could spend forever rambling over the hills with Rose: walking, picnicking, gossiping, laughing till their eyes water and their stomachs ache. There's no avoiding it, though; she's already prolonged her stay by a couple of days, and if she tries to spin it out any further she'll lose her job at the cosmetics counter in Browns of Chester. Miss Whelan is already sceptical of the new girl. ("Wipe off that bored expression," Nina has been warned, on more than one occasion, and she's only had the job since August. "My customers don't come in here to get scowled at.")

Nina wants to explain to Miss Whelan that she's not so much bored as uneasy. Up until she finished school, Nina had been counting on a vaguely conceived but thrilling future: life was just around the corner, just beyond the horizon, just a question of waiting. Whenever she's with Rose, she recovers some of that conviction, but when it's just her and Dad, and the job at Browns—which she only keeps because it kills time and earns her a bit of pin money—then a suspicion tugs at her sleeve. What if this *is* the future? What if she's the victim of a practical joke? What if the punchline to growing up is (wait for it) that nothing changes. Nothing that matters.

For Nina, the highlight of a normal day consists of glimpsing the man from Hawthorn House—Guy Nicholson—as she dashes past his office on her way to catch the Cottenden bus. *There*, she thinks, *that tells you all you need to know about my existence*, although in actual fact she hasn't told anyone about her secret crush—not even Rose. Mr. Nicholson never comes into Browns. Occasionally his wife comes in with the little boy to buy a pot of face cream, or a compact, and she always smiles and says, "Hello," but not in a way that invites conversation. She's probably remembering that disastrous dinner party, when Nina made an absolute fool of herself by stealing a dress off the Allens' washing-line. Not that she *did* steal Lyn's dress . . . but never mind that now.

"Suppose there is a war," says Nina. "What will you do?"

"Join the effort, of course! Like a shot. And if Mum and Dad don't like it, they can lump it."

"But what will you actually do? Specifically?"

"I don't know; something that involves a uniform. Whoever has the most flattering look. The ATS, perhaps?"

"You sad child, the Auxiliary Territorial Service is part of the army. Their uniforms are khaki."

"What's wrong with khaki?"

"What's *right* with khaki? Honestly, Rose Allen, you used to have a smashing dress sense. Your tastes are obviously deteriorating with age."

"You're the one that's deteriorating, Nina Woodrow; you used to be above such superficial concerns. Any sign of Dad yet?"

Nina is sitting in the lookout's corner of the windowsill. She presses her cheek against the glass, screws up her eyes, and peers down the street.

"No. All clear."

As soon as Mr. Allen comes striding up the hill from town, briefcase in hand, the girls will stub their cigarettes and duck away from the window. The other day he caught sight of them and wasn't best pleased, although he doesn't get cross in the awful, quiet way Nina's father does. Mr. Allen described them as looking "like a pair of lizards in a tank, soaking up the sun" and expressed surprise, as he tucked into his dinner, that they didn't have anything better to do with their time. Mrs. Allen rolled her eyes and wondered, mildly, what on earth the neighbours must think, before urging Nina to help herself to more potatoes.

"Girls!" Mrs. Allen calls up to them now, from the hall. "Are you going to give me a hand laying the table?"

They lock eyes in mutinous silence before shouting, in unison, "Coming!"

Rose swings her feet and sighs. Nina closes her eyes and takes a final pull on her cigarette. When she opens them again she says, "Oh

Lord! He's here!" and they slide down the wall and onto the floor in a heap of smoky coughs and giggles. Rose reaches for the cracked teacup that serves as their ashtray.

"Did he spot us?"

"I don't think so; he was too busy chatting to a tall, youngish chap. Oh goodness, Rose, has your dad brought a guest for dinner? I bet he has, you know! A man! For you! They're going to marry you off."

Rose drops her head onto Nina's shoulder.

"Don't joke." She is as close to seriousness as she's been all afternoon. "Honestly, Nina, don't joke. Did the chap in question have slicked blond hair and a long chin?"

"I can't comment on the hair, because he was wearing a hat, but yes to the chin."

"Hell's bells, I bet it's Harold Lamb."

"*Who?*"

"Harold Lamb. He works with Dad. Apparently he's going to be a big noise in the world of Buxton banking, one of these days."

Nina thinks that's funny and wants Rose to think so too. "Mrs. Lamb," she taunts, in a sing-song whisper, swaying from side to side, bumping her friend's shoulder on every other beat. "You're going to be Mrs. Lamb." At first, Rose is irritable ("Get *off*, Nina!"), but eventually she gives in to a reluctant smile.

"Girls!" Mrs. Allen calls again, from the bottom of the stairs, as Mr. Allen's key turns in the lock.

The two of them hobble to their feet, shaking out their pins and needles and smoothing the creases from their skirts.

"We're coming!" Rose shouts as Nina retrieves a bag of mint imperials from underneath her camp-bed. They take two each and chew earnestly.

"Okay?"

"Okay."

In as far as this breath-freshening exercise is meant to delude the parents, it's futile, since the smoke clings to their clothes, skin, and hair. In as far as it constitutes a shared ritual, Nina wouldn't dream of calling it into question.

. . .

ROSE AND NINA ARE SUPPOSED to lay the table for each meal, without being asked. *That's the deal,* as Mrs. Allen occasionally puts it, in a tone more hopeful than resolute. As they descend the stairs this evening, Nina expects a telling-off, but the atmosphere in the hall is strange, and not the least bit cross—quite the opposite.

Mrs. Allen laughs as she says, "Girls! Oh, girls! You won't have heard the news!" The strange young man says, "Hello there . . . Harold Lamb . . . Wonderful . . . So glad," whilst shaking their unresponsive hands and pecking at their cheeks. Subtly, the girls move closer together, until their arms touch. Harold is wearing an abundance of musty-smelling aftershave, and Nina knows by the pressure at her elbow that Rose has noticed the same thing, at exactly the same time. It seems to her that their thoughts are identical, and as plain to one another as speech.

"Peace for our time," says Mr. Allen, kissing his wife and the girls, and clapping Harold on the back. "Peace with honour, no less. Marvellous news."

For a moment, Nina thinks something must have happened at the bank—perhaps the crabby old manager, the bane of Mr. Allen's life, has retired or died at last—but then she sees the evening paper he's waving, and although it's rolled up she can make out, or guess, the words *Munich* and *Chamberlain* and, in large capital letters, PEACE.

Over the jabber of introductions, apologies, and do-let-me-take-your-hat-and-coat, Mr. Allen reads excerpts from the front page in a booming voice.

"*Referring to the successful conclusion of his talk with Herr Hitler, Mr. Chamberlain went on, 'We regard the agreement signed last night and the Anglo-German Naval Agreement as symbolic of the desire of our two peoples never to go to war with one another again.'* Excellent news, eh? Jolly good chap, Chamberlain. My dear, we ought to telephone Michael and Lyn after dinner; they *will* be relieved."

Mrs. Allen is doing her level best to offer Harold Lamb a warm welcome, but he is ignoring her in his eagerness to apologise.

"Your husband *insisted* that I wasn't to spend this evening all alone like the poor old bachelor that I am," he explains, for the third or fourth time. "I hate putting you out, but he really was most insistent." Producing a brown paper bag from his briefcase, he adds that he's brought "a little bottle of something" to make up for the inconvenience of his visit, and to celebrate the success of the Munich talks.

As he draws the bottle from the bag, he makes a sly face and winks at the girls—but it's only ginger ale. Nina makes the mistake of catching Rose's eye and is forced to convert a snort into a cough. Over the course of the last week, the two of them have been making discreet forays into Mr. Allen's drinks cabinet, and they have concluded that vermouth is their favorite, followed by gin, followed by port. (Actually, Nina likes cherry brandy, but it's such an obviously childish choice that she's not about to admit it.)

"*Mr. Chamberlain concluded, 'My good friends, for the second time in our history, a British Prime Minister has returned from Germany bringing peace with honour. I believe it is peace for our time.'*"

Rose and Nina press elbows. *No war, after all*, is what that means. *Alas, no war! Poor me, poor you, poor us.*

"It's wonderful news," they say, out loud. "Really wonderful."

. . .

DINNER IS GOING TO TAKE forever this evening, and Nina wants to cry. There's still so much to talk about with Rose before they part tomorrow morning.

The five of them don't even head for the dining-room straight-away—no, this evening they have to stand about in the sitting-room, sipping ginger ale and nodding along to a blow-by-blow account of Harold Lamb's Day at the Office, while the parents mix gin cock-tails. (Mrs. Allen offers Harold one, but he's a teetotaller; it doesn't even *occur* to her to offer gin to the girls.)

Nina watches Harold's unenchanting mouth move and thinks about Guy Nicholson. If she blurs her focus, she can turn Harold's lips into his, but the effect requires a lot of concentration and only lasts for a moment. Guy Nicholson's mouth was playful and mys-terious, that twilight evening in the summer of '34, and he didn't yatter on and on; his Canadian friend did all the talking. When he touched her hand with a feather-light kiss, he might as well have stabbed her; she is certain her knees would have buckled if she hadn't been leaning her back against the cherry tree. They might give way now if she thinks about him too intently.

Oh, wouldn't you know it: Mrs. Allen has produced an entrée out of thin air, in honour of the occasion. As she leads the way to the dining-room she says that she hopes everyone likes cold consommé, and everyone replies, "Oh yes!" or "Lovely!" but Nina loathes cold consommé; one might as well eat a jellyfish. Besides, it will add a quarter of an hour to the meal.

Rose is seated to the left of her father and Nina to the right, with Harold and Mrs. Allen opposite. Thanks to Mr. Allen's intervening bulk, the girls can't even communicate by nudges or looks. If Nina slides her eyes sideways, she can see the soup spoon in Rose's right hand, poking listlessly at the consommé. She is sorely tempted to bring jellyfish into the conversation, just to make Rose laugh, but how does one casually introduce the subject of marine life into a discussion that is currently ranging between the politics of Buxton's high street bank and the politics of Czechoslovakia?

"You have to understand," Harold is saying, "that it's a very fine desk with a green reading lamp, in one of the larger first-floor offices, and Cunliffe has had his eye on it for a long time. But Miller told him in no uncertain terms; he said, *Mr. Cunliffe, that particular desk has been earmarked for Mr. Lamb.* Well, as you might imagine, *I* said—"

While Harold continues to talk, Rose puts her spoon down and rests her fist on the tablecloth. Mr. Allen places his large hand over his daughter's and gives it a little pat, and Nina hates him for it, even if she can't quite understand why. Mrs. Allen smiles at Rose across the table—and is there a trace of apology in the gesture, or does Nina simply feel there ought to be?

Rose pulls her hand free and stands up.

"I don't feel well," she says, dully. "Will you excuse me? I'm awfully sorry."

Everyone stops eating to watch her slip through the door, and nobody speaks while she pounds up the stairs. Mrs. Allen catches her husband's eye and subtly shakes her head.

"Shall I . . . ?" Nina asks, half standing.

"Thank you, dear; if you would."

. . .

IS ROSE ACTUALLY BEING SICK? Surely not, though she's all hunched up with her back to Nina and her shoulders are shaking.

"It's only me." Nina kneels down. She lifts her friend's dishevelled hair and tucks it behind her ear. "Are you crying or laughing?"

"I'm not sure," Rose moans into her hands.

"You're not upset about *Harold*, are you? Your parents aren't literally going to force you to marry him, you ninny; they're not that bad."

"I know." Rose uncovers her face. "It's not him, or even them. It's just . . ."

Nina strokes her hair. "Tell me."

"It's just *life*. There are so many things I want, but none of them are going to happen, are they?"

Nina nods, but at the same time she says, "Really and truly, it *is* good news about the war. Think of all the men who would have been killed, and won't be. Think of your brother. Isn't it nice that Michael can carry on milking cows and being married to Lyn, instead of—"

"Yes, yes, I understand all that, and it's not that I want a war, as such. It's just that I remember being a kid, sitting in your treehouse, poring over the atlas, dreaming up all sorts of schemes for the future . . . and now here I am eating jellied consommé with Harold Bloody Lamb, while he blathers on and on and on about nothing whatsoever, and my parents send me meaningful looks across the table."

Rose pauses to draw breath and Nina says, "Perhaps we should go ahead and open our own pet shop? That was our great ambition, wasn't it, about five years ago?"

"Perhaps we should."

A shadow brushes Nina's memory, and the coarse bark of the cherry-tree trunk presses through the back of her dress. In a spirit of honesty she admits, "I would like to experience one spectacular love affair before I tie myself to the pet shop for life."

"Naturally," Rose agrees. "The trouble is, he might be hard to shake off once you've finished with him. Spectacular lovers are notoriously difficult to get rid of."

Now they've got the giggles.

"I'll make sure he abandons me," Nina says. "Or dies, or something."

"But of course he must *die*! Imagine how badly it will reflect on you, if he leaves you for someone else!"

"That's true. All right: I'll treat him to a few weeks of whirlwind romance, and then I'll bump him off."

There are footsteps on the stairs: they must stop, but the pressure to be quiet makes everything doubly funny.

"Poor man," Rose whispers, squeakily. "You must make sure it's a pain-free death."

There's a tap on the door.

"If not actually *pleasurable*."

Mrs. Allen pokes her head round the door.

"Rose?" she begins, gently, but when she sees the two of them spluttering and sprawling on the floor, she sets her shoulders and folds her arms.

"Sorry, Mum," Rose whimpers, sitting up and pushing the hair from her face. "I wasn't completely pretending; I did feel a bit queasy."

"Did you? Well, you appear to have made a stunning recovery, so I suggest you get downstairs now—both of you—and start again."

There is a rebellious pause, during which nobody moves. In the blue dim of evening, it's difficult to read Mrs. Allen's face. She might be teetering on the brink of fury; she might be nowhere near.

"If we refuse?" Rose's voice is tiny. "What happens then?"

"If you *refuse*?" Mrs. Allen is never quite without a sense of humour, even when she's cross. "Oh, in that case I shall send Mr. Lamb upstairs to fetch you."

. . .

IT'S GONE TEN O'CLOCK BEFORE they're alone once more, sitting cross-legged on Rose's bed. Nina rummages through her handbag for the cigarettes and offers the box to Rose, but she shakes her head and says, "Let's do something really wicked. I don't know what, exactly, but something one heck of a lot worse than smoking. Something that would completely horrify Mum and Dad, if they ever found out."

Nina picks uneasily at a hole in the quilt. Heaven knows, she understands the lure of rebellion, but there's a hard-eyed quality that takes possession of Rose every now and then—it's there now—which makes her jittery.

"What kind of thing? You must have some idea."

Rose rests her chin on her hands and stares at the flapping curtains. They've been keeping the window open at night for the sweet, heathery air coming off the hills, but all of a sudden the summer has ended, and the wind that gusts down the street smells of dying leaves and sadness. Nina feels a strong urge to close the window and the curtains and to switch on all the lights.

"We could get drunk?" Nina suggests.

"On what? Harold Lamb's ginger ale? Dad will notice if we pinch any more of his stuff."

"I suppose."

They sit very still. Rose is deep in thought, but Nina is listening to the end-of-day sounds from downstairs: the clink of empty milk bottles, the gush of a tap, the low rumble of voices from the cluttered kitchen. Harold left half an hour ago, and the girls embarked on the washing-up, unasked, but then Rose went and broke a plate and her father lost his rag. "Absolutely bloody hopeless," he began, and there was obviously more to come, not just about the plate, but Mrs. Allen intervened and packed them off to bed.

Rose sits up tall. She grabs Nina's hands and gives them a shake. "Let's hold a séance."

"A séance? What, you mean talking to the dead?"

"Yes!" Rose is thrilled. "Let's summon the dead and ask them—"

"—what?"

"Anything! Whatever you like!"

The wooden sash rattles and they both jump: Nina feels the pulse in their linked fingers. She gets up to shut the window and roots through her packed suitcase for a cardigan. *Back home tomorrow*, she thinks, for the hundredth time. Back to dusting the shelves in Browns, and rearranging lipstick displays. Back to quiet evenings with Dad and a scratchy wireless tuned to the BBC Regional Programme.

"All right," she agrees. "We'll hold a séance. But how will we know what to do?"

"It'll be fine; we can make it up as we go along."

Nina buttons her cardigan up to the neck as Rose paces the narrow gap between their beds.

"Don't you have to rest your fingers on an upturned glass?" Rose ponders. "I'm sure . . . yes, and then you say, *Is anybody there?* and the ghosts come and move the glass around, and you get them to spell out words and things?"

"Okay, but don't you need a big round table?"

Rose drums her fingers on her chin, thinking.

"I don't suppose we *need* one. We can shove your camp-bed aside and use the floor."

Nina can't see any escape from this experiment, and she's not certain she wants one, but some instinct makes her try.

"If we can't do it properly, is there really any point? I mean, if we don't follow the right steps, it's not likely to work, is it?"

"Says who? We'll invent our own ceremony, and if the dead don't like it, no one's forcing them to show up."

Nina shivers and pulls her woollen sleeves over her hands.

"But, Rose?" she lowers her voice to a whisper. "Do you think it's safe to dabble with this sort of stuff? I mean the occult, and all that. My dad would have my guts for garters if he knew."

Rose is busy wedging a chair beneath the door handle, but Nina's question makes her stop and turn.

"Isn't that rather the point?" she whispers back, hands on hips. "And anyway, what's so wonderful about feeling *safe*? Aren't you just sick of feeling *safe*? I tell you something . . ."

"What?"

"I bet you Harold Lamb would never dare do a séance. Not in a million years."

Nina smiles, despite herself, and begins clearing a space on the floor.

. . .

THEY DECIDE THAT BARE FLOORBOARDS will work best, so they roll back a section of carpet, and Rose sets to work with a chalk, drawing a wobbly ring and inscribing the letters of the alphabet all the way round it. She makes adjustments with spit and a handkerchief until the circle is fairly even, and the letters are spaced to her satisfaction.

"Candles!" she exclaims next. "We can't do this by electric light."

The girls unearth a couple of candle stubs from the back of a desk drawer, along with two wax-encrusted holders: a porcelain one in the shape of a podgy Cupid and a tarnished silver one with *Blessings on Your Christening Day* engraved around the base. Rose crouches down to draw a series of overlapping triangles inside the circle, and when Nina asks what they signify, she answers, "No idea, but they look right, don't you think?"

"What else?" asks Nina. "We need a glass, don't we?"

Rose chews her lower lip as she looks round the room.

"I reckon our ashtray will do the job."

Nina empties the cracked teacup into the wastepaper basket and places it upside down in the middle of the circle. Rose lights the candles with matches from Nina's handbag, places them at intervals around the circle, and flicks off the ceiling light.

"There," she declares, and her voice drops like a pebble into the well of silence. The bustle of preparation is over. Nina listens for sounds beyond the bedroom—Mr. and Mrs. Allen putting their clothes away in drawers, or talking to one another, or brushing their teeth—but there is nothing. She strains her ears. Nothing at all. It's very odd, and if she had the courage to speak, she would say so.

The two kneel opposite one another, either side of the circle. The bedroom curtains are in Nina's eyeline: the familiar, faded curtains with their blowsy white flowers against a blue background. The flowers are glowing, because there's a street lamp right outside the house, and Nina searches their shapes for friendly faces. Sometimes she can see a cartoon elephant in the folding petals of the largest rose, but she can't make it out tonight.

"Well?" whispers Rose.

"Well!" Nina gives a shaky laugh, which peters out as she stares into her friend's face. The flames are illuminating Rose from below, making her chin, nose, and brow shine like gold, and turning her eyes into empty hollows. It's hard to decide whether seconds or hours have passed since the house fell silent.

"What do we do now?" Nina breathes.

Rose taps the teacup with her left hand and nods, so that Nina understands to do the same. Their fingers touch at the very tips.

"And now?"

If only Rose would speak! Then again—what if an alien voice were to emerge from her oddly lit mouth? It looks so unfamiliar, all of a sudden, with the candlelight playing across the upper lip and expunging the lower one.

"Is anybody there?" demands the voice which may, or may not, belong to Rose.

All of Nina's senses seem to have gathered in the tips of her fingers. When the cup jerks, she sucks in a huge breath and almost chokes.

"That was *you*!" she hisses, but Rose shakes her head. Is there someone else in the room, then? Someone standing very still at Nina's elbow?

There is.

There *is*.

She can hear a presence, although it makes no sound; she can feel it, though it's not quite touching her. The air inside the room has shifted and darkened. If she turns her head she will see it, so she gazes straight ahead, into Rose's empty eyes.

A minute passes—two minutes—with the cup quivering under their fingers.

"Are you a ghost?" asks Rose, and the cup jumps.

Nina searches for the friendly elephant in the curtains. There he is! But his nice smile has turned nasty, and all he does is stare and stare.

"Your turn," murmurs Rose.

"But I don't know what . . . Help me, I don't know what to say."

"Just ask it something quickly, before it goes away!"

"All right . . . Ghost? Tell us what it's like to be dead."

No response.

They wait.

"Maybe it prefers yes/no questions?" urges Rose. "Try again."

The two of them shuffle forwards on their knees, and the shadows shift again over Rose's face. There's a glint in the depths of her eye sockets.

"Did you die a long time ago?" asks Nina.

The cup wobbles.

"In Queen Victoria's reign?"

Nothing.

"*This* century?"

Another tiny lurch.

Nina sits back on her heels, anxious for Rose to take over. The cup is wide awake under her touch, vibrating with readiness.

"What did you die of?" asks Rose. "I mean, sorry, did you die of natural causes?"

Nothing.

"In an accident?"

Nothing.

"Not—suicide?"

Nothing.

"Were you murdered?"

The teacup shoots violently to the left, bumping over the floor-boards and toppling onto its side. The girls' arms shoot with it. Rose loses her balance and bumps her head on the bed-frame.

"Are you all right?"

"Yes, yes!" Rose snatches up the teacup and slams it into the centre of the circle. "Quick! Your turn!"

Slowly, reluctantly, Nina returns her fingers to the cup.

"Who *are* you?" she asks, and Rose is starting to say, "Yes/no question!" when the cup moves, darting across the circle with speed and certainty, stopping for a second as it touches on particular letters. The girls recite them under their breath:

"T . . . E . . . O . . . D . . . O . . ."

Nina tears her hand from the cup and her eyes from the chalk circle. She scrabbles to her feet and falls against the wall switch, flooding the room with light.

"What is it? Oh Lord, Nina, whatever's the matter?"

Nina stands very still until Rose comes and wraps her arms around her, and then her body slackens and she finds herself shivering uncontrollably. She's cold—cripplingly cold—it's like being ill with a fever. Goose pimples sweep up her arms and legs in a rushing wave.

"My mother's name was Teodora," she explains, but Rose doesn't hear over the sound of her own voice.

"Shh!" she keeps murmuring, as she strokes Nina's back. "It's all right."

"No, it's not—"

"Shh."

Nina rests her chin on Rose's shoulder and watches the teacup rocking from side to side, next to the letter R. She waits until it falls still.

"Listen to me. My mother's name was Teodora. T-E-O-D-O-R-A."

Rose pulls a little way away, so that she can see Nina properly. They search one another's faces for a practical joke.

"I wouldn't make that up!" Nina says, savagely, at the same time as Rose is insisting, "I didn't know!"

Rose continues, "I swear I didn't know her name, and even if I had, I would *never* . . . Anyway, Nina, your mother wasn't murdered!"

"Oh, I know *that*!" Nina is trying so hard not to cry that she can hardly get her words out. "It's not *that*!"

"What is it?"

"It's just that we shouldn't have done it. I wish, I *wish* we hadn't done it. There was something evil . . ."

"I'm sorry." Now Rose is coming close to tears as well. "It's my fault. I'm sorry."

They cling tightly to one another. Nina closes her eyes, and presses them against Rose's neck, unable to shake the panicked suspicion that they've done something immutable; that they've flung themselves down a swirling, slippery slide, with no way up again. Then Mrs. Allen taps on their door, on her way to the bathroom, and says, "You two! Enough nattering; turn that light off and go to sleep," and the terror fades slightly.

Together, they extinguish the candles and roll the carpet over the chalk circle. ("I'll wipe it clean tomorrow," says Rose, "after you've gone.") They try to put Nina's camp-bed back, but one of the legs must have broken when they shoved it aside, because it won't click into place anymore. "Oh, Dad's going to love me when he sees this," grumbles Rose, and by the time she's said that, and Mrs. Allen has knocked again, on her way back from the bathroom, and called crossly, "*Girls!*" Nina feels she has returned from the dark mirror-world and come home to the regular one. She takes a decision not to think deeply about what happened. It was probably her subconscious mind playing tricks—or Rose's—or both. It was fear; it was tiredness; it was a longing for something to happen. Somehow, in some way, it was explicable.

They sleep together in Rose's bed, like they did when they were children.

4

Kate

September 2–3, 1939

I CAN'T FIND THE LIST! OH, FOR HEAVEN'S SAKE, MY MOTHER used to say I'd lose my head if it wasn't screwed on, and she was right. What if Guy gets hold of it? Only an idiot would have committed such things to paper in the first place, but to misplace it straightaway . . .

I sit on the spare bed with my eyes squeezed shut and my fingers pressed to my temples, retracing my steps.

All right, let's start with Guy driving my sister Deb, her husband, Mike, and their three children to Chester Station, earlier this evening. I stayed behind with Pip, since there was only so much room in the car, and after they'd gone the most terrible sadness washed over me, so I got to work, putting the house to rights. In between chatting to Pip, collecting used teacups, shaking out rugs, etc., I pondered the mysteries of Deb and Mike's brilliant marriage. Observations, ideas, and questions were swirling round and round inside my head—some memorable, some not; some graspable, some not—and I decided (*idiot!*) to try to pin them down, by putting pen to paper. I went into the kitchen and sat down at the table with an old brown envelope and a pencil, and after I'd jotted down three of my points (only three, so matters could be worse), I heard the car pulling into the drive. Guy came in through the back door and said, "Oh, are we not having any supper?" and I said, "I'd no idea it had got so late!" and then I put a pan of soup on the stove and fetched some bowls from the cupboard—*but what did I do with the list?*

I've searched the kitchen, and it's nowhere to be seen. Did I put it in a drawer? Inside a book? I'm pretty sure I didn't throw it in the bin.

It's late now. Pip is asleep. Guy is in the sitting-room, listening to a Tchaikovsky symphony on the wireless and reading the newspaper. I sat beside him for a while, but the slow second movement was too much to bear, so I came upstairs for an early night. Somehow I wandered into the spare bedroom instead of my own, and here I am now, ostensibly stripping the sheets from Deb and Mike's bed, actually idling about and thinking.

Deb wanted to help me with the beds, but I wouldn't hear of it. I said I'd be glad of something to do when she was gone, to stop me feeling lonely.

"You're not lonely!" she exclaimed, "You've got Guy and Pip!" and of course I replied, "No, no, I'm not lonely in any serious sense; I just meant that I'll miss you." The true (or truer) answer to the question is awkward, so I ducked it, coward that I am.

There's a tangle of brown hair in the wastepaper basket, scrapings from my sister's hairbrush. The pillowcases smell of her too—not just her perfume, but the special Deb scent that carries so many subtle associations, none of which translate into words. The best I can do is to call it *the scent of home*, or *of childhood*, but those labels are too broad to be meaningful.

Here's Guy coming up the stairs, so I get to my feet and make myself busy.

"Kate?" he calls, finding our own bedroom dark and spotting the light on in here. "Ah, here you are!" I peel the sheets and woollen blankets from the bed while he leans against the door-frame, his arms crossed, watching.

Deb says Guy is handsome ("Hasn't he turned out handsome? Such a little shrimp he was, as a boy!") and she's right, although that isn't as much comfort as one might assume. Mike is pug-ugly—not to put too fine a point on it—and Deb used to worry about that when they were courting, but I doubt it crosses her mind anymore. Mike is Mike, and that's all there is to it. Objective standards no longer apply.

If war *is* declared tomorrow—please God it won't be, but if it is—Guy intends to cut a dash in air-force blue. He's going to join the RAF, not because he knows the first thing about flying, but because he thinks it will be more exciting than the army, and because he'd be seasick in the navy, and (not least) because Joey Roussin intends to join the Royal Canadian Air Force. Guy writes letters to Joey in Winnipeg, and Joey writes back, and from what I've seen it's all a lot of hearty joshing, and how they can't wait to get their hands on old Adolf, etc., etc., but beneath the sparks of excitement there's a fierce, desiring heat, which disturbs me. We all pray that the prime minister gives us "Peace for Our Time" tomorrow, as he did last September, but I suspect some of us are more sincere in our prayer than others.

"Are you all right?" I ask. What I really mean is, *Can you not shift yourself from the doorway and help me fold this enormous double sheet?* but Guy fails to hear the unspoken aspect of the question and answers, simply, "Yes, I'm fine."

The corner of his mouth keeps quivering; something has amused him. What? Is it my irritable tone of voice? Guy thinks I'm funny when I'm snappish.

He slides a cigarette from one pocket, and a piece of brown paper from the other.

Oh Lord, he's got hold of my list.

"Aha!" I say, airily. "I think that's mine."

"Yes, but what *is* it? It was on my chair when I sat down to supper. I didn't like to ask in front of Phillip, so I stuffed it in my pocket and forgot all about it, till now."

"It's nothing." I finish with the huge sheet and start work on the pillows, folding the cases with pointless care, since they're only going to be bundled into the wash. "Can I have it back, please?"

"Why do you want it back if it's *nothing*?" The unlit cigarette waggles at the corner of his mouth as he speaks.

"All right, it's not *nothing*. It's *private*."

"It was in the kitchen! On my chair!"

"Well, it wasn't supposed to be. Can I have it back, please?"

When I hold out my hand, he laughs and says, "Oh, Kate." An outsider, looking on, would probably describe his tone as *kindly* and *teasing*, and Guy would agree, I'm sure, in all sincerity. Look at the crinkles round his eyes, which accentuate his good looks! Look at the playful twitch of his lips! The outsider would think, *What's wrong with his wife? Where's her sense of humour?* Yes, yes, I know what I am: a plain woman who can't crack a smile.

"*D and M's Marriage*," Guy quotes, in a grandiose tone that isn't his own. He sounds like a character in a comedy sketch: the secretary of some absurd society, reading the agenda at an annual general meeting. "Item number one: *D's ankles on M's lap*."

He questions me, lightly, with a look.

"Guy..."

I toss the last pillowcase onto the floor, as he continues: "Item number two: *The way they argue*."

There's no point in protesting. I fold my arms, lift my chin, and wait.

"Item number three: *Talking without words.*"

Thank goodness I got no further than three. Guy hands the envelope back, though I no longer want it. I sit down on the edge of the bare mattress and re-read my own words—not because I need reminding, but because I need to direct my eyes at something that isn't my husband's face.

This room is no place for a heart-to-heart: it's pure Hawthorn House, with its high ceilings and empty echo. When we first moved in, I hung a Renoir print (*Dance in the Country*) between the two windows. It used to dominate my bedroom at home—my childhood home, I mean, in Carlisle—but all its warmth ebbed away when I brought it in here. Far from brightening the room, it has paled, in keeping with the place, and Renoir's vigorous, ruddy-cheeked girl is now blue-tinged and limp. She looks as though she's dying, rather than dancing, in her lover's arms.

Deb dislikes Hawthorn House. I know she does, though she doesn't say so directly. Whenever she comes to stay, she makes observations like *You've got such a lot of space*, or *The kitchen's so light*, as if hoping I won't spot the difference between a statement of fact and a compliment.

"Come on, darling," says Guy. "Tell me about your list. I'm fascinated!"

He's still lounging and smiling, but he's got that clenched look about his jaw, which means he isn't going to let this go. I wish we were in bed with the lights off, because that's always been the best place for Guy and me to talk. There's no distracting physicality in the dark; we stop being awkwardly matched bodies and become a pair of whispery, confidential voices.

Yes, all right, I do see the irony; I accept that's an odd way to sing the praises of my marital bed.

"I take it *D and M* refers to Deb and Mike?"

"Yes."

"And the items on the list? Go on, tell me. Are these what you see as the secrets to a functional marriage?"

I take a deep breath and square my shoulders. "I think their marriage is rather more than functional."

"Unlike ours."

"I didn't say that."

"You strongly implied it."

He's taken the unlit cigarette from his mouth, but he's still lounging in the doorway and his voice remains blithe. I can't decide whether his detachment is real or forced.

"I suppose I did. I'm sorry."

I sit with my head bowed, reading the list over and over. My mind picks on superficialities and worries at them, as if they matter: *my W's look too much like U's; that pencil needs sharpening; why do we never use a paper knife when opening our post?*

"You envy Deb and Mike?"

"In some ways."

We are positioned a long way apart—a good three paces—and starkly illuminated by the ceiling light. I am sitting down while my husband is standing up. From a rational point of view, these differences are easily solved, but in the moment they seem hopelessly fixed. Guy takes a box of matches from his pocket and gives it a little rattle.

"*D's ankles on M's lap?*" he asks, as he lights up.

I shrug unhappily and try to explain.

"The other evening they were reading on the sofa, and at one point Deb kicked her shoes off and swung her feet up onto Mike's lap, and he rested his hand on her ankles. Neither of them looked up from their books, and it was so—oh, I don't know how to put it—so instinctive; so intimate. They didn't even notice what they were doing."

"And?"

"And if that was you and me . . . well, you know . . . I'd be all clunky and self-conscious, and you'd be taken by surprise and say,

Oh goodness! What are you doing? and we'd both be put off our books."

Guy lowers his eyes and takes a long, slow drag on his cigarette. His thoughtfulness makes me briefly hopeful. Maybe this is the moment our life changes? Maybe, all of a sudden, he will see things the way I see them, and we will laugh at ourselves and begin to mend? But when he speaks, he adopts the aggressively jovial tone that he usually reserves for Pip.

"You do talk nonsense!" He plumps himself down beside me, on the mattress. "Come on, swing your feet up and I'll show you how *instinctive* and *intimate* I am. Up you come!"

He pats his knees, as if encouraging a small dog to jump up.

"Guy..."

"Come on!"

"No."

"But I thought you wanted to? I thought resting one's wifely ankles on one's husband's lap was the sine qua non of a perfect marriage?"

"You're turning it into something silly."

"Not at all! I accept that it's extremely important and entirely serious. Come on, do it."

Awkwardly, unsmilingly, I lift my legs across his lap and he pats my thick and unpretty ankles.

"Better?"

"No."

Guy raises his eyebrows a fraction and makes no objection when I take my legs away.

"Oh well." He pulls too furiously on his fag, and bursts into a coughing fit, but he moves off as soon as I start slapping him on the back.

"What else was there?" He ambles about the room, from fireplace to window to wardrobe to door. "*The way they argue.* I didn't know they argued?"

"Oh, but they did, a couple of times."

"And what's so enviable about their methods?"

I decide to answer naively, as if I can't hear the sarcasm. My only other option is to shrivel, and fall silent.

"When Deb and Mike argue they light up with loathing for one another, you can practically see the sparks fly—"

"Sounds terrific!"

"—but it passes quickly, and afterwards they're so, sort of, *giddy*, as if they can't believe their luck at having come through."

Guy waits for me to go on, and when I don't, he adopts a weary expression.

"Go on, Kate, draw the telling comparison; you know you're dying to. When they argue, they go all giddy, whereas when *we* argue . . . ?"

"You already know."

"But I want to hear it from you."

"Well, when we argue, we're the opposite of fiery. We're cold and sulky and the aftermath doesn't come for ages, and even when it does, it feels like we're weaker than before. Like we've taken a blow, and another tiny fragment of—well, of us—has been chipped away."

Guy pauses at the window and gazes out. Since it's night-time, I suppose he only sees himself and the reflected room. Or perhaps he's looking at me? I pretend to study the old envelope again.

After a while he murmurs, "*Talking without words*," which is the third item on my list. I make no attempt to explain it, and he doesn't ask. I avoid looking at his shadowy reflection and run my eyes, instead, over his broad shoulders, and the back of his curly head, and the sturdy way he stands with his hands in his pockets. It crosses my mind that he might be trying, right now, to talk to me without words, but I can't hear anything.

Turn around and see me, I beg, silently, but he just stands and smokes, jiggling the loose change in his left-hand pocket.

I wait a minute or two—perhaps we are both waiting for each other—before leaving the room with a mumbled excuse and an armful of dirty laundry.

. . .

WHILE I'M GETTING READY FOR bed I listen to Guy loping downstairs, pouring himself a drink and flicking the wireless back on. The music is jazzier than it was before, and pretty soon he switches it off again. There's a clink as he unstoppers the decanter and tops up his glass, and then silence.

When he comes upstairs, I pretend I'm asleep. He gets undressed without bothering to wash, and once he's in bed he lies on his back with his hands behind his head, stinking of brandy and tobacco smoke. His elbow brushes my ear, but it's not an intentional touch, let alone a tender one.

If he says my name I'll answer with a kiss and we'll talk properly; if he doesn't, I'll carry on feigning sleep.

He doesn't. In fact, he doesn't say anything, he only sighs, and the house answers with one of its strange, low groans.

Guy lies awake for a long time—but whether he's thinking about Hawthorn House and its restless spirits, or the likelihood of war, or our marriage, or something else altogether, it is (of course) impossible for me to say.

. . .

I DREAM OF OUR CHILDHOOD, and when I wake up I'm convinced he's here: five-year-old Guy, kneeling on the bedroom floor in his pyjamas, playing with a wooden train. I watch drowsily as the dream melts away, and I realise that the boy is my son, and that I'm a grown woman, and that this is Cottenden, and that the real Guy

Nicholson (aged twenty-eight) is outside on the driveway, tinkering with his car.

There's a cup of tea by the bed, on top of my stack of books. I take a sip, but it's cold; Guy must have brought it ages ago. How late *is* it? I reach for the alarm clock and grimace.

Pip hasn't noticed I'm awake, he's too busy pushing his train around and murmuring urgently at—or on behalf of—the characters in his game. Since I'm too slovenly to make it to church on time, I might as well give in to the luxury of watching him from my warm bed. I lie on my side and half close my eyes, trying to recall my dream. We were little and Guy was feeling poorly, but . . . but what? I don't remember. It's gone.

We did fall ill with the chicken pox once, in real life. All of us had it at the same time: Deb, Ron, Janey, Guy, and me. It must have been 1916, because I'd just had my seventh birthday, which means Guy was five; I remember him crawling over the rag rug, playing toy soldiers, while I umpired from my bed and tried not to itch my spots. I don't know where the others were that morning: perhaps they were feeling worse than us, or much better, or perhaps they were bored by Guy's shyness. That happened, from time to time. All the things that bound me to love him—his parents' distaste for toys and games, for example, or the quiet surprise with which he observed our own family interactions—never harrowed my siblings in the way they harrowed me. "Don't your mother and father ever give you cuddles?" Janey once asked, and when he replied, after a long think, "I sometimes shake hands with my father," she shrugged and said, with the cold gaucheness of a child, "What an oddity you are!"

Even in those days, Guy and I didn't talk a lot, but we stuck together. I enjoyed muscling in on his private games ("Guy? Let's make the soldiers trek across the desert; the floor is the desert and my bed is the ice mountain they have to get to, but there are snakes everywhere . . ."), and although he was diffident about admitting me, I felt he liked me for trying.

Sometimes, when the weather was warm and the windows were open, I heard awful noises from next door: his father giving him the belt, or his mother shouting. I used to cry wildly when my parents told me off, but Guy was cold and prickly after these incidents, and took offence at gestures of sympathy. I remember discovering him in tears on one occasion, all bundled up with his head buried in his knees, and I don't know what made him so different—so unguarded—that day. He crawled into my arms and let me comfort him, and after a while he said, *Oh Kate, I wish it was just you and me.*

I probably took those words more literally, and treasured them more devoutly, than I should. Until recently, I assumed he meant *forever*, but I suppose he needn't have done. Or perhaps he did mean it in the moment, but changed his mind later on. We were only children, after all.

"Mummy, when can we have breakfast?"

My eyes have been open all this time, but I don't notice Pip standing right beside my pillow until I start at the sound of his voice. I haul him under the covers and shower him with kisses till he squeals with laughter. Guy comes into the bedroom, catches the smile from my face, and takes it as his—though really and truly it belongs to Pip. He smiles back, and somehow, most unexpectedly, the day is off to a hopeful start.

. . .

DEB AND I CLEANED THE kitchen yesterday, and now it feels cold and stagey, like a kitchen in a magazine. I belong in it even less than I usually do, with my shabby old dressing-gown and my hair in need of a wash; the photographer would have a fit if he caught me wandering on set. Anyway, I'm not the only thing that's out of place: so is the homely whistle of the kettle, and the spit and sizzle of bacon and eggs, and the smell of burning toast. This is a kitchen for looking elegant in—perhaps, at a stretch, for mixing a dry martini in—not for comfort. We should have painted the walls a bright, primary colour, but Guy says it would be a waste of time and money to change it now.

I stand at the window and swish hot water round the teapot, as a prelude to making the tea.

"Let's go for a walk after breakfast." The early September sunshine is pouring over the lawn, edging the summer trees with gold, and the hills are gathered like clouds on the horizon. "We could drive into Wales; take a picnic up Moel Famau?"

"The car's out of action," says Guy, lowering his newspaper. "I'm in the middle of cleaning the spark plugs. Besides, we can't go anywhere till after eleven."

Of course. The prime minister's statement.

"Afterwards?" I persist. "It doesn't matter about the car. We could walk over the fields to the watermill, or along the canal."

"Maybe."

I refer to the prime minister's statement in terms of *before* and *after*, as if it's going to constitute one episode in a normal day of many episodes—on a par with eating breakfast, or going for a walk, or listening to *Children's Hour*—and yet the world may be tipped on its axis at eleven o'clock. My head foresees it and understands, but my heart can't take it in. I'm keeping an eye on the frying pan, and watching Pip struggle to butter his toast, and biting my tongue, because it won't occur to Guy to lend his son a hand, unless I ask him to.

Current affairs, I think, as I turn the rashers, loosen the eggs from the bottom of the pan, and scald the tea, *are surely the least of my worries.*

. . .

BY THE TIME WE'VE EATEN and washed up, it's five to eleven, so I shoo Pip off to the sitting-room to play with his trains. While Guy fiddles with the wireless, I sit at the clean kitchen table and place my clasped hands in my lap. The wet cloth is hanging over the tap, and it drips into the sink with a mesmerising pitter-patter. I am thinking of that, and studying the shape of Guy's head in profile, when the wireless yowls into life, and it's only then—when the man says, "This is London"—that my gut begins to dread what my brain has already foreseen.

When Mr. Chamberlain's grave voice crackles over the airwaves—"I am speaking to you from the cabinet room at 10 Downing Street"—I realize, before he's said the words, that it's going to be war.

"This morning the British ambassador in Berlin handed the German government a final note, stating that unless we heard from them by eleven o'clock that they were prepared at once to withdraw their troops from Poland, a state of war would exist between us."

I glance up at Guy. He is leaning forwards in his chair, smiling a tiny, twitchy smile, and his eyes are very bright.

"I have to tell you now that no such undertaking has been received, and that consequently this country is at war with Germany."

I start a prayer inside my head ("Dear God . . ."), but I don't know how to go on. Guy puffs out his cheeks and makes a sound like *phew*.

The prime minister is still speaking ("what a bitter blow" . . . "Hitler would not" . . . "can only be stopped by" . . . "that you will all play your part"), but I'm not listening anymore. Did Guy actually say . . . ?

"Did you actually say *phew*?"

"What? No."

"Do you *want* to go off and get killed?"

There's a dribble of egg-yolk on the tabletop. I scrape at it, slowly, with my thumbnail. If I don't press Guy for an answer, and don't call Pip from the sitting-room, and don't look up from the table, and don't get to my feet, then nothing need ever change. The three of us can stay here, just as we are. I know we're not entirely happy, but we're not entirely unhappy, either. We love each other, in our way, and we're safe.

"Of course not." Guy switches the radio off and gives my slumped shoulders a pat as he passes behind my chair. "Naturally, I want to do my bit for my country. You wouldn't have it any other way, would you?"

He goes to the window and stretches his arms wide. Guy would look perfect in my imaginary kitchen catalogue: a spirited young Briton greeting the new dawn with cheer and resolve. The camera would love him.

. . .

WE SET OFF FOR A walk, but get no farther than the playing field beside the village pond. Pip begs to be allowed to stop and play, so we sit on a bench while he clambers up the steps to the slide and whizzes down, over and over again.

"Goodness," says Guy. "He's keen on that slide, isn't he? What about the climbing frame and the roundabout?"

"He only likes the slide. You knew that, didn't you?"

"Can't say I did. I've never brought him here before."

I start to protest, but it's probably true. Guy isn't drawn to village life: he is either pottering about at Hawthorn House, or working in Chester, or taking the car out for a spin. People think him standoff-ish (which he is), and then they tar me with the same brush, because I'm his wife. In fact, I have tried to fit in, but I struggle to get beyond the *Good morning, how are you?* phase. Everyone in Cottenden is long established: fresh acquaintances are welcome enough, but nobody is in need of a brand-new friendship.

There's hardly anyone about today; I suppose they're all at home, digesting The News. Guy and I don't discuss it. We talk about trivial things instead—the various problems with the car, and what time to have lunch—but my tone of voice is dull, whilst his is lively and quick.

"Everything will be fine," Deb whispered into my hair, yesterday, with her goodbye hug. It was the last thing she said before climbing into the car, and she was referring to the possibility of war, of course, but she meant other things too. She was touching on our private worries and sadnesses; the sisterly secrets we share, or half share, or hint and guess at.

I replied conventionally ("Everything *will* be fine!"), but there was a little part of me that rebelled against the cliché and the ease with which we bandied it about. Why not tell the truth for once? Why not say, *For God's sake, Deborah, how can you possibly believe that?*

Naturally, I resisted the urge—Guy had already started the engine, Pip had taken my hand, everyone was waving and calling goodbye—and do you know what? I'm glad I let it go. Sometimes I think brave banalities are all we have, and that the only sensible course is to repeat them over and over again, to ourselves and others, in spite of all probability.

"Aren't you bored of the slide by now?" calls Guy, but Pip ignores him.

There's Henry Woodrow, over on the other side of the playing field, with his dog. I almost point him out and ask Guy whether he remembers the dog's name, but I think better of it. Guy will only make some withering remark about that awful dinner party, all those years ago. The dog has become old and plodding, but Mr. Woodrow doesn't seem to mind; he waits inside his own thoughts whenever it stops to sniff.

Biscuit. That was it.

Guy takes my hand and says, "I do love you, Kate. I'll miss you, when I go away."

"I never said you didn't. Or that you wouldn't."

"That's all right, then."

I free my hand and wonder whether Henry Woodrow will go to war. Didn't he say he'd fought in the last one? In which case, I reckon he'll be too old, this time round. If he *were* to join up though, he would do it gravely. There'd be no jubilation, suppressed or otherwise; he would see the reality, as I do.

I watch him walk the length of the field in his smart woollen coat and hat. How can I possibly claim to know what Henry Woodrow would think or do in a given situation? As if anyone can judge a stranger (which is all he is, really) by the quality of his coat! Other people's lives have a habit of looking simple from the outside—free from peculiarities and troubles—but I don't suppose they are, deep down. They can't be.

And yet . . . he strolls along, keeping pace with his well-behaved dog and blowing his nose on a neatly pressed handkerchief, and it's impossible to visualise life with Mr. Woodrow as anything other than calm and pleasant. I imagine the two of us returning, arm-in-arm, to 7 Canal Road, and enjoy the straightforward conversation we have on the way. It's so genial; so free of perilous undercurrents. *I love you* means something sweetly simple to me and my alternative husband. When we reach home I take his coat, and he says, *Thank you, dear*, and kisses me on the cheek. We are one of those made-in-heaven couples that populate the short stories and advertisements in *Good Housekeeping* and *The Lady*. We surpass Deb and Mike. We talk without words at every moment, with every glance.

I'm not sure where Pip fits into this fantasy, let alone Mr. Woodrow's daughter, Nina. I've seen her once or twice, working behind the cosmetics counter at Browns of Chester, but I suspect she's forgotten me.

Guy is looking at me, so I turn to him.

"I love you too," I say, belatedly. "I'll miss you horribly." If I sound more angry than loving, it's because I'm anxious not to cry. My husband—the real one—smiles absently and we hold hands again.

Mr. Woodrow and Biscuit are leaving through the wrought-iron kissing-gate. He did a whole circuit of the playing field without glancing our way, even when Pip hurtled down the slide shouting, "Mummy! Dad! Watch me!"

Or perhaps he did spot us and turned away with an inward shrug? He can't possibly have forgotten the dinner party, but I doubt he turns it over in his mind, like I do. Ideally, I should like him to forget the party whilst remembering me, but I suppose that's a bit of an ask.

"Phillip?" Guy calls. "Come and sit on the roundabout; I'll give you a push."

Pip whooshes down the slide and crouches at the bottom, wiping his runny nose across his sleeve.

"I don't like the roundabout."

"Don't be silly. All little boys like roundabouts."

"I don't."

(*I think you're awfully patient*, Mr. Woodrow said that evening, and although the sentiment itself left me cold—I mean, patience is all very well, but it's not the most breathtaking of the Virtues—the way he said it did not.

I think you're awfully patient. We were going through to the dining-room, and he was helping me up from the chair. *It's a quality I admire.*)

Guy goes over to the slide, and crouches down to talk to Pip, who pouts and recoils. Stern words are spoken and Pip shakes his head. Guy lifts him up by the armpits, carries him to the roundabout, and places him on the seat, where he slumps like a sack of potatoes.

"Come on!" Guy starts to push. "You'll love it!"

I watch them from the edge of my seat. Pip seeks me with his eyes as he starts to spin, and I'm not sure what to do for the best. I twist my handbag straps into knots and send him my brightest smile.

Everything will be fine.

5

Nina

November 18, 1942

The Waafery
RAF Charlwood
Lincolnshire

November 18, 1942

Dear Dad,
You remember that dinner party, years ago, when we
invited that couple from Hawthorn House? Guy Nich-
olson and his wife, and their Canadian friend? Well,
you'll never guess

Nina screws the page into a ball and starts on a fresh one, which is annoying, because there's hardly any notepaper left. Everything's running out today.

"When's coal day, again?"

"Day after tomorrow," says Joan from the opposite side of the hut, and they both make the same face.

When Nina put the blackout curtains up, half an hour ago, she found that the windows had iced up on the inside. Joan had returned from her shift shortly afterwards, and now the two of them are sitting in their respective beds with greatcoats on, breathing clouds of mist. Joan is darning a jumper, Nina is trying to write, and from time to time they exchange a few words. There are ten beds altogether in Hut 9, but everyone else is out.

The storm lamps throw strange shadows over the curved ceiling, and when Nina blurs her eyes she can imagine herself into an older, quieter century—especially now, when there are no aircraft taking off or landing. It's a comforting pretence, for as long as she can keep it up. Dolly Brown has pinned a photograph of her parents onto the hardboard wall over her bed, and they too seem like people from another time and place. Nina likes looking at their camera-shy smiles, and the sun-speckled trees in the background.

Nina's own family photograph lives in the suitcase under her bed. Occasionally she takes it out when she's alone in the hut, and searches the three faces: slack-cheeked toddler, serious father, unknowable mother. There's never anything new to see.

The Waafery
RAF *Charlwood*
Lincolnshire

November 18, 1942

Dear Dad,
In your last letter, you said that my address—The Waafery—always makes you chuckle. Well, I'm pleased to think of you chuckling! It used to amuse me

too (it sounds so appropriate, doesn't it, like a ruffling of feathers?!), but I've grown used to it now, and stopped noticing its oddness. I hope you agree it rolls off the tongue more easily than "The Women's Auxiliary Air Force Quarters"!

Are you well? I hope your earache has cleared up, and that you feel happy, in a general way, despite everything. I do worry about you, all on your own, with nobody to talk to. Good for Jessie, going off to work in munitions, but it leaves you in the lurch. How will you manage without a daily help? Don't just live off digestive biscuits and things—that would be enough to lower anyone's mood! Try to cook something hot and nourishing, now and again. Soups and stews are quite easy.

I am as busy as ever, both on duty and off, especially now that preparations are well and truly underway for the Christmas concert. The choir is going to sing "For unto Us a Child Is Born" from Handel's Messiah, as well as some lighter numbers from the musicals. I wish you could be in the audience, but never mind, I expect to get leave over the New Year and I'll see you then. (I'll show you how to make a good soup, if you haven't worked it out already!)

Is it cold at home? It's freezing here, and I've never been more grateful to be a parachute packer, because the room where we air the parachutes is kept lovely and warm. It's a rather dreamlike place, with high windows and long tables, and row upon row of parachutes hanging down from the ceiling, like giant jellyfish waiting to pulse into life. However, despite the clement temperatures, it is not a cushy job! In fact, sometimes the responsibility weighs on my mind so much that I almost

*wish I were a kitchen orderly again. (Almost!) I keep
having the most hideous nightmares, in which I can't
fold the silks correctly, try as I might, and the cords are
all twisted up and knotted.*

*Speaking of the weather turning cold, it was very
kind of Mrs. Dempsey to knit me some bedsocks. I am
wearing them now, on top of two pairs of my usual socks!*

*A funny thing happened today. Do you remember
that man the Nicholsons those people that day eight
years ago Do you remember Guy Nicholson?*

No, no, no.

Nina screws up the sheet with a vigour that's meant to attract
notice, and Joan duly looks up from her sewing to ask, "What's
up?"

"Nothing. I'm writing to my dad, but I can't seem to say what I
really . . . Do you ever talk to yours about—you know—men?"

"Do I talk to my *dad* about *men*?"

"Mmm."

"No!"

Nina caps her pen and leans back to stare at the lamp-lit ceiling. A line of trucks rumbles through the Waafery, onto the airfield,
spoiling her old-world illusion.

"It's stupid, really, because I'm only trying to tell him that I
ran into a neighbour of ours, but I can't seem to phrase it without
sounding . . ."

"Keen?"

"Either keen, or falsely casual."

"Who is he, this neighbour of yours?" asks Joan.

"He's an officer. Ludicrously handsome."

"Safely married?"

"So I thought—but I found out today he's a divorcé."

Joan looks up. "Blimey!"

"I know!"

"I wouldn't breathe a word, if I were you. If your dad is anything like mine, he'll have kittens." She affects an old-womanish croak: *"Men like that . . ."*

"You're right."

Joan laughs and turns back to her mending, as if the question is closed—but it's not closed. Nina needs to tell someone about Guy Nicholson. Not that there's much to tell, it's just . . . it's the wonder of the encounter. The thrill of coming face to face with her secret love in the midst of this everlasting wartime winter, and discovering that he no longer has a wife.

Nina sits up again and turns to a new sheet of notepaper. She writes her address and the date swiftly, but hesitates before starting the letter itself.

Dear Rose,

I was so glad to see you in October, despite the sadness of the occasion. Michael was a fine man, and you must be proud to have had such a brother. Every time I see that poster for the Merchant Navy (the one with the man in the woollen hat holding binoculars), I think of him. I hope Lyn is managing, and the little ones too; please let them know I was asking after them.

I hope you are well and continuing to enjoy life in the ATS. You looked very glam in your uniform—they ought to photograph you for recruitment purposes!

Oh, Rose, I was so glad to see you at the memorial service. I can't explain what a relief it was to talk <u>properly</u> with my oldest friend. Was it the same for you? Everyone here at Charlwood is nice, but there's nobody

I can talk to the way I talk to you. You and I can say
everything and anything that's on our minds, because
we really know each other. Because we're us!
On which note, I've been dying to tell you

Susie Macaulay bursts in with a rush of cold air, and kicks the door shut. Her boots squeak on the polished linoleum as she crosses to the bed, and the three of them exchange low-key greetings. Nina tries to return to her letter, but there's a new turbulence in the hut, which makes it difficult to concentrate.

Susie sits heavily on the adjacent bed. While she's grappling with her bootlaces she glances up at Nina.

"I met Lucky on the way back, and he made me stop just so he could tell me what a peach you are. Oh, and did I know whether you were on duty tomorrow teatime?"

Nina draws an absent-minded swirl on the cover of her notepad. "What did you say?"

"That I don't happen to carry Nina Woodrow's shift pattern round in my head."

Susie levers one boot off and starts on the other, before giving up with a groan. She flops sideways onto the bed and covers her eyes with her forearm. Joan sticks the needle into her mending and puts it aside.

"I'm going to the cookhouse to see what I can scrounge. Try and get warm, Susie."

Susie doesn't move. When Joan's gone she says, "Lucky wants to marry you."

"He told you that?"

"No, but it's obvious. I'll bet you anything he's going to propose tomorrow."

Nina looks at the girl splayed gracelessly, hopelessly, on the bed, her eyes concealed behind her sleeve, her mouth drawn down. Susie's fiancé was killed in November, during a training exercise. Wait, it's still November. Nina shuts her eyes while she works it out. Susie's fiancé was killed last Wednesday.

Last Wednesday. That's a long time in the accelerated universe of RAF Charlwood; long enough to cry a bit, put him from your mind, and move on. Susie has cried every night for a whole week, which is frankly idiotic. Make friends with these airmen, by all means, thinks Nina—kiss them, dance with them—but don't mistake them for your future. They're sketches in the sand, and the waves are roaring up the beach. Marriage is an exotic custom from somewhere far away; it makes no sense here.

"Well," Nina says. "If he does ask, I'll refuse."

Susie lifts her arm away from her eyes and turns her head. Her nose and lips are chapped—perhaps from the weather, perhaps from weeping—and her voice is so tired, it sounds misleadingly gentle.

"God, you're a cold-hearted bitch."

Nina blushes and swallows. She pretends to re-read her letter, but in fact she is picturing Flight Sergeant "Lucky" Lucas in the rear turret of his plane, crouched over the machine gun, his baby face made alien by goggles and respirator. Sometimes, when he's away on ops, she thinks she's desperately in love with him; it's only when he's earthbound that she realises she's not, and that they hardly know one another. When they're sipping beer and holding hands in the Poacher's Arms, she feels stuck for words, or bored.

Lucky is Nina's fourth proper boyfriend. She's liked them all, more or less—Sammy, Mac, James, and Lucky—but the first three are dead, and the fourth is on borrowed time. Meanwhile she's alive, and somehow still all right. Or if she's not all right, she's moving too fast to tell.

On which note, I've been dying to tell you something. You'll never guess who I saw today. In fact, I've spotted him several times before, but this morning we actually came face to face. It was Guy Nicholson, the man we met at Hawthorn House, on that awful day when we quarrelled about the dress! Do you remember? I already knew he was in the RAF, *because I've seen him around Cottenden in his uniform, but still, what are the chances of him being stationed here, at the same base as me, of all places! What's more, it turns out he and his wife have divorced! A friend of a friend told me all about it, and I didn't believe her at first, but I did some digging around and it's true. I don't think I've ever met a divorcé before. Have you?*

He can't be much more than thirty, but the war (along with a doomed marriage, perhaps?!) has made him look older—or rather, more serious. Also his hair is shorter now, and Brylcreemed. It's funny to think how young he must have been when we met him that day (about our age now, I suppose), and yet he seemed so grown up. Do you remember how we showed his Canadian friend the way to Hawthorn House, and then we sat in his garden drinking some extremely lemony lemonade? It seems so long ago! They were quite flirtatious, in a boyish sort of way (didn't they dub me "Greta Garbo" and you some other film star?), and we were suitably overawed! Do you remember?

I don't believe I've spoken to him since that day, although I've seen him whizzing through the village in his car, and I've seen his wife (ex-wife!), Kate, and their little boy in church, and around and about. Rumour (i.e., Mrs. Powell at the village shop) has it that Kate Nicholson almost died giving birth that summer, and that she can't have any more children, but I don't know if that's true.

Anyway, here he is, at RAF Charlwood: Warrant Officer Guy Nicholson. He's the navigator for one of the bomber crews, which proves he's brainy as well as good-looking. I always think navigating must be the hardest job of all—like doing a life-or-death geometry exam at several hundred feet, whilst being shaken about and shot at (!).

Officers aren't supposed to fraternise with WAAFs. A lot of them keep aloof, and don't really approve of "petticoats" in the air force, but I don't think he's one of them. I've walked past him three times before—twice on the airbase and once in Lincoln. The first couple of times he glanced my way; the third time he smiled, although I don't believe he recognised me.

Early this morning, however, he came into the parachute-packing room (which is where I work now) to return his kit. It was busy, and I was chatting with a friend as we logged the kits back in, and at one point she said, "You come from Chester, don't you, Nina? Sara here comes from Chester." I waved down the table at Sara and said, "I actually grew up a few miles out of the city, in a village called Cottenden," and as I uttered the word "Cottenden," Guy Nicholson wheeled round (he was standing a few feet away, talking to someone) and looked right at me.

Joan returns with a tray of steaming cups, followed by Dolly Brown, who's lugging a steel bucket. Nina stops writing to draw breath and shake out her wrist.

"I pinched some coal from outside Hut 12," whispers Dolly, theatrically, kneeling in front of the stove and opening the door.

Joan brings tea and fruitcake to Susie's bedside, while Nina gets up and helps herself from the tray.

"Fruitcake!" she exclaims, as if gladdened by the sight, although she had some yesterday and knows it tastes like sawdust. All wartime pleasures involve a measure of make-believe. Susie shoots her a sceptical look, but no one has a chance to speak before the shuddering and thundering starts. A few hundred yards away, the bombers are coming to life.

"I thought ops were off tonight?" Nina raises her voice above the din.

Dolly drops a lighted match into the stove and hauls herself to her feet. "Fog's lifted."

They sit in a cluster and drink their tea. Nina can feel the engines through the soles of her feet, as when a cathedral organ is playing its deepest notes. When she swings her legs onto the mattress, she feels the bedstead trembling too. She tries to imagine the men inside the bombers, but even though she knows they are nearby and real, she can only think of them as far away and insubstantial, like actors on a cinema screen.

Nobody mentions what's happening out there. Susie hardly talks at all, but Nina, Joan, and Dolly discuss coal rationing, and different sorts of cake, and the rehearsal schedule for the Christmas concert.

The stove is slow to warm the hut. After tea, Nina gets back into bed and re-reads her letter to Rose, but the tone strikes her as shallow and disingenuous, and she shifts uncomfortably inside her coat. *What are the chances of him being stationed here?* squeals the letter excitedly, without admitting that the chances are high enough when you create them for yourself.

Well, she might as well finish it off and post it, because she's sick of wasting notepaper, but she won't write anything else about Guy Nicholson. She's too shy to tell Rose about the way he echoed the word *Cottenden* and took a step towards the table, or the way his face lit with recognition, as if he'd come across a friend in a strange land.

"I know you," he'd said, and she'd wanted to reply memorably, but hadn't been able to draw breath.

He was about to say something else—he must have been—but dozens of airmen were pouring into the room, and there was too much commotion for anything else.

. . .

IT'S FOGGY AGAIN, THE NEXT day. At three o'clock Nina is loitering outside the WAAF guardroom with her bicycle, breathing into her scarf for warmth, wishing Lucky would hurry up.

They'd met briefly, in the grey light of dawn, as she made her way to work. She'd taken a short cut through a hangar, and when he shouted, "Nina!" his voice echoed round the mighty, metallic space with such force that he sounded angry—which of course he wasn't. Nina tried to wave in a passing, friendly way and called out, "Perhaps see you later?" but he ran over and made her stop. The wing of a Lancaster bomber jutted above them, casting Lucky's face in shadow.

He was sweet—Lucky was always sweet—but all the same, Nina disliked being held by the wrist. She disliked the way he gently shook her arm, if she didn't answer straightaway.

"Are you free this afternoon?" he wanted to know. "How about we cycle into Lincoln, and I'll take you for tea at Annabelle's? I've got a briefing after lunch, but I can be with you by three."

She'd dithered, but ended up saying yes. That business about him popping the question was probably Susie's nonsense, and tea at Annabelle's Café was always nice.

It's half past three now, and the light is dwindling. Mist shrouds the airfield, but Nina catches the occasional glimpse of runway, or the outline of a grounded plane. If the place feels haunted now, how much more haunted will it seem once the war is over (if it ever is)? She can't be a completely cold-hearted bitch, or she wouldn't feel so sick at the thought of Charlwood unpeopled and forgotten: its runways overgrown with nettles, its barbed-wire fences rusted, its windows broken, its doors unhinged. Maybe she'll visit as an old woman, and wander round the ruins, remembering. Or maybe she won't. The nostalgia might kill her.

Nina frowns and fiddles with the bell on her bicycle, but *nostalgia* is the right word; she can't think of a better. The war is hellish, and Nina prays as hard as the next English man or woman for a prompt victory, but even in the thick of it, she feels a stirring of regret; a premature homesickness for this terrible time and place.

She balances the bicycle against her hip and wiggles her frozen fingers inside her gloves. The briefing room is on the other side of the road, and it keeps fading and emerging through a ribbon of mist. Someone inside switches on the lights and draws the blackout blinds, and she perks up, thinking it means the end of Lucky's meeting, but five minutes pass and nobody comes out.

It takes forty minutes or so to cycle to Lincoln; Annabelle's will probably be closed by the time they arrive. They'll end up at the pub, and she'll ask for a sherry, but Lucky will talk her into having a beer on the grounds that it goes further. She's still trying to like beer.

Nina walks her bicycle in a tight circle, stopping where she started, with a sigh. Nobody else is around on such a bleak afternoon: everyone is either on duty, or holed up in their billets. That's where she should be too. Nina pulls the collar of her greatcoat as high as it will go, but the dampness has worked its way through the wool, and it's impossible to get warm. She decides to return to Hut 9—Lucky will know where to find her—but as she's turning her bicycle she sees a man walking briskly with his head down and his hands in his pockets. It's Guy Nicholson, marching out of the airfield, onto Roman Lane. God knows how she recognises him—he's only a moving silhouette; a long coat and an officer's cap—but she does.

Roman Lane goes all the way to Lincoln, running roughly parallel to the modern, tarmacked road. In summer it's enchanting, with its banks of cow parsley and overarching elms. In winter the delicate shades of green turn to grey, the skeletal trees crowd too close, and it's muddy underfoot. Nina wavers, thinking of her bed, but in the end she follows Guy, treading in his footprints. She's sorry she oiled the bicycle chain so thoroughly last night; if he were to hear it squeaking he might turn round, and then he'd have to speak to her.

Perhaps he's not in a noticing frame of mind: the bell jingles when she catches the front wheel on a stone, but Guy simply strides on with his shoulders hunched up to his ears. They walk like this for five minutes. Ten. Fifteen. The cathedral towers materialise darkly, up ahead, as the trees dwindle. Nina begins to feel foolish. She will follow him round the next bend, and if nothing happens she will turn quietly and retrace her steps.

Nina rounds the bend—and he's gone, which is impossible. The path does not split, and there are no buildings just yet, only hedges and fields. She stops and stares round, feeling worse than foolish.

Is he—was he—a ghost? Nina hates to frame the question, but it's unavoidable. At RAF Charlwood, the veil between death and life is threadbare, and reliable people have odd experiences. When Dolly Brown started as a radio operator, she swears she spoke at length to one particular pilot, giving him permission to land—only he never did land, because he'd crashed into the North Sea several hours before. There are several girls who have heard the tread of flying boots on corridors at night, and gone to look, but found nobody there. Only a couple of evenings ago, Susie Macaulay wanted to experiment with a Ouija board, and the others in the hut were quite keen, but Nina's refusal was so withering that the idea died a death.

A little way along, on the left, there's a five-bar gate standing open. She props her bicycle against the hedge and peers inside the field, and there he is—her quarry, her ghost—sitting on a ridge of ploughed soil, with his cap scrunched up in one hand, and a sheet of paper in the other.

Nina recoils. Over the past couple of years she's witnessed a number of airmen lose their minds: she recognises the ones with the staring eyes; the ones who weep; the ones who get the shakes and can't pick up their beer without slopping. Her second boyfriend, Mac, used to ask, with unsettling frequency, whether ops were on tonight. He barely said anything else the week before his death, even during their jaunt to Stratford-upon-Avon. (*Nina, darling, are ops on tonight? . . . Mac, you know perfectly well you're not on ops, you've got forty-eight hours leave! . . . I know, I know, but I like to hear you say it.*)

On the upside, Guy isn't talking to himself, or making funny noises, or swaying backwards and forwards. On the downside, it's not normal to sit in a muddy field, on a winter's evening. Nina takes a deep breath and begins picking her way towards him. He takes no notice until she reaches his side, and even then he hardly affords her a glance. She decides not to mind his coldness too much; at least his eyes aren't vacant.

"Hello," she says.

"Oh!" His expression softens. "It's you."

Nina looks at her shoes. She'd polished them up rather well this morning, but never mind.

"Are you all right?"

When he doesn't answer, she crouches down, bringing her face on a level with his. There's a smudge of mud on Guy's forehead, just over his left eyebrow, and she touches it lightly with her woollen thumb. He seizes her hand, and she thinks he's going to fling her away, but instead he presses her knuckles against his head, and she does well to keep her balance. He's breathing hard and squeezing his eyes shut, as if it's an effort not to cry. Perhaps it's an effort not to scream.

What would RAF Charlwood be like, she wonders, if everyone who wanted to scream, screamed? In a flash she sees the whole lot of them—airmen, ground crew, and WAAFs—standing or kneeling on the runway, their faces lifted to the skies, their mouths stretched open as wide as they'd go. She frees her hand from his grasp with a shudder.

Nina can't keep on crouching, because it's uncomfortable, and she doesn't want to stand up, because it would look unfriendly, so she sits beside him on the soil. The damp chill seeps through her clothes, and practical questions flicker through her mind, as if to distract her from what's really happening. (*How badly muddied will my coat be? Should I clean it with a damp cloth? No, better to hang it near the stove and brush it when it's dried.*)

Guy doesn't try to recover her hand. Nina watches him from the corner of her eye as he draws his knees up to his chest. The crumpled paper he's holding is key to all this, she's sure. There's a flashy signature at the bottom—*Joey*—and after a moment's thought she exclaims, "Joey! Your Joey? Canadian Joey?"

Now he's looking at her properly, and she feels less like an attractive shoulder to cry on, and more like Nina Woodrow.

"You knew him?" he says. "Of course you did, I'd quite forgotten."

"You'd *forgotten* . . ."

If he had forgotten, then what was yesterday's flash of recognition about? How could Guy have remembered her, in the parachute room, without remembering the circumstances of their meeting eight years ago? In her own mind, Guy Nicholson is inextricably bound up with Joey Roussin, lemonade, rye whisky, August heat, and Rose's sister-in-law's dress. (Especially the dress. Black silk, lacy sleeves, red cherries.)

"That awful dinner party," says Guy.

She nods, her eyes on the letter. When she takes it, he doesn't resist.

"You got drunk," she recalls.

"Joey got drunk. Well, all right, I got drunk too. Your father didn't like us."

Nina can't deny it.

Guy goes on, "There was a tree with a treehouse, and Joey and I knelt beneath it and kissed your hand and apologised for being such drunken idiots."

"You swore to be my knights errant—whatever that meant."

"I remember. You were terribly embarrassed and worried your father might see. You kept saying, 'Get up, oh please, just get up.'"

"May I read the letter?"

Guy passes it over and drops his head onto his knees. Even in the fading light, it's easy to decipher Joey's big, bold handwriting.

RAF Fairlop, Essex

Nov '42

Dear Guy,

If you're reading this letter, it means I've bitten the dust. Worry not, I won't come over all heavy—these aren't the last words of Seneca. (Remember Cain the Cane going misty-eyed over the death of Seneca, when we were in the fourth form? Or was it Socrates? You know who I mean—the guy in the bath.)

Anyway, there's a "big show" tomorrow, as they say, so we've been encouraged to scribble our adieus this evening. I've never bothered before, but I seem to have caught the writing bug tonight, and I reckon if I owe anyone a fond farewell, it's you. (I've written one for Mum & Dad et al., and another for Aunt Calla and Uncle Bram, and I thought of doing one for Patty and the kid, only her hubby might not like it. Besides, chances are she'll read to the end and think, "What the hell? Joey who?")

Remember one time at school, we were feeling pretty low, and we hatched a plan to run away to Canada? We were going to begin by sacrificing our Latin Grammars and rugby kits to Lake Winnipeg—according to some spooky ritual of your devising—and then we were going to spend the rest of our lives rounding up cattle and cooking over campfires. Remember? But then what happened? First I became a clerk, and you an accountant—which was bad enough—and then the war came along to put us out of our misery. Boy, what a waste.

Well, whenever I'm feeling fed up, that's where I go in my head—to our ranch in Manitoba. Big skies, big horizons. Horses and cattle. Lake swimming in summer. Snowshoeing in winter. Whisky swigging all year round, straight from the bottle . . .

I guess I just wanted you to know about that.

Cheerio, old pal. Safe flying.
Joey

Nina doesn't try to come up with comforting words. She doesn't even touch him. She just hands the letter back and moves a little closer to his side, and they stare out across the field together. The twilight is deepening, but the mist is thinning, and there's a misshapen moon above the far hedge. (*Waxing gibbous*, she thinks, irrelevantly, at the same time as she's remembering Joey Roussin, with his sunburn and swagger.) She starts to shiver, but holds it at bay by clenching her jaw, because she doesn't want him to think she's restless.

It's Guy who says, "We should go," in the end, when there's more darkness than light in the sky, and the land has lost its contours. Nina is so frozen she can hardly stand up, but she is also pleased: she can tell by the softness of his voice that he's understood her stillness. Not everybody would. Some people—civilians—would have fussed and wept and said, *How awful! Poor Joey! Poor you!* but not Nina. That isn't the way at Charlwood. When you receive a bitter pill, you don't chew it up with lots of mess and noise, you swallow it discreetly, in one.

Not for the first time since joining the WAAF, Nina feels a flash of scorn for the ordinary people—people like her own father—who haven't the faintest clue. Cosy Cottenden hasn't experienced a single air-raid, whereas she has smelled burning flesh, and stepped over severed arms and legs, and administered first aid to a man who begged her to shoot him in the head. (She didn't, but she stayed with him while he died.)

Lucky likes to say, "I reckon the ones who suffer most in this war are the ones at home, with nothing to do but wait," but this drives her mad. What, *them*? They're all right! What's the worst they've got to fear? The sharp sting of a telegram (*deeply regret to inform you* ...) softened by kindly neighbours and sweet tea.

Guy helps her to her feet, and they hold on to one another as they make their way to the gate. Once they're back on firm ground they move apart. Nina retrieves her bicycle from the hedgerow, and wheels it along between them. They're quiet, except for the *tick-tick* of the wheels.

"Are you on ops tonight?" she asks, at last.

"Yes, if the fog keeps lifting. Our usual kite's C:Charlie, but she's in for repair, so we're flying V:Victor instead."

"Oh, I see."

Nina looks at him anxiously, as he sighs a bluish cloud into the darkness. She wants to say, "A plane is a plane; it makes no difference," but she knows she won't convince him. Crews are funny about their kites. He's thinking, *V:Victor is bad luck.* He's thinking, *Tonight's the night I bite the dust too.*

Perhaps he's also thinking, *So what?*

"Was Joey a fighter pilot?" she asks.

"Mm. Yes."

Nina tightens her grip on the handlebars and keeps walking, although she's finding it difficult to breathe in the normal way. Every time she inhales, her stomach tightens.

"Well... I think it's harder for you," she says.

"Harder than what?"

"Harder than it was for Joey."

"How so?"

"I mean, fighter pilots only have themselves to worry about. You've got five other men to bring home safely."

Guy laughs drily. Nothing else is said until they've left the lane, and they're back outside the WAAF guardroom.

"Here we are," he says. "Thank you for your company."

"Not at all."

Their pace slows, but they never quite stop.

"Goodbye then," he concludes. "All the best."

The words *Safe flying* are on the tip of Nina's tongue, but they're the final words of Joey's letter, and it seems presumptuous to use them.

"All the best," she echoes.

Nina turns left, while Guy heads on towards Barrier C and the airfield.

. . .

NINA SITS ON THE WOODEN chair between her own bed and Susie's. Mary Crawshaw is fast asleep in the bed nearest the window, but otherwise the place is empty. There's a whole hour to kill before her own shift starts.

She dozes and dreams she's in the lane again. There's a legion of Roman soldiers marching towards her, filling the space from hedge to hedge, and she has to escape, but her bicycle is so cumbersome, and the hedges are higher than they were, and there's no gate . . .

Nina sways forwards and starts awake. She rubs her eyes and wonders about removing her damp coat and going to bed, but it hardly seems worth it for fifty minutes. There's always the cookhouse—she wouldn't say no to a cuppa—but it will be full of bright lights and people, and she'll have her fill of them when she goes on shift.

She leaves the hut and wanders back to Roman Lane. The mist is gone, and the moon is up, but it's still too dark for a proper walk, and she has to be careful where she puts her feet.

After the second bend, she comes to a sharp halt. Some distance away—how far, it's hard to tell—a tiny light flares, shrinks, and glows red. Her first thought is of the ghostly legionaries, but she knows enough about Roman Britain to know that they didn't march along with fags hanging out of the corners of their mouths. That was definitely a match being struck to light a cigarette—no, a pipe. The smell is distinctive.

Perhaps *she* is the ghost, straying into a peaceful future world? Perhaps the pipe-smoking man will be frightened when he sees a woman in the faint moonlight, dressed in an old-fashioned uniform from the 1940s war?

The thought makes her laugh unexpectedly, and she walks forwards, to test her theory out.

"Hello?"

The man turns towards her voice and takes the pipe from his mouth.

"Hey!"

It's Nina who takes a sharp breath and steps back; it's she, after all, who has seen the ghost.

. . .

RUNNING IS DISCOURAGED AT RAF CHARLWOOD, unless it's a matter of life and death. Even when the air-raid sirens blare, you're not supposed to pound so forcibly that your cap flies off. Nina doesn't care. This is an emergency, as far as she's concerned. Joey Roussin is not dead, after all. He's alive; he's come here, to Charlwood, and he wants to see Guy Nicholson.

She has to pause at Barrier C to show her papers, but as soon as she's through she breaks into a run again: past a couple of battle-axes from WAAF admin who call out sternly; past a wolf-whistling sergeant.

The airfield is busy and noisy. Near the control tower she stops one of the ground-crew boys, and catches enough breath to ask, "Warrant Officer Guy Nicholson?" but he looks at her blankly. Before she can resume her search, Lucky emerges from who-knows-where and catches her round the waist.

"Darling!" he says. "I'm sorry the wretched briefing dragged on; I couldn't get away. What are you up to, same time tomorrow?"

They might be at a dance, going by the dreamy look on his face, but they're not at a dance, for God's sake!

"Lucky, I can't talk now. I need—"

"I'm on ops in an hour. Thank goodness we ran into one another; I was afraid I might not see you."

"I need to find Warrant Officer Guy Nicholson. I've got an urgent message for him; terribly urgent. I simply must find him."

"Guy? I know Guy. I've played billiards with him down at the Poacher's Arms. Is it official or unofficial?"

"What?"

"This urgent message. Is it from on high . . . or is it from you?"

He smiles reproachfully and tilts her chin, but she bats him off.

"Lucky . . . don't be . . . it's not like that. It's important, that's all. There's someone here to see him; it's too complicated to explain."

They loiter together while others rush around them: men going to get kitted up; trucks delivering crew to hangars; tractors with bomb trailers bouncing along behind.

"Well, I don't know where he is. With his crew, I suppose."

Lucky tries to pull her close. She lets him kiss her closed lips, but then she's off.

"I'll see you tomorrow," she calls over her shoulder. "I'll try, anyway."

The first of the Lancaster bombers is lumbering away from its hardstanding, followed by another, and another, and another. They advance on the flare-lit runway with menacing intent, their wingtips blinking green and red. The earth vibrates under Nina's feet, the sky vibrates in her ears, and the hairs rise along her arms. She is used to most things now, but she will never be used to the Lancasters. They are more monster than machine: they remind her of the flesh-eating dinosaur in her *Children's Encyclopaedia*. She used to love that page—the dead-eyed Tyrannosaurus rex with the herbivore flailing between its jaws—although it gave her bad dreams, and she wasn't allowed to look at it before bed.

The first plane gathers speed and takes off. Guy might be boarding V:Victor right now, settling at his map table, adjusting his Anglepoise lamp as the engines roar into life.

Even if he's not, she's run out of time. Her shift starts in two minutes.

"Damn it."

It's tense in the parachute-packing room. There's a teeming queue for kits, and another for the logbook, and brisk conversations on all sides. Nina glimpses a familiar dark, clipped head, but it might not be Guy's, and she's needed at once, and anyway . . . She stands on tiptoe and peers around the throng. Anyway, whoever he was, he's gone.

. . .

NINA'S SHIFT ENDS SHORTLY AFTER dawn, and she dawdles back along the perimeter fence. She's in no hurry—although she should be, because she needs sleep. Sometimes she stops and peers at the clouds, and the trails of flares along the runway. Far away, in the early-morning gloom, she can make out a few wounded monsters rolling back to their hangars. There have been losses, but only one plane is unaccounted for, and it's V:Victor. Of course it is. The gods of this world have a taste for sick jokes.

It's like the plot of a lousy film. *Girl falls for unattainable local man and makes him the subject of her most private fantasies. War is declared. Man joins air force, so girl joins WAAF. Man is stationed at RAF Charlwood; girl leaps at unexpected opportunity to work there too. Weeks pass. Girl worships from afar. Girl discovers man is divorced, and engineers a meeting. Man and girl share a moment of restrained intimacy in a field, during which she strokes a piece of mud off his forehead (albeit with her woolly glove on). The same night, he is killed in action. The End.* It's the sort of film that would have Joan and Dolly weeping into their handkerchiefs, and Nina saying, "What an absolute waste of half a bob."

Guy Nicholson is dead. She makes herself say it under her breath, as she pictures him kneeling under the cherry tree at 7 Canal Road and touching her hand to his lips like a real knight—like Lancelot or Percival—and making her fall in love with him. Joey Roussin had wanted more than her hand—he'd started moving his lips up her arm—but Guy had cuffed his friend round the head and told him not to be an ass, and Joey had obeyed.

A black dot is emerging from the low clouds. The dot turns into a dash; the dash turns into a plane. Nina leans back against the fence and grips the wires with her cold fingers. *V:Victor*, she thinks, but she's too superstitious to say it out loud.

A little yellow biplane flew over Hawthorn House, that summer's day in 1934. Mrs. Nicholson said a person would have to be crazy to want to fly, but Guy said, *I'd do it!* and Nina said, *Me too!* When the war began, five years later, Nina made a secret bet with herself that Guy Nicholson would join the RAF, and a week later she glimpsed him at church in a blue-grey uniform, with the wings embroidered above his breast pocket, and his uncrazy, earthbound wife at his side. *Didn't I say?* she thought, gleefully. *Didn't I just know?* A few days afterwards, she joined up herself.

It *is* V:Victor, but something is wrong. It's approaching too fast and at a funny angle, and the landing gear isn't down. One of its engines is smoking. The plane ought to sound lighter, having ditched its bombs, but it sounds strained, as though it's only kept airborne by a collective, waning belief.

People are running and shouting; there are racing trucks and clanging sirens. The bomber roars, furiously, in its desperate search for lightness and poise. The seconds stretch, and there is just enough time to start hoping before the wings overbalance and the big beast spins, nose first, into a clump of trees about a quarter of a mile away from where Nina is standing. There's a momentary stillness before the inevitable flash and boom.

Nina runs with everyone else, only stopping when the heat crashes, like a wave, against her face. She tries again, but someone grabs her by the arm and a voice shouts, "Nina! Nina, don't. You can't do anything."

She flinches at a second explosion and turns towards the voice. It's Guy Nicholson. His face is bright yellow in the light of the blast.

"God almighty," he's saying. "I'm so sorry, Nina. I'm so sorry."

She only half listens to his words, because it doesn't matter what he's saying. It's as much as she can do to grasp the fact that he's speaking at all. Someone is screaming. There's another explosion, and more sirens, and a lot of shouting.

"There was a mix-up with the kites—too many in for repair at once—we got C:Charlie after all, and Lucas's crew was assigned V:Victor—I knew him a little—I saw him last night—he mentioned you—God, I'm sorry—such bloody awful . . ."

As Guy's lips move, Nina becomes aware that Lucky is in that plane, and that her thoughts should be with him. Even here there are moments—brief, brief moments—where you're allowed to acknowledge death, and feel sad, before duty moves you along. This is one of those moments. She is being offered the gift of a pause, but all she can do is watch Guy's lips move.

"Joey's alive," she says, stopping his flow of words. "I tried to find you last night, to tell you, but you'd gone. His Spitfire did go down, but he made it out all right. He's here—he turned up on a forty-eight-hour pass, looking for you."

. . .

JOEY IS VISIBLE THROUGH THE cookhouse window, exactly as he was when Nina left him yesterday evening, joshing with a couple of girls, smoking a fresh pipe, handing out sticks of gum. They've brought him yet more tea and an egg on toast, which they wouldn't do for everyone. There's something extra exciting about a Royal Canadian Air Force man or a Yank: perhaps it's the accent, or the allusion to unspoiled places far, far away. The wireless is playing dance music, and it's clear that nobody has noticed—or chosen to notice—the disaster on the other side of the airfield.

"Bloody glamour boy!" Guy bites the inside of his cheek as if to stop himself from laughing. *Glamour boys*: that's how fighter pilots are disparaged by Bomber Command, and Joey fits the bill with his roll-neck sweater and silk scarf. He is clean-shaven now, and thinner than he was in 1934, but his smile is as dazzling as ever.

Guy makes for the entrance hall, but Nina doesn't follow. She lets the door swing shut, and walks away. There's an oily, acrid stench in the early-morning air: the carcass of V:Victor is still in flames, as are the leafless trees that caught it in their arms. The fire engines remain, a frantic cluster of lights and hoses, but the ambulance has gone. There was never any realistic need for an ambulance.

A friendlier sort of smoke is issuing from the tin chimney of Hut 9. The coal delivery must have arrived early, or else Dolly has "borrowed" from another hut. It's just as well. Nina looks at the lowering clouds and predicts rain, or even snow, for today.

There goes Joan, red-faced and tear-stained, rushing back from the scene of the accident.

Nina will go inside too, in a minute, and warm up—but not yet. She hides in the muddy gap between Hut 9 and the wash-house, searching her pockets for a cigarette she doesn't have, and doesn't really want. She overdid smoking when she was eighteen, and now it makes her sick.

Everyone will know it was Lucky's plane. Joan will say, "Are you all right?" in her softly-softly voice and insist on fetching a cup of tea, and a slice of that god-awful fruitcake.

Better to wait for a while—at least until Joan's gone on shift.

"Nina?"

It's Guy.

"Nina, what are you doing here? Why did you disappear?"

She might ask what he's doing here, when he should be in the cookhouse with Joey. Still, she's glad of the chance to drink him in again; she can't help it. That mouth, and the shadow of a dark beard, because he hasn't shaved since yesterday morning. Those cryptic eyes.

"Why aren't you with Joey?" she asks.

"Because I want you to come too."

"*Me*? But he's your friend, and anyway..."

"Please come."

It's a trivial conversation, yet they manage to burden it with meaning. When Nina relives the scene later on (which she does, again and again), she can't work out how they did that—how they turned something so light into something so weighty.

Guy removes his cap and twists it in his hands. Then he shoves it into his greatcoat pocket, and moves towards her, just as she is moving towards him.

It's as much Nina's kiss as Guy's, so she can't claim to be taken by surprise, but she's as panic-stricken as if they've stumbled together off the edge of a rickety staircase. She has to cling to something as she falls, so she clings to him, and he clings to her.

Nina has kissed plenty of boys—even if her father doesn't know it—but never, ever like this. She has never feared the end of a kiss before, or enjoyed the sensation of being smothered, or resented the capacity to breathe again.

Who wants to breathe chill November air? Any old fool can breathe air.

6

Kate

January 15, 1943

PIP IS SUFFERING WITH HIS CHEST TONIGHT. I'VE MANAGED
to sit him up in bed, and now he's leaning over a bowl of boiling water
with a towel over his head, while I stroke his back, saying, "Deep, steady
breaths! That's it!" I'm trying hard to sound jolly and encouraging.

He'll be nine in August, but he looks about six; there's nothing
but skin and bones under that striped pyjama jacket. The last time
Guy came home he ruffled his son's hair and said, "Hello there!
How's the runt of the litter?" No doubt he meant it affectionately—I
think that's how they talk in the RAF—but I told him off for being
patronising, and he got quite indignant. ("Says she, who shortens
the poor kid's name to *Pip*!" I argued back on the grounds of literary precedent, but it didn't wash. Guy dislikes Victorian novels, and
Dickens in particular.)

"Shall we pop your dressing-gown on?" I say, in my jolly-and-
encouraging voice. "We can't have you shivering."

Pip manages to get his arms in the sleeves, and I retrieve the hot water bottle from the floor and tuck it in beside his feet.

I'm shivering as well, but not—or not entirely—because of the cold. There are two subjects on my mind, but both are so momentous that I can't manage them at the same time, and I keep bouncing from one to the other, in a state of repeated shock. Whenever Pip's breathing eases, I resume the train of thought I've been following all evening ("Guy is having an affair? *Guy* is having an *affair?*"). Then Pip starts coughing again, and I jump to attention, unable to think of anything other than fresh kettles of boiling water, and mustard plasters, and *Please God, let him be all right.*

And so it goes on: Pip's cough, Guy's affair, Pip's cough, Guy's affair . . . I can't imagine having space inside my brain for anything else, ever. There isn't even enough room for The War.

Just as I'm about to telephone Dr. Lupton again, and implore him to come over, Pip starts showing signs of improvement. When I say, "You sound like a steam-train, wheezing up a hill," he chortles, and I know we're over the worst. True, the laugh turns into a coughing fit, but it subsides quickly, and when I poke my head under the towel to give his cheek a kiss, he smiles. A couple of hours ago, he could only stare at me wide-eyed and grip my hand.

"Do you know, I've always suspected you might be half boy, half steam-train."

"Can you tell me a story about it?"

"A story about Pip, the steam-engine boy?"

I move the bowl from his lap so that I can put my arm round his shoulders and swing my feet onto the bed. He rests his head on my chest and sticks his thumb in his mouth. ("Now, that's a habit that needs nipping in the bud," said Guy, on his last leave.)

"You'll have to give me a minute to think," I say, stroking Pip's damp curls and suppressing a sigh. With any luck he'll fall asleep in the meantime, because I'm all out of ideas tonight.

I slow my breathing right down, so that his body rises and falls in a gentle rhythm. After a while, I manoeuvre my left arm carefully, and switch off the bedside lamp.

Hawthorn House and I have never made friends, but over the years I've made my peace with one of its rooms. Murdered ghosts are no match for my son's bedroom: not when his inside-out clothes are strewn over the floorboards, and his steam-train drawings are tacked to the walls. I feel at home here, in a transitory way. The other rooms continue to repel me, but I don't care about it as much as I used to.

Pip's night light is glowing on top of the bookcase, and silvery remnants of steam wind upwards from the bowl that I placed on the floor. All is quiet, except for a single fluty note each time he breathes in. The peace is beautiful, but there's nothing I can do in response, except to feel sad and watch it pass by. I suppose that's often the way with beauty.

So: Guy is having an affair.

My husband has a mistress.

My child's father . . .

I'll never be able to read tonight, let alone sleep. It would be a relief to talk to a fellow grown-up, but I'm too ashamed to tell my friends, and none of my siblings will do. Deb will feel desperately sorry for me, and cry down the telephone. Janey will snap, "Frankly, Kate, in the context of what's happening to the *world* at the moment . . ." Ron will swear and call Guy a bastard, which might be quite cheering, except that Ron has been posted to India, and can't be reached by telephone.

Pip and I used to lie together like this, night after night, in the autumn and winter of 1940. We used to listen to the German bombers swarming overhead, homing in on Liverpool; it was impossible to sleep inside that noise, safe as we were in our rural darkness. A public warning notice had gone up in the village about how to recognise hostile aircraft, and I knew the illustrations by heart—the

Messerschmitts and Heinkels, the Dorniers and Junkers—but I never set eyes on a single one; only ever heard their low growl. All I saw of the Liverpool Blitz, through the landing curtains, was the red haze on the skyline, where the docks were burning. I would have given anything, back then, for this depth of peace and quiet.

"Come and talk to me, Ghost!" I whisper into the darkness. "I'd rather have your company than none."

Pip whimpers in his sleep. Minutes tick by on his alarm clock, and the night light gutters and fades.

. . .

I'M SURPRISED IT'S ONLY HALF past ten by the time I leave Pip sleeping and come downstairs; it feels like the dead of night. For a few minutes I perch on an armchair in the sitting-room, next to the electric fire, but I'm worried I won't hear Pip if he calls, so I return to the hall.

The blackout curtains are up, so I can't see what sort of night it is, but I can feel the crackle of frost in my bones. I fetch my old tweed coat from under the stairs, along with the rabbit-fur stole that Guy gave me for Christmas, and once I'm bundled up, I sit on the stairs. I look like an intruder in my own home.

The stole smells of oranges and cloves, just as it did when I chose it in the shop, and when Guy handed me the box on December 22. (He had to return to Lincolnshire on the twenty-third, so we held our celebrations early.) I remember pressing it to my face and say-ing, "How lovely!" because in my limited experience, furs can smell dreadful. He stood at the window, lighting up his new pipe, and said, "Glad you like it." Even at the time I noticed that he didn't kiss me, or watch me put it on, but I thought he was worrying about going back to the war. It never crossed my mind that he might be in love with another woman.

Rabbit. I suppose it's the cheapest sort of fur one can buy, isn't it? Even in wartime, there's no shortage of rabbits. I pull the stole off my neck and fling it half-heartedly into the darkness, dislodging the telephone receiver from its hook without quite knocking it off.

What a typically pathetic gesture. What a meagre person I must seem, in the eyes of my husband the War Hero. I wonder how he refers to me in front of his lover? I can't imagine him saying *Kate*. Perhaps he says *the wife*, with one of his wry smiles? *The* wife, rather than *my* wife. Yes, I bet that's what he does, if he mentions me at all.

As I get up to set the telephone to rights, I wonder again about calling Deb. If only she wasn't so solidly married herself, I might endure her sympathy, but, as things stand, I want communion with a fellow sufferer. I want to lament with someone who has recently sustained a vicious kick to the gut.

I put the receiver to my ear and pinch my lower lip to help me think.

I could call Henry Woodrow. It seems a bit mean to administer the kick myself, just so that I can have someone to talk to, but then again, in many ways, he is the obvious . . .

No, Kate.

No.

What's got into you? You can't call Mr. Woodrow! You barely know the man! You'll sound desperate and ridiculous.

Don't do it.

Please don't.

· · ·

"COTTENDEN 108?"

He picks up at once, so there's no time for second thoughts. Oh Lord, he'll think I'm mad or drunk. I wish I *were* drunk, but we're out of alcohol, and the most potent substance in the house is an ounce of poor-quality tea. I pass my hand across my tired eyes. There's nothing for it but to put on a voice: the pleasant-yet-brisk one that I've honed in my dealings with Mrs. Powell at the village shop.

"Mr. Woodrow? How do you do, this is Mrs. Nicholson here. Kate Nicholson."

I wait a moment, but there's no reply. (*Do please call me Henry,* he'd said, all those years ago, but I can hardly presume on that now. We never managed to make good on the intimacy that flared into life that summer evening in 1934—for which I blame Guy and Joey's rudeness, as well as my own shyness and Henry's profound reserve. Sometimes, in church, I look at him through my fingers when I'm meant to be praying, and think how brooding he looks, like a man with a secret love and/or a mad wife in the attic. Sometimes—well, twice actually—I've caught him looking at me.)

"Mr. Woodrow? You may not remember—"

"I remember, of course. Kate Nicholson. Hawthorn House."

"Yes, that's right. Listen, I'm awfully sorry to telephone so late."

It's funny that my name puts him in mind of Hawthorn House; it's not as if he's ever been here. Following that peculiar dinner party I half wanted to invite him over in return, but to begin with it felt too awkward, and then it felt too late.

"How may I help you, Mrs. Nicholson? I hope nothing's wrong?"

"Well, in fact, I'm afraid something is."

"Oh?"

"And I realise it's late, and you'll think me a frightful nuisance, but I think we ought to discuss it in person."

"In person? You wish me to come to Hawthorn House?"

"If you would."

"Now?"

"I'm sorry to trouble you, but it's rather a delicate matter for the telephone, and if we leave it till morning . . . The truth is, I don't know what I'll do with myself if I have to wait."

God almighty, Kate! I screw up my face and bang my forehead gently against the wall. It's not as if I look like a seductress—not a successful one, anyway—but that's no guarantee of pure intentions. I readjust the elements of my pleasant-yet-brisk tone, in favour of briskness.

"Mr. Woodrow, I hope you don't think I'm the worse for drink, or anything of that sort."

"Mrs. Nicholson . . ." The line buzzes, as Mr. Woodrow clears his throat. "Mrs. Nicholson? Perhaps if you could give me some idea what the matter is?"

Oh, hell's bells: apparently I'm in danger of crying. I will not have Mr. Woodrow writing me off as hysterical, on top of everything else. My only hope is to speak in the abstract. If I say *Guy* or *my husband*, all will be lost.

"I'm afraid I've made a rather terrible discovery."

Mr. Woodrow is silent for a long time.

"A discovery?"

"Yes. This afternoon. My son and I were alone in the house, but then something odd happened, and I made . . . I made, as I say, a rather terrible discovery."

Silence again. Perhaps there's a delay on the line. His voice sounds fainter too.

"I see, and . . . if you don't mind my asking . . . are you alone in the house now?"

"Yes. Well, I mean, Phillip is here, but he's in bed. Phillip is my son."

"I see."

"Will you come?"

No answer.

"Mr. Woodrow, will you come? I know how queer this must sound, but we do need to talk. Please?"

There's no answer, but I can hear his breathing.

"Wait," he says, and the line goes dead.

. . .

MR. WOODROW LOOKS SO UNLIKE himself when I open the door that I'm half tempted to shut it again, without letting him in. He's panting, as if he's run all the way, and he seems much larger than he did on Sunday, when he stood behind the lectern in his dapper suit and read from the Psalms. Perhaps it's just the bulky coat he's wearing, and his relative proximity, and the strangeness of seeing him in the dark. Moonlight does odd things to people's faces.

I have to admit, the dog doesn't help. The Woodrows used to have a waggy old spaniel called Biscuit, but it appears to have been succeeded by a bull terrier. Doesn't Bill Sikes have a bull terrier, in *Oliver Twist*? I almost say so, but manage not to.

"Goodness! What a dog!"

"Don't mind Shirley. She's nicer than she looks."

Which is just as well, given the psychopathic gleam in her little black eyes. By the time I've said a standoffish, "Hello there, Shirley," and Mr. Woodrow has said, "All right if I bring her in?" they're both inside and there's nothing for it but to lead the way to the sitting-room.

The standard lamps are on, as is the electric heater, so this lofty-ceilinged, white-walled, much-neglected room is as cosy as it ever gets. I invite Mr. Woodrow to sit down, but he won't. He suggests that I shut the door, but I tell him I can't, because my son is poorly and likely to shout out.

"Would you like anything? I'm afraid I haven't much to offer, except some very weak tea."

"No, no, no." He flaps his hand impatiently and paces the rug. "Thank you, anyway." Shirley lies down beside the sofa and rests her chin on her paws.

"Well?" he demands, at exactly the same moment as I beg him to *please* sit down, upon which he apologises and flings himself into an armchair. I sit down on the other side of the fire, and try to get warm, but only succeed in par-grilling my ankles. I'm still wearing my frumpy tweed coat—partly for insulation, partly to signal that my purposes are categorically chaste.

Mr. Woodrow is fidgety. He takes his scarf off, and keeps winding it round his wrists, or running it through his fingers. He is not glad to see me, not even a little bit, and I repent of having picked up the telephone. I just thought . . . I don't know what I thought.

"Mrs. Nicholson? Please! Out with it!"

"Of course. I'm sorry. It happened this afternoon."

"*What* happened?"

"No, wait, I have to go further back than that: about a week before Christmas. Before I begin, though, may I ask a question?"

He nods faintly.

"Are you familiar with a shop in Carlisle, called Cooper and Reid?"

"Am I familiar . . . ?" He runs his fingers through his grizzled hair. "I've never even been to Carlisle."

No. I thought not. I close my eyes and gather my thoughts. I rarely drink or smoke, but I'd pay over the odds, just now, for a double brandy and a cigarette.

. . .

I TELL HIM THAT WE travelled to Carlisle in mid-December—Guy, Phillip, and I—to visit the family. On the second day of our stay, we went into town to do some Christmas shopping, and it all got rather tedious.

"Darling, I'd like you to have something nice," Guy kept saying. "Name it, and I'll buy it."

I'd already suggested a few ideas (a bottle of scent? peppermint creams? a new novel?), but nothing suited him. (*Oh, but I gave you scent for your birthday . . . Surely you can think of something better than sweets . . . Haven't we got enough books cluttering the house? Are you telling me you've read them all? And anyway, we've already done the bookshop.*)

Of course we had "done" the bookshop. Pearson's Books is my brother-in-law's shop, and Deb is running it single-handedly while he's away fighting. Mike's in North Africa at the moment, and she hasn't seen him since May 1940; she thinks I'm terribly lucky because Guy is based in England. When we went into Pearson's she was rushed off her feet, and barely had time to wave.

"So what's it to be?" Guy insisted. "There must be something you want?"

What I actually wanted was to get out of this rasping wind and catch the bus back to Mum and Dad's house. We were only going to be in Carlisle for three days, and I'd hardly seen my lot yet—not properly. Yesterday afternoon had been squandered on musty cake and stiff conversation in Guy's parents' drawing-room; I couldn't bear to waste another.

When Guy said that about the books I shrugged helplessly and looked at Pip, who was even colder and wearier than me. His woolly hat kept slipping over his eyes, no matter how many times I tried to adjust it, so he'd taken to walking around with his head tilted back. I followed his eyes upwards, to the dark-green sign with the gold lettering.

"What about something from Cooper and Reid?"

"Yes!" Guy looked surprised. "Yes, all right, if that's what you'd like."

Guy's mother is an enthusiast for furs—amongst other items she owns a startled-looking stoat, which she drapes over her shoulder on leaving the house—but I have never gone in for them. Pip took my hand, and we stood in the amber glow of the shop window, studying the dummy in the long black coat. Someone opened the shop door, and an expensive fragrance—musky orange spiked with cloves—wafted out.

"What do you think?" I said. "Shall we . . . ?"

Once inside, Pip and I went to the window display and took turns to stroke the long black coat. I imagined putting it on and changing into something non-human: some supple, dangerous creature that would slink from the shop on all fours and disappear into the hills.

"If you got it, we could play dressing up as bears," mused Pip.

"I might turn into a real bear. A grizzly."

He sniffed and pushed his hat out of his eyes. "If you were a bear, would you go round eating people?"

"Oh yes. I mean, I wouldn't bother with you until you'd grown a bit bigger, but I'd definitely eat Daddy."

I tried to catch Guy's eye, but he wasn't having it. Guy no longer seems to approve of nonsense talk. He used to, when we were children, but not anymore.

"Would Madam like to try the sable coat?" said the woman at the counter.

"Oh . . . I'm not sure . . ." I caressed the sleeve again. There are at least two women who wear sable coats about the village and look very fine indeed: Sir Godfrey's wife, who holds court at Cottenden Hall, and Mrs. Mills-Amersham, who used to visit Paris regularly, before the war, with the express purpose of buying clothes.

"What do you think?" I turned to Guy. "Can you picture me in furs, giving Mrs. M-A a run for her money? Of course, it'll mean abandoning our favourite tea-shop when we go into Chester. I couldn't settle for less than lunch at the Grosvenor, wearing a coat like this."

Guy ran his knuckles gently down the sleeve. Then he flipped the price tag that was dangling from the cuff.

"Oh," I said.

"Heavens!" he agreed.

I folded my arms and cast my eyes about the shop.

"Ah well. Perhaps something a bit . . ."

There were some cosy hats and mittens on display behind the counter, but I chose a rabbit-fur stole in the end (sans head and paws). I wasn't at all sure, but Guy said, "Lovely. Very stylish."

The woman wrapped it in tissue paper and put it in a green-and-gold Cooper and Reid box, which lent it a certain glamour, and made me feel I'd chosen well, after all.

"Thank you, darling," I said, as Guy put the parcel under his arm and gathered the rest of our shopping. The woman wished us a happy Christmas and held the door, and when she smiled at me in passing, I could see her thinking: *What a delightful man. What a lucky little family.*

. . .

I WOULD HAVE FORGIVEN MR. WOODROW for telling me to get to the point, and I'm rather touched that he doesn't. He watches my face with fixed concentration, both while I'm speaking, and when I pause.

"You wore that stole to church, on Christmas Day," he observes.

"I did."

Does Henry Woodrow remember what everyone in the congregation was wearing that day? Surely he didn't single me out? No, I think he is generally observant, which I am not, and yet I know he wore a burgundy scarf on Christmas morning that matched the band on his dark-grey trilby.

I go to fetch a glass of water, and check on Pip. When I return, I thank Mr. Woodrow for his patience, and he replies with a grave nod. His manner has changed since his arrival: he's stopped fidgeting with his scarf, and he's smoothed down his hair, and he's even leant back in his chair and crossed his legs. It's as if he'd been harbouring certain fears, which my story has allayed. When I think of what I'm going to tell him next, I feel sick. I sip some water, and set the glass by my feet.

The dog, Shirley, looks as though she's asleep in the shadow of the sofa, but she's not. When I look carefully, I can see a pinprick of light in each of her black eyes.

I resume my tale.

. . .

THIS AFTERNOON, AS I WAS washing up the lunch things, I spotted a woman loitering by the gate.

Since the start of the war, I've grown afraid of visits from strangers. It's the same for everyone, I'm sure. The telegram boys are the worst, of course, but anyone might be a harbinger of doom, and as soon as I saw her, the hairs rose along my arms. All I could think was: *Guy*.

I wiped the mist from the kitchen window to get a better view, and the flash of my palm must have caught her attention, because a moment later she raised her hand in a cautious wave, which seemed a good sign. You wouldn't wave, would you, if you were about to deliver grim news? It's too sprightly a gesture.

What with the steamed-up glass, and the distance between the gate and the house, I couldn't see her in detail. She was wearing a dark fur coat, which reached all the way down to her ankles, but she wasn't Sir Godfrey's wife, or Mrs. Mills-Amersham. It was obvious, by the way she held herself, that she was young and exceptional, but it never crossed my mind that she was Nina.

("What do you mean by *exceptional*?" asks Mr. Woodrow. It's the first time he's interrupted my narrative. If I were him, I'd have picked on the words *dark fur coat* as the most curious aspect of the narrative so far. We are both on edge now; both sitting forwards in our chairs.

"Exceptionally attractive," I clarify.)

Pip was sitting at the table, flicking through a book called *Anyone Can Bake*. I took my time—swooning over the chocolate cake recipe Pip wanted to show me, tidying half-heartedly around the kitchen, hanging the damp tea-towel over the warm stove—but when I returned to the window, the woman was still there, so I took off my apron and went outside.

I think she had a moment's doubt when she saw me coming out of the house. Or perhaps I'm mistaken. Knowing what I know now, it's easy to suppose she *must* have had a moment's doubt, but that would be to judge her by ordinary standards, and Nina is not an ordinary person.

Nina Woodrow, aka Greta Garbo. I'd recognised her by now. She gathered herself, and made herself smile, and made herself walk towards me.

"Is it . . . Miss Woodrow?" I asked.

"Yes. Hello . . . ?"

She appeared to have forgotten my name.

"*Mrs. Nicholson*," I supplied.

Nina stopped and I went forwards to meet her, tugging my sleeves over my hands and trying not to shiver. She had raised her collar to cover her ears, and her cheeks were warm and pink inside the layers of fur. The coat gleamed with newness, and it carried the same spicy fragrance as my rabbit stole. I thought all furrier's shops must smell of oranges and cloves.

"I didn't expect you to be in," she said. "I thought you'd be collecting your boy from school."

"Phillip's at home with a cough." It wasn't until much later, when she'd gone, that I realised what I should have said. (*If you believed the*

house to be empty, why did you come?) These things always occur to
me too late.

When I invited Nina in, she accepted, and when I offered her
tea, there was none of the usual fuss about using up other people's
rations. She just said, "That would be nice, thanks."

I was conscious of her eyes on my back, as we crunched over the
gravel and entered through the side door. She studied everything
intently—me, Pip, the kitchen clutter, the view from the window
over the sink—as if to catalogue it all, and make sense of it later. Pip
hid the recipe book on his knees when she came in, and slid lower in
his seat.

Nina hung her coat on the back of her chair and sat down, while
I filled the kettle. The coat was far longer than the chair was high,
and its skirts pooled like black oil on the floor. She laid one of the
sleeves across her lap, for the duration of her visit, and stroked it with
her thumb.

"You must be Phillip?"

People usually affect a special voice for children, but Nina didn't.
In principle, I approved of this; in practice, Pip looked scared. I
slipped him a smile, and raised my eyebrows, until finally he nodded.

"He looks like you," said Nina. "He's got your husband's hair, but
mostly he looks like you."

When she said *your husband*, she looked at me, as if I was bound
to react, and I got the feeling she was disappointed when all I said
was, "Oh, do you think so?"

Pip darted glances at our guest from under his lashes, whilst
making tiny rips in the cover of *Anyone Can Bake*.

"Pip?" I shook my head, and he looked at me anxiously, uncon-
scious of what he was doing. I took the book from his lap and
returned it to the shelf.

Nina is very attractive. Have I said that already? I feel I ought
to say it at fixed intervals during my story, like a chorus that recurs

and recurs. There's much to say about Nina, but her beauty is the solid fact that grounds it all, whether I want it to or not. It would have been true if she'd been dressed in civvies, but the WAAF outfit made it doubly true. The fur coat had given her a seductive air, but the blue-grey uniform made her heroic, like a modern-day Greek goddess.

"He—my husband—is in the RAF too," I remarked, since her uniform had to be acknowledged one way or another.

"Yes, I know," she said hurriedly, her eyes fastened on my face. "We've bumped into one another a few times. It's the strangest thing, that we should both end up at Charlwood. It's not even a large airbase, as airbases go. Two people from the same small village—what are the odds?"

"I don't know."

That was when I felt the first stirrings of unease. It wasn't because the odds seemed so remote (maybe they were, maybe they weren't, I simply couldn't say), but because she pressed her questions with such force, making them into more than rhetorical devices. *Isn't it the strangest thing? What are the odds?* She might as well have said, *Do you believe it's a coincidence, Mrs. Nicholson, or don't you?* And then there was the way she had of scrutinising my face and body, as if there was something she needed to find out; or something she knew already, but wanted to confirm. I glanced into the little mirror on the dresser—dry lips, shadowy eyes, untidy hair—and wondered what she thought she saw.

"How's your dad?" I asked.

"Fine, thanks."

"Still living at Canal Road?"

"Yes. Same old dad, same old house."

I took my time making tea, setting out cups and saucers, rooting in the tin for biscuits. I couldn't think of anything else to say, except *Why are you here?* and it was difficult to phrase that without sounding unfriendly. Perhaps Nina was sociable, and enjoyed drop-ping in on random acquaintance (very random, in my case) for the fun of it? Cottenden people tend not to be dropper-inners, but—I reminded myself sharply—Cottenden is not the measure of all things. *Come on, Kate,* I told myself. *There must be something you can say. Ask her about her work . . .*

Nina got in first, however: "Do you ever think about that din-ner party at our house? I do. I remember it all, as if it happened yesterday."

"The dinner party!" I laughed. "Phillip was born the very next day; that's all I really remember."

Not true. Ever since Nina turned up in her sable coat, I'd been contrasting this January afternoon to that August night. I kept trying to name the quality she'd lost, in the intervening years. A cer-tain innocence, I suppose, although I wouldn't normally hold that against a grown woman.

"I'm heading back to Lincolnshire shortly," she said, changing the subject and taking another biscuit. She ate absently, as if her mind was elsewhere.

Now that I'd stopped clattering about the kitchen I could hear the whistle inside Pip's lungs. It was a delicate sound and I don't sup-pose Nina noticed, but it hadn't been there before lunch. I sat down beside him and laid my hand across his back.

"It must be nice," said Nina.

"What must?"

She gestured all around. "To live here, safely tucked away from all the horrible goings-on in the world."

Pip's ribcage fluttered beneath my palm. Inside my head, I listed my war "ordeals": trying to grow vegetables, making do, organising church bazaars, writing letters to prisoners, volunteering for the vicar's wife's "Knit for Victory!" group, even though I hate knitting, and the vicar's wife says my stitches are "awfully *sloppy*, dear." What else? The tiredness that is no less crippling for feeling unjustified. The waiting for bad news. Worrying about Guy; worrying about Pip; worrying about my brother, Ron; worrying about my brothers-in-law; worrying about my sister Janey, who drives ambulances in London.

"I looked after a group of evacuees for two years," I said. "Four brothers. They've gone to live in Wales now, to be nearer their grandparents."

Nina smiled politely. "That sounds fun! Nice for your son, too."

I made myself smile back. When they first arrived, the boys would only speak amongst themselves. The younger two wet their beds every night for six months, and the others were morose with homesickness. Sometimes the eldest broke things on purpose, or shouted at me, and Pip would retreat into his shell. At the time, I'd congratulated myself on coping rather well, but Nina made me see I'd done nothing at all. Sheltering a handful of needy children is not plucky. Choosing to knit of an evening, rather than read, is not an act of heroism.

I ought to have asked what she did, as a WAAF, but I didn't. No doubt—no doubt at all—Nina Woodrow does Great Things, all day, every day, in her immaculate blue-grey uniform.

"Was there any particular reason you called round?" I asked, instead.

She took a slow sip of tea, and kept her eyes on the cup as she laid it carefully on the saucer.

"No." She shrugged. "I set off on a nostalgic walk, and somehow ended up here. Whenever I think of long, hot peacetime summers, I think of your house, and that funny August day."

"You're a bit young to be taking trips down memory lane."

She looked up. "To you it's only—what—nine years ago? To me it feels like another lifetime."

"Yes, I suppose it must."

I put the lid on the biscuit tin and began stacking the plates and saucers.

Nina drew a long, steadying breath.

"Actually . . . I need to ask you something."

As she spoke, she reached across the table for my hand. I might have softened, if I hadn't suspected her of wanting to test my reddened knuckles; to make sure they couldn't compete—by some secret quality, apparent only to the touch—with her own lily-white skin.

"Oh?" I said, but my tone was discouraging, and she drew away, shaking her head.

"Actually . . . it doesn't matter."

We drank our tea in an awkward silence and then Nina said, "I suppose I should go. My train's at half four; Dad and I are getting the bus to the station."

She stood up, flicking the crumbs from her skirt. While she was checking her strawberry-red lips in the mirror, I lifted the sable coat off the back of the chair, and found the label. I was conscious of Pip watching me.

Yes.

Nina turned round and saw me holding up the coat. "Thanks!" she said, slipping her arms inside the sleeves.

Yes, it was true, but I couldn't comprehend it yet. I felt as though a mysterious object had been placed inside my hands—something unspeakably heavy and grotesque—but I wasn't allowed to look at it, until she was gone.

("I'm sorry, I don't understand," says Mr. Woodrow. "What label?"

"The label inside the coat," I explain, patiently. "It said, *Cooper and Reid Ltd, Carlisle*.")

Before Nina came, Pip and I had been chatty and cheerful, but after she'd gone we fell quiet.

"That lady was wearing a grizzly bear coat," I said. "Did you notice?"

Pip drew a laboured breath and made no answer.

"Pip?"

"Mummy, can we play Snakes and Ladders?"

I trailed my hand back and forth through the washing-up water and stared through the window, at the empty gateway. The water was tepid and greasy, but the rhythmic swashing distracted me from thought.

"Mummy? Please can we—"

"Not now, Pip. Maybe later."

. . .

"THE LABEL INSIDE MY DAUGHTER'S coat read *Cooper and Reid?*"

"*Cooper and Reid Ltd, Carlisle.* Yes."

"The shop you visited with your husband, before Christmas?"

"Yes."

"And from this you deduce . . ."

Mr. Woodrow can't bring himself to utter the words. He has withdrawn from me entirely. His eyes, which I remember as unusually searching, are unusually cold.

"What else? Barring the most extraordinary coincidence, it's clear that your daughter . . . that Nina and my husband . . ." (*oh for heaven's sake, Kate, spit it out*) ". . . that they're involved with one another. That they're having an affair."

The corner of Mr. Woodrow's mouth flickers in what looks like a smirk, but may be an expression of pain. He moves his hands to his lap and folds them, with studied calm, one inside the other. I lean forwards in my chair, elbows on knees and hands cupped like a begging bowl, but he remains straight-backed, and the more earnestly I seek his eyes, the more resolutely he addresses the space above my head.

"What a bizarre conclusion," he says.

"Is it? Then how do you explain the coat?"

His mouth twists and he shakes his head. There's a daydream I've been toying with for nine years: middle-aged Mr. Woodrow and youngish Mrs. Nicholson, barely acquainted, yet conscious of a natural affinity; two honourable people with a bond that must never be owned. I'm not saying it meant a lot to me—as private fantasies go, it's not the best I've got up my sleeve—but it did mean something, and I'm sorry to have to let it go. I knew he was likely to be upset, but I never imagined he would turn cold; in the back of my mind I had a vision of him bursting into tears and reaching for me, blindly.

Mr. Woodrow stands up, winding the scarf round his neck, and beady-eyed Shirley scrambles out from under the sofa. I sit on my hands, so that he won't see them shaking.

"Didn't you ask Nina how she'd acquired such a luxurious coat?" I persist. "You must have wondered."

Mr. Woodrow fastens the buttons on his gloves.

"I did not ask her. She told me—unprompted—that it was a Christmas present from a friend."

"Well then!"

Mr. Woodrow purses his lips and I slump backwards in my chair, as much as to say, *I give up.* He straightens his gloves, clips the lead onto Shirley's collar, and graces me with one last look.

"I suppose I ought to thank you for your hospitality, but I can't and won't. You have insulted my daughter, offended me, and humiliated yourself, and frankly I would feel sorry for you, if—"

"But Mr. Woodrow—Henry—if you would only *listen*! You know, the first time we met—"

"The first time we met was an out-and-out fiasco. Who'd have thought the second and last time could be even worse? Your husband and his friend were louts, but at least they didn't pretend to be anything else. You, however . . ."

"What about me?"

"You are a fraud and a disappointment."

As he says the word *disappointment*, a speckle of spit catches his lower lip. He wipes it off, immediately, with the back of his hand.

"How crushing," I say, conscious that I'm spoiling the sarcasm by looking thoroughly crushed.

Mr. Woodrow leaves the room, and I decline to get up, which means listening to him and Shirley bumping about in the dark hall, searching for the front door.

He was wrong to dismiss our first meeting as an out-and-out fiasco, despite Guy and Joey's bad behaviour. Henry liked me at the time, and praised my patience, and I know that's true because it's where my "kindred spirit" daydream sprang from. I'd felt the gratitude of an unnoticeable person who is suddenly, unexpectedly, noticed.

"Jane Eyre-itis," I mutter to myself, and the sound of my voice makes him pause, but he doesn't respond.

Eventually I follow him into the hall, where he's struggling with the latch. The key is rusty, and it takes a certain knack to turn it, which is not terribly conducive to magisterial exits.

"Mr. Woodrow, what did you think I was going to tell you?"

"I beg your pardon?"

The door squeaks open, at last, and the hall is washed by frosty air and starlight.

"When we spoke on the telephone you seemed to guess what I was going to say, and it made you agitated, but not unpleasant. You weren't expecting it to be about Nina. There was something else."

The silhouette man puts a silhouette hat on his head.

"I have absolutely no idea what you're talking about," he says. "Goodnight, Mrs. Nicholson."

He tips his hat, out of habit or mockery, and goes away without closing the door.

After I've locked up, I bury my head in my arms and lean them against the wall. I'm suspicious of self-pity, and I do guard against it, but sometimes it's hard to resist.

I don't want to go to bed—the sheets will be freezing and Guy's side will feel even emptier than usual—so I creep to Pip's room and drop into the sagging armchair beside his pillow. I'm still wearing my tweed coat, which is neither thick enough to keep me warm, nor thin enough to force me to fetch a blanket, so I curl up as tightly as I can, with my knees almost touching my chin. My neck ends up at an odd angle, but it doesn't matter.

Pip's head is a concentration of darkness at the centre of the pillow, and I would like to reach out and stroke his hair, but I daren't disturb his sleep.

You're daft about that child, says Guy's voice in my head, but I don't smile and shrug him off as usual. I answer spitefully, *So what if I am?*

Pip's lungs are easier than they were, but if I lie very still I can hear them whistling to themselves, like a pair of soft and strange little birds.

7

Nina

January 15–16, 1943

"SO YOU'RE STOPPING ONE NIGHT WITH ROSE, AND HEADING back to the airbase tomorrow? I've got that right, haven't I?"

It's almost the last thing Dad says, as the train pulls in, and he knows full well he's got it right because he asked Nina the very same question at breakfast, and again on the bus to Chester station. The first time she answered, "Yes, I'm seeing Rose. It's handy that our leave overlaps." The second time, she smiled and nodded. The third time she made no response. Such is the level of communication to which her secrecy—and his innocence—has reduced them.

The very last thing Dad says, as the train labours to a halt and carriage doors start banging open, is, "Darling? You are all right, aren't you?" The timing of the question is uncharacteristically point- less, but helpful too. What can she possibly be expected to say, in these last few seconds? *Well, Dad, since you ask: I'm supposed to be spending tonight with my divorced lover, only it turns out he forgot to tell his wife they were divorced, which makes him a liar and a cheat, but I can't work out how to stop loving him, and to cut a long story short, I'm out of my depth, and don't know what to do.*

"I'm fine," she replies, pecking him on the cheek.

The train is crowded, but Nina finds a seat between a soldier and a woman with a toddler. What with the crush, and the filthy windows, there's no seeing out or in, so it's hardly been worth Dad's while to come onto the platform to wave her off. In her next letter home, she must remember to write what a shame that was, although she won't mean it. Dad's proximity has become unbearable, even behind a steamed-up pane of glass: that's why she wandered off to look at Guy's house this afternoon; it's why she stayed for tea with Mrs. Nicholson and the boy, against her better judgement; it's why she walked the long way home and almost missed the bus.

Except for those times when he's depressed, and temporarily out of reach, Nina and her father have never been stuck for things to say to one another. When she was growing up they were famous for their weird and wonderful conversations; none of her friends had such an original parent. *How do you know I exist?* Dad might ask, casually, over supper, or *Do dreams contain messages from God?* or *Is a lie ever excusable?*

Someone has cleared a patch of steam from the window, and the Cheshire fields and hedgerows are visible, going by in a blur of blue dusk. The soldier offers Nina a cigarette. She accepts, and immediately wishes she hadn't, because it gives him an opening, of which he makes full use, asking whether that's a WAAF uniform he glimpsed under her coat, and where she's off to now, and does she ever get down to London? She answers civilly ("It is a WAAF uniform, well spotted . . . I'm visiting a girlfriend in Buxton . . . Almost never, I'm afraid. What about you?"), and when they've finished their cigarettes, he offers to share his sandwich.

"No, thanks."

On the seat to her right, the toddler is clambering about and poking its fingers into its mother's mouth. Nina shudders slightly, buttons the sable coat up to her chin, and pretends to doze.

The coat has been problematic; she ought to have foreseen that. When Guy gave it to her—or rather, when the parcel arrived at the Waafery, just before Christmas—she was over the moon, partly because of the extravagance of the gesture, and partly because warmth is a luxury in wintry Lincolnshire. Naturally, it provoked comment—*Ooh, Nina, who's the sugar daddy? What will you be giving him in return?* etc., etc.—vulgar stuff, but endurable. Nina doesn't mind a bit of teasing.

No. When she tells herself it's been problematic, she's thinking of Dad.

"What a splendid coat!" he'd exclaimed, four days ago, when he came to meet her at Chester station. "I hardly recognise you! What a shame we have to catch a bus; I feel I ought to be wearing a chauffeur's uniform and driving you home in a Bentley."

Nina had answered with a self-deprecating shrug. All the way home she'd blocked further discussion with rapid-fire enquiries after the neighbours, and the new dog, and how Dad had spent Christmas, but by the time they were traipsing from the bus stop outside the post office to the house on Canal Road, she'd run out of topics. There was no one else around, and it was abruptly quiet, except for the ringing of their footsteps.

"You never paid for that coat all by yourself?"

Dad's tone had been confidential; almost shy.

"No," and then, before he could ask: "It was a Christmas present from a friend."

"Ah!" Dad shifted the suitcase from his left hand to his right, and back again. "Well! He must think very highly of you, this 'friend.' When will I have the pleasure of meeting him?"

"But I never said it was that sort of friend! It's . . . for goodness' sake . . . I didn't even say it was a man."

"All right! Forgive me for prying."

She hadn't known her affair was adulterous, at that point, but then it didn't have to be adulterous in order to be beyond the pale. (*Adulterous*, God, what a word. *I have committed adultery*, she tells herself now. *I am an adulteress*.) Guy kept sending flowers and letters to Canal Road during her four-day leave, until she telephoned him at the base and begged him to stop.

Dad didn't mention the mysterious "friend" again. Whenever they went out together she wore a scruffy old jacket with horrible boxy shoulders and clinging dog hairs. The sable coat hung at the back of her wardrobe, reserved for solitary outings.

The train judders over a set of points. Wearily, Nina opens her eyes. The soldier spots that she's awake, and starts going on about some West End revue that everybody ought to go and see, and surely there are lots of trains from Lincoln to King's Cross, and what about it, one Saturday? Bother him.

"I hate and loathe London," she says. "I avoid it on principle, as far as I can."

Well, that shuts him up. The toddler fondles Nina's sleek, black sleeve and says, delightedly, "Cat!" at which the soldier mutters, "Too bleeding right." The mother gives the child a little shake and says, "Don't touch the lady's coat!" Nina shuts her eyes again and thinks about Guy.

Whenever she and Guy are alone together (*Whenever*! They've only managed it three times, so far), she assumes that the memory will nourish her forever, as a source of perpetual bliss; that she'll be able to relive it as many times as she likes. Why doesn't remembering work like that? It seems to for some people. Susie Macaulay, for example, who has the neighbouring bed in Hut 9. Susie ekes out her entire existence on cups of weak tea and bittersweet memories of her dead fiancé.

Nina wishes she had the same knack, because, as things stand, she'll be left with nothing once she's ended it with Guy. Even now, and at best, her memories of their encounters are blurry and unspecific, like poorly developed photographs. At worst, she has long felt that to see their affair truthfully is to see it from the outside, through unsympathetic eyes, in all its indignity: the fumbling with buttons and belts; the noises they make, despite their best efforts to be quiet; the slapstick rocking of the car behind the hedge.

The train clatters through the darkness towards Manchester, where Nina will change for Buxton. Icy rain slashes the windows along one side of the carriage, as the soldier tears into another sandwich, and singing breaks out in some of the seats farther down. The toddler starts rubbing its eyes and whingeing on one note. Nina reprimands herself, vaguely, for calling it "it," but small children are much of a muchness to her. She chews her thumbnail to the quick, and makes a list of her worries.

She's worried about Mrs. Nicholson and Pip, and regrets having met them today; ignorance would have been bliss, in a very literal sense.

She's worried about Dad, because she's always worried about Dad, even when she can't articulate why.

She's worried about Rose, and wishes she hadn't stood her up via telegram this morning.

Most of all Nina is worried about Guy. What if he has a plausible explanation? What if he doesn't? What if she can't resist the delectable smell of his skin, and the coaxing whispers in her ear? What if she *can* resist, and has to spend the rest of her life lamenting her own moral courage?

Guy will be dead soon. He will. The statistics don't lie. One of these nights his plane will explode in the night sky, somewhere over Europe.

Technically, this makes no difference to the adultery question—a sin is a sin—but it nags at her, all the same.

. . .

BUXTON RAILWAY STATION IS BLACKED out, except for a single porter with a lantern. There's a sleety wind coming down from the Peaks, and Nina stands with her suitcase at her feet, glad of the sable coat. Every now and then the door to the station café swings open, and a slice of light falls across the platform.

Somebody is hurtling along the platform, calling her name, and all at once there are hands around her waist and she's turning to meet him. Guy drops a quick kiss on the rim of her ear, another on her cheek, and a lingering one on her lips, which she begins to reciprocate, before pushing him away.

"Your train's not due for another half hour!"

"Hitched a lift," Guy explains, breathlessly, and then, "What's wrong?"

She shakes her head, grateful for the darkness. Even if his face were visible, she doubts her own ability to read it.

"Nina?"

Oh God.

"Guy, you told me you were divorced—"

"No, I didn't!"

She blurts a sharp, angry sound.

"Getting divorced," he clarifies, hastily. "I'm *getting* divorced; we haven't yet dotted the i's and crossed the t's, but it's the same difference."

"And are you sure your wife knows that you and she are *getting* divorced? Only I bumped into her, in Cottenden—"

"What did you say?"

"I didn't say anything. Not even when she referred to you, in passing, as her husband. *My husband is in the RAF.*"

The silence that comes between them is as frightening as total solitude. Guy ends it, eventually, by saying, "Nina, I love you," and she can't help feeling relieved, both by the words themselves, and by the human warmth of his voice.

"I love you too, but that's entirely beside the point."

"Kate knows, of course she does—what do you take me for? But she's not about to announce it to the world. There's every chance she'll strike lucky and become a widow before the divorce goes through, and no one will be any the wiser."

The café door opens, spilling light, and she has a fleeting vision of him standing there looking sad and lost, and very beautiful. At the same time a new voice cries, "Nina!" and she finds herself spinning away from Guy, and into someone else's arms. Rose has come, and to judge by her excitement, she's not received the telegram.

"Sorry I'm late," Rose picks up Nina's suitcase. "Let's go! Dad lent me the car, so no need to trudge up the hill on foot. What on earth have you got in here? A corpse? Oh gosh, I am glad to see you . . ." She drops the suitcase for another hug. "It's ages since we had a proper talk!"

Nina returns the hug with force and at length, but says nothing. When Rose urges, "Come on, you, let's get going!" Nina steps away, shaking her head, and says, "You didn't get my telegram, did you?"

The café door flashes open again and Nina has her first proper glimpse of Rose's face: immaculate hair; shrewd eyes; bright-red, faltering smile.

"Telegram? Saying what?"

Telegrams can make anything sound businesslike and above board; that's why Nina sent one. (*REGRET CAN'T COME TONIGHT STOP LUNCH TOMORROW STATION CAFE 1 PM HOPE OK LOVE ALWAYS NINA*)

Nina takes hold of her friend's arm. "There's been a last-minute

change of plan. I'm sorry, I only found out myself this morning . . .
Listen, let's go and sit down. I'll buy us all a drink."

"*All*?"

Nina pulls towards the café, but this time it's Rose who resists.

"What do you mean, a *change of plan*? Have they ordered you
back to the airbase?"

"No, it's not that." Nina's voice wants to plead and shrink, but
she won't let it. "You'll understand, once I've explained. You will.
Come on, let's go inside, we can't talk properly out here."

Rose won't budge. "I don't want to sit in a café; I want to go home.
Mum's keeping the dinner warm and I promised we'd be quick."

"But Rose, there's something I need to tell you."

"Tell me on the way! She's made a rabbit pie, with bacon in it."

"I can't!"

Nina has the feeling that Rose can see in the dark. She has all the
dour stillness of a watchful cat.

"Nina Woodrow, are you throwing me over for a man?"

Guy has found a torch in his kit-bag, and when he switches it on,
the beam is a whirl of sleet. At last they can see one another, albeit
in rapid, blinding fragments. As the downpour hardens to hail, he
draws his open coat around Nina and holds her against his side.

"Rose?" says Nina. "You remember Guy Nicholson?"

She tries to say it with a light smile, but it's no use; her tone is
anxious and pleading. She wants to shake Rose by the shoulders and
say, *Please, see what I see! Please see a beautiful love story!*

"I remember Mr. *and* Mrs. Nicholson," says Rose, and when Guy
murmurs a greeting and holds out his hand, she ignores him. "Nina,
you can't do this. I left Mum making up your bed. She was taking all
the sheets off, because she'd forgotten to put the electric blanket on
underneath."

Nina is silenced for a few seconds. Then: "I'm sorry."

"Are you, though? I suppose you two have got some fancy hotel lined up. The Palace, is it?"

"Gosh, no, nothing so grand!" Nina answers eagerly, as if lack of grandeur makes all the difference. "What was the address you said, Guy? Cheap Street?"

"Number 36, Cheap Street," Guy confirms. "I only booked this morning; I had to take what I could find. It's run by a Mr. and Mrs. Meeny."

And then Nina makes things worse by pretending to laugh; pretending to find it *funny*. Oh, but it is! Mr. and Mrs. Meeny of Cheap Street! Why won't Rose see that it's funny, instead of standing there, chattering her teeth and glaring? Guy understands; *he* can see the funny side. In his exuberance he turns her round and kisses her full on the mouth, as a group of men clatters down the platform in army boots, snaring them all in torchlight. A few of the men whistle and one yells at Rose over his shoulder, "Three's a crowd, blondie!"

Nina breaks away and follows her friend towards the exit. When Rose pauses at the gate, Nina braces herself for a tirade, but Rose simply says, "Please come with me?" and Nina almost replies, "Yes."

"I'm sorry," she repeats instead, touching Rose's arm. "Please believe me. I know you think I'm vile, and maybe if I were you—maybe if I were anyone other than me, in this place, at this moment—I'd agree."

No response.

"Oh, why won't you understand?" Nina cries. "I need you to understand! Why should I be principled, when the whole world has gone wrong? I don't want to be an old woman lying on my deathbed thinking, *Oh well, I missed my one chance of real happiness, but at least I didn't do anything especially blameworthy. At least I was never rude to Rose's mum.*" Rose remains silent and Nina lowers her voice still further. "If his plane went down tomorrow, how could I live with myself, knowing I'd turned down the chance of seeing him one last time? How could I carry on existing, knowing I'd preferred your mum's rabbit pie—as superb as I'm sure it is—over the love of my life?"

"*The love of my life*," Rose echoes, mockingly. She turns on her heel and leaves through the station building.

"He's not married anymore!" Nina calls.

But Rose doesn't look round.

. . .

IN THE DREAM, EVERYONE IS standing around a large, rumpled bed. There's a corpse underneath a sheet and someone is crying. The mood is angry. Lucky is there, and so is Dad. Rose's mother says, "Perhaps there was a fault with the electric blanket," and Rose says, "No, no, the fault was with Nina."

"What's up?" Guy's voice is ropy with sleep.

"Nothing," she mumbles back. "Nightmare."

She dozes and dreams of gentle Mrs. Allen working the pastry for a rabbit pie, chopping onions, frying bacon . . . Her eyes flick open onto the lamp-lit room, and there's a pressure in her chest that resembles fear. She reminds herself that she's in bed with Guy, in Mr. and Mrs. Meeny's guesthouse, with the certainty—the luxurious certainty—that all is well, and will be well, till morning.

Guy pulls her close and she grows calm again. The air on her face is chilly, but it's warm under the covers. Guy's skin is tacky against her own legs and back, and he stinks of sex and sweat, but this doesn't disgust her. No doubt she smells too. They are feral, like two foxes in a den, and the squalor of their intimacy is comforting.

Until tonight, they have never seen one another without any clothes at all, and she worried about her own imperfections: the itchy patches on the insides of her elbows, for example, and the short, dark hairs on her legs. The ceiling light rinsed the room like dirty dishwater, and Nina wanted to turn it off before they began, but Guy begged her to leave it, and he was right. Not that either of them is flawless—even Guy is no silver-screen god; he's too thin—but his faults are more endearing to her than his perfections. "Don't be timid," he kept saying, and in the end, she wasn't. When she tried to hide the chapped patches on her elbows, he made a point of kissing them.

Now they are quiet, and Nina listens to the night-time sounds of the guesthouse: a tap running; a man snoring; the flush of the upstairs loo; someone rolling over on squeaky bedsprings. The floorboards creak on the landing as the lavatory user returns to bed; maybe he or she is feeling the effects of Mrs. Meeny's Woolton pie? Those semi-cooked swedes and potatoes were a bit rough on the guts, but they still comprised the most romantic dinner of Nina's life. She and Guy ate with the other guests, in a dining-room that smelled of stale gravy, and the BBC news—Soviet gains on the Eastern Front, and German losses in North Africa—was turned up to such a volume that conversation was impossible. Nina could only communicate with her "husband" via nudges under, and glances over, the communal table.

Rain beats in regular flurries against the ill-fitting window. The Meenys' guesthouse is an odd sort of heaven, but Nina can't enjoy it because her thoughts keep reverting to the hell beyond the present moment. Tomorrow, she and Guy will venture into another January day, and go back, via more draughty trains, to their chaste beds at RAF Charlwood. Back, as far as Nina is concerned, to tepid hot-water bottles, and the nearness of death, and girls jollying one another along, like overgrown pupils at a boarding school.

"I know you're awake." Guy sounds more alert than she'd taken him to be. "What's up?"

Nina sifts through the several matters, large and small, that are bothering her. She has the feeling that she ought not to keep things from Guy; that having become a liar to everyone else, she must make a special effort not to lie to him. Rose is at the forefront of her mind, but it's easier to talk about Kate.

"You know I said I bumped into your wife, when I was in Cottenden?" (The muscles tense along Guy's arm, but she carries on.) "Well, it wasn't quite like that. I went to look at Hawthorn House, thinking they'd be out, but she saw me through the kitchen window and invited me in for tea, and I said yes. Your son was there too."

Guy is about to roll away, but she seizes him before he can. She worries he'll go quiet—as far as she can tell, from so brief an intimacy, he's a brooder rather than a shouter—but then he asks, in a fairly ordinary way, "What did you make of her?"

Nina hesitates and Guy goes on: "Did you feel terribly superior?"

"Superior?"

"Yes, what with being younger and prettier. A woman of the world, with a lover, and no domestic ties?"

"No!" She can't quite catch his tone. Is he angry with her? Teasing? She turns to look at him, and remains unsure. They lie, facing one another, under the dingy ceiling light. She rests her hand on his cheek.

"Maybe that's what I wanted to feel, at first. When she came down the drive, and invited me inside, there was a part of me that hoped to find someone ugly and small-minded, who'd never deserved you in the first place."

Guy doesn't ask what she actually found, and Nina doesn't tell. It's just as well: she struggles to explain her feelings to herself, let alone to him. When she recalls Kate and Pip's shared world, with its homely baking smells, and piles of tattered books, and the small socks and vests on a pulley-dryer above the stove, she is confused by equal pangs of fear and longing, like a die-hard atheist at a candle-lit mass.

Nina and Guy are silent for a long time, and the house is still, as if everyone else is fast asleep.

"You know, I never actually proposed to Kate," Guy says, out of the blue. "It was simply a given that the two of us would marry, as soon as we were old enough."

"You mean other people expected it of you? Your parents?"

"Oh no, not them, they couldn't have cared less. I mean it was a given between us; between me and Kate."

Nina is not in a position to be jealous—not when Kate's husband is lying here, stroking her bare thigh—but it needles, all the same. What's that line from *Wuthering Heights*? Something about a love that's lively but passing, like the leaves on a tree, compared to a love that's silent but enduring, like the rocks under the earth. Kate would know, what with being so well-read. Nina watched the Laurence Olivier picture, a year or two back, with a couple of WAAF friends.

"We hadn't a clue what we were doing," Guy continues. "At least, I didn't."

Nina isn't sure what this implies (*No clue about the practical aspects of marriage, like finances and housekeeping? No clue about the emotional toll that comes with living together? No clue about sex?*), but all she can think to say is, "Do you still love her?" Inwardly, she mocks the naïveté of the question, and hopes he's not doing the same.

Guy thinks for a while.

"I've always been good at going through the motions," he says. "Sometimes I think I've been too good, like a kind of con artist, though I didn't mean to con anyone."

"A con artist?" she repeats, uneasily.

"I mean, I knew how to make paper boats with my son, and how to praise my wife's cooking, and how to write suitably touching messages on her birthday cards. I knew how to come across as the kindly paterfamilias. I'm not sure they noticed the difference between a husband—a father—who was fully present, and one who wasn't. Or maybe Kate did suspect, a little bit, sometimes . . ." He twitches his shoulders. "The fact is, I did everything that love required—I could probably have fought and died for them, if it had come to that—but I couldn't seem to do it with the right feeling."

Nina rummages through the bedclothes for his hand.

"People always blame other people for having the wrong feelings," she says. "It makes no sense. How can anyone help what they feel?"

"Or don't feel."

"Exactly."

Guy strokes her wrist with his thumb, and she resists a childish impulse to add, *This doesn't apply to us, though, does it? We'll always feel the same?*

"Kate and Phillip exist in their own world," he goes on. "They have their in-jokes, their ways of thinking; their little day-to-day routines. It used to be the same with her and me, when we were children, but then I grew up . . ."

". . . and she didn't?"

"Well, I suppose not, in some ways. Kate is very . . ." He searches for the right description. "She's a very *innocent* person. Of course, when we were little it wasn't particularly noticeable, but it is now."

Innocent. Is that a slight? Nina begins to defend Kate ("I have to say, she struck me as pretty astute!"), but Guy says, "Don't let's talk about them anymore," and kisses her on the mouth.

"Do you want to sleep?" says Nina, after some minutes have elapsed.

"I'd rather talk."

"So would I. What shall we talk about?"

"I don't know . . ." He moves his lips through her hair, pressing them against her scalp, her ear, and her jaw-line. "Let's talk about what you'll do, once the war is over. I can't imagine you not being a WAAF."

Nina suppresses a shudder.

"When you say, what will *I* do, you mean, what will *we* do?"

He holds her so tightly that she struggles to breathe.

Yes," he assures her. "That's what I mean."

It's a long time before their embrace slackens, and by the time it does, Nina is close to sleep. Guy strokes her hair.

"We'll start a new life, far away from here," he murmurs.

"Mmm."

She's on the brink of a dream, peering into its dark depths, when she hears the word *Canada*. It's hard to tell whether the word is coming from Guy, or from the dream, but it doesn't matter.

"Canada," she murmurs agreeably, tumbling into sleep.

. . .

NINA SITS UP AND SQUINTS at Guy's wrist-watch. It's gone ten. Sunlight is seeping through the thin curtains. There are children playing outside in the street, calling to one another and rattling sticks along the railings.

"Guy?" she whispers, but he's well away. Nina slips out of bed, flicking the light switch off and the electric fire on. Yesterday's clothes are strewn across the floor, and although she's shivering, she slumps at the prospect of putting her uniform back on, just yet. There's a dressing-gown on the back of the door: a frothy, peachy monstrosity made from fabrics that are trying, desperately, to pass themselves off as satin and lace. Nina fingers the sleeve and sniffs it. It smells cleanish and faintly perfumy.

"If you absolutely have to wear something, wear that." Guy's voice rumbles sleepily from the bedclothes.

"Really?" She throws him a look that mingles horror with amusement, unhooks it from the door, and holds it up for inspection. "I suppose someone left it behind. Can't think why."

Nina puts her arms through the sleeves, knots the belt, and performs a slow twirl. Guy props himself up on one elbow.

"It's utterly indecent," she says.

"Yet strangely compelling. I dare you to go downstairs like that, and cadge us some breakfast."

"Mrs. Meeny might throw me out on the street."

"Yes, and poor Mr. Meeny might have a stroke."

Nina is impressed that she and Guy can still joke, with the arrival of morning. She resolves to stave off gloom until the moment they're forced to part, like polite acquaintances, at the entrance to the airbase.

"Maybe I should put my coat on top . . ."

"Oh no! That would ruin the effect entirely."

Nina retrieves her coat from the floor, but it's still damp from last night's rain, and besides, she likes the way he's looking at her. She drapes the coat over the back of a chair.

"Very well, darling." She half closes her eyes and affects a sultry Hollywood drawl. "I'll risk it. For you."

"You will?" Guy laughs and sits up. She blows a pouty kiss from the doorway, and he blinks like a man who has caught the attention of a bona fide goddess.

. . .

EVERYTHING CHANGES AS NINA STEPS onto the landing and closes the door behind her. All at once she's just an ordinary woman wearing an inadequate dressing-gown in someone else's house. A man clears his throat in the bedroom across the way, and the clarity of the sound makes her wince. The walls in this place must be paper thin.

Nina goes down the stairs and along the hall, to the kitchen. Mrs. Meeny is standing at the sink with her back to Nina, washing dishes, while a sheepdog dozes by the range. The BBC Home Service is playing Wurlitzer music, and sometimes Mrs. Meeny jerks her head from side to side, in time to the beat. There's a plywood gate, waist-high, which has been bolted shut to keep the dog in, or the guests out, or both. Nina leans over and says, "Excuse me? Good morning?"

The woman swivels round. Nina places a hand over her lacy chest, though it's a bit too late to be coy.

"Breakfast was between seven and nine," says Mrs. Meeny.

"I know, I'm sorry, we overslept. I wondered—that is, my husband and I wondered—whether we might scrounge some tea? Perhaps a few pieces of toast?"

The woman is in no rush to finish washing the crockery in the sink. When she's done, she pulls the plug on the dirty water, squeezes and folds the dishcloth, and dries her hands on her apron. Only then, and with a sigh, does she fill the kettle and place it on the stove.

"Toast, you say?"

"Please."

She hacks two meagre slices from the loaf and puts them under the grill.

This is Nina's first proper encounter with Mrs. Meeny, apart from the briefest glimpse on their arrival; it was Mr. Meeny who showed them to their room and served dinner. Last night's welcome had hardly been warm, but it hadn't been this bad. It seems they've been rumbled—but how? Was it the lazy lie-in that betrayed them? Don't real husbands and wives sleep till ten? Perhaps it's the dressing-gown, or . . . Nina catches sight of her own reflection in a glass-fronted cupboard. Perhaps it's something about the way she looks and carries herself. The air of apparent poise that led a married man to kiss her behind a Nissen hut, and Susie Macaulay to call her a cold-hearted bitch.

But he's not a married man, he's divorced. Divorc*ing*.

The kettle boils, the toast browns, and Mrs. Meeny places cups and plates on a tray. Nina's surest defence would be to make fun of her, and perhaps that's what she'll do when she gets back upstairs. There's plenty of material for a comedy routine, after all: the horn-rimmed glasses; the hefty bosom; the thick legs, lumpy with varicose veins. On the other hand, it's a bit difficult to despise other people when you've just spent the night with a man who isn't your husband, and you're wearing a diaphanous dressing-gown in the middle of the day, and you're very much in need of a wash, and you've been brought up—for better or worse—to be something quite different from what you are.

Nina watches Mrs. Meeny shave two thin curls from the margarine block, and lay them on top of the toast. She remembers versions of this woman from childhood, when she and Dad spent summer fortnights in Rhyl, or Llandudno, or Pwllheli. The guesthouses were always run by middle-aged matrons in floral housecoats, but in those far-off days they were benevolent figures who fussed over Nina; pulled her into bosomy cuddles; slipped her sweets. "*Cariad bach*," those Welsh Mrs. Meenys would call her, and Nina would like it, without understanding the language.

"Thanks," Nina says, taking delivery of the tray over the half-door. Mrs. Meeny doesn't answer, *That's all right*, or *I'm sorry there's so little milk for the tea*. She says, "Oh dear, Mrs. Nicholson, I hope you haven't lost your wedding ring?"

They both look at the fourth finger on Nina's left hand, bare of any ring, or any telltale imprint of a ring.

"Actually, I have." Nina looks the older woman in the eye. "It's very upsetting. I took it off at work, in case it snagged on the parachute silks—I'm a parachute packer, you know, at an RAF base—and then later on, when I came to get it from my pocket . . ."

She shrugs regretfully, and the two women hold one another's gaze for an impolite length of time. Nina is the first to look away.

"Well." She turns to go. "Thank you for the tray."

"Very good, Mrs. Nicholson. If you could avoid dropping crumbs on the bed-sheets I'd be much obliged; and if you could tell your husband the same."

Nina makes her way along the hall and up the stairs. The dressing-gown is slowly, but surely, sliding open, and she has no free hand to stop it. Ten minutes ago, this would have made her giggle, but now it doesn't.

. . .

THE ELECTRIC FIRE HAS WARMED the bedroom nicely. Guy is sitting up in bed with his hands behind his head, looking content, and for the first time since she's known him it strikes her that this is unusual; that Guy is not, essentially, a contented man. As she enters, struggling to balance the tray on her hip and kick the door shut, he grins at her, and she tries to grin back, but it's not the same as before.

"Everything all right?" he asks. "Mr. Meeny still in the land of the living?"

"I didn't run into Mr. Meeny."

"Probably just as well."

Nina hands him his tea and remarks, accusingly: "You seem very chipper this morning."

Guy holds out his free hand and Nina sits beside him on the counterpane.

"Are you not happy?"

"Yes. No. It's just—I don't know—you don't seem very sad about going back. I think you love the men in your crew, in a way I could never love the girls in my hut. I think you miss them."

At this point, according to the script, Guy should deny that he loves anyone other than her. When he doesn't, she wishes she'd kept her mouth shut, or given an amusing description of Mrs. Meeny's hatchet face. She takes his proffered hand.

"Don't let's talk about going back," says Guy. "We've got hours yet; the train isn't till three."

"Two fifty-four. But you're right."

She passes him the plate, with its snippets of toast, and when he snorts with laughter she can't help joining in.

"What a banquet!" he says. "Mrs. Meeny has surpassed herself. I hope we can manage all this between us."

Nina swings her legs onto the bed and nestles into the crook of his arm. Guy's right, they've got hours yet, but it doesn't stop her from stealing repeated glances at his wrist-watch.

"Well? How about it?" he says, offering her a sip from his teacup, since she can't reach hers.

"How about what?"

"Canada. We talked about it in the night, remember? After the war, we're going to leave it all behind, and set ourselves up in a log cabin in the wilds."

Oh Guy, she thinks. She doesn't say it, because it sounds like a reproach, and he shouldn't be reproached for dreaming. Nina runs her fingers along his arm and tries to believe that it's impossible for Guy to die in action, since it is impossible to imagine these taut muscles, springy hairs, and delicate blue veins curling up in flames—perhaps tonight, perhaps tomorrow night—before dwindling to gristle and ash.

"We'll fish through a hole in the ice," she says, "and keep a pet elk."

"And drive a dog sled, and learn to ski."

They trade dreams of how it will be, and it isn't until later that she notices how innocent they sound, like children. Guy will show Nina how to ride a horse (not that he's very proficient himself), and Nina will teach Guy about the constellations (though the little she knows comes from a book someone bought her for Christmas one year). Winter is the season they fantasise about the most, when the landscape will be changed by snow, and they can hide away inside its alien simplicity. They picture snowdrifts piling higher than their windows, making the daylight strange, and keeping them safe at night.

"Why a Canadian wilderness, in particular?" Nina asks, through a mouthful of toast. "I suppose it's because of Joey Roussin."

Guy bursts out laughing, but, for the first time, Nina doesn't feel in on the joke. It's as if he's locked eyes with someone who isn't there—with Joey Roussin—and they're keeping the source of their amusement to themselves.

"Oh, absolutely," he says. "Most things are Joey's fault in the end, you know."

She starts to ask, *What else is Joey's fault?* but stops. Let them have their private jokes, if they must. Sometimes Nina tries to imagine Guy without Joey—she refigures the 1934 dinner party so that there's no whisky drinking and no bawdy talk and no drunken kisses up her arm, only Guy, under the cherry tree, looking at her as if she's the loveliest thing he's ever seen—but it's pointless. Joey was there and Joey is here now, and that's how it has to be, because he matters to Guy.

"Did Joey grow up somewhere rural?" she wonders, instead. "Somewhere like the place we're imagining?"

"No, no, the Roussins are from a little town near Winnipeg. His father is some kind of clerk in the local registry office, and that's where Joey worked too, after he left school. But his aunt and uncle owned—or own—a farm a few miles farther north, on the shores of Lake Winnipeg, and he used to go and stay with them most summers. In September he'd come back to England all muscled and sunburned, and about a foot taller than he'd been when he left. Some of the boys at school used to sneer at him for being so un-English—*redneck Joe*, they called him—but not me. I just wanted to be like him."

Their conversation is interrupted by a frantic rat-a-tat on the front door, followed by a long-drawn-out shrilling of the doorbell.

"Blimey, someone's desperate for a room," says Guy.

"Or desperate to get their money back," she retorts, nibbling his earlobe to make him squirm. "The Palace Hotel next time, yes?"

"All right, all right! The Palace! I promise!"

Over the sound of their own breathless laughter they listen to the slap of Mrs. Meeny's slippers as she makes her way down the hall and opens the front door.

"But what on earth was Joey doing at an English public school, if his family was over in Canada?"

"Oh, it was all to do with his English grandfather—his mother's father—being an alumnus of Shrewsbury; the old man reckoned his eldest grandson had a God-given duty to follow suit. It was tough for Joey. He missed his folks terribly, but he couldn't get home very often, not even every summer. Most of his holidays he spent at school. It's amazing, really . . ."

He combs his fingers through her hair, and coils a loose strand.

"What's amazing?"

"The way Joey has managed to remain Joey, despite everyone's efforts to fashion him into something else; something smaller."

Nina ponders Guy's words. She doesn't know why she's itching to dispute them, and to undermine Joey's appeal in some small way. Really, there is no good reason; she hardly knows the man.

"I suppose—" But whatever she supposes, she never says, because at that moment the bedroom door bursts open. Nina twists round inside Guy's arms, a muddle of peach-coloured rayon and bare flesh, and there is her father, standing on the threshold, breathing very quickly, as if he's run all the way from Cottenden.

. . .

NINA HAS HEARD ABOUT THE Windmill Theatre in London, and the revue shows with their nude tableaux vivants. Susie Macaulay's late fiancé used to rave about them, which made Susie sulk, and the other Hut 9-ers roll their eyes. The Windmill Girls and their infamous tableaux flash through Nina's mind, as everyone stands—or lies—stock-still in Mr. and Mrs. Meeny's second-floor bedroom. The scene seems to last forever, as if they are in competition not to move or speak.

It's Guy who breaks the spell by sliding out of bed and reaching for his clothes. He moves cautiously, as if he's in the presence of someone—or something—fearsome, which must not be provoked. Gently, he drapes the blanket over Nina's body, so that only her face is visible, lying sideways on the pillow.

"Dad," she whispers, addressing his shoes, since she can't look at his face.

Mr. Woodrow wheels about and rushes downstairs. The front door opens and slams shut.

"I'll go after him," says Guy, who is more or less dressed. He grazes his cheek against hers, in the approximation of a kiss, and dashes away, throwing his greatcoat over his shoulders as he goes. He is wearing shoes, but no socks.

Mrs. Meeny has been standing in the doorway all this time, but Nina only spots her now. There is no light in the older woman's face, yet she manages to look triumphant.

"I don't know what your game is," she says, "but I want you out. You've got a quarter of an hour."

. . .

THIN CLOUDS SCUD OVER THE hills and rooftops, and the wind is cold. Nina loiters at the corner of Cheap Street, out of sight of the guesthouse. She can't think where else to go, if Guy is to find her again.

Mrs. Meeny wasn't joking about the fifteen-minute deadline. She stood guard outside the bathroom while Nina was washing, and outside the bedroom while she was dressing, shouting out time checks: "Twelve minutes . . . ten minutes . . . five minutes . . ." As a result, Nina isn't properly dry, and now she's shivering inside her coat. There wasn't time to mess about applying make-up, or combing her hair. As for whether she's managed to collect everything from the floor and dressing-table, she really couldn't say. Not that it matters. Nothing matters anymore.

A couple of kids run past and give her a sideways glance. When they are farther down the street they slow, and the one with the football under his arm whispers to his friend, who laughs. Perhaps it has nothing to do with Nina, but she feels it must. They've probably noticed the way her hands are trembling, and the shallow way she's breathing, and written her off as a drunk.

Nina stuffs her hands in her pockets, hunches against the wind, and obsesses over things that don't matter: the weeds growing between the paving slabs (*Now why should that line be thick with withered grass, and that one have none at all?*) and the net curtains in the opposite house (*So annoying, the way it rucks up in the middle! If I could just reach through the glass and give it a tug . . .*). After a while Mr. Meeny walks past. When he spots her, he stops jingling the change in his pocket and opens his mouth to speak, before thinking better of it and quickening his pace.

Whenever she considers what just happened, it's like a blade slipping under her ribs, and she thinks, *I've lost my Dad, forever.* And if no Dad, then no Cottenden, no neighbours, no home. No kindly Mrs. Dempsey posting out knitted bedsocks, because she will take the correct view of things. Everyone in their right mind will do the same. Rose's parents will turn against her. Rose already has, of course: Who else could have let slip about the guesthouse at 36 Cheap Street? It hadn't crossed Nina's mind to swear her friend to secrecy.

The cold is making her nose run. It's crazy how much she's shaking: she can hardly manage to pull the handkerchief from her pocket and bring it to her face. If she saw someone else in this state, she'd think they were play-acting.

And where is Guy? Where is he? Here comes Mr. Meeny, back from the newsagent's with a *Daily Express* under his arm, and this time there is no awkwardness, because their eyes don't meet; he even whistles a jaunty tune under his breath as he strides past. But where is Guy? Nina loves him more than anything in the world, but she doesn't know him that well. What if it turns out he has a violent side? What if . . .

He's here, rounding the corner briskly, his head lowered, and she waits with the handkerchief clenched in her fist. There's no blood on his clothes, or anything like that—but of course there isn't—and no sign of Dad, either.

"All right?" she breathes as they meet, although she can barely get the words out, and it's an idiotic question.

"All right," he replies, but his face tells a different story.

He pats her arm and she attempts a laugh.

"Mrs. Meeny threw us out."

They pick up their bags—his kit-bag, her suitcase—and leave Cheap Street behind.

. . .

AT THE RAILWAY STATION CAFÉ he buys them both a brandy and they sit at a small round table in the corner. There are a few customers milling about, so they whisper.

"Drink up," he says. "Go on. It'll help."

Nina downs it briskly, like medicine.

"Tell me what happened with Dad."

Guy rests his elbows on the table and frowns into his glass.

"There's not much to tell. We walked. Or rather, your father dashed along like a lunatic, while I did my best to keep up. I told him that I loved you, and that I had every intention of marrying you, but he took no notice. He just kept walking."

"Oh, but surely he must have said something?"

Guy's frown deepens. "Nothing to the point. When we turned into the Pavilion Gardens he started going on about your mother."

"My *mother?*"

"Yes, he started telling me about—you know—the manner of her death. It was quite bizarre . . ." He takes Nina's hand. "I'm sorry."

She grips his cold fingers.

"He said nothing at all about me?"

"Not really. I suggested that what had happened to your mother, although truly terrible, was irrelevant to the here and now . . . He started walking even more quickly, almost running, and I had to shout to make myself heard. I didn't want to shout—we were already attracting glances—so I let him go and came back to you."

They hear a train heaving into the closest platform. Disembarking passengers crowd into the café, and suddenly there's a lot of chatter and scraping of chairs, and the woman behind the counter does something to the hot water urn that makes it roar and hiss. For a while, it's too noisy for a whispered conversation. Nina thinks Guy says, "Your father is bloody scary," but she can't be sure. For the avoidance of doubt she retorts, "My father is a good man; better than either of us," but Guy gives no sign of having heard.

It's not until the bustle has subsided, and their fellow customers are chatting quietly over rock cakes and cups of tea, that Guy says, "I meant it, you know."

"Meant what?"

"About marrying you."

She squeezes his hand and tries to smile. "Thank you."

There is a plausible world, well within reach of Nina's imagination, in which this proposal would bring her comfort, even happiness, but it's not the world they inhabit. He knows it. She knows it. There are people who try to strike deals with the odds (*If a bomber crew has a 5 percent chance of being shot down on one*

op, then they've got a 5 percent chance on every op, therefore a 95 per-
cent chance of surviving the war!), but this isn't Nina's brand of
dishonesty.

They keep hold of one another's hands across the table, and sit
with their own private thoughts, waiting for their train.

8

Kate

March 12–13, 1943

THE SITTING-ROOM WINDOW DOESN'T NEED CLEANING (NOT by my usual standards), but the sunset is illuminating a dribble of bird-muck, which keeps catching my eye, no matter how I angle myself on the sofa. I'm supposed to be reading, or carrying on a conversation with Mrs. Cox—I'm not entirely sure which—yet my attention strays, time and again, to that streak on the glass.

Hilda Cox and her twins (a boy and a girl, a couple of years younger than Pip) are my new evacuees, and it's not quite accurate to call this a "conversation," it's more a case of Hilda rattling on in her mildly risqué way, while I nod and smile. I don't mind so much when she's talking about people she knows, or the latest programme on the wireless, because all I have to do is say, "Hmm," or "Quite so," or "Yes, isn't it?" as appropriate. It's when her focus turns on me that I get fidgety.

"How's that delicious husband of yours?" she asks now, as I stare at the bird-muck.

Delicious! What a way to describe Guy! Hilda has only met him once, that Saturday in January when she and the twins first arrived. Guy had chosen the same day to come home, in order to tell me (a) that he and I were going to get divorced because he wanted to marry Nina Woodrow, and (b) that he was very sorry to cause me pain, and (c) would I please stop looking at him like that. To be fair to Hilda, she had no idea of the circumstances of his visit. She only glimpsed him as he was leaving, and he *was* piercingly handsome that afternoon, with his perfectly adjusted RAF uniform and sorrowful face.

"Oh, Guy's fine," I say, although we haven't spoken in weeks. Presumably someone official would let me know if he was dead. I follow up with a non sequitur about clothing coupons, which, thankfully, she pursues.

In another life, I might have found Hilda Cox good company. In the life I've been leading since January, I find her oppressive, and I'm disturbed, rather than entertained, by her use of the word *delicious*. I picture a life-sized model of Guy, made of ice cream and spun sugar, with everyone invited to come and take a lick.

"Hilda? Do excuse me . . ."

She stops mid-prattle as I shoot out of my chair. A minute later I'm outside on the gravel, hurling a bucket of steaming suds against the glass, making her jump. The children are traipsing into the sitting-room as I do it—the twins and Pip—and I can make out the little ones shrieking and bouncing on the settee, while Pip stands and stares at me. I can't see his expression through the froth, but I notice the way Hilda Cox smiles at him and smooths his hair. *Poor boy*, she's almost certainly thinking. She doesn't like me. I don't like me either. I work the crusty bird-muck with the sopping cloth, and chip at it with my fingernails, but it won't budge.

Deb will telephone shortly, which is one good reason to wander off into the garden instead of returning inside. At the inevitable moment when Hilda opens the front door and shouts, "Kate? It's your sister on the phone!" I'll hide behind the shed, or among the rhododendrons. It poured down this afternoon, and the Cox family seem to have an inborn horror of damp feet, so I know she won't venture far to look for me.

This March evening is deeply scented and swathed in blue shadows. A blackbird is singing in the hawthorn hedge, and wet grass brushes my ankles as I walk. I wish I was wise enough to be soothed by this beauty, but I'm not; it only deepens my consciousness of what I have become. Up until January, I took it for granted that I was an element of the natural world; that my job was to push forwards and grow and struggle alongside everyone, and everything, else. Before Guy left, I thought I was bobbing along quite adequately, but it turns out I wasn't; it turns out I hadn't even made a proper start. I don't belong. I'm one of nature's blunders: a smashed bird's egg; a cankered sapling; a spring bulb that's failed to put out shoots.

Deb has called every evening since January. As soon as she's home from the bookshop, and even before she's fed the children, she's on the phone to me. I know she means to be kind, but I wish we could write to one another instead. My words dry up when I'm standing in the echoey hallway with the receiver pressed to my face, constantly begging her to "hush," whereas I might be able to explain myself on paper. Whenever I suggest a correspondence, Deb retorts, "That's all very well, but a letter only tells me you were all right two or three days ago. I need to know you're all right now." (*All right*, in this case, being a euphemism for "not suicidal," which is silly. Deep down, she knows I would never go to such extremes. Apart from anything else, I have Pip to consider.)

I stop at the gap in the straggly hedge, and look out at the Welsh hills. That one, straight ahead, is Moel Famau, the highest hill in the Clwydian Range. There's a ruined tower at the top, which looks like a pimple from here. Guy and I climbed Moel Famau the summer after we were married, and we always said we'd do it again with Pip, but never got round to it. Nina Woodrow has probably climbed every single one of those hills, many times. She'll be good at things like that. I'll bet she never complains that her legs hurt, or that she's out of puff.

If Deb must ring every single evening, you'd think we could keep it brief (*Hello, Kate. Still ticking along? . . . Not dead yet, Deb! Bye for now!*), but she seems determined to spin it out with pep talks and words of wisdom, none of which help. I think she knows this, but struggles for anything else to say—and anything has always been better than nothing in my elder sister's book.

"For goodness' sake, don't become one of those embittered women!" is the sort of thing she comes out with, which is like telling someone not to get sick after gorging on iffy oysters. Or, another of her favourites: "Guy is only a man! You can't let your life be ruined by one wretched man!"

What Deb doesn't understand, and what I can't explain over the phone, is that the wretched man himself is not the point; it's his place in my life that matters. If my husband and I were separate people, I could avert my eyes and think distracting thoughts until the sadness of his going had faded, but we're not separate people—or not separate enough. Guy's exit changes me—damages me—and that's not a coy way of saying I love him, it's a statement of fact. I've known Guy since I was six and he was four. We got engaged when we were still at school. If a person's life can be said to resemble a tapestry, then a crucial thread has just been yanked from mine, leaving all the other threads snapped, frayed, and out of joint.

"I had an image of myself, and the world, and where I fitted in," I began, once, when I knew Hilda and the children were outside, but Deb misunderstood my reference to *image*.

"If you're worried about people looking down on you for being a divorcée, don't. Honestly, don't. The people who really love you—"

"That's not what I meant," I said, but the front door opened as I was searching for the right words, and the children poured into the hall.

"What then?"

"Nothing. Never mind."

That was the last time I tried to justify myself to Deb. Perhaps I'll try again, the next time we meet face to face.

The rain is soaking up through my soles, and my shoes are probably ruined for good. It doesn't matter; they're only cheap things. I leave the view of the Welsh hills and make another circuit of the lawn. When I duck under the empty washing-line I graze it with the top of my head, and the suspended raindrops flick away, leaving the cord bare. Soon it will be summer, and I will be hanging out the laundry again, and the thought of it appals me, though it's not bothered me overmuch before. If it wasn't for Pip I would give up on all the jobs—washing, ironing, cleaning, tidying, mending, scrubbing bird-muck off windows—that only need doing again, the second you've finished. I'd live in solitary squalor, and let the garden grow wild. Local children would make up stories about me, and dare one another to ring the doorbell.

I've just realised that I'm clutching my hair with both hands, as I walk. How melodramatic! Perhaps I do need to hear Deb—or someone equally kind—urging me to pull myself together. I hope to goodness Pip hasn't been watching from one of the windows. The low sandstone wall, which divides the garden from the lane, is out of sight of the house, so I make my way over and sit down. Here I can rest my elbows on my knees, rake my fingers through my hair, and make whatever histrionic gestures I like.

Isn't it the twelfth of March today? I think so. In which case the purple hyacinths will be laid at the gate tonight. (You see: I'm not entirely self-absorbed. I can think of things outside myself.) Yes, I'm pretty sure that's right: today *is* the twelfth of March, and every year since we moved here, on the morning of the thirteenth, I have discovered a posy of purple hyacinths by the gate. It took me a few years to notice that the date was always the same, and a little longer to conclude that the flowers must mark the anniversary of "our" murder—the Hawthorn House strangling—twenty-odd years ago.

("Kate?" Hilda's voice floats, predictably, across the garden. "Your sister's on the telephone!" I'm minded to sit still and keep quiet, but guilt gets the better of me. "Tell her I'm fine," I shout, over my shoulder. "Tell her I'll call later.")

I've often wondered about the furtive mourner with the purple hyacinths, and idly planned to keep a lookout, but whenever March the twelfth rolls around I forget, or find I'm too busy. Well, here I am now, with nothing more pressing to do than sit and wait. Mind you, I don't know what time he or she usually comes; for all I know, it might not be till the middle of the night. The flowers are always left beside the wall, half-concealed in the long grass, and there is never a note. From where I'm sitting I can see the withered stalks and scraps of string, which are all that remain of last year's offering.

Deb would be frantic if I admitted to envying the murdered woman. Naturally, I don't envy the manner of her death, but I sometimes think wistfully about *being* dead, and I don't think that's especially grotesque, whatever Deb might say. How divine to sink into sleep, with the prospect of never having to get up again, and never having to reassume the responsibility of living.

What's that poem by Charlotte Mew that keeps rattling round my head? The one in which she declines any glitzy idea of heaven involving pearly gates and martyred throngs and suns that never set. I forget what it's called, and I can't find it in any of my anthologies, but I remember the last four lines:

> *And if for anything we greatly long,*
> *It is for some remote and quiet stair*

Which winds to silence and a space for sleep
Too sound for waking and for dreams too deep.

I dwell on these lines a lot—but then, as ever, my thoughts circle back to Pip. There wouldn't be any joy or peace if he were left behind.

Pip knows about the divorce. That horrible Saturday in late January, when Guy came home to break the news, he took Pip for a walk across the fields. I watched them from an upstairs window, until they disappeared from view. They were holding hands as they left (Pip still instinctively reaches for a hand when we're walking side by side), but there came a point, halfway across the second field, as they were skirting the tree-fringed pond, when Pip shook his father off and plunged his mittened fists into his pockets. I know I was a long way away, but I'm sure it happened that way round, though it's usually Guy who's keen to discourage childish habits.

I couldn't read anything from Pip's manner when they got back. He can be awfully self-contained when he wants to be, and I resisted the temptation to sweep him up in my arms and give him a kiss. I simply said, "Are you all right?" to which he replied with a shrug and a studiously casual, "Yep."

Guy ruffled his hair and said, "Run along." Turning to me, he added, "I think he understands."

I barked with laughter, but the vicar's car rolled up with my new evacuees just then—Hilda and the twins—and I never got the chance to add a biting retort.

The daylight is getting meagre, and I'm starting to feel chilled, but I don't want to leave the garden. I know Pip may be alone in his bedroom feeling lost, and that I ought to go to him, but I worry I'll lose my temper, or burst into tears, and that these things will be worse for him than my temporary absence. Besides, my son is maddeningly unpredictable: there's every possibility that he and the Cox children are currently whacking one another over their heads with pillows and laughing themselves silly. One of the great advantages of the Coxes is that they get on well with Pip. The twins admire him for being two years their senior, which surprises and pleases him. Hilda is instinctively maternal, and loves all children just because they're children. I think she also pities him for being my son.

I shift about on the damp wall, trying to get comfortable, and my wet shoes make sucking sounds whenever I move my toes. I find myself thinking of Joey Roussin, and my eyes prickle, though I've never been sure how much I liked him. Joey is surely dead by now— or as good as dead—but in the early hours of August 25, 1934, he was my accidental midwife. He'd only delivered calves before (he told me, afterwards), and was badly hungover at the time, but he saved two lives that day. He wrote to me in February, you know, a week after Guy's visit; a week before his Spitfire went down for the second and final time. *Dear Kate, I'll love Guy like a brother till the day I die, but as far as "Nina" is concerned, I think he's a class-A jerk. She's not a patch on you. "Chin up," as the Stoics might have said. (Don't you just hate the Stoics!?)*

Yes. Chin up, Kate. There are so many things I need to do when I eventually go back indoors: telephone Deb to reassure her I'm still in the land of the living; chat to Hilda whilst we listen to nonsense (or horrors) on the wireless; knit my millionth pair of khaki socks. If I'm lucky, I'll find time to read, although even that's lost its savour since Nina Woodrow came for tea in her sable coat, and Guy told me our marriage was dead. I have taken to gulping books down at a desperate pace, as if they are pills to be swallowed with a mouthful of water and a grimace (Do Not Chew). This is neither effective nor pleasant (when it comes to books, the more chewing the better), but it seems to have become my way, and I don't know how to change.

Someone's coming along the lane.

I reckon those footsteps belong to a man, although I'm not sure how I can tell; I can't see anyone yet, for the curve of the hedge. I think about sliding off the wall and spying from behind the horse chestnut tree, but in the end I stay put. It's good to feel disquiet—even the faintest tingle—after weeks of grey gloom.

His eyes are downcast as he rounds the corner, fixed on the bunch of purple hyacinths in his hands.

"Oh!" I exclaim. "It's *you!*"

I speak without thinking, and immediately wish I hadn't. After our last encounter, I swore I wouldn't say a word to Henry Woodrow ever again, in any circumstances.

Henry Woodrow knows about his daughter's affair with my husband, yet he has never thought to apologise for his unkind remarks, or admit that I was right all along. I know he knows, because when Guy came in January I asked him outright, "Is Nina's father aware of what's going on?" and he replied, "Oh yes," as much as to say, *I could tell you a fine old story about that, if I chose.* (I desperately wanted to hear the story, but couldn't very well ask for it there and then, having so recently hurled a wet dishcloth at his face and invited him to drop down dead.)

Sure enough, when I observed Mr. Woodrow in church around that time—in fact, every Sunday since—he looked pale and hollowed-out, as if he'd pretty much given up on food and sleep. He looks like that this evening—in fact, he looks worse, without the extra veneer of smartness he reserves for Holy Communion.

He stops in his tracks.

"Mrs. Nicholson!"

A number of sarcastic rejoinders suggest themselves ("Merely the *first* Mrs. Nicholson . . ."), but sadness is descending again, like a fog, and I can't be thinking of things to say, let alone witticisms. I move my toes around inside my shoes and make them squelch.

Perhaps it's an effect of the dusk, but Mr. Woodrow actually does seem slighter and more stooped than before. The way he held himself used to imply, *Take me or leave me*, but now it says, *Try, if at all possible, not to notice I'm here.* He removes his hat with the shy hesitancy of a much younger man—a boy—and says, again:

"Mrs. Nicholson."

"I really would prefer to be called Kate."

"Kate," he echoes obediently. I note that the Bill Sikes dog hasn't come along for the walk; it's a solitary pilgrimage tonight.

Sometimes, over the last couple of months, I've resented Henry Woodrow more than anyone else involved in this sorry tale. He and I could have been comrades in humiliation, if only he'd admitted to being in the know, or apologised for calling me names (specifically a "fraud" and a "disappointment." Every Sunday, he skulks away from morning service without meeting my eye, and I have to endure the vicar's wife's musings about how "poor, dear Mr. Woodrow" is looking peaky, and how she keeps recommending him to drink stout.

Oh God, listen to me; I'm becoming "one of those women." I wish Deb could tell me how to avoid embitterment, instead of hurling maxims at me. The one I hate most is "What doesn't kill you makes you stronger," because it assumes my husband's betrayal is not killing me, whereas—don't tell Deb—I fear it is. I feel the fracture lines creeping avidly across my soul, multiplying like cracks in a sheet of ice. One day, in the not-so-distant future, I might split and shatter at the lightest touch.

Henry and I look at one another in the twilight, and I make no effort at all to rearrange my expression. I care about presenting a cheerful—or at least, acceptably neutral—face to Pip, and the Coxes, and people in the village, but I don't care one jot when it comes to Henry Woodrow. It's a relief, to tell the truth.

"Kate," he says, effortfully. "I owe you an apology."

He offers me the hyacinths, but I make no move to take them.

"You didn't bring those for me."

He inclines his head; doesn't deny it; seems to think.

"I would like you to have them, nonetheless."

He holds them out again, insisting, but my arms—like my spirits—are too heavy to lift.

"Why do you bring flowers every year for the murdered woman?" I ask.

He runs his fingers through his hair and peers down at his hat. It takes him a good while to answer.

"Because she was my wife."

I recoil.

"Your *wife*?"

"Yes."

"But that evening, all those years ago, you told me—"

"I know. I know what I said that evening; our conversation is as vivid to me as if it happened yesterday. I'm very sorry."

"Your *wife*," I repeat, wonderingly.

Whatever I may (or may not) feel about this man, I regret that my first instinct was to shrink from his admission. I don't know what to say now. It seems wrong to quiz him when he looks so broken, and equally wrong to change the subject.

"I should like, very much, to talk to you," he says. "Not now; I don't mean now."

He waits for my acceptance, and I nod.

"May I call on you tomorrow?" he goes on, pressing the posy into my hands. This time I take it.

"You may, but Hawthorn House is full to bursting with evacuees at the moment." (This is an exaggeration, but it's a mild one. The house is full to bursting with Hilda Cox.)

"Ah . . . then perhaps you will call on me? You remember the house, I expect: 7 Canal Road."

"I do remember."

"But will you come?"

If I hesitate, it's because I don't want to seem eager. Of course I will accept, for curiosity's sake, if nothing else.

"I'm busy in the morning." (I'm not really, except that Hilda thinks we should drag all the rugs outside and give them a good beating. Spring cleaning is one of her many enthusiasms.)

"A cup of tea, mid-afternoon, then. Three o'clock?"

"All right. Three o'clock."

It crosses my mind—and I think it crosses his—to shake hands, and we both start forwards before suppressing the impulse. My relationship to Henry Woodrow is an almighty puzzle. We've had nine years to decide whether we are polite strangers, enemies, or intimates, and we still seem unable to commit ourselves.

"Goodbye, Henry."

He bows slightly and says, "Till tomorrow," before turning and walking away.

Perhaps *enemies* is too strong a word. I'm not sure. I hope so.

When I'm halfway up the drive the light comes on in Pip's bedroom, and I see the children's shadows bouncing across the closed curtains. Pip is always forgetting his blackout blind; I'd better go up and see to it. Perhaps I'll read a bedtime story while I'm there, to settle the three of them down. It's a while since I read to Pip.

As I enter the hall, I stop to look at the hyacinths. They are a beautiful shade of purple, like the sky when it's neither bright nor dark, but a vivid blend of both. I'm comforted in the way I ought to have been earlier, when I heard the blackbird and felt nothing.

Nevertheless, I return to the gate and lay them in their usual place beside the wall. Whatever Henry says, I don't believe these flowers are mine to keep.

. . .

AFTER LUNCH THE NEXT DAY, I go upstairs to make myself smart, and on the way down I meet Hilda. It's not as though I've gone to great lengths—little more than washing my face and tidying my hair—but she stops and says, "Ooh, are we meeting someone?"

Hilda Cox is perfectly natural with the children, but she can't talk to adults without adopting a roguish manner; she makes *Will you pass the marmalade?* or *What's tomorrow's weather forecast?* sound like double entendres. Her husband is fighting in the Far East, like my brother, Ron, and I wonder whether she's the same with him when he's at home, and whether he finds it seductive, or irritating, or a bit of both.

"*I'm* meeting someone. I'm going to tea with a friend."

"Very nice!"

Hilda stands over me as I root through my small collection of shapeless hats. When I select my navy beret she says, "Hmm. A gentleman friend?"

She takes the beret out of my hands and positions it on my head, at a debonair angle. I glimpse my reflection in the mirror, and make her "tut" by rearranging it to my own, unadventurous, taste.

Pip is also in the hallway, swinging lazily on the sitting-room door, the very image of childish boredom. He doesn't look as though he's eavesdropping, but that doesn't mean he's not.

"A family friend," I say, crisply. "You won't have met him. Henry Woodrow."

Hilda's lips twitch.

"Henry Woodrow? I haven't met him, but I've seen him out and about. The suave widower."

She is watching me tie my scarf, so I can't experiment with it, as I'd like.

"Well," she goes on, confidingly, "we'll see you when we see you. Don't rush home on Pip's account; I can see to the children's supper."

"Heavens, I won't be out that long!" I turn to face her. "Anyway, Pip is coming with me."

It's a snap decision, with no other purpose than to wipe that arch smile off Hilda's face, and of course Pip is listening. He lets go of the door-knob with a snap and drops his arms to his sides.

"Mummy, no! Me and the twins have got plans."

"*The twins and I.* What plans?"

Pip shrugs moodily. No doubt he's thinking of his latest favourite game, German Spies, which (so far as I can tell) involves donning his father's old trilby, hiding pencilled messages in the hedge, and bossing the twins about. Pip plays German Spies with great seriousness. I think the twins are a bit fazed by it, though they play their parts obediently, and get terribly excited when Pip lets them wear the hat.

"Well, I'm afraid you'll have to move your plans to tomorrow," I say. "Go and change your shirt, and make sure your shoes are clean."

"But I don't even *know* this person," says Pip, defiantly. "Henry Woodlouse, or whatever he's called. Henry Wood . . . pecker."

The twins giggle, from wherever they're hiding, and Pip makes every effort to hold his scowl steady, and not to undermine it with a smirk. Hilda watches from the sidelines, eyebrows cocked.

"Mr. Wood*row*." It takes me all I've got to say it calmly. "Now that's enough back-chat. Go and fetch your gas mask."

. . .

I WORRY THAT HENRY AND I are back at square one when he invites us inside with such subdued politeness and starts commenting on the weather. It is rather windy today, which makes the indoor silence all the more marked when the front door closes behind us.

Henry ushers us into the kitchen, where two cups and saucers and a plate of biscuits have been set on the table. He doesn't seem put out by Pip's presence, he simply fetches a third cup, and tells Pip he's sorry there are no chocolate biscuits, and asks whether he owns a kite, since "today would be a jolly good day for flying one, don't you think?"

If Henry is tense, it only shows once, momentarily, when Shirley—the bull terrier—growls at Pip, who has stepped backwards onto her bed. "Bad dog," Henry murmurs, twisting her collar so sharply that her eyes boggle. I begin to protest, but it's over in a flash, and Henry is reassuring my son so kindly ("All right there, Pip? She's a silly old lady, but her bark's much worse than her bite.") that I let it go.

"Can we leave soon?" Pip stage-whispers, as Henry makes the tea. It'll only make things worse if I tick him off in public, so I check him with my most awful frown and say, "Why don't you go and run around the garden while I talk to Mr. Woodrow?"

"Because I don't want to *run around the garden*," he retorts, swivelling in his seat and returning my frown in full.

Henry brings the teapot to the table and starts talking about the damned weather again. I catch Pip's eye.

"Mr. Woodrow has a piano," I assert, rather suddenly, regardless of speculation as to whether this cold front will, or will not, last into the beginning of next week. "Perhaps, if you ask nicely, he'll let you have a go?"

"Ah," says Henry politely, "so you're a musician, are you?"

"No!"

"No, but you would *like* to be," I insist.

We troop into the sitting-room. It's not quite as polished and tidy as it was in the summer of 1934, and it feels smaller, as remembered things often do. Other than that, it's eerily familiar. There is the cherry tree beyond the french windows, and the Gothic desk with its complex drawers and compartments, and the piano stool, where Nina sat in her stolen dress.

Henry opens the piano lid and plays a quick trill.

"It's terribly out of tune, I'm afraid, but you're more than welcome to try."

Pip hesitates. He's in the mood to disconcert us with a lofty refusal, but he's also a small boy being authorised to make a din. He touches middle C, quietly at first, then more loudly, then with gusto. He spreads all his fingers wide, and brings them down to make a jangling chord. I smile at Henry, and we return to the kitchen.

There's a shyness between us, now that we're alone. Henry riffles at *The Times* and resorts to war-talk ("Seven U-Boats destroyed this month alone, so they say; I reckon the war's taking a turn for the better . . ."), but I am conscious that the piano's appeal won't last forever, and that there are matters we've waited nine years to discuss.

"I think it's lovely that you lay flowers every year, in memory of your wife."

He bows his head.

"I was afraid you'd think it presumptuous," he says, quietly. "It's your house, after all."

"I don't think anything of the sort!"

I watch him stir and pour the tea. *Your turn to speak, Henry.*

"Sugar?" he offers. "Have a biscuit; I'm sorry they're only shop-bought."

I shake my head and wait. Henry stirs his tea, though the milk is already well blended, and he hasn't taken any sugar.

"You didn't realise it was my wife who had died?" he asks. "I assumed you'd have had the full story from someone, at some point over the years."

"No! Nobody told me. I don't really have those sorts of friends, at least not in Cottenden."

"Those sorts of friends . . . ?"

"Gossipy friends."

"Ah." Henry nods. "Nina—I mean, my daughter, as was—do you mind my mentioning her?"

"No."

"Well, she never knew either. I couldn't burden her with such horrors while she was small, so I told myself to wait till she was older, but the longer I waited, the more impossible it became. I ended up swearing friends and neighbours to secrecy, and sending her to school in Chester, so that she wouldn't mix with the village children. Nina grew up thinking that her mother had died in an accident; that she'd been run over and killed by a car."

Henry sets the spoon on the saucer and there's another lull. I think about *My daughter, as was*. It's a chilling phrase. I try to imagine the circumstances which could, one day, compel me to say, *My son Pip, as was*. Perhaps if he committed some awful crime: rape or murder? But whatever he did, he'd still be mine, whether I liked it or not.

"Shall I tell you about her? My wife, I mean."

Henry looks as though he's asking the teacup.

"Only if you want to."

For the first time since we stopped talking about post offices and shop-bought biscuits, he meets my eye.

"I do want to."

. . .

IF HENRY SAYS HE WANTS to tell me, I suppose I must believe him, but goodness, I wish I could be so restrained, whenever I feel the need to talk! It makes me blush to recall that January evening when I told him all there was to tell about the sable coat: how I tumbled over my words, barely pausing for breath, scouring every incident for its inmost meaning, in my eagerness to make him see things exactly as I did. Henry tells his story slowly and concisely, and he keeps being sidetracked into trains of thought that he's unwilling to share.

"What was her name?" I ask, in an effort to get him started.

"Teodora. She was Italian. You know, Kate, when I lied to you about it, all those years ago—implying that I hardly remembered the murder—it wasn't because I minded you knowing. It was just—"

"—it was just that you were in the middle of hosting a dinner party, and it was entirely the wrong place and time to discuss it. Henry, you don't need to explain, let alone apologise."

"All right. Well, thank you."

The piano's muffled *plinkety-plonk* fills the stillness, as Henry plunges back into thought. I rack my brains for another prompt.

"Did you meet Teodora during the Great War? In Italy?"

"I did meet her during the war, but in London, while I was on leave. I've never been to Italy; my battalion fought in Belgium."

He stirs his untasted tea again.

"She was clever and pretty, and a waitress at a rather seedy bar in Soho. A fish out of water. I think I might have a picture . . ."

He reaches inside his jacket for his wallet, and hands me a dog-eared photograph. *I think I might* is surely disingenuous; this little square of paper must burn a hole in his shirt, day in, day out. She's beautiful. In fact, she is an exaggerated version of her daughter: the hair is even darker and glossier than Nina's; the eyes more impish; the rosebud mouth more blooming. For an instant, I have a sense of someone vividly real, but the longer I look at her, the more lost she seems. *I can no more fly to the moon*, I think to myself, *than come face to face with Teodora Woodrow, in the flesh.* Maybe I'm stupider than I realised, because it's hardly an original thought, but it still has the power to disturb me.

"She wasn't happy in London," Henry says. "She didn't like waitressing. There are so many unkind men—lewd men, if you'll forgive me—in the world, and I'm afraid young soldiers on leave are no exception to the rule . . ."

He tails off, and I glimpse the dazzling roar of a Soho bar, and a waitress with a tray chock-full of glasses, trying not to spill as she steps over khaki legs, and dodges groping hands.

"So you rode to the rescue?"

"In a manner of speaking." He smiles thinly. "When the war was over I married her and brought her home to Cottenden. My parents had died during the war: Father had a stroke after my brothers were both killed on the same day, and Mother just . . . gave up, a few months later."

I draw a sharp breath. "Two brothers on the same day?"

"August 16, 1917. Passchendaele. God, what a year. Four of my school friends, two of my cousins, both my brothers—then my parents. Teodora was a gleam in the darkness. No, not a gleam so much as a burst . . . a blast . . . an *explosion* of light."

Pip has stopped playing the piano, but Henry doesn't appear to have noticed. I'd like to do something—to touch him, or say something helpful—but I'm afraid of intruding on his faraway thoughts.

"There was a man—a boy—a friend of hers. George Tyler. He was a pianist; played in the same Soho bar where she worked."

Yet another frowning pause.

"Were they . . ." I want to ask whether they'd been lovers, but I can't bring myself to say the word in front of Henry. It doesn't matter; he knows what I mean.

"George liked everyone to think so, but Teodora laughed at the very idea. She told me she'd sooner fall in love with her own little brother. I gathered that they'd known each other as children, and she'd been fond of him for a long time, but that they'd grown apart. By the time Teodora met me, she actively disliked George; she couldn't wait to leave him behind and move to Cottenden."

"What sort of person was he?"

Henry shudders. "Nasty, pushy little fellow. Took himself too seriously. Didn't like to be crossed."

I nod, and Henry smiles at me.

"Anyway, not many months after our marriage, this George chap called on us, unannounced. Said he 'happened' to be driving through

Cottenden, on his way to Liverpool—but I'm not sure. Teodora was pregnant with Nina at the time, and I was terribly worried about the effect on her health. Not that George was openly antagonistic—in fact he was chillingly polite—but my goodness, the looks he gave her! The looks he gave *me*, for that matter."

Henry sighs and shakes his head.

"What an afternoon. We walked to the Red Lion together, the three of us, just for something to do. I shall never forget that we stopped at Hawthorn House, on the way—a tumble-down farmhouse, as it was then, with an overgrown paddock instead of a garden—to take in the views."

Naturally, I want to know what happened next, but I'm distracted by the hush from the sitting-room. What on earth is Pip doing in there? Please God he's not nosing about; poking through the desk; playing German Spies. My toes curl at the thought.

Henry goes on: "Eventually he left, without further ado, but a few weeks later he started sending letters."

"To you?"

"To Teodora."

"What sort of letters?"

"She burned most of them without showing me; afraid I'd be upset. I got my hands on one or two. Outrageous stuff, it was—jealous—menacing—shamelessly theatrical. Told my wife in no uncertain terms that she 'belonged' to him; that she'd no right to marry another; that he was going to exact his revenge, et cetera, et cetera. I laughed, at the time; it seemed so overblown."

Henry passes his hand over his face.

"Well, Nina was born, and time went by, and the letters kept arriving—more often, I believe, than Teodora let on. Finally, George must have told her he was returning to Cottenden, and that he wanted to see her. She didn't say a word about it to me; perhaps she hoped to spare me a scene by speaking to him in private. At any rate, it appears she agreed to meet him on the evening of March 12, 1922. Whether it was she who suggested the tumble-down farmhouse on Manor Farm Lane, because she didn't want the gossip-mongers to see her with a strange man, or he who suggested it, because he needed somewhere secluded to do . . . what he was going to do . . . I don't know.

"As it happened, I felt unwell that evening and took myself off to bed. Our two-year-old daughter was fast asleep. I didn't hear Teodora leave the house."

Henry stops and shuts his eyes. I'm worried he's going to break down, in which case I'm not sure how I'll resist gathering his hands into mine and kissing them.

"He strangled her with a silk scarf, or a stocking—something of the sort," he says, striving for matter-of-factness. "The police don't know for sure, because they never found it. I suppose he must have hidden it very cleverly, or destroyed it."

I manage to nod.

"There's not much more to tell. I got up at midnight to go to the bathroom—I was still feeling off-colour—and that's when I discovered she was gone. It was odd, to say the least; odd and alarming. I went outside, but there was no sign of her, so I roused the local bobby, Sergeant Murray—Constable Murray as he was then. It was Murray who discovered her, around dawn, inside the old farmhouse. *He* was there too—the murderer—sitting with her among the nettles and long grasses."

"He admitted to it, then?" I ask.

"Oh no, he made out it had nothing to do with him. Apparently he'd arranged to meet Teodora at the Red Lion, and when she failed to turn up he went off in search of her, and some mysterious *instinct* led him to the old farm . . . None of it stacked up."

"And so . . . ?"

"And so that was the end of George Tyler. I'm no Judge Jeffreys— believe me—but the hangman has his place."

We sit in silence, and I feel oddly comforted in the wake of this bleak, bleak tale. Does that sound callous? I don't mean to be callous. It's just... here Henry is with his great grief, and here I am with my lesser grief, and we don't need to pretend everything is fine, or make small talk, or say anything at all. The plate of biscuits remains untouched, and our half-drunk cups of tea have gone cold, and I wish I could sit like this forever.

If only Pip hadn't gone quiet.

The longing to touch this man is on me again—just to take his hands, or cup his face, or brush his forehead with my lips—but I can't, I *can't*. It would be like rushing up to the King at some public event and caressing him, on the grounds that he looks lonely. The possibility of a smiling response is outweighed by the awful, and very real, possibility of annoying him.

Henry gathers up the teacups, while I slip away to check on my son.

. . .

"PIP! WHAT IN HEAVEN'S NAME do you think you're doing?"

I shut the door softly, before swooping like a bird of prey. Hastily, Pip tucks a pile of receipts into one of the desk's pigeonholes and shuts Henry's address book.

"What about this?" I snatch at the drawstring purse he's clutching in his left hand. The colour rises to his face, but he doesn't say anything. The purse is made of black velvet, and I can't tell what's inside—a paper, I should think, judging by the way it crackles, and something soft—*not* that it's any of my business.

"Where does it go? Quick, Pip! Where did you find it?"

Henry will come, any moment now. Naturally he'll be cross, and I'll have to make Pip apologise, and yet I'll also defend him, because, after all, he's only an eight-year-old boy with a German spy obsession . . . and at the end of it all, Henry and I will be at odds again. Knowing us, we won't speak for another decade or two.

Damn it!

Pip removes a small drawer from the bizarre desk, and reaches into the space left behind. He retrieves a carved ebony box—integral, by the looks of its matching Chinese dragon design—flips it over, and removes a false base. What a desk! I've never seen such an eccentric piece of furniture in all my life, and if I had time to marvel at it, I would.

"Quickly, quickly," I whisper, as Pip places the purse inside, closes the box, and slots everything back into place.

When Henry enters, we're sitting quietly on the sofa, flicking through a book called *Easy Piano Sonatas*. Neither of us can read music, but Henry doesn't need to know that. I glance up with a smile, conscious that my cheeks are pinker than they were before. Pip's hands are trembling, but he does his best to hide it by pressing them between his knees.

. . .

AS WE ARE PARTING OUTSIDE the front door, Henry says, "You're a good listener. Thank you."

I feel pleased, as if I've won a prize. I know I shall be tempted to tell someone—Hilda Cox, most likely—so I make a mental note to do nothing of the sort. If I blurt out that Mr. Woodrow praised me, Hilda will raise her eyebrows meaningfully, and make me feel like the fool that I am.

"I'm sorry I monopolised the conversation," Henry says.

"But you didn't; not in the least! I'm glad you felt able to tell me about Teodora."

"We never discussed your concerns. We didn't even touch on . . . you know . . ."

I check that Pip is out of earshot. He's on the opposite pavement, picking leaves off a neighbour's privet hedge.

"You mean, we didn't touch on the subject of Guy and Nina," I say, just to prove I can. "The future Mr. and Mrs. Nicholson."

Henry winces, and I don't know what comes over me; I don't even glance over my shoulder to check Pip is still distracted before seizing Henry's hand and pressing it to my lips. It's the same idiotic impulse that made me telephone him that desolate night in January, and I know I'll cringe for it later. It's not a kiss I can explain away; there's nothing light, or playful, or dignified about it. It's more like the staunching of a wound than a kiss.

Still he maintains his reserve.

"My dear Kate," I hear him say, as he frees his hand. "You are the only Mrs. Nicholson. There will never be another."

. . .

SLEEP IS MORE EXHAUSTING THAN wakefulness tonight. Figures loom over me with their backs to the light—Guy, or Henry, or some monstrous fusion of the two—and just as I'm sure they're about to embrace me, they wind a silk stocking round my neck and start to pull.

I wake up, to the extent that I'm conscious of being in my own bed, in my own house, but there are footsteps going up and down the stairs. It's probably Hilda (a chronic insomniac) going to the kitchen to fetch a glass of water, but I picture Teodora Woodrow climbing out of Henry's photograph and walking about my house, with her smiling eyes and her mouth like a blown rose.

All in all, I'm glad when my bedroom door creaks open, and a slight figure whispers, "Mummy?"

I lever myself up on one elbow.

"Pip?"

"I've had a bad dream."

I lift the sheets to let him in, and wrap my arms around him. Pip is real and warm, and the scent of his skin is milky, like an infant's. I shut my eyes and breathe it in. I know it won't last. Deb's children smell dreadful now that they've reached their teens.

"What happened in your dream?" I ask, stroking his hair.

He hesitates. "I can't really remember."

Goodness, but I was cross with him, after we left Henry's. I decreed that he couldn't have any jam with his rice pudding, and you should have seen the way the Coxes looked at me. You'd think I'd proposed to skin him alive.

Nevertheless, it's me he comes to at night, when he's frightened.

"Mummy?"

"What is it, Pip?"

He wriggles round to face me.

"I'm scared of that man."

"What man? Do you mean Mr. Woodrow?"

He nods, but I make the mistake of laughing, and he hides his face in the pillow.

"You know, I'm pretty sure he's not a German spy," I say, as solemnly as I can, dropping a kiss onto his ear.

"I didn't *mean* that."

"What then?"

"Nothing."

"Oh, go on, tell me what you meant. I'm sorry I laughed."

But the moment has passed. Pip turns away, rigid with resentment, and pretends to fall asleep.

I close my eyes, and my thoughts drift from my unknowable son, to our strange afternoon at 7 Canal Road, to Henry Woodrow.

Henry said I was a good listener, and described me as his *dear Kate*. I turn the words over, like a miser with a small horde of coins, and when I'm done, I remember the fierce kiss that I planted on his knuckles, and his last few words, before we said goodbye.

You are the only Mrs. Nicholson. There will never be another.

Was it reassurance—as much as to say, whatever Guy and Nina do, Kate remains real and valid and whole? I wonder. I recall the sadness of his tone, and the gentleness with which he drew his hand from my lips, and pushed me away.

I roll onto my side, turning my back on Pip.

Why will there "never be another" Mrs. Nicholson?

Don't be stupid, Kate. There will never be another Mrs. Nicholson for the simple reason that I—and only I—am the woman who married Mr. Nicholson in the first place, for better or worse, till death do us part. Henry wasn't reassuring me, he was urging me to endure, because he doesn't believe in divorce. Of course he doesn't. Neither do I. We were brought up the same way.

What therefore God hath joined together, let not man put asunder: I've always thought it a rather magnificent line. Tonight, for the first time, it strikes me as dreary.

I turn onto my back, and then onto my side again, and put my arms around my sleeping son. The sadness is coming down on me again, after a twenty-four-hour reprieve. Good grief, what's wrong with me? What's wrong with the lot of us? We're all obsessed with sexual relations—Guy, Nina, me, even Henry—either wanting them for ourselves, or despising others for wanting them, or both. I would very much like to step off the treadmill and concentrate on something else, but it's easier said than done.

Pip's hair tickles my lips when I sigh.

Poor Kate (as a plainer-speaking man than Henry might have put it), *whatever you might wish—whatever I might wish—an honourable man like me can never accept a kiss like this, from a woman like you.*

9

Nina

May 19, 1945

RAF Beaulieu
Hampshire

Monday, May 14, 1945

Dearest, darling Nina (also known to the world as <u>Mrs.</u>
<u>Guy Nicholson</u>!!!)

"Hmm," Nina says to herself, and looks up. It's not the first time she's read this letter, so she doesn't need to hurry to the end.

St. James's Park is busy, as you would expect on such a fine Saturday morning, with couples ambling arm-in-arm, or lounging on picnic rugs, and children throwing crumbs for the birds. Every so often, someone important-looking strides among the pelicans and ducks on his way towards Whitehall, oblivious of the scattering and squawking. In fact—wait—that tall man with the wing collar:

Isn't he in the cabinet? The minister for . . . something or other; Dad would know. Anyway, it might not be him. Nina looks back at the letter, so as not to be caught staring.

Best not think about Dad. She wrote to him three times after Buxton, and on the third time he replied, in a manner of speaking. The note read, *I cannot forgive you.* That was all. No ranting or raving; no lamenting or pleading or counselling. It didn't even start *Dear Nina,* or end *From Dad.*

But she won't think about that again. Not now.

Dearest, darling Nina (also known to the world as <u>Mrs. Guy Nicholson!!!</u>)

Guy has made quite a habit of that "also known as" line. It's her own fault, because she kept going on about it during their four-day honeymoon in Yarmouth. "Mrs. Guy Nicholson! How can that be me?" she used to wonder aloud, far too frequently, with a mixture of pleasure and unease—but Guy heard only the pleasure, and turned it into a running joke.

Six months since the wedding, and she still isn't used to it. It's like a lovely pair of shoes that's taking an awfully long time to break in. Of course, it hasn't helped that the two of them have been stationed at different bases for a year and a half—he at Beaulieu in Hampshire, she at Upper Heyford in Oxfordshire—but things are bound to change, now that the war in Europe is over. Their married life will begin properly.

I'm glad they gave you a good VE-day at Heyford. It wasn't too bad at Beaulieu either—there was beer aplenty, and a great deal of larking about, although everything was touched with a funny sort of sadness. I suppose it's inevitable: too much has been lost for joy to be unbounded. (Besides, what self-respecting man can properly celebrate when his adored wife is a hundred miles away, having the time of her life without him? Tell me, I need to know: Are those blasted Yanks still based at Heyford?!!!)

Roll on Saturday. Eleven o'clock at "our" bench in St. James's Park? All being well I shall have a marvel-lous surprise for you, but I'd better not say more in case it doesn't come off.

Any news re when you might be demobbed? Things appear to be moving fairly quickly here, so fingers crossed. To think we might both be free within weeks! But I know what you'll say, and you're right: best not get ahead of ourselves.

Sorry to be so brief. I'm a dreadful letter writer—always was. We'll talk properly on Saturday.

I love you.

Guy
(aka Mr. Nina Nicholson)

Big Ben strikes eleven as she folds the letter and slips it back inside her coat pocket. She's read it six or seven times now. It's one of the most straightforward letters Guy has ever written—a gush of relief and love—and she ought to enjoy it on its own terms, instead of por-ing over it with a half frown, like a puzzler in search of clues. The silliest things worry her: the "marvellous" surprise (Nina has grown wary of surprises); the prospect of being demobbed within weeks (because what then?); his slapdash brevity (whatever he may claim, he *did* write at greater length when he first moved away to Hampshire).

VE-day was awful, actually, though when she spoke to Guy over the telephone last week, she lied and said it had been fun. The celebrations at RAF Upper Heyford were pretty wild, but Nina went to bed early, pleading a headache. She switched the wireless on right in the middle of the King's victory speech, and lay on top of the covers, half listening, and wondering how late a woman's monthly bleed could be, without it meaning the worst. "Together we shall all face the future with stern resolve," said the King, "and prove that our reserves of willpower and vitality are inexhaustible." Nina had shut her eyes tight. At that point, her period had been two weeks late. Now it's three, going on four.

Without it meaning the worst. Maybe—just maybe—it's wrong to think like that. She looks around at the people in the park. There are children everywhere, once you start worrying you're pregnant. A couple of benches down, a woman takes a sturdy little baby from its pram and lifts it high, before bringing it down to face level for a kiss, and as she does so it chortles and flaps its fists. Presumably there would be moments like that, even for Nina—sunny Saturdays in the park, birthday teas, lighting the candles on the Christmas tree— when everything feels perfect, and there's nothing to detract from the primal love and contentment that makes a woman a Mother, with a capital *M*.

Then again, look at those three on the footbridge: a woman with two small children in tow, both of them squirming and tugging at her hands, threatening to sit down on the spot because "My feet are *so* tired, Mummy," and "I want a carry!" Not just the woman's face, but her entire body, express a desperate sort of boredom. The kinder passers-by simply avoid her eye; the less kind purse their lips. A good-looking man in a morning coat tuts and shakes his head as he glides around them and continues on his unencumbered way.

Nina places her little suitcase squarely on her lap, so that nobody can see her pressing her fingertips against her abdomen. It can't be true, can it? If someone were to ask her to describe exactly what the sensation amounts to, she'd be hard-pressed to say. Perhaps she feels completely normal! Perhaps. She shifts her weight, and twists in her seat, to see if it makes any difference. There: that faint tightness; that tenderness?

Nina fiddles with her gloves, and straightens her green dress. Clothes rationing notwithstanding, she looks a million dollars—if she wasn't already sure of it within herself, she'd know by the glances she'd been getting all morning—but she also looks ordinary. Just an attractive woman; just someone's wife; just another mother-to-be. A group of ATS women pass by in their khakis, and Nina wishes she'd worn her uniform too. It's looking a little worn these days—the jacket collar is pale at the edge, where it's rubbed against her neck, and she's had to mend her skirt in a couple of places—but her heart still swells when she puts it on. None of the other WAAFs feel the same, or if they do, they're not admitting to it. When Nina told her roommate, Angela, that she was having two days off to see her husband, Angela said, "Lucky you! A chance to wear civvies!"

She scans the people strolling through the park, knowing at a glance that none of them is Guy. Nina will recognise him the moment he enters the corner of her eye, no matter what he's wearing. He's ten minutes late, but it's far too early to fret. The possibility of ironic catastrophe (ironic for a soon-to-be ex-member of Bomber Command) haunts Nina, if she lets it, so she absolutely won't. Her young husband will not have been hit by a bus, or electrocuted by a faulty plug socket. He will not have scratched himself on a rusty nail and died of blood poisoning.

A heavily pregnant woman passes by with a man, and Nina watches till they disappear from sight, conscious that her forceful curiosity makes no sense. What can she possibly learn from a glimpse of two total strangers? Just because the woman smiles and whispers with the man as she tucks her hand through his arm, it doesn't mean they're both happy deep down, or that their love will last forever, or that they're going to be wonderful parents. All it proves, if anything, is that ambling beneath tall plane trees, during peacetime, on a sunny May morning, puts people in a good mood.

Big Ben strikes the quarter hour. Nina crosses her legs, feels the twinge again, and uncrosses them. The twinge remains.

The question is, when to tell Guy? Should she get it over with, as soon as he arrives, so that it's not weighing on her all day? But if he's annoyed, then it will weigh on both of them, and spoil their reunion. Oh, what a drag! And after they'd been so very careful—or thought they had.

Of course, he *might* be pleased.

Nina fidgets unhappily with the buttons on her gloves, remembering a party they attended last year with some of Guy's old accountancy friends, and the couple they met—Johnny and Vera—who were expecting their first child. After everyone had downed a few glasses, Johnny asked the room, "What's it like, then, being a father?" Some dealt with the question earnestly (*a huge responsibility, I'd have to admit, but terrifically rewarding*). Some were jokey (*say goodbye to what little hair you still possess, old man*). Amidst much laughter, Johnny turned to Guy and said, "You're a father, aren't you, Nicholson? What's it like?" and Guy replied, without so much as a smile, "Vastly overrated."

Later on, the mother-to-be, Vera, had cornered Nina in the cloakroom. They were both a little worse for wear, by then. Everyone was.

"Tell me," Vera slurred, fumbling to get the lid off her lipstick. "Is your husband mean, or unhappy? Which is it? I want to know."

"Neither!" Nina had cried, and Vera had raised her eyebrows a fraction, and that was all.

The whole incident amounted to nothing, really. Too much shoddy gin all round, and not enough to eat.

Nina looks up. Here he is now! She stands, then sits again. Will it ever feel less than miraculous to lay eyes on Guy; to think, *He's still alive, and whole, and walking towards me*? He looks boyish and energetic in his claret sweater and tweed jacket, his hair tufting in the breeze. She decides, there and then, to tell her news straight off. It will be fine. They'll make a joint decision to be contented parents, and that's what they'll be.

Guy waves cheerily from the bridge, before pointing with comic emphasis at the person walking beside him; the tall, lean man with the walking stick. Nina stands again, and waves uncertainly, as Guy takes hold of the stranger's elbow. Should she recognise . . . ?

"It's the surprise!" Guy calls. "I told you I'd bring a surprise, and here he is!"

The tall man lifts his hat as they meet on the path.

"Hey there, Nina."

The voice is her best clue, but even so, she's tentative.

". . . Joey?"

The muscles inside his face lack their old flexibility, which may be why there's no warmth to his smile.

"Isn't it terrific?" Guy plants a kiss on her cheek. "Sorry we're late. I had to go via East Grinstead to collect the old crock."

Nina wants to study Joey's face properly, and absorb its strangeness, but she daren't. She shoots him quick glances, instead, and keeps smiling. One of her old boyfriends at RAF Charlwood, James Wylie, suffered burns to his face, though they were nothing like as bad as Joey's. "Can you not even bring yourself to look at me?" James used to complain, when they were sitting opposite one another in the Poacher's Arms. It was either that or, "For Christ's sake, girl, stop staring!"

Nina proffers a gloved hand. "You had us worried, Joey," she says. "I'm so pleased you're all right now."

Joey eyes her outstretched hand in silence before touching it, briefly. Blast it, she's gone and struck the wrong note. Just over two years ago—shortly after his visit to Charlwood—Joey fell from the sky inside a tiny, twisted, blazing cockpit, so of course he's not *all right*. Perhaps he never will be. He wasn't wearing his goggles when it happened, and it's a miracle he didn't lose his sight. According to Guy, both his eyelids burned away entirely, and the plastic surgeon had to take skin from the inside of his arm, in order to make new ones.

"Just look at him!" Guy claps his friend on the chest. "He's more than *all right*! What a stroke of luck, finding someone who was willing to remake that ugly mug from scratch. Haven't I always said it was the only solution? Good old Archie McIndoe, plastic surgeon extraordinaire! No wonder they call him The Maestro."

Nina tenses, but Joey's face contorts into something like a smile and he barks with laughter.

"Ugly mug yourself. What about this lunch you promised me?"

"It's barely half past eleven!"

"So? I'm hungry right now. You're not going to argue with an invalid?"

"Invalid! Greedy bastard, more like. Come on then." Turning to Nina: "Darling? Are you ready?"

"Ready!"

She prods her stomach one last time, under the guise of smoothing her dress. Guy gives his left arm to his wife, and his right arm to his friend, and they process through the park like Dorothy and Co. from *The Wizard of Oz*. When they hesitate at a fork in the path, Nina says, "Follow the yellow brick road!" and Guy smiles, to show he gets the reference. Neither he nor Joey pick it up and play with it, though, and Nina is surprised to find herself blushing.

Joey walks fairly well, with the aid of Guy's arm and his walking stick. Nina has never been sure how bad the injuries were to the rest of his body; she only knows that his face took the brunt of it, and that everyone was relieved he had, at least, been wearing his flying gloves. His hands are shinier and lumpier than they were before, but their essential shape is more or less the same.

They pass a cluster of yellow primroses, and Joey says, "Guess I should have brought flowers, or something. For Nina, I mean, not for you."

"Don't be daft; Nina doesn't expect flowers."

"No, of course I don't!"

She almost adds something conventionally polite, about how seeing Joey up and about is the best present anyone could wish for—but why say it, when it will only fall flat? The day has barely started, but it's going wrong. Nina makes a conscious effort to think one positive thought, and it takes a while, but it comes to her as they're leaving the park: her husband is happy. He really is.

Of course, this is a good thing in itself. Also, it might make him more open to her news, when she finally has the chance to break it.

. . .

LONDON, RATHER LIKE GUY, HAS an air of triumphant exhaustion. She noticed it this morning, even before she arrived, as her train was rattling through the western edges of the city.

Nina has grown used to travelling between Oxford and Paddington, ever since she and Guy were reposted at the end of '43—the capital being the obvious place to meet up. There was nothing wildly novel about the view from the train today—the same heaps of charred, weedy rubble where houses used to stand; the same crude graffiti under the railway arches; the same tattered recruitment posters on grimy station walls—and yet something had changed. The people she glimpsed on the streets seemed less dogged and hunched; they had ungritted their teeth. Several bombed-out terraces sported streamers and lopsided strings of bunting, and someone had scrawled *We beat the Heil out of Hitler!* in drippy paint, on a factory wall. In a small park, where a man was throwing a ball for his dog, Nina spotted the relics of a huge bonfire.

Something of the same spirit is alive in the august streets of Westminster. Strangers smile complicitly when you catch their eye. Distinguished-looking men stand around with their hands in their pockets, joking amongst themselves, as if they have all the time in the world. Even the grumpy-looking people (and there are still plenty of them) look more at ease in their ill humour.

Two girls run past, doubled over with giggles, and Nina struggles not to think about Rose. She says, "It's nice to see people laughing again."

"We laughed through the war," Guy objects. "In fact, we laughed a lot; we hardly stopped."

"Yes, but in a different way."

Nina spots a scrap of paper—a little Union Jack—that's been swept up against the curb. Its colours have run in the rain, but even so, she'd like to rescue it, and keep it as a VE-day souvenir. By now, though, the men have set a good, rhythmic walking pace, and she doesn't like to disrupt it, for Joey's sake.

. . .

THEY END UP AT A crowded café, off Piccadilly, eating corned beef sandwiches and drinking weak tea. Joey has to sit with his left leg sticking out, because he can't bend it properly at the knee, but nobody complains. Whenever the waitress has to step over his foot—which is pretty often—she bobs her head and murmurs, "Sorry." She adds a currant bun to their lunch order, and puts the extra plate in front of Joey.

"On the house," she says, shyly.

"Lucky sod!" says Guy, when she's gone. "That's what you get for sporting the all-out war hero look."

"Guy . . ." Nina frowns.

"Yeah." Joey's unreadable eyes are fixed on the plate. "A free currant bun and a whole ton of pity. Aren't I the lucky one?"

Guy leans forwards, lowering his voice. "It's not *pity*! She doesn't *pity* you, you nitwit; she thinks you're a god. They all do."

They meaning "females in general"? Nina glances swiftly at Joey's new face and takes a large bite from her sandwich, so that she can't be expected to chime in. It's his eyes that are difficult to get used to: they don't crease at the corners anymore when he smiles, and the lids seem outsized and puffy. Then there's the stiff, white, hairless upper lip, which was also grafted using skin from his arm, and the scarring all over his scalp. Joey's hair is cut short—shorter than a soldier's; more like a convict's—and it looks as though someone has been drawing lines on his head, in red ink.

The last time Nina saw him, some months ago, at the Queen Victoria Hospital, his face was masked by a sheet of white gauze. She and Guy had called at a bad time, shortly after he'd been wheeled back to the ward after yet another operation, and they'd sat hand in hand by the bed for an hour or more, watching him sleep. There was a slit in the gauze where his mouth should be, and you could tell he was still breathing by the way it fluttered.

Nina thinks of Frankenstein's monster, pieced together from dead body parts, and rebukes herself for shallowness. If Guy had suffered the same injuries, she would love him as much as ever, if not more. She would kiss his mouth with the same fervour, if it lost its familiar shape and sensitivity; if it were a white slab . . .

"Are you all right, darling?" says Guy. "You've stopped eating."

"I'm not terribly hungry. Have my sandwich, if you like."

She feels strange again, and shuffles discreetly in her seat, but it makes no difference. *God help me*, she mouths, silently, over the rim of her teacup. *I'm pregnant.* She doesn't intend anyone to lip-read—not really—and they don't.

Nina rests her chin on her hand and looks around, while the men pick at her sandwich and natter about their schooldays. Clouds of cigarette smoke curl through the sunlight and hover above the tables. An old man frowns over a coffee-stained menu; a middle-aged couple share a slice of cake; a mother and her adolescent daughter conduct a whispered argument at the table in the window. Nina's attention lingers on these last two. The girl is angry and talkative; the mother, patient and tired. She's one of those unselfconscious women who don't know how to make the best of themselves—are clueless, in fact, when it comes to clothes and hair—but who possess a certain spark, which saves them from out-and-out frumpery. Nina is put in mind of Kate Nicholson, and turns away at once.

She often sees things that put her in mind of Kate and Pip. A lush summer garden will do it, or a willow-pattern teacup, or clothes hanging on a pulley-dryer. It's a bit like being haunted, she supposes—only it might be simpler to exorcise a couple of bona fide wraiths, than these spectres of flesh and blood. Sometimes she thinks she'll write a letter to Kate, laying out her excuses (*Guy insists your marriage was over before we began our affair, and I want to believe him, but the truth is I've never been sure, and I know I should have made sure . . .*) and begging forgiveness (*if you could find it in your heart . . .*)—but why should Kate give a fig for Nina's youth, and her run-of-the-mill faults, and her commonplace excuses? Why on earth should she forgive? There's nothing in it for her.

Nina offers the teapot round, but Joey shakes his head, so she shares the stewed remains with Guy.

"What's next, then?" Joey asks, addressing her. "Where does the yellow brick road lead from here?" When she looks blank, he clarifies: "What are your peacetime plans?"

Nina reaches across the table for Guy's hand. This is a better train of thought. It is exhilarating, and frightening, to remember that the two of them have a future; that she no longer has to accept the likelihood of her husband's death, if not this week then the next. She might not be a widow till she's a very old woman; she might die first, and not be a widow at all. Just as she's about to say, "We haven't really discussed it yet," Guy tells Joey, "Canada! That's what's next!"

Ah, thinks Nina, fondly. *The log cabin in the snow-bound forest, with the bears prowling round, and maple syrup for breakfast.* She smiles, and begins to explain the joke, but Guy interrupts.

"Seriously. Nina and I first started talking about this... goodness knows when. I thought it best to wait till the war was over, and you were properly on the mend, before bringing you in on it. I'm not sure I ever believed the day would come, but now it has; it really, truly, honest-to-goodness has!"

Guy slaps the table, making the teacups rattle, and heads turn all over the room. He bursts out laughing, although he sounds as close to crying.

"How about it, Roussin? We always said we would, as kids, but I'm not sure I ever meant it till now."

Joey looks at Guy, his face warping into something that conveys affection, even if it couldn't rightly be called a smile. He cuts the bun into thirds and shares them out. Nina picks at the currants. *Canada?* She hasn't even thought of it as a real country before now. Surely, surely, Joey will tell Guy not to be such an ass, and the conversation will move on to some smaller, safer topic.

"Y'know what?" Joey says, once he's swallowed his chunk. "It's funny, but I had a letter from Aunt Calla, only last week. She's talking of selling up the farm now that Uncle Bram is dead—this is the farm I spent my summers, as a kid—and I was thinking—just idly thinking, y'know—that I might put in a bid. I reckon she'd give me first refusal."

"You might put in a... but that's... good heavens! Why on earth didn't you tell me?"

"I'm telling you now, aren't I? I was working round to it, only you got in first with your little speech."

"But Roussin, that's marvellous! Your own farm!"

"Hey, I only said I was *thinking* about it. Even if I could afford the old place, I wouldn't be fit enough to manage it by myself, the way things have turned out. Of course, a farm in rural Manitoba mayn't be what you and Nina have in mind ..."

Guy squeezes Nina's fingers so fiercely, she's afraid the bones will crack. People are staring at their table; even the adolescent girl by the window has forgotten her grievance for a moment, and turned round. Nina wants to say, *Hang on a minute!* but she can't; not here and now; not with everyone watching. She frees her hand from Guy's grasp and wraps her fragment of bun in a paper napkin. The men are talking over one another, unable to give voice to their rapture except via a lively discussion of practicalities.

They talk and talk—about property valuations, milk yields, bank loans, and acreages—until Canada is no longer a far-fetched dream for two, but a realistic proposition for three. Nina slips the paper napkin inside her coat pocket. She would give all the coupons in her ration book to be by herself, with space to think, but there's no hope of solitude for hours.

. . .

GUY FLOPS ONTO THE BED with a sigh, while Nina sits on one of the chintz armchairs and kicks her shoes off. The curtains are drawn against the darkness, the pink-shaded lamps are glowing, and the only sound is the crackle of the wood fire.

"Nina?"

"Mmm?"

"Why are you sulking?"

"I'm not sulking!"

"You've been like this all day."

"I have not!"

"Is it to do with Joey?"

There's a tap at the door and Mrs. Wallace enters with a tray.

"Sorry to disturb. I thought you might need a little something after your long drive."

The old lady has been a darling, considering that they arrived at the guesthouse—the Maltings—two hours later than expected. It was getting dark by the time they dropped Joey at the convalescent home in East Grinstead, and then they managed to get lost in the lanes of rural Sussex. It's true that they haven't talked much, since saying goodbye to Joey. During the drive, Nina pretended to doze, her head bumping against the car window, while Guy focussed on the road and smoked his pipe.

Mrs. Wallace unloads the tray onto the table by the fire: two cups of cocoa and a plate of bread with butter and honey. They thank her warmly, as befits such a lovely young couple (that's what she called them, when they were signing in), but their expressions fade the moment she leaves. Guy slumps back on the bed and Nina stares unseeingly at the fire.

"You didn't seem very pleased to see him," Guy resumes.

"Didn't I?"

"Do his injuries offend your aesthetic sensibilities?"

The question demands an immediate retort (*What a horrible thing to say!*) but Nina hesitates, out of a desire to answer truthfully. She and Guy have always prided themselves on being brutally honest with one another; ever since the start of their affair, they have brandished their ability to say the unsayable as proof of their own specialness. Then again, it's not too difficult to be brutally honest about other people—Rose, for example, and Henry, and all the other people who have given them the cold shoulder since they got together. It occurs to Nina that she has said the words, *Darling, I feel that I can tell you anything*, more often than she has actually ventured a risky idea. She frowns, now, and stirs the cocoa.

"Of course it's hard to look at his poor face," she says, "remembering how it used to be."

"There's nothing *poor* about Joey Roussin."

"You know what I mean. Anyway, it's really nothing to do with his face. I was so excited to see you, after weeks and weeks of being apart; I admit to being a little disappointed when your *marvellous surprise* turned out to be a third party."

Guy stares wordlessly at the ceiling. Nina gets up and places a cup of cocoa beside the bed.

"Also," she says, "there's the question of Canada."

He turns his head in her direction, as she sits back down.

"Question?"

"Yes. I didn't realise it was something we genuinely intended to do. We've only ever talked about it in bed, on the edge of sleep. I thought it was a fantasy. A dream."

"It *was*. At times I thought it impossible that the war would ever end, let alone that Joey and I would still be alive when it did. Forgive me for being pleased that it did, and we are."

"*Joey and I*," Nina echoes, as if to herself.

Guy rolls onto his side and props himself up on one elbow.

"Yes! Joey and I! How in God's name do you suppose we'd cope on a dairy farm without him? You wouldn't know one end of a cow from another, and no more would I!"

"Shh!" Nina holds up her palm for quiet. It would be dreadful if Mrs. Wallace heard them quarrelling. "All right. Listen, I'm not saying emigration is a bad idea. Maybe it's a very good idea. But it's not our only option, is it? We ought to think about it, and talk together, just the two of us, before jumping in with both feet. I know Joey is your dearest friend, practically a brother—I understand that—but I am your wife!"

Silence.

"That *is* how the hierarchy goes, isn't it?"

The fateful dinner party flashes into her mind. August 1934. Guy and Joey as a two-headed beast, getting drunk together; insulting Dad together; belittling Kate together; stalking her—Nina—into the dark garden. The flicker of Joey's tongue on her bare young arm. She shakes her head and it's gone again.

"Don't be childish, Nina. Tell me what you mean when you say emigration isn't our only option. What other possibilities are there?"

"Oh, what a question!" She laughs incredulously. "We could do anything!"

"Such as?"

Nina shifts in her seat. Her hands are trembling, ever so slightly, and she puts her cup down in case the cocoa spills.

"Oh goodness, I don't know." She pretends to rack her brains. "We could . . . we could buy a house in Lincoln and start a family."

"*Lincoln?*"

"I love Lincoln! It's where we met—sort of—if you discount Cottenden, which I try to."

Guy laughs, sourly. "Even so, I can't say my happiest memories—"

"Oh, fine, not Lincoln then! You're missing the point. I only meant—"

"Are you trying to tell me that you want to have children?"

Nina shrugs, shakily. "Not necessarily. It was only—"

"Well, if you are, the answer is no."

Guy rolls onto his back and flings his arm across his eyes. Nina watches for a softening of his posture; a relenting look, or word. A minute passes, and another, but nothing changes.

"Guy . . . ?"

"I'm sorry, darling, but no. Fatherhood is one possible future I won't consider, not even for you." He drops his arm onto the bed and looks at her, sidelong. "I thought you knew that? I thought you agreed with me?"

"But I just wonder—now that the war is over—why not? Or, at any rate, why so emphatically not?"

God, they must remember to keep their voices down.

"Because!" Guy slams his fists on the mattress. "Because I've tried it once, and made a bloody hash of it, and I don't care to repeat the experiment."

Nina picks up a slice of bread. It's got real butter and everything, but she gives up after one bite and returns it to the plate.

Poor little Phillip Nicholson, with his weedy frame and chesty cough, and no father to speak of. And yet, like Joey, not "poor," when you think about it. He has a lovely house with a big garden, and a doting mother who bakes biscuits, and reads to him, and calls him, rather soppily, *Pip*. It seems a fair bet that Kate never harboured any doubts about motherhood. A warm glow of complacency would have nourished her throughout the nine months of pregnancy, and beyond. She'd have talked about nothing but babies, babies, babies, and bored Guy rigid with facts about feeding schedules, and weaning, and . . . whatever else.

Those two, again. Nina's personal ghosts. Oh God, if only Pip *were* a spoilt brat with everything going for him; if only Kate *were* soppy and complacent and uninteresting.

If only Nina could make it so, by wishing.

"Just because you left your first wife and child, it doesn't mean you're incapable of loving me and *our* child."

The words sound even more searing than she intends, and she regrets them at once. She looks at her husband fearfully, as he swings his feet to the floor and stands up.

"Don't, Nina!"

"Don't what?"

"Don't tell me what I do, or do not, feel for my own son!"

Nina wishes she could weep on demand, like the best actresses, but she can only stiffen her shoulders and stare at the embers. She actually means it when she says, "Sorry," but it sounds as though she doesn't.

Guy drains his cup in one gulp, grabs a towel from the stand, and stomps off down the landing. She can hear him in the bathroom, running the taps at full pelt, and cursing when he drops the soap. Nina puts her head in her hands and wonders—since it's the least of her several worries—what on earth Mrs. Wallace must be thinking.

. . .

GUY AND NINA UNDRESS SHYLY, like strangers forced to share a room. Guy climbs into bed first, and turns his back, while Nina pulls her nightie over her head. A bath would be nice—London has left her feeling stale—but it's far too late now. She potters about, folding their clothes and stacking the cups on the tray, and when she can think of nothing else to do, she switches off the lamps and slides between the sheets. The fire is too low to lift the darkness, and she can't see Guy at all, but she can feel the faint movement of his breathing, and knows he's not asleep. The brushed-cotton bedding smells of wind and sunshine, and the mattress is divinely soft. Dad would say it was bad for the posture—but she must stop thinking about Dad.

Nina opens her eyes as wide as they'll go, forcing herself not to blink, but the tears won't come. If she were to cry Guy would have to turn round and comfort her, or at any rate, he'd have to do something; say something. She recalls the weeping fits she used to have as a child, and the way her father would lift her onto his knees, and dab at her flushed face with his handkerchief. It was never a ploy on her part—the stuttering sobs were real—but goodness, it was handy when it came to breaking stalemates.

Ah, but she was little and innocent then. It might not work now.

"Guy?"

Nina reaches out and rests her hand on his side. He doesn't respond, but he doesn't pull away, either.

"Guy? I'm sorry I said that about Phillip. It was stupid. I didn't mean it."

He shuffles his legs and sighs, and eventually reaches round for her hand. The silence is taut, and Nina is loathe to break it. When it comes to Phillip, Guy's guilt runs deep; she's always thought it must be so, and now she's sure. *Tread carefully*, she thinks. Her mouth is dry, and she has to swallow twice before she can continue.

"I like Joey," she says, although it's not entirely true. "I don't want you to think I don't." (That part is true.)

Guy strokes her fingers with his thumb. "I suppose I should have told you he was coming along today."

"It doesn't matter."

Nina wriggles closer, until their bodies are almost touching.

Guy draws breath, as if to speak, but seems to have second thoughts. Nina waits, and eventually he says, "As for Canada—"

"I think it's the right thing to do."

"No, you don't."

"I do! Really! Why would I want to stay in England? My career is about to fizzle out; my father has disowned me; all my old friends have written me off as a bad job."

"But darling... Maybe you need longer to think about it."

"No. I'm sure."

Guy swivels onto his right side, so that they're lying face to face. He tries to kiss her lips, but misses them in the darkness, and finds her nose and chin instead. At least it's something for them both to smile about.

They don't fit so well this way round, but she can stroke his hair and feel his breath on her cheek. Now is the time to break the news about you-know-what.

Now?

Yes. Now.

Nina takes a deep breath. Downstairs, a clock chimes the half hour.

Oh, but how to find the right words? She's darned if she'll be apologetic, since it's as much his doing as hers. On the other hand, a panicky tone will make everything wrong, and God help her if she tries to put a positive spin on things. Even a neutral tone is likely to rile him (*Good grief, Nina, how can you be so calm?*). If she tries to be herself, she'll end up sounding sulky—because that's how she comes across when she's upset—and it's already been established that she can't weep to order.

The clock strikes quarter to. Nina counts every chime before moistening her lips and whispering, "Guy?"

His body jolts reflexively and he mutters, from the depths of a dream, about Leipzig and the towers of Lincoln Cathedral.

"*Guy?*"

"To the . . . to the left . . . when I've plotted the course . . . but I can't . . ."

Nina gives up. It will have to wait till tomorrow. When the clock strikes midnight she disentangles herself from his arms and gets up. She paces stiffly round the bed, her arms wrapped across her stomach, trying to remember whether there's a bottle of aspirin in her sponge bag. Even if there is, she'll never be able to find it in the dark; for all her clumsy groping, she can't even locate the light switch.

It takes her ages to get down the landing to the bathroom, and she stubs her toe twice on the way. The light comes on with a rackety *clack* when she pulls the cord, and she is careful to bolt the door quietly. The pink tiles are nice and cool against the soles of her feet, but their fleshy colour makes her feel faint.

What is it? she wonders, meeting the eyes of the pasty-faced woman in the mirror. *What's happening?*

Nina is still asking the question when the answer comes. Outwardly, she remains perfectly still, but internally she trips and falls, and the sensation is weird enough to make her whimper. She hitches up her nightie in time to see gore dropping down the insides of her thighs, spattering the floor and pooling between her toes. Most of it is ruby red and liquid, but there are stringy bits as well, and clumps like black jelly.

"Oh . . ." says a reedy voice that must be her own, and it occurs to her that it might be better if she didn't look. She grasps the rim of the basin with both hands, and stares straight ahead, at the mirror.

Her reflection smiles back, but it's a feeble effort, a grimace, worse than no smile at all. She shudders as an icy wave washes her from head to foot. It's all right, though. From this moment on, everything will be all right. The gush has dwindled to a trickle; the trickle is stopping; she's not going to die; there'll be no baby anymore.

No baby.

"Thank you, God," whispers the woman in the mirror, at the same time as her features waver and crumple. "Thank you."

Nina clutches the sides of the basin, hangs her head, and cries as silently as she can. If she could explain these tears away as tokens of relief, she would, but that's not what they are; not entirely. Dad always held that women were illogical creatures, and it looks like he was right, after all. Her mother would have understood. Or Rose.

A door opens farther down the landing, and slippered feet come flapping to the bathroom door. There's a subdued tap.

"Mrs. Nicholson?"

Nina wipes her face on her sleeve.

"Mrs. Wallace?" It's almost more than she can manage, her voice is so clogged with tears and mucus.

"Can I help you, dear?"

Maybe, thinks Nina, hopefully, but on reflection she shakes her head and croaks, "No." She wants to add *Thanks*, but it's beyond her powers.

She hardly dares look at the slaughterhouse floor. How can she possibly clean it up, on her own, in secret? She has a dressing-gown in her suitcase, and a spare blouse. If she uses the blouse to scoop up the worst, and then soaks the dressing-gown under the hot tap, and smears it with a bit of soap . . .

"Mrs. Nicholson?"

Go away, lovely Mrs. Wallace.

At long last the old lady sighs and shuffles off, and Nina sinks to her knees. Now that it comes to it—now that the problem is not an inability to cry, but an inability to stop—she finds it's better to be alone, after all.

✳10✳

Kate

December 6, 1945

AS OFTEN AS NOT, I WILL DROP IN AT 7 CANAL ROAD, ONLY TO find Henry sitting by himself in the cold and semi-darkness. I say *sitting*, although I don't actually know what he's doing before he opens the door: he could be doing circuits of the kitchen to keep warm, for all I know, or lying face down on the floor.

Oh, he'll gladly light the fire and make the place snug for a visitor, but he won't do it for himself. He says it's because of coal rationing, but I'm sure there's more to it than that. We had a row on the subject, only a couple of days ago. I accused him of needing to be mothered all the time, and he said, "Is that so very terrible?" to which I replied, "As long as you don't expect *me* to do the mothering." Henry has a temper, especially if he feels he's being ridiculed (I called him an *overgrown child*, which did not go down well), but at least his outbursts are short-lived. We parted on bad terms, but he telephoned within the hour to apologise.

"You won't give up on me—on our friendship—will you, Kate?"

"Don't be daft."

"You won't though, will you?"

It's windy this afternoon, the rain is ice cold, and I've forgotten my gloves. It's only because I'm meeting Pip from school that I'm out of doors at all, otherwise I'd be huddled by the range in our oversized kitchen, tackling my darning, or writing a list of groceries, or (more likely) reading the last few chapters of *Frenchman's Creek*. Don't most people long for interior light and warmth, on days like this? Yet here's Henry, drifting towards the frosted-glass panels on the front door, like a ghost emerging from the gloom. I dare myself to say that to his face, but teasing Henry Woodrow is a risky business, and we mustn't fall out again.

"Kate!"

"Hello."

I resist the temptation to kiss his cheek (for months—years—I've been resisting this temptation, yet it still presents itself, every time) and ask, "Any chance I can warm my hands at the fire that's surely blazing in your ever-so-cosy sitting-room?"

"Sorry, sorry, sorry, I'll light it now." He smiles. "Come on in."

Henry leads the way to the sitting-room, where the hearth is not only unlit, but bare, except for a twist of newspaper and a few sticks of kindling. He reaches for the scuttle. "I'll just dash outside for some coal. Won't be a second. Make yourself at home."

It's too chilly to remove my coat, or even to sit still, so I bunch my hands in my pockets and pace about. There's a pale-pink envelope on the desk, propped between the lamp and the paperweight, addressed to *Mrs. Nina Nicholson, c/o Mr. Henry Woodrow, 7 Canal Road, Cottenden, Chester.* It's the surname that catches my eye—for a jolting second I think it must be for me—and I pick it up, and look it over, before putting it back in its place. The postmark says *Buxton*. I wonder who the letter is from, and what Henry feels when he reads the name *Mrs. Nina Nicholson*, and whether it will ever reach her, in Canada. I shiver and turn on my heel, to stop myself from staring at it.

The room feels horribly damp and draughty. How on earth can Henry bear it all day? It's a pity his parents left him a house and a private income, because it saves him having to work, and a job would do him good. I wonder what prevents him from joining the Home Guard, since he's too old to enlist in the regular armed services, but I suggested it once, and he looked at me as if I'd handed him a white feather for cowardice. "I do my bit, Kate," he said, to which I replied, rather too bluntly, "Do you? What does that amount to then?" and you can imagine how *that* was received.

Well, since he won't deign to keep busy (barring his voluntary roles at church), and will insist on brooding in Rochester-like solitude, what on earth stops him from doing so in comfort? Even at his most blind and broken-hearted, Mr. Rochester didn't say no to candles and a fire.

There's a chipped saucer on the windowsill, holding three cigarette butts. One of them still glows with a tiny orange spark, which greys and dies while I watch. Henry started smoking a couple of years ago, though he never lights up in public, or even in front of me. I picture him standing right here at the window, smoking one fag after another, watching December days shrink into December evenings. The sad thing is, there's nothing very comforting about the view from the french window: just shrubs, and a muddy lawn, and the remnants of a treehouse in the bare, dripping branches of the cherry tree.

"Hello, Shirl," I say softly as I wander over to the bookcase. She's watching me from her favourite spot, under the sofa. Shirley's all right, really; she just gets on edge when people talk loudly, or look at her too directly. When I touch one of the books, she makes a little rumbling noise in her throat, so I put my hand back in my pocket.

I wonder how often I've perused the spines of these books, since my friendship with Henry began? Starting from the top shelf, working from left to right, they go (and you'll have to take my word for it, that I can do this with my eyes closed): ancient history books, modern history books, Arthurian legends and Greek myths, gardening manuals, a complete set of Shakespeare, *Encyclopaedia Britannica*, the *Oxford English Dictionary* in thirteen volumes, an *Illustrated Atlas of the World, Caring for Your Dog* by R. M. Stewart, *The Interpretation of Flowers* by Dora and Emily Pettit, *Mrs. Beeton's Everyday Cookery and Housekeeping Book*, and a collection of nineteenth-century poetry books, which he inherited from one of his uncles. Henry says he reads, and I'm sure he does, but everything is always in its place and gathering dust. I think he prefers *The Times* to books.

Mind you, there was one occasion when I did notice a volume out of place, and I count it among the most peculiar events of my life. This would be over a year ago, in the summer of 1944, and the volume in question was *The Poems of John Clare*. It was lying on the arm of the sofa—closed, but bookmarked with a pencil—and when Henry disappeared to the kitchen to put the kettle on, I picked it up and opened it to a short poem called "The Secret." Well! Not only had the first two lines of the poem been underscored, but the word *Kate* had been written beside them, in the margin. The lines in question go:

I loved thee, though I told thee not,
Right earlily and long

I stared for some time—a tad more slack-jawed than your ideal romantic heroine, perhaps—but I was sufficiently self-possessed to put the book back before Henry returned from the kitchen. I didn't say anything, partly because I couldn't bear the awkwardness, and partly because—I admit—I rather enjoyed the romance of it. What if Henry had said: "Oh, that? Uncle Bob must have written that, when he was a young man . . . Why? You didn't think that *I* . . . ?"

The whole incident remained a sacred mystery for an entire afternoon, until I went and told Deb over the telephone. Mike had been killed earlier that month—two days after D-Day, in fact—and the grief was making her angry.

"For God's sake, Kate, stop asking me how I am. Talk about something else, can't you?"

So I did.

"Well, of course this Woodrow fellow was referring to you!" she exclaimed. "And of course he meant you to read it! Honestly, Kate, for a middle-aged divorcée you can be terribly naïve."

"I'm not naïve! You make him sound . . . I don't know . . . predatory. Henry's not trying to seduce me, or anything; he's not like that."

"No? Well, why isn't he? You're in your mid-thirties, and you reckon he's pushing fifty. That makes you both too old for unrequited passions and sappy poems."

"Deb! Look, let's just change the subject, shall we?"

I couldn't hang up, or get in a huff, given how recently she'd been widowed. We ended up talking about our parents' cats again—we always seem to be discussing the various ways in which Inky bullies poor Olivia, and what should be done about it—but our hearts weren't in it, that day.

My mind is still on Deb when Henry returns with the coal scuttle. I can smell the fresh air on his clothes, as he kneels to lay the fire.

"I spoke to my elder sister, yesterday," I say, perching on the arm of the sofa. "She thinks Pip and I should move back home; she says she could find me a job in the bookshop."

Henry strikes a match and moves the flame along the edge of the newspaper. He doesn't seem to have heard me, and I'm about to repeat myself when he says, "I thought *this* was your home? Cottenden, I mean."

I'm surprised.

"Did you?"

I study Henry's slender shoulders, and the back of his head. His greying hair is kept tidy by Mary Fellowes, four doors down, even though she's really a ladies' hairdresser. There are all sorts of people—mostly women—eager to do kindnesses for poor Mr. Woodrow. Mrs. Dempsey seems to spend half her life knitting him belated Christmas presents, or early birthday presents, or vice versa, depending on the time of year. The blue-grey pullover he's wearing now is one of hers.

I know what you're thinking. You're thinking, *Less of the supercilious tone, Kate Nicholson.* And you're right; it's true; I'm one of them; I'm a top-ranking member of the "Poor Mr. Woodrow" brigade. There was a time, not so very long ago, when I couldn't have contemplated leaving the village because I couldn't have contemplated leaving him. Deb reckons I had some kind of mental breakdown in the spring of '43, and she's probably right, though she assumes it was all Guy's fault, whereas I know there was more to it than that.

Mental breakdown is Deb's term for whatever it was that got me. I like it. It makes everything sound fixable, as if the vagaries of the human mind are no more disturbing than the vagaries of a conked-out lawn-mower. Mind you, that's not what it felt like at the time. In 1943, and early '44, I thought I was losing my soul, and slithering head first into hell. My whole being consisted of Henry, Henry, Henry. I used to pray, *Please God, let Guy be killed soon, so that Henry will do away with all his scruples and have me*—and this wasn't only when I was twisting and sweating in my bed at night, but when I was helping Pip with his homework, and when I was beavering away at the "Knit for Victory!" group, and in church, as well, when I was kneeling in my Sunday best and saying all the right words from the Order of Service.

"We would never see each other," Henry says now, "if you moved to Carlisle."

"That's not true, and anyway, we could write. I'd like that. I'm a better letter writer than I am a conversationalist."

His head and shoulders slump, and he doesn't look round.

"Henry?"

He prods at the smoking coals with the brass poker.

"My brother will be home soon," I add, a touch sharply. "That's another factor. I'm not sure it would be fair to leave my parents and sisters to look after him on their own. Not that Janey will be able to do much, anyway; she's still down south. Everything will fall to Deb, and she's already got three adolescents on her hands, not to mention a business to run."

Henry replaces the poker on its hook and sits back on his heels.

"I thought your brother had come through all right?"

"Ron has survived," I clarify. "He can function, more or less. He can walk and breathe and talk, although he's got a stammer now, which he never used to."

I think of the few, strange letters I've had from Ron, and the one very expensive, very fuzzy telephone call from Australia, where he's convalescing. For want of a better idea, I fired questions at him, which he answered vaguely and with effort, or not at all. I remember asking whether he was starting to feel stronger, to which he replied that he'd "g . . . g . . . gone up to . . . s-s-six and a half stone." In September, when the Japanese surrendered and the camps were liberated, he'd weighed five.

Henry maintains his silence, and momentarily I loathe us both: two well-fed decadents playing at being lovelorn; wallowing in the romance of self-denial; acting as if our finer feelings mattered one jot. When I'd asked my brother if he was sleeping okay, he'd started sobbing down the telephone. I said, "Forgive me, Ron, I didn't mean to say the wrong thing," but he kept on crying, and in my mind's eye I saw him as a little boy in blue-striped pyjamas, prone to bad dreams, like Pip.

"I'm sorry," Henry says now. "Of course you should go, if that's where you're needed. I only wish—"

He hesitates, and my irritation melts, as usual. I kneel beside him, on the hearthrug.

"Oh Kate, I wish things were different; I wish I could give you a reason to stay."

Henry can't bring himself to touch a married woman—we don't even shake hands—but sometimes he will say something that's as close to a caress as words can ever be. We both fall quiet, and Henry stares at his inmost thoughts, while I stare at his face in profile. The unsteady firelight gives him a less definite expression than usual. Any second now he will say something down to earth, because that's what he always does at moments of danger—or possibility—when we are sitting so close that our elbows almost touch, and the silence is stretched to breaking point.

"I'd offer you tea," he says, "but I've run out of milk."

I laugh, and he glances up, as much as to say, *What's funny?*

"Or if you don't mind drinking it black . . . ?"

"No, I'm fine, thanks."

Henry rattles a few more coals over the bright flames. Conversation is obviously not going to flow today.

"There's a letter on the desk, addressed to Nina," I remark, and although he doesn't move a muscle, I feel him withdraw.

"I'm aware of that. It's from an old friend of hers: Rose Allen. She and Nina were as thick as thieves when they were children. Not that I've read it, I hasten to add; I just recognise the handwriting."

"Rose Allen . . . I think I met her, once."

He keeps piling on the coals, which looks like a mistake to me, because the flames are smothered and the whole thing starts smoking again. I might be wrong, of course. I don't have the knack for lighting fires.

"Are you going to send it on to Nina?"

"No."

"Why not?"

"Why should I? Anyway, I haven't got a forwarding address."

"I've got Joey Roussin's childhood address, I think. It might be worth a shot."

"No."

He's lost that restless, querying expression, which I think of as typically "Henry," and which I've grown fond of over the years. I hate it when that happens.

"What a pair," he says. "Neither of them turned out to be any better than they should be."

"Who? Nina and Rose?"

He nods, and I frown. Whatever bad things Nina has done—never mind this Rose character—I'm not keen on Henry's purse-lipped tone, or the implication that he and I belong together on the complacent side of the weighing scales. If he thinks the goody-goodies are the ones who win out in the end, he can't have read enough fairy tales in his childhood.

Henry gets up from his knees and sinks, with a sigh, into his armchair.

"Don't become embittered," I plead, as if I didn't know it never works that way; that you can't tell even your dearest friends to be this, or be that, and expect them to obey.

He lifts his arms in a wide shrug, and drops them over the arms of the chair. I swivel round, so that we can look at one another as we talk, and spot Shirley watching from under the sofa. She never comes to greet Henry when he enters a room, but once he's there, she can't take her eyes off him.

"Nina is dead to me," he intones. "I don't have a daughter anymore."

"Don't be so silly," I snap, startling us both.

That was mean; Henry is obviously very low today. I will resist doing what I was about to do, that is, telling him to count his blessings and to be grateful he's not spent the last two years in a Japanese prisoner-of-war camp. That's the sort of logic that really ought to work, when it comes to rousing people from their doldrums, but never does—or not in my experience.

I frown at my scarf, and plait bits of the woolly fringe.

"Nina will always be your daughter," I point out. "Maybe you should consider forgiving her."

Henry gives me one of his narrow-eyed looks.

"Does that mean you've forgiven Guy?"

I consider the question, and find it surprisingly difficult to answer. Have I forgiven Guy? How would I know? Is forgiveness something you proclaim, or something you do, or something you feel . . . ?

"Well, I don't rail against him in my head all the time, like I used to. I had a phase, after he left, of fantasising I had the power to do awful things to him—to both of them—with a click of my fingers. You know, like, *Let Guy break his leg*, or *Let Nina's hair fall out*, or . . . well, much worse things than that, actually. I haven't had those thoughts for a while."

Henry is still slumped like a broken doll, with his arms hanging over the sides of the chair, studying me in silence. Slyly, soundlessly, he clicks his dangling fingers.

"Is anything forgivable, in your book?" It's not a neutral question. He used the same tone of voice when we were walking across the fields, last summer, and Shirley got waylaid by a cowpat. After slapping her across the shoulders with the lead, and dragging her away, he said, "What a bad dog you are. Honestly! Is anything edible, in your book?"

"*Is* anything forgivable?" This time there's a little less censure in his tone, and a little more curiosity.

"Yes!" I affirm. Then I remember the British Pathé film I saw in April, after Bergen-Belsen was liberated, and all the other photographs and reports that keep coming out of Europe. I think of Ron weighing in at five stone.

"No," I contradict myself. "But I'm pretty sure Nina and Guy are."

Henry neither agrees nor disagrees. Shirley crawls out from under the sofa and snuffles at his loosely curled hand, before plumping down at his feet.

"Anyway, never mind what's good for them," I say. "What about you? Don't you think it would be good for you to move on?"

Henry rubs his eyes. He looks very tired. Perhaps he's thinking about it; more likely, he's trying not to.

Poor Henry.

For nine years, in between meeting him for the first time and making friends with him again, I carried an image of 7 Canal Road in my mind. I always pictured it as sun-filled, rose-scented, and comfortable: a domestic paradise that we Nicholsons—not to mention Joey Roussin—were too crass to appreciate. These days, I picture it as it is now, with rain dribbling down uncurtained windows, a fire failing to take, and a coating of dust on all the books and paintings. There's a patch of mould on the ceiling, and a stain on the carpet where a spillage has been half-heartedly mopped up.

"How about a walk?" I suggest, and Shirley's head whips round. "Shirley says yes! Why not come with me to meet Pip from school?"

"But the weather's so . . . and I've only just lit the fire."

"We won't be long; it'll heat the room while you're out."

Henry shakes his head and smiles from some distant place in his mind.

"Thanks anyway, Kate."

. . .

I NEVER THOUGHT I'D SAY it, but I'm warming to Shirley. She hauls me along the pavements of Cottenden, all but yanking my arm from its socket, while the wind tries to shove us in different directions. "Steady on!" I shout, as we round the corner of Canal Road, and she barks back at me, wild with glee. Together we charge through puddles—leaky boots and wet paws be damned—turning our faces up to meet the rain. I wish Henry had come: it would have done him good, and I'd have welcomed a bit of extra muscle power. When we reach the main road I have to clutch the lead with both hands, and tug with all my might, to stop Shirley from charging across. A lorry hurtles by, shooting spray from under its wheels, and while I cry, "Urgh!" she makes bouncy circles on the spot, yapping her enthusiasm.

I wonder what December is like on the shores of Lake Winnipeg, and whether Pip and I would be there now, if we hadn't been replaced by Nina. Fierce, clean cold under big blue skies, and snow on snow: that's how I picture it, in my head. Whenever resentment floods my bloodstream, like a toxin, I tell myself that Pip would be happier and healthier on a Canadian farm, and that Guy must have known that, and done what he did in spite of it. It's probably untrue. I'm sure there are also Canadian boys who pick relentlessly at their scabs, and seem to have no close friends, and avoid confiding in their mothers.

Shirley has set such a pace that we arrive early at the school gates. The other mothers turn to survey us, but I keep my distance from their cluster as I stop to catch my breath. In the summer months, you know for sure when you're being shunned (I'm thinking of the little clique which refers to me as *that divorcée*) or pitied (the "Poor Kate" brigade is smaller and less fervent than the "Poor Mr. Woodrow" brigade, but it's still a force to be reckoned with). It's much easier in the midwinter dusk, with everyone wrapped up against the cold; it feels quite natural not to wave or talk.

One of them—the smart woman with the tight perm, whose umbrella never seems to blow inside out—glances at me and whispers, and a couple of the others laugh and say, "Shh!" It's funny to think that if Guy had been killed in the early years of the war, these women would dote on me and Pip; they'd be falling over themselves to invite the war hero's widow to their "dos," and his darling boy to their own children's birthday parties. Pip and I have been shoved into an inferior category of being, not for anything we've done, but because Guy lived, and took an executive decision to leave us. I don't mind for myself—I've no desire to simper and make small talk at their blessed coffee mornings—but I mind for Pip.

Shirley sits heavily on my foot, and I bend down to scratch her head and tell her she's a treasure. The walk must have put her in a good mood, because she accepts my attentions without demur, and it's obvious, to anyone who cares to look, that I'm perfectly at my ease.

Mrs. Tight Perm is saying something about Henry Woodrow. There are trees all along the edge of the playground, and the soughing of the wind in their branches makes it difficult to eavesdrop, but I catch the words "men will be men" and "Poor Mr. Woodrow" and "lady friend." Shirley blinks at me, wickedly, and I shrug back at her. None of this is news to me. Sometimes I wonder whether Henry has heard rumours of our torrid affair, but I'm too nervous to ask. It's safe to assume he wouldn't see the funny side.

There's the school bell now, and here come the children, bursting through the double doors: the shouters and gigglers, the scabby-kneed racers, the satchel twirlers, the chatterboxes, the solitary trudgers.

Pip is a trudger. He comes down the steps with his head lowered and starts for home without noticing us. Shirley and I have to set off in pursuit, and it's only after I've said his name twice—I won't shout, for fear of annoying him—that he turns. He doesn't have much to say, but I'm grateful for the nod, and the willingness with which he matches his pace to mine and Shirley's.

"You didn't need to meet me," he says, but he doesn't sound cross. Yesterday he came home with a cut under his eye, and when I asked where he got it, he muttered, "Just . . . I don't know . . . on the way home."

"I meant *how* did you get it?"

"I don't know. It was nothing."

"Pip?"

"Mum! Stop asking me questions *all the time*! You're like the bloody Nazis!"

I docked one week's pocket money for *Nazis* and another for *bloody* and sheer cheek, but it hasn't stopped me from worrying. It's enough to make me wish the Coxes were still with us, Hilda and all, but they went back to London in May. I watch, with suspicion, the boys pouring out of school—especially the large, confident ones—but I don't glean anything. Perhaps I'll make a habit of giving Shirley a walk at half past three on weekdays.

Perhaps I'll think more seriously about this proposed move to Carlisle.

"Good day?" I ask, when school is well behind us.

"Not bad."

We've passed the village pond and let Shirley loose in the playing field before he thinks to say, "You?"

"*You* what?"

We catch one another's eye, and I'm grateful for the half-smile, even if it does come with an eye-roll. He answers, with cartoonish over-emphasis: "Did you have a good day, Mum?"

"I did. Thank you."

We follow the dog round the edge of the field, past the football pitch and the swings and slides, and I resist pulling my son's arm through mine. It feels like a long time since I last pushed him on the swings, or waited for him at the bottom of the slide, and I have to remind myself he's only eleven. Sometimes he seems older than that—much, much older—as if every year of the war has cost us a peacetime decade.

Shirley gambols over, dragging a stick twice the length of her own body, and drops it at Pip's feet. He picks it up, with a show of reluctance, and flings it across the grass.

"You're honoured," I say, as Shirley hurtles after it.

Pip grunts, but when she brings the stick back he wrestles it off her and throws it again, and then again.

"I suppose we'll have to take her back to Mr. Woodrow?"

"Yes, but we won't stop."

Does Pip murmur, "Thank God," or do I just imagine it? Either way, spoken or not, it hovers in the space between us. I'm about to change the subject when he goes on, rapidly, with his eyes on Shirley and the stick: "I've told you before: I don't think you should have anything to do with that man."

"Pip! Listen, if people have been gossiping—"

"It's not about *people*; it's about Mr. Woodrow. I don't think he's a good man, Mum. I don't think you should go to his house on your own."

"Oh, Pip! Why do you say that?"

"Because—"

"—because of the 'creepy old letter' you found when you rifled through his desk?"

"I suppose."

Pip yanks the stick from Shirley's jaws and hurls it as far as he can.

"But what was it, Pip? What did it say?"

"I don't know, it was just horrible."

"But how can you say it was horrible if you don't know what it said?"

"Mum! I don't *know*!"

I suppose I should be thankful he's stopped referring to Henry as "Mr. Woodlouse"; we had to have stern words about that, a year or two back. I have pressed Pip to tell me about the afternoon when he went poking about in the Gothic desk, and I've got as far, but no further, than the "creepy old letter" he found. And then I think about the Henry I've come to know—soft-spoken, melancholy, prin-cipled Henry—and I can't believe my son discovered any real reason to dislike him. It's much more likely that he's suspicious of men in general, and if there's anyone to blame for that, it's Guy.

Guy came to see us, you know, in August. I spotted the car from the kitchen window, as it pulled up across the end of the drive, and I carried on washing the dishes while my former husband and his new wife talked together in the front seats. After five minutes or so, they kissed and he got out. She stayed put, looking as lovely and serene as ever: lipsticked, nail-varnished, headscarved, and masked by a pair of round sunglasses. If it were me, sitting outside the family home of the man I'd run off with, I think I'd squirm and sink a bit lower in my seat. Or wear a bag over my head. Or not be there at all. Nina just leaned one elbow on her open window, gazed down the leafy lane, and smoked. It must be wonderful to live your whole life in the certainty that you are the right person, doing the right thing, in the right place, at the right time—no matter what the critics say. I don't even mean it ironically; I'm serious. What a lot of heartache that would save.

As soon as I'd opened the front door and we'd said our hellos (a coolly surprised hello, on my part, a cautiously affable one on his), Guy came straight out with it: they were going to emigrate to Canada in a month's time, and he'd come to say goodbye. Was this a suitable time? Perhaps he should have written or called in advance . . . ?

Oh, but he was cocksure, standing there in his shirtsleeves, all tanned and healthy-looking, with a smear of lipstick at the corner of his mouth. *Nina and I*, he kept saying: Nina and I are off to Winnipeg; Nina and I were just passing through; Nina and I were hoping you'd be in.

How annoying to be here, precisely as expected, with a berry-stained apron and no pressing engagements. I was more than half inclined to make something up (*my car will be here shortly . . . new job in London . . . all rather hush-hush I'm afraid*), but the smell of simmering jam was a giveaway. I ushered him inside. He followed me to the sitting-room, and sat down on one of the blue armchairs we'd chosen together, shortly after our wedding.

"Canada!" I said.

"That's right."

He sounded like himself, briefly, when I offered him a drink ("Ah, bless you, Kate! Just the ticket!"), but perhaps tap water wasn't what he had in mind, because after he'd sipped, and masked a grimace, he turned into a visiting acquaintance again.

"So . . . ?" I prompted.

"So our plan is to buy the family farm off Joey's Aunt Calla—"

"Joey's in on all this?"

"Uh-huh. The first six months or so we're going to stay with his parents in Rossett Falls, near Winnipeg, and get some funds together—Joey's going back to his old job as a clerk at the registry office, and I'm going to join him there, all being well. Then once we're ready, and Aunt Calla's ready, we'll make the move."

"Farmers! You and Joey!"

"That's the idea!"

And Nina?

I thought of her waiting in the car, headscarf knotted elegantly beneath her chin; lips a perfect Cupid's bow. Whoever she was, she wasn't the shy tomboy I met eleven years ago, with bruised shins and scruffy jumper. Presumably Guy had noticed that. He, of all people, would have the measure of her.

"What does Nina make of your scheme?"

"Oh, she can't wait! She and I have been planning this for years; ever since we met."

I made no reply, and the room's chilly echo seemed to accentuate the clumsiness of his statement. Guy—even Guy—must have noticed, because he added, in a much smaller voice, "Sorry."

I shook my head.

"Don't worry. I've done all my crying and shouting. I wish you both well."

He nodded his thanks, and a page seemed to turn in my mind. *Finis*, I read there. *The End.*

I did not imagine, and I don't imagine now, that we would ever meet again. We had been married for a long time, and been friends longer still; that was why I'd asked him in, rather than keeping him on the doorstep. Of course we would have important things to say to one another at the end—the very, very end—wouldn't we? Or perhaps not. How strange. Guy had a lot of water left in his glass, and he seemed to be sipping it ever so slowly.

"You don't have to finish that, you know."

Guy returned the glass to the table, and placed his hands on his knees, which looked like a prelude to standing up. It wasn't. He said, "Phillip . . . Pip . . ."

I shivered. "What about him?"

Guy cleared his throat, and I waited, but he didn't seem able to go on.

"I ought to check on the jam," I said, eventually.

He followed me to the kitchen and leaned against the countertop, watching as I stirred the jam and inspected it, to see if it was ready. (I never can tell.) He used to hang about like that in the old days, and I used to say he was like a pet dog on the lookout for titbits. He used to pass me things I needed—a sieve, a tea-towel, a cup— while we chatted about humdrum things: his day at work, or the news in general, or our small son's latest antics.

"What sort of jam is it?"

"Gooseberry. What did you want to say about Pip?"

"I just wondered whether he might see me . . . whether I might be allowed to say goodbye?"

My head went light for a second, as if I was about to faint, though it passed without Guy noticing. What on earth had I expected?

That Guy was going to take Pip with him, to Canada? That he had come armed with court orders, to fetch him away? Ridiculous, Kate. Quite apart from anything else, it was difficult to imagine Nina Woodrow—I do beg her pardon, Nina Nicholson—wishing to take on an antagonistic prepubescent stepson. I reached for the ladle and began transferring the jam (a bit runny? never mind) from the preserving pan to the warmed jars.

"He's in his room," I said. "I can tell him you're here, if you want."

"Would you?"

"In a moment. Let me finish these."

"How has he been, Kate? I haven't seen him since Jan—"

"—since January '43. Yes, I know. He's all right, thank you. We get by pretty well."

This is the problem with my feelings for Guy: one minute I'm all neutral and wise, and the next my blood is at a rolling boil. Just then, for example, as I heard myself say, *He's all right*, my inner banshee started screeching, *No thanks to you, you cheating bastard*, and it was all I could do to keep ladling the hot jam with steady hands.

. . .

"MUM?"

Pip shakes my arm. It's not August, it's December, and the rain is coming on again.

"Mum, you're miles away."

"Sorry, I was thinking."

"You're dragging Shirley along too fast. I think she wants to stop for a wee."

"Yes. Sorry, Shirley."

We pause to let the dog do her business, pressing against the hedge whenever cars come along with their headlights ablaze.

"What were you thinking about, Mum?"

"Just . . ." I hesitate. "Just how cheerful it is to see so many lights, after all those years of blackout. Have you seen the Christmas lanterns they've strung around the village green?"

"Mmm." Pip isn't interested in Christmas lanterns. It occurs to me—it's crossed my mind a few times lately—that he might not be utterly dismayed if I admitted I was thinking about his father. He might even welcome the chance to talk.

One of these days, I'll put my theory to the test—but not now.

· · ·

GUY WAITED PATIENTLY WHILE I sealed the jam jars and wiped their sticky sides. When I'd finished, I slung my apron over the back of a chair and went upstairs.

"Pip?"

I knocked, waited a few moments, and poked my head round the bedroom door.

"I won't," he flashed, before I could speak. "I know what you're going to say, but I won't come and see him. I hate and despise him. He's a son of a bitch."

"Phillip Nicholson!"

He was sitting cross-legged on the bed, nursing a toy gun across his sharp knees. He looked fierce and grubby, like a child soldier in a guerrilla war. *Son of a bitch* merited a telling-off, of course (and I'd very much like to know where he picked it up from), but that could wait.

"Your father—"

"He's not my father. You can call him Nicholson, if you like, although actually even that's pretty annoying. If I were you, I'd go for 'son of a—'"

"*Pip!*"

I sighed and leant against the door-frame. It was too hot for jam-making. I should have waited and done it this evening.

"Listen, he's going away in a few weeks. Going away for good, I mean, to Canada. He came because he wanted to see you, to say goodbye."

Pip sat, tensed and glaring. All at once he leapt from the bed and rocketed downstairs, toy rifle in hand. I listened for the sounds of confrontation, but all I heard was the click of the front door as it opened, and the crash as it slammed shut. I walked to the head of the stairs just as Guy was emerging from the kitchen.

"Was that . . . ?"

"Yes," I said. "That was him. I did my best, but he wouldn't listen." There was a satisfied edge to my tone, which I'm ashamed of now.

. . .

THE RAIN IS SPIKIER THAN it was. All three of us—woman, child, dog—walk defensively: heads down, shoulders up. We're almost back at Henry's. I ought to be thinking useful thoughts, such as what to cook for dinner (something involving half a pound of greying mince, that's for sure), but my mind keeps reverting to that day in August. Gooseberry jam day. I made nine jars in the end, and it did cross my mind to give one to Guy and Nina, but I couldn't decide whether it would be a fine gesture, or a weak one, and in the end I decided not to risk it.

. . .

"I'LL WRITE TO HIM," GUY had said. "If you could spare me some paper and an envelope, I'll write Pip a letter, and you can give it to him whenever you see fit. Is that . . . ? Would you . . . ?"

When Guy is very upset he talks rapidly, crossly, and small red patches appear on his cheeks. He almost never softens, let alone cries, and is therefore difficult to soothe. Not that it was my place to soothe him, anymore. I fetched notepaper and an envelope from my desk.

Guy sat at the kitchen table and folded himself over his writing, just as our son does when he's absorbed by a piece of homework. I pottered about, making labels for my jam jars, and watching from the corner of my eye. He wrote with all his concentration: not fluently, but carefully and at length. Sometimes he chewed his left thumbnail, and at one point he tugged so hard it began to bleed. He didn't complain—just folded his thumb into his palm, laid his hand on his lap, and carried on.

As I passed the sink I saw Nina strolling about on the lawn, hugging herself around the waist and smoking. Her bearing, whether she stands, or sits, or walks, is . . . I was going to say *elegant*, but it's more than that. It's momentous, significant, expressive. That summer afternoon she looked less like a woman deep in thought, and more like an actress playing a woman who is deep in thought. There ought to have been a Rachmaninoff piano concerto drifting across the garden, by way of an accompaniment.

It was only when I caught her eye (or rather, her dark glasses) that her poise crumpled. She couldn't seem to work out what to do. First she raised her hand in the nervy likeness of a wave; then she dropped her cigarette and stooped to pick it up; then she turned her back on me altogether and pretended to be spellbound by the view. Poor girl. Her gaucheness surprised me; almost managed to touch me. Perhaps she wasn't an actress, after all; perhaps I just preferred to think of her that way.

Do you know, if she hadn't been Nina Nicholson, and my husband's preferred choice of wife, I could have crossed the lawn quite easily at that moment, and offered her a cup of tea.

. . .

PIP IS WALKING AHEAD OF me as we turn into Canal Road. Even in his duffel coat he looks spindly from the back; small for his age. I hope his chest won't play up this winter.

Guy's letter is still in my bedside cabinet, underneath my reading glasses and a scattering of bobby pins. It's not that I want to hoard it: Pip can have it tomorrow as far as my own feelings are concerned, but I'm terribly afraid of getting the timing wrong. It would be just like him to make some theatrical gesture: throwing it unopened onto the fire, say, or ripping it to shreds without reading it first. *This is what I think of that son of a bitch!* A whim like that could haunt him forever.

Pip stops at Henry's gate and stands aside to let me pass—less an expression of politeness, I suspect, than a reluctance to go first. He loiters behind as I ring the bell, kicking at the loose stones on the path.

"You can't go home in this!" Henry insists, as soon as he's greeted us. "Look at that rain, it's coming down like stair-rods! At least stay until the worst has passed."

Pip communicates his opposition by (more or less) discreet sighs and shuffles, but Henry is insistent.

"Just five minutes," I say, with a quick smile for both of them. "Thank you."

. . .

NINA'S LETTER HAS DISAPPEARED FROM the desk—not that it's any of my business. The fire has all but expired, leaving the chill intact. I decide not to sit down. However fond I am of Henry (and I'm sure I still am, even if my love no longer classes as a Grand Passion), I want to be elsewhere, just now. I have a longing for home, which is not a longing for Hawthorn House, but for something more elemental. It's a yearning for warmth and gentle light, and for the feeling of security that used to seem real in my childhood, and now seems strange.

Pip asks if he can use the loo. Henry says, "Certainly," and removes Shirley to the kitchen, to towel her off. Alone in the sitting-room, with the rain blistering the windowpane, I spot Rose Allen's letter to Nina in the wastepaper basket—or rather, I spot a pale-pink, crumpled-up ball.

Guy's address book is still at Hawthorn House, in the middle drawer of the Welsh dresser. It's one of the many things he left behind: a tatty object with dog-eared pages and half a front cover. On the first page, in a round, childish hand, is written:

Guy Robert Thomas Nicholson,
Shrewsbury School,
Shrewsbury,
Shropshire,
England,
Great Britain,
Europe,
Northern Hemisphere,
The World,
The Solar System,
The Milky Way,
The Universe,
Whatever-is-beyond-the-universe,
Whatever-is-beyond-whatever-is-beyond-the universe,
Etc.,
Etc.,
Etc.,
Ad infinitum.

Inside the pages, under *R*, there's an address for *Roussin*, though whether it refers to Joey's parents' place, or his aunt and uncle's, or even his own set-up, I couldn't say. I only know that Guy used to send a Christmas card to that address every year, before the war came along.

On balance—and I don't say this glibly—I've reached the conclusion that it's better to be a forgiving sucker than an unforgiving sage. I glance over my shoulder to check Henry's not there, before fishing the balled-up paper out of the bin, and slipping it into my pocket.

11

Nina

February 8, 1946

"THERE'S A LETTER COME FOR YOU, MISSY," SAYS JOEY'S father's voice, from the other side of the bedroom door, and Nina pauses in her packing to let him in.

Nina likes Mr. Roussin Senior. She likes everyone in Joey's family, more or less, but Mr. Roussin is her favourite. He doesn't say much, compared to the others, but he notices more. Right at the very beginning, when they first met, Joey's mother swept Nina into a hug and cried, "Honey, you must call us Ma and Pa," but Mr. Roussin took one look at her face and said, "Or not. Not if you don't want to."

Nina and Guy have been lent a room at the top of the house, right under the eaves, and Mr. Roussin has trekked all the way from the basement kitchen, just to bring her a letter and a cup of coffee. For once, Nina is too happy to be cursory.

"How kind, thank you! Why don't you come in for a minute and sit down? All those stairs!"

"Oh, well . . ."

"I don't mean you look like you need a rest, because you don't; you never do. It would be nice to see you properly, though, before we set off. I'm going to miss you!"

"Oh, well now . . ."

Nina reddens, even as she smiles. Throughout the five months of this stay with the Roussins, she has never spoken with such warmth, and rarely at such length. She glances at the pink envelope (redirected twice and horribly crumpled . . . British postage stamp . . . who . . . ? *Rose* . . . ?) and puts it away, hastily. She won't open it until she's alone.

"It's done the rounds, that letter," Mr. Roussin remarks, taking one of the chairs in the window. He's big and fair, like his son, but he doesn't sprawl like Joey; he sits with a straight back and places his hands on his knees. "Looks like it went to the wrong address in England, first of all; then to our old house, the other side of town. Hope it's nothing urgent."

"I'm sure it isn't." She affects nonchalance in order to deter questions, but she can hardly keep from singing. Unfriendly letters don't come in pink envelopes.

Nina sits opposite Mr. Roussin and sips the coffee. She's wearing her sable coat over her ordinary clothes, which might have come across as rude back home, as much as to say, *It's a pity you can't heat your house properly*, but nobody is offended by anyone else's extra layers here; not in February. The house at 124 Quincy Street is centrally heated—even up here in the attic rooms, the pipes clank and gurgle day and night—but central heating is only one weapon against the murderous Canadian cold, and you need as many in your arsenal as you can muster. Mr. Roussin has been going round in that caribou-hide jerkin since November, and sometimes he matches it with caribou-hide trousers—or *pants*, as Nina flatly refuses to call them.

("Why won't you call them pants?" Joey's sister-in-law once asked, over dinner, sending Guy and Joey into fits. "That's what they are."

"Because . . ."

The whole table had fallen silent, which was unheard of in Nina's experience of Roussin family meals.

"Because in British English, *pants* are, you know . . ."

When Nina hesitated, Joey said, "Ah, but they *don't* know."

"Well, they're underwear," she clarified, sounding all the more prim for her efforts not to.

"Underwear!" yelled the eldest child, in a fair imitation of a British accent, and soon all the children were shouting, "Underwear!" and the whole table was laughing, including Nina herself. It was the most successful conversational gambit she'd made, in her entire stay, and she wishes she could have broken through her own reserve, like that, more often. It wasn't for want of effort—but then, to make an effort to be easy-going is to fail before you've begun.)

"The coffee's very good," she tells Mr. Roussin now.

It is. It's wonderful. Everything is wonderful since last night, when Nina screwed up her courage for a proper heart-to-heart with Guy. If only she'd done it sooner! She ought to have trusted him to listen, but was afraid of another quarrel. It seems to her—or it did seem, until last night's grace—that they quarrel rather a lot, for a young couple in love.

Now that an escape route's opened up, Nina can finally see the charm of their Canadian adventure. For the first time in five months, she feels affection for it all: for the little town of Rossett Falls; for sleepy Quincy Street with its clapboard houses and wooden sidewalks; for No. 124 in particular, and the welcome they've had. Most of all, she likes the thought of looking back on it with Guy, in years to come—even the parts involving Aunt Calla's farm—and saying, *What a time of our lives that was.*

"You look happy, Missy."

"I am happy. Everything's going right today."

She's even come round to Mr. Roussin's habit of calling her *Missy*. It offended her at first (*he must think me childish*, she assumed, *or improperly married; or perhaps he can tell, just by looking, that I'll never be a mother*), but now she knows it's just his way.

"Guess you're glad to be going out to the farm, at last, and setting up for yourselves?" He sounds a mite doubtful, especially when she fails to answer.

"This place is kind of a sardine can," he goes on, with a greater confidence. "Not a whole lot of space, or privacy, and always fighting to be heard over everyone else at dinner. It's only natural you'll be glad to move out."

There's no denying that 124 Quincy Street is a full house. Mr. and Mrs. Roussin, Joey himself, two of Joey's siblings and their respective spouses, five children under the age of ten, and the Nicholsons makes fourteen, and that's before you add the three dogs and the several cats, whose numbers seem to wax and wane (but mostly wax).

"It's been wonderful." Nina's answer is truthful today, though if she'd said the same thing yesterday it would have felt like a fib. "*You've* been wonderful to put up with us for so long."

There's no need to mention the situation with the farm. Quite apart from anything else, Guy has asked her not to, and she's minded to do whatever he likes at the moment.

Last night, as their talk was winding down, Guy had said, "Let's carry on with the move tomorrow, as if nothing's changed; as if everything's going ahead as planned. No big announcements; we need to work out the details ourselves, first."

Nina had reached for him under the weight of quilts and blankets and laid her face against his back.

"Shouldn't we tell Joey?" she'd whispered. It was easy to be considerate, with her mind at ease for the first time in months.

"Joey? Oh, he can wait." It was the only time, during their whole exchange, that Guy showed a trace of vexation. "I need time to think this through, Nina; it's one hell of a lot to get my head round."

It was a surprising answer, coming from Guy—after all, such a sudden decision to abandon the farm project amounted to the yanking of a pretty hefty rug from under Joey's feet—but Nina was too content to probe.

Mr. Roussin leans forwards in his chair and rattles the lower half of the sash window, in order to dislodge the drifted snow. He peers down into the street.

"Ma tells me Guy went back into the office, this morning?"

"Mmm."

"It's only a couple of days since he and Joey had their big send-off."

"Oh, well, he's not gone *in*, as such; I mean, he won't be stopping." Nina peers out, too. "I think he said he left a pair of gloves behind, and didn't like to leave them."

Was it gloves? At one point he'd said gloves, and then he'd changed it to hat. He'd been rather cagey altogether, when she woke at first light to find him out of bed and dressing, but it hadn't seemed right to push for an answer.

Still, she hopes he won't be too much longer; they must set off for the farm in good time. The journey was quick enough by car, in balmy mid-September, but with a horse-drawn wagon, and in the snow . . . Not to worry. It'll be all right. Sunset's not till half five.

"I'll miss Quincy Street," she says, her breath clouding the glass.

"You won't recognise it, next time you come; they're gonna lay tarmac in the spring, and pave the sidewalks."

"Oh, what a shame! It's so picturesque, as it is."

Mr. Roussin laughs his quiet laugh, and although there's no malice in it—none at all—she feels she's chalked up another small failure to fit in.

The snow wasn't heavy last night, so the gritted road is clear, and the neighbours' dug-out paths remain passable. It's gone half eight, and now that the office workers have left for the day, hardly anyone is out and about. Old Mrs. Picoult is letting her dog out the front door for a quick pee, and Mr. Fry is sweeping his steps, because *passable* isn't good enough for him; everything must be neat at No. 119, whatever the weather. Oh, and there's Dirk Milne, who wears a fur hat with a tail hanging down, and busks with a mouth organ when the weather is clement; he's striding eastwards, away from town, with a rifle over his shoulder. Joey always refers to Dirk as "the old Injun," which makes Mr. Roussin Senior cross; he says Dirk is an Anishinaabe Indian and deserves a bit more respect.

A-n-i-s-h-i-n-a-a-b-e: Nina will never forget the spelling, because it was the very first word she'd written in her new notebook; the forlorn enterprise that was meant to be her own private encyclopaedia of Canada. It had seemed like a perfectly reasonable ambition at the time: to try to condense her new life into a list of facts and impressions; to fit it all, by force, inside the pages of a school exercise book. The second entry she'd made, after *Anishinaabe Indian (Dirk Milne)* had been *Caribou (reindeer)* alongside a sketch of Mr. Roussin in his jerkin and trousers. The third entry—after which she'd admitted defeat, ripped the first page out, and donated the exercise book to one of Joey's nieces—had read: *Aunt Calla's Recipe for Muskrats à l'étouffée: skin muskrats and clean carcasses, making sure to remove scent glands, and I want to go home, I want to go home, I want to go HOME.*

Nina puts her coffee cup down and caresses her left hand with her right, running her thumb over her ring finger. That was how the conversation had started, last night: with Guy touching her hand. She'd been lying very still, staring up at the darkness, envying the ease with which he always tumbled into sleep, when he'd reached for her and said, "What's wrong?"

Before she could deflect him with *There's nothing wrong*, or *I thought you were asleep*, he said, "Please talk to me. This has been going on for months, and it's no good."

She almost said, *What's been going on for months?* but his tone was too direct, and too gentle, to be lied to. So she confessed everything, in a rush of relief, and with no expectation of being understood.

"I can't do it, Guy. I can't be a farmer's wife. I can't live in the middle of nowhere, without a single woman to talk to, and nothing but forests and farmland for miles and miles around, skinning muskrats and gutting fish. I'm not like you and Joey, I don't *feel* it, I don't *want* it. I want to want it, for your sake, but I don't know how to make myself."

It seemed to Nina that she ran out of words before she'd even begun to explain herself, and when Guy didn't answer immediately she braced herself for bitterness. After a long silence he brought her hand to his lips and kissed it softly—sadly, even.

"It's all right," he whispered. "Everything will be all right. We'll sort it out. There's no point in doing it if you're unhappy."

Nina touched her husband's face, and was shaken to discover that his cheeks were wet. Guy had never cried before, to her knowledge. The Canadian dream had meant a lot to him—an awful lot—and it was kind of him to mourn its passing with tears, rather than by getting cross. In many ways, though, it would have been better if he'd shouted.

"If you were to leave me, and go back to England—" Guy began, but Nina interrupted, and the sentence was never completed. In years to come, she will wish she'd heard him out. She will also wish she'd expressed herself sincerely (*Leave you? Never!*), rather than flippantly, in an effort to lighten the mood. Nina thought her love for Guy was understood—that its realness went without saying—and statements of the blindingly obvious were not her style.

"Back to England? Heavens, can you imagine the humiliation? *That Nina Woodrow*, they'd say. *She married another woman's husband, the little trollop, but she couldn't hang onto him for more than a couple of years . . .* Oh, the indignity! The shame!"

But Guy had been too withdrawn to laugh.

Nina shivers, in the gauzy light of morning, as old Mr. Roussin wipes their breath from the window.

"Here comes Guy now," he says. "Joey too."

"Oh! I didn't know they'd gone together."

Nina watches the pair make their way down the street. They're so wrapped up against the rawness that she only knows them by the way Joey drags his left leg, and by the glint of eyes in the gap between hats and mufflers.

"Joey's scars are healing well," says Nina, with a cautious glance at Mr. Roussin. He nods, wholeheartedly.

"Good old Canadian air, that's what it is. That's what's doing the trick."

"Maybe so," she agrees, although privately she doubts it. Her own hands and lips have never been so cracked and sore, and Mrs. Roussin's greasy ointment just makes them more itchy.

"This farming venture will be the making of Joey," says Mr. Roussin. "Your husband, too. Gosh, but they're keen; I don't reckon they've talked of anything else all winter."

His smile falters as he meets her eye. Maybe he wants to say, *It'll be the making of you, too, Missy,* but can't get the words to sound natural.

Suddenly Joey's eyes narrow with laughter and he throws an arm round his friend's shoulders, mid-stride. It's such a swift, rough hug that Guy nearly falls.

"Ah, but they're fine boys," says Mr. Roussin. "Fine boys, the both of 'em."

. . .

ONE NIGHT IN DECEMBER, WHILE she was sleeping, Nina's left foot had slipped out from under the mountain of quilts. The following morning she told Guy what had happened, and that she'd had a nightmare about a polar bear circling the bed with bared teeth, dripping seawater on the rug, sniffing at her toes.

Guy mentioned it at the breakfast table, and the children were scornful ("There aren't any polar bears in Rossett Falls!"). Old Mr. Roussin smiled at Nina, though, and said it was a true dream. "The cold out here is a predator, as fierce as any bear. It will hunt you down, and if you're not on your guard, it will eat you up."

Nina often recalls the draughty Nissen huts, the smoky stoves, the low clouds and endless rain of her wartime winters. "I'm freezing to death," she used to whimper—she and Joan and Dolly—and they'd exaggerate the chattering of their teeth, and hug each other, and laugh, and Dolly would make them do star jumps. Here on Quincy Street, there's a man who lost three fingers and part of his nose to the cold, but when Nina had asked what exactly that meant, the answer came with a shrug. "Frostbite," Joey's sister had said. "You've got to be careful, that's all."

Nina slips on two thermal vests and two pairs of long johns, before strapping a hot water bottle round her middle with a scarf, in a system of her own devising. Once it's secure, she dons as many layers as she can, including the new sealskin kit that all three of them have acquired, at Joey's insistence. By the time she's done, she looks like Humpty-Dumpty, and bends with difficulty at the elbows and knees. She tries to complete the ensemble with the dear old sable coat, but she can't get her arms through the sleeves, so she carries it downstairs instead. It will do as an extra rug.

Guy and Joey are in the lane, finishing loading up the covered wagon. Nina strokes the horses, and whispers to them, but they toss their heads and look the other way when she fails to produce any sugar from her pockets. "Can't we just hire a normal removal van?" she'd asked, the other day, but Joey had snorted. According to him, the horses would manage the snow much better than a van, especially during the last few miles from the main road to the farm. *Why not wait a few months, and move when the weather's fine?* she'd wondered next, but she was damned if she was going to say it; he'd only treat it as a stupid question.

The men help her on board, and she makes a den for herself between a large crate, packed tight with newspapers and crockery, and a chest of drawers. As soon as she's settled beneath the sable coat, she realises she's forgotten to make her farewells to the Roussins, so she clambers to her feet, but there's a chorus of "Don't go climbing out again!" and "Honey, it's okay, you stay put." What a fool she must look, standing over them in her ungainly layers, waving her stiff, fat arms.

Joey's mother emerges from the back gate with a casserole dish. "Barley soup and dumplings for tonight," she tells Nina, confidentially. "You won't want to start cooking the minute you arrive." Under Mrs. Roussin's direction, Nina wraps the dish in spare rugs and furs, so that it won't freeze solid in transit. There are other last-minute gifts, too: a bar of chocolate, a recipe book, a sack of coffee-beans, a crumpled collection of children's drawings, two bottles of rye whisky. By the time they're all set, and the wagon is heaving away with Joey and Guy up front, Nina has shouted, "Thank you!" and "Goodbye!" so many times that the phrases are starting to sound alien to her own ears.

"Thank you," she whispers to herself, as she settles under her coat, with her back against the packing crate. "Goodbye." This was one of her favourite private games, as a child: trying to hear English as if it were a foreign language; a string of sounds without meaning.

"Thank you and goodbye."

She found it practically impossible, back then, but she can do it today.

. . .

ROSSETT FALLS IS A SMALL town, and Quincy Street is on its northern edge. Nina watches through the open end of the wagon, as the houses and factories fall away, shrink, and disappear. A smoky smudge remains on the horizon, but even that vanishes in the end, and Nina is no longer sure where the pale land ends and the sky begins.

Joey and Guy have visited the farm several times—almost every weekend before the snows came, and a couple of times since—but Nina has seen it only once, in September. Aunt Calla was there, packing up her own life into boxes; letting go of her old home; showing them the ropes with a diligent ferocity that terrified Nina.

"Why is she so cross?" Nina had whispered, looking to Joey for reassurance. "Doesn't she want us here?"

"Oh, don't mind Aunt Calla," Joey had replied, as his aunt and her walking stick hobbled into earshot. "You've always been a crabby old sourpuss, haven't you, Aunty C?"

Aunt Calla smacked Joey over the side of his head (scars or no scars) and ordered him to mind his manners. The interaction had all the hallmarks of a serious falling out, and Nina assumed that was that—they'd all have to leave—but Joey just yelled, "Ouch!" and rubbed his ear, sheepishly, and a few minutes later, Aunt Calla was ruffling his hair and pretending not to find his jokes funny. "You rascal," she kept calling him fondly, or "You good-for-nothing," or "You young scoundrel." She never mentioned his injuries, at least not in Nina's hearing, but she was always slipping him treats: slices of apple, offcuts of pastry, little tastes of whatever she happened to be baking. By the Saturday evening she'd begun to do the same for Guy, albeit shyly, but she never included Nina.

"So you're planning to kick me out of my own house, and take my place, are you, Mrs. What's-your-name?"

That was the very first thing she said to Nina, after she'd greeted the men, and they'd headed off to the fields to look at the stock. No *pleasure to meet you* nonsense from Aunt Calla. Nina took such a long time to work out how best to reply (humour? indignation? dogged politeness?) that she ended up saying nothing at all.

"Sullen," muttered the old woman, as they turned and headed for the house.

Nina smiled, to show she was nothing of the sort. "It's a beautiful place. You'll miss it."

The old lady ground her stick into the dusty ground, with every other step. "Fifty-three years," she said, accusingly. "That's how long I've lived on this farm. Fifty-two years a wife; one year a widow."

Nina looked up at the house, properly. It *was* beautiful, in its own way: a sprawling, generous, irregular building made of wood, with shutters on the windows, and a veranda all along the front. She would have enjoyed coming across it in a picture book, or a film, or a dream. Its outline wavered and wobbled, ever so slightly, as if it were a hand drawing, brought to life by magic. In the beginning— whenever that was—it must have been red, but the paint had flaked away over the years, leaving the silvery wood bare, with rust-coloured streaks between the slats.

Behind the house loomed the forest. On either side of it lay outbuildings—a huge barn, a row of stables, a couple of shacks— and fields of grazing cattle. When Nina turned, so that the house was at her back, she faced Joey's parked car, and beyond that a kitchen garden and an apple orchard, and then more fields, and more cows, and finally the diamond-bright glint of Lake Winnipeg. The sunshine was warm that day—not hot, simply pleasant—and as Nina slipped her cardigan off and tied the arms round her waist, she felt a moment's pleasure, a flash of hope, which ended when Aunt Calla said, "You know how to churn butter? Yes?"

"No."

They resumed their halting walk to the house.

"Or how to make cheese?"

"No."

"You ever worked a cider press?"

"No."

Nina had always thought of herself as reasonably competent, but apparently she was mistaken. The list of things Aunt Calla understood, and Nina didn't, seemed to go on forever. She didn't know how to pluck geese, or can vegetables, or stretch animal pelts on willow moulds to dry them out. She didn't know how to split logs with one blow of an axe, or fashion snares out of wires and sticks, or catch pike. She didn't know how to skin rabbits, or mend fishing tackle, or assist a cow in labour. She didn't know how to cook muskrats à l'étouffée.

"I'm pretty good at folding parachutes," she offered, but Aunt Calla said she didn't see what bearing that had on anything.

"It doesn't. I was being humorous."

"Huh."

Thank goodness Aunt Calla has gone now, and won't be there to greet them. She moved out a few weeks ago, leaving the farmhand, Martin, to hold the fort. Now—believe it or not—she's living a life of ease in some suburb of Winnipeg.

Nina sways loosely with the motion of the wagon, as they pass through a grove of silver birches. The snowfall is hypnotic. She fastens her eyes on a particular flake, and tries to follow its leisurely zigzag, but loses it almost at once. She tries again, and fails again. The snow, like the landscape, goes on, and on, and on, and there are no distinct colours or forms, just a thousand subtle gradations of white. Grub white; pearl white; sugar white; fish white; milk white; stone white; bone white. The birch trees are the only solid shapes in sight, and even they start to look abstract if you stare at them for long enough.

It's hard to imagine Aunt Calla—that tall, rangy woman with the sun-bleached hair and the wind-dried skin—living happily in suburbia. Nina wouldn't mind it, one bit. She likes Winnipeg. Her favourite day, since their arrival in Canada, was when they went sightseeing in the city: browsing the art gallery and shops; strolling along the river; admiring the stately buildings; eating fancy pastries in a French café. If Guy wants to settle in Winnipeg, and visit Joey at the farm for the odd weekend, that will be fine by her. Or they could think of moving to a different Canadian city, or crossing into the States. They could go back to England, and try somewhere new to them both: Cambridge, perhaps, or Bath, or York; somewhere restful and attractive, but populated. Whatever makes Guy happy. And she won't even hint at her longing for a baby—not yet. Perhaps never.

They pass a broken-down logging truck, tilting drunkenly in a ditch. It must have been abandoned, because there's nobody in sight. Snow is piled thickly on the roof of the driver's cab and on the long, stacked trunks behind. It's proof that human life exists beyond their wagon, thinks Nina grimly. Or rather, to be strictly logical, it's proof that human life did exist, once, in the not-too-distant past.

The daylight has mellowed, and the shadows are longer and more distinct, by the time Joey halts the horses, to give them a breather. He and Guy jump down to stretch their legs, but Nina stays put. Without the creaking of wheels, and the muffled clop of hooves, the silence of this place is extraordinary. She burrows down inside her coat and covers her ears against the vastness, finding comfort in the warm, pulsing resonances of her own body.

Vastness: that was the whole point of the Canadian adventure. Vastness, and the radical freedom it implies. Nina closes her eyes as well as her ears, and tries not to think about the wildness of the forest they're journeying into, or the deepness of the cold, or the advance of night.

As a child, growing up in a Cheshire village, she'd enjoyed imagining vastness. It was pleasant to sit up in bed with the atlas open on her knees, trying to picture what those bright-blue lakes would look like in real life, and noting the scarcity of towns, the farther north her eyes travelled up the page. Within the confines of the atlas, these places used to thrill her, but in reality they leave her desolate.

She did try to explain herself on their return from the farm in September, but Guy had refused to understand, back then.

"Wasn't it wonderful, though?" he'd cried, flinging his arms wide in the Roussins' attic bedroom, and sending a hairbrush flying. "All that *space!*"

It wasn't a real question, it was a demand for agreement, and Nina longed—more than anything, she longed—to fling her own arms wide, and jump up and down, and shout, "Yes, it *was*! It *was* wonderful!"

"I don't know," she'd said, retrieving the hairbrush from the floor and returning it to the chest of drawers. "We'll see."

Nina gets the feeling that Guy's soul has expanded to fit the scenery, according to plan, while hers hasn't altered at all. They will have to stay in Canada, for his sake; he will want—need—to be in striking distance of the wilderness, now that he's encountered it. Cambridge? Bath? York? Not in a million years; not if she knows her husband. Nina will have to content herself with looking them up in the atlas.

The wagon jolts and sways as the men climb back up. Joey is laughing. She hears him say, "Come on, you're allowed to see the funny side," but Guy replies, "Shh," and murmurs something in a low voice that she can't quite catch.

"All right back there?" Joey calls, through the canvas flap. Nina unburies her face to answer, "Fine!" and they whip the horses on.

It's all very well thinking, *Thank goodness Aunt Calla has gone*, but how will they manage without her? The antique cooking range, for example: Aunt Calla explained its numerous subtleties at length, in

September, but that was ages ago, when Nina wasn't even half listening. The old woman had still been in full flow (*On absolutely no account turn this knob, here, without first opening this vent, here—*) when Nina had decided she couldn't stand any more. She'd half walked, half run, for the kitchen door, throwing some witless excuse over her shoulder. (*Sorry, but I'm a bit . . . I don't know. I need some air.*)

The men had been far away across the fields, in deep discussion with the farmhand. Nina slipped through the fence and strode through the grass to meet them. The cows watched her steadily, except when she came too close, at which point they startled and shambled off, showing the whites of their eyes.

Guy slung his arm around her shoulders, as she reached his side. Joey said, "Hey Nina, this is Martin, he's been Uncle Bram and Aunt Calla's right-hand man for God knows how long. Forever."

It was hard to tell whether Martin was really glowering, or whether it was just an effect of his wiry eyebrows and beard. Nina said, "Hello there!" with a smile and a nod, which came across as charming in precisely the wrong way. She wished she'd worn slacks and wellington boots, rather than a tea dress and sandals.

"Martin, you were saying about the wind-breaks?" prompted Guy, but Martin itched the back of his head and said, "Ah . . . that was it. I'd finished."

They made an awkward grouping: Martin kicking at a tussock with the toe of his boot; Nina frowning in annoyance—at herself, at Martin, at the general situation, at the way in which the other two kept glancing at one another and trying not to laugh.

Joey cleared his throat. Guy hugged Nina to his side and said, "How about a bathe in the lake before the sun goes down?"

Martin clapped an oily old cowboy hat on his head.

"I'll leave you to it, gents," he said, shaking hands with them both. "Missus," he added, glancing slightly at Nina and touching the brim of his hat.

Nina hoped they would all laugh together when he was out of earshot ("Missus" indeed!), but it didn't seem to occur to Guy or Joey.

"How about it?" Guy asked, giving her shoulder another squeeze. "A swim?"

It was all very well for them, but there was no way Nina was going to jump in the lake without a costume; not in front of Joey.

"I'm not sure," she said, although she was. "I don't think the weather's quite hot enough for my liking."

She walked with them, though, down the sloping fields towards the shore. As soon as the beach came into sight Guy darted off, shedding his clothes as he ran and whooping like a boy. Joey followed as fast as his lopsided stride would allow. He was still supposed to be using his walking stick, back in September, although he'd insisted on managing without it during their trip to the farm; said he couldn't face Aunt Calla's teasing.

"It's as big as the sea!" Guy yelled.

"It's Lake Winnipeg!" Joey retorted. "What were you expecting, Limey? Some lousy little English pond?"

They splashed, and shouted, and dunked each other's heads, and blew huge spouts of water into the air. If you were to judge by the noise they made, you'd think there were a dozen men in the lake, not two.

Nina sat with her knees drawn up to her chin, sketching spirals in the sand. She remembers wishing that Rose was there, or if not Rose, then Kate Nicholson—which was probably the stupidest of all the stupid thoughts she'd taken to entertaining lately.

That May afternoon kept coming to mind, when Guy had called at Hawthorn House to say goodbye. Nina had stayed in the car, trying to look impervious in her big, dark glasses, and Pip had hurtled down the drive with a toy gun, peppering the windscreen with imaginary bullets. When he'd disappeared into the fields, she'd tried to escape into the garden, but Kate had spotted her through the kitchen window, and Nina had read kindness in the other woman's eyes—such a baffling kindness—and it was like being gunned down, all over again.

. . .

IT'S DARK BY THE TIME they reach the turning to the farm. The clouds that muted the sunshine all day have scattered, giving way to a real night sky: not the Cheshire version of a night sky, or even the Lincolnshire one, but a darkness like the depths of the universe, in which everything has sunk away, except the stars.

"Magnificent!" breathes Guy, as they come to a standstill on the smaller road, their wheels wedged in a drift. The wind is getting up, and the storm lanterns swing from the hooks at the front of the wagon, sending rays of light spinning across the tree-trunks on either side. Sometimes a gust will catch at the snow on the ground and whirl it into a topsy-turvy blizzard.

"This could be heavy going," says Joey, jumping down. "I'll bet there's been no traffic on here for days."

The tired horses strain forwards, and the wagon inches along. Joey hands Nina a crowbar and a spare lantern, and she scrambles down to join him in the road, so that they can beat the claggy snow from the wheels. Guy stays on board, shouting encouragement at the horses and flicking the whip across their hindquarters.

"What's that noise?" Nina asks, as she and Joey work together on the rear wheels. She stands still a moment, trying to hear past the *thwack* of the crowbar, and Guy's "gee-ups," and the groan of the wagon, and the shrilling of the wind, to . . . there! That.

"Oh God, what is it?"

It sounds like a troop of crying children; small, lost, desperate children. She must be losing her mind. She braces herself for Joey to say, "What noise?" but in fact he says, "Coyotes."

"Oh!" Nina scrapes at a snowdrift until the straining wheel surges forwards. The cries sound again—lingering and bereft—before fragmenting into a high-pitched, doglike yapping. It's hard to tell how close they are; it depends on the direction of the wind.

"Are they dangerous?" she asks, and of course—of course—Joey laughs at her.

"Are they dangerous! Uncle Bram's sister's first baby was taken from her cot by a coyote. You can't live here and not know that; it's part of Roussin family lore."

Nina gives the spokes a spiteful wallop. *Just as well I don't intend to live here much longer*, she thinks.

She looks at Joey. In the lamplight, his face is a shifting network of yellow lights and black shadows.

"Just as well you don't intend to live here much longer," he says, or seems to say. But how can he possibly say it, unless he has the power to pluck the thoughts from a person's mind, word for word? Before she can respond, he's disappeared up front again and Nina is walking alone in the wake of the lumbering wagon, the snow squeaking and crunching beneath her boots. The coyotes wail again, but she hardly notices; her unease is not chiefly on their account.

"Farm ahoy!" yells Joey or Guy; she's not even sure whose voice it is. She wades around the side of the wagon, to see a golden bead of light ahead, and with the next burst of gritty wind she catches the homely scent of wood smoke. As the minutes pass, and her legs begin to ache with exhaustion, the light grows larger and squarer, and turns into a window.

"Martin!" yells Joey, though they're much too far away to be heard. Perhaps Joey needs to make a noise for the sake of it, as an outlet for his glee. He is striding along with the horses now, tugging at their halters, breaking into a jog whenever it's sound enough underfoot. Gathering all her strength, Nina manages to clamber back on board the wagon, and join Guy up front. She sits down, close to him.

"Did you tell Joey about our plan?" The wind is gathering pace, and it's necessary to shout.

"Yes," Guy shouts back. "I know I said I wouldn't, but I had to. I needed his help."

"What do you mean? Help with what?"

"Look, Nina, let's just get there. I'll explain everything, later on."

If they weren't so bundled up and roly-poly, like a couple of snowmen, Nina would kiss her husband on the cheek. She makes do with patting him on the arm.

"I don't *mind*," she bawls. "I'm just surprised he seems so chipper; I thought he'd be devastated."

It's not a question, so it doesn't require an answer, which must be why Guy looks straight ahead and says nothing at all. Either that, or he hasn't heard her properly; or he's too tired to talk; or all his focus is on directing the horses. There'll be a good reason.

"We'll discuss it properly later on," she murmurs reassuringly, into the folds of her scarf.

. . .

JOEY RETURNS TO THE SUBJECT of coyotes at supper. He's in his element by then: sprawling on Aunt Calla's old settee with a bowl of food in his hands and a half-drunk bottle of whisky on the floor, at his feet. Martin lit the range earlier in the day, so the kitchen is warm, and they worked out how to heat Mrs. Roussin's barley soup without any difficulty.

From time to time, Joey swaps the bowl for the bottle and takes a swig, before handing it to Guy, at the other end of the settee. After Guy has had a drink he offers the bottle to Nina, who is sitting at the table, but she declines and passes it back to Joey. She did have a mouthful when they first sat down, but one was enough. She feels on edge, and it's stopping her from wanting to eat or drink, although she's sure she must be hungry. The prospect of opening Rose's letter is her great comfort, but she can't remember where she put it for safe-keeping, and it keeps nagging at the back of her mind.

"I was telling Nina about the coyotes," says Joey. "About Uncle Bram's sister's baby. You know that one, right?"

"You've mentioned it before." Guy takes two generous slugs of whisky when his turn comes round. He doesn't sound drunk at all, even though he's had more than Joey, whose voice is starting to slur.

"Yeah, well. This place isn't for the faint-hearted. There's a whole lot of lousy ways to die out here; one hell of a lot more than you'll find in Cheshire."

Sheshire: that's how he pronounces it. Nina stirs her soup and brings the spoon to her lips. It smells savoury and good, but she can't persuade herself to want it.

"For example," Joey uncurls his thumb from his fist, as he starts to count. "The cold. You get lost in a blizzard, or you go out there without the right gear, you're dead. So that's one way."

He uncurls a second finger. "You might get attacked by a predalat . . . pretadtad . . . you know what I'm trying to say. Coyotes, bears, wolves . . ." He waves extravagantly, to imply plenty of other possibilities.

"Secondly—no, thirdly—we're a heck of a way from any hospital, so if you get sick, it's too bad. Blood poisoning, brain fever . . . burst appendix. Oh boy, yeah, that's a real bad one. Appendiss-whatsit. Appendicitis. Yeah. I had a good friend who died from that."

He crosses his eyes, lolls his head, and sticks out his tongue, which makes Guy smile very slightly, but Nina not at all. Joey glances from one to the other and settles back against the cushions, with a genial laugh.

"Let's see now. Well, it's a farm, isn't it? And a farm is a dangerous place: powerful machinery, sharp blades, stampeding cattle, fire haz-ards, big horses with big hooves who aren't afraid to kick. And then there's the lake: you can drown there in the summer, or fall through the ice in the winter, as you prefer; either way, you're food for the fishes."

Guy is staring into the middle distance, his fingers steepled against his lips. When Joey stops talking to fetch his pipe from his pocket, Guy asks wearily, though still with a degree of amusement, "Anything else?"

Joey lights his pipe with some difficulty, and puffs away. The kitchen smells delicious, what with the barley soup, the tobacco smoke, and the wood burning in the range. Even with their boxes lying about—corded, or half-unpacked—this room is the picture of cosiness. It's a perfect winter's night, just as August 24, 1934, had been a perfect summer's night. The red-and-white-checked curtains are drawn against the night, and the wooden house is singing in the wind.

"There's murder," Joey suggests. "You could get murdered."

Guy reaches across the sofa and removes the whisky bottle from his friend's hand.

"I'll bet even you have never known—"

"Don't you believe it! There was a real nasty murder round here, back in the olden days—maybe fifty, sixty years ago. Okay, so before I was born, but still. It was on a farm not ten miles from here. Old Mitchell's pig farm. They had a servant girl, who was raped and strangled—"

"Joey! That's enough." This time there's no trace of humour in Guy's tone.

Joey is momentarily startled. He throws himself across the settee, shedding sparks from his pipe, and flings his arms around his friend.

"Hey! I'm not trying to scare *you*, little guy. 'Little Guy' . . . ha ha, that's funny."

"I'm thinking of Nina," says Guy, shoving him away. "You fat-head."

Nina looks up from her soup. She's been stirring it slowly, all this time.

"Oh, don't mind me. Please carry on, Joey; you're so vastly entertaining."

Joey narrows his eyes and sucks on his pipe.

"All that about—you know—about strangling," Guy tells her. "You shouldn't have to hear that."

"Nor should anyone." She sets her spoon down. "What do you mean? Why should I not have to hear it, in particular?"

Guy picks at the label on the whisky bottle, as if he's too flustered to meet her eye.

"You know why. Because of what happened to your mother."

"My mother died in a car accident."

Guy stops fidgeting and looks at her. Their silence is broken by Joey's low whistle. He wrests the bottle back from Guy, smooths the torn label, and takes a long drink. There's only an inch or two left by now.

"What do you mean?" Nina's voice is hard. "What do you think happened to her?"

Guy looks at her strangely and rakes his fingers through his hair.

"What do you think happened to my mother?" Nina persists. "Tell me!"

"It was your father who told me. He said she was murdered. He said that she was having some kind of a liaison—"

"My *mother*?"

"—yes, and that her lover strangled her. That's what he said, so I assumed it was true, and it never occurred to me that you might not know. I'm sorry. Truly. I wouldn't have breathed a word if I'd thought you didn't know."

Nina wants to study her husband's face, but he's dropped it into his hands again. Some kind of reaction is necessary, but how can she react when she doesn't understand what's happening? Maybe she is drunk, after all. Maybe one sip of whisky can turn the world on its head.

"Why would you say that? I don't understand why you would invent such a horrible lie."

"Invent! Nina, I'm telling you what he said! It was that time in Buxton, when I had to chase after him—you remember. He kept muttering, *Like mother, like daughter,* and he went on and on about her scandalous behaviour, and the way in which she'd died, as if it were a moral lesson. A warning. *Look what happens to women who mess around*; that kind of thing."

Nina sits and stares, clinging for dear life to the sides of her soup bowl. She feels the tremble of an upside-down teacup and hears the whisper of long-ago voices. *Ghost? Were you murdered?*

"Guy—"

"Nina, I swear I'm only telling you what he said."

It's not Guy's fault that Joey chooses this moment to snigger, but it tilts Nina's perspective, nonetheless. She'd been on the brink of believing her husband, but now she sees the pair of them, side by side on the settee. Joey and Guy, the famous double act. The naughtiest boys in the school.

"I don't know what you're playing at, or how you can find it so funny. You're toying with my mind again; you've been doing it all day, both of you, and I don't know why—"

"Nina!" Guy is the only one to protest. "Your father—"

"My father is the most upright person I know."

This sets Joey off again, and Nina bursts out of her chair, onto her feet. It's tempting to hurl the soup in his face, but he'd probably find that amusing as well.

As she makes for the stairs, she swipes the bottle from Joey's clutches, and drains it in one breathless gulp.

. . .

NINA AND GUY HAVE ALREADY dumped their luggage in the big spare room above the kitchen, so she makes her way there. Once she's closed the door she doesn't know what to do, except walk about, wrapped inside her own arms, and try to breathe normally. The wailing of the wind disguises the creak of the floorboards beneath her feet.

Where's her framed photograph? The one she's kept all her life, with Mum and Dad, and herself as a baby? It's never far away; it'll be here somewhere. She switches on the bedside lamp and a watery yellowness—barely a light—seeps through the shade. She might have packed it in this cardboard box. Or does this one belong to Guy? She rummages through the folded clothes and pulls out a wallet, a toothbrush, a couple of old tram tickets, and an official-looking document on stiff paper. Ah, no, these are his things. Where's her own little suitcase? She needs to search her mother's face again. She needs to ask, for the thousandth time, *Who are you?* Only this time she'll express the question with such urgency that the picture will be compelled to answer. Reticence will not be an option.

Nina places an ice-cold hand around her throat and squeezes slightly. She can picture her mother's sturdy neck as it appears in the photograph, strung with beads and skimmed by a satin collar.

She feels no interest in her husband's belongings; she only glances down at the official-looking document because it happens to be in her hand.

Province of Manitoba

Certificate of Death

Registration Division of the town of Rossett Falls

This is to certify that the following particulars are from a registration filed in the said Registration division:

Name: Nicholson, Guy Robert Thomas
Age: 35

Sex: Male
Date of death: February 5, 1946
Place of death: 124 Quincy Street, Rossett Falls
Cause of death: Appendicitis
Name of physician: Dr. H. W. Alexander, Coroner

This is to certify further that the said registration was so
filed during the preceding three months prior to issue
hereof.

Given under my hand this 8th day of February, 1946

B. P. Chapman
Divisional Registrar

Nina reads it three, four, five times, but it still makes no sense.
The eighth of February is today, and Guy Robert Thomas Nicholson
did not die three days ago. He is here in this house, climbing the
stairs, pushing open the door to the spare room, advancing towards
his wife.

"Nina?"

They stare at one another. She advances on him and presses the
paper into his hands.

"I said you were playing with my mind. I said so, didn't I? What
is this?"

"Nina—"

"What *is* it?"

She retreats, her arms tightly folded across her chest, and he
makes as if to stroke her.

"Guy, I don't need to be soothed. I need to understand what it
means."

He looks down at the paper, and up at her.

"I was going to explain everything later this evening, when we were alone. This was never supposed to be a secret—far from it—this document belongs to you."

He tries to pass it back, but she swerves away. She won't say another word, or touch him, or express anything by so much as a look, until it's all explained and understood. She will be as mute as her mother's photograph.

Guy sits down on the edge of the bed and studies his own death certificate—or pretends to. Nina stands by the window, watching and waiting.

"Darling, you and I understand—I think we've understood for weeks, months—that we are going to have to go our separate ways. When it first dawned on me, I racked my brains to find a way out, but it was no good. This life is for me, but it's not for you. I long for it with every particle of my being; you loathe it. That's the case, isn't it? I'm not wrong, am I? I know I'm not wrong; not after our talk last night."

Nina says nothing, so Guy carries on.

"I would rather die than return to England. To be close to my son, yet estranged from him . . . I think that would hurt too much. But going back is what you want, deep down, isn't it?"

She shrugs.

"You want to go home, but it's hard for you—our affair has made it hard—because people are so malicious."

"When we started our 'affair,' you told me you were free," she objects. "I never meant to be a marriage wrecker."

"We're not talking about what actually happened; we're talking about what people think. If you were to return home as a divorcée, their spite would be unrelenting; they'd say you'd picked up a married man and dropped him again. They'd never get over it; never forgive you."

He turns the certificate round and round in his hands, as if he's trying to work out which way is up.

"Whereas if you went home a widow . . ."

He won't look at her and she won't speak to him.

It's true that Nina feels homesick, but not in the sense Guy means. She doesn't yearn for long-lost places. All she wants, just now, is for the woman in the photograph to come alive, so that Nina can sit on her lap again, and feel the particular quality of her skin, and smell her particular scent: the aspects of her mother that she can't possibly remember (Dad has said so, several times), but decidedly does. Mum would still love her, even now, when nobody else does. That's not a matter of fantasy or faith; she knows it's true.

Guy is explaining his scheme, at tedious length: "It came to me last night, while I was lying awake. I was thinking about what you'd said—about the indignity and shame—and I thought how much easier it would be if you could tell everyone I was dead. But then, the more I dwelt on it, the more convinced I was that you'd need documentation. If you had a death certificate to wave around, then nobody would suspect a thing; it wouldn't even occur to anyone to start digging.

"So I got up early, to go to the office. I was intending to go on my own, but Joey was up and about, and I ended up consulting him. Actually, it was much easier with his help, because I am—I mean I was—on the bottom rung of the ladder, whereas Joey was old Chapman's right-hand man."

Guy hesitates, as if hoping for a nod or a word of encouragement. *What clever boys. What a marvellous wheeze.*

"Anyway, off we went, first thing, and filched a blank certificate. I typed it up and Joey forged Mr. Chapman's signature. The whole thing was a piece of cake. God knows what laws we've broken, or what the penalty would be if anyone found out, but it doesn't matter. Dear Nina, I'd risk more than that for your peace of mind."

He reaches across, trying to hand her the paper again. When she doesn't take it, he looks around and places it on top of her small suitcase.

Nina slides her back down the wall, until she's sitting on the floor with her knees bent. The wind is working itself up into a frenzy, and the lonely cries of the wild dogs are bound up within it, forming a crazy braid of noises.

"I would have stuck it out for your sake," she tells her husband. "I'd have stayed, just to be with you."

Guy sighs and looks down at his hands.

"Nina, you can still stay, if that's how you feel."

"No, I can't."

"Why not?"

"Because now I know I'm dispensable."

The wind and the coyotes are doing all the shouting, and Nina wonders what's stopping her from joining in. She sounds—much like her husband—passionless and spent. It could be that she's going mad.

"So Guy doesn't love me," she thinks, before noticing she's said it out loud.

"I do love you."

He sketches a vague gesture in the air with one hand—an allusion to tenderness—but he doesn't do anything else, or move closer.

"Not enough, though," she retorts, laying her head on her knees. "Not nearly enough."

12

Kate

March 16, 1946

I'M VERY GLAD THAT MY BROTHER, RON, HAS COME TO STAY,
but I've hardly slept a wink since his arrival, and it's starting to show.
I keep doing stupid things, like losing my ration book, or forgetting
to lock the house, and Pip says I stare for too long before answering
the simplest questions.

Daytimes have been all right, by and large. This morning, for
example, we went for a blustery walk along the canal, and in the afternoon Ron showed Pip how to do conjuring tricks with coins and an
old silk scarf. Ron's wartime memories hide away in the daylight, but
we all know they're there, hiding in the nooks and crannies, ready to
scuttle out when darkness falls.

"Talk to me," I said at breakfast, his first morning, after Pip had
left for school. "Tell me about the prison camp. It might help."

It's not that he got angry or upset. There was no wild eruption—
he took a careful sip of tea and continued scraping margarine across

a piece of toast—but his reticence felt like a slap in the face. For all Ron's gains in weight and strength, something inside him has weakened, since he went to war. He is like a burned stick that continues to hold its shape, though it may be no more than ash.

Sometimes I hear him shouting in his sleep. He dreams about beatings and men with bayonets, and sometimes he begs for rice or water, or weeps for "Charlie, my old pal." I don't know who Charlie is, or was, but I know better than to ask.

Whenever Ron's nightmares are frenzied, I hover in my dressing-gown between his bedroom door and Pip's, unsure what to do for the best: afraid of waking my brother and afraid of abandoning him to his dreams; afraid of the effect this might be having on my son. But the silent nights—like tonight—are worse than the noisy ones. When Ron makes no sound at all I am afraid that the memories have swarmed across his body, once and for all, and stripped him to the bone. I worry about what I'll find between the sheets when I go up with his morning tea.

It's gone two o'clock in the morning and, for the life of me, I can't lie still in bed. I put my ear to Ron's door and satisfy myself that he's breathing, before heading downstairs, careful not to stub my toes on any of the removal men's boxes.

There's still a lot of packing to be done in the kitchen. Quietly, one by one, I take the remaining plates from the dresser, wrap them in newspaper, and add them to the half-filled crate. In just over a week's time, the three of us will leave Hawthorn House for good and head for Carlisle. There's a narrow terraced house a few doors down from Deb's, which I'm in the process of buying. Ron will live there with me and Pip, until he's ready to find a place of his own.

Just over a week! Henry refuses, point-blank, to believe it. Whenever I broach the subject he responds with a smile—one of those sorrowful, maddening smiles that he does so well—and when I ask what on earth *that's* supposed to mean, he says, "You won't leave."

Henry. I wonder how many times that name has orbited my brain, over the last three years. I pause in the wrapping of a willow-pattern dinner plate, and study my reflection in the little mirror, tracing my thumb over the shadows of my mouth. The only light is coming from the hall, and in this semi-darkness my face could amount to anything at all, from freakish, to ordinary, to beautiful. How strange—how unutterably strange—to think that these lips have finally been kissed by Henry Woodrow, after an eternity of wishing and wondering.

I haven't told Deb about The Kiss, but I will, once we're together. I hope she'll understand. When it comes to Henry, the things I feel most deeply are always the things most difficult to grasp and explain; they are like liquids that slip through my fingers, leaving nothing of substance behind, only faint stains on my skin.

I pull out a kitchen chair and sit down, resting the half-wrapped plate on my knees. Hawthorn House is silent, but not at rest.

The danger is that Deb will say, *I see: so, this Henry Woodrow chap kissed you, and you found you didn't like it very much?* and I'll say, *Yes, that's about it,* and she'll say, *Ah well, never mind,* and I'll say, *Quite.* Because, in a way, that *is* all I've got. A non-story. Something and nothing.

And yet, in another way . . .

When I'm telling Deb, I'll begin with Sunday morning—last weekend, six days ago—when Henry came up behind me, at the end of church, and seized me by the arm.

. . .

HENRY AND I NEVER TOUCH—YOU know that—so I almost cried out, in front of the whole congregation. In actual fact I didn't make a sound, but people still turned and stared.

"Kate!" he said, excitably. *Kate* rather than *Mrs. Nicholson.*
Thank goodness Pip wasn't there that morning—he'd have died of
embarrassment—and Ron hadn't arrived in Cottenden yet.

"I have news!" Henry brought his face too close to mine and
hardened his grip on my arm. Mrs. Tight Perm (real name Mrs.
Susan Dankworth, it turns out) would be swooning with disgust.
I tried to forget about her, but I knew she was about—she and her
cronies—gossiping by the hymn-book table while they signed people
up for the Lenten Lunch.

It seems ironic now, but I remember wishing that I could be
alone with Henry.

"What news? Is something wrong?"

I flinched when he laughed in my ear. He was obviously trying
to maintain a whisper, but his voice kept rising. "Kate, something
astonishing has happened. Something miraculous. Come and see
me this afternoon—just you—no need to bring Pip."

I think he wanted me to clutch him right back and shower him
with questions, but I wasn't in the mood to play ball, not with everyone watching. Also, I'd been probing a gumboil with my tongue for
the best part of an hour, and it was starting to hurt.

"All right," I said, disappointingly. "Three o'clock-ish?"

I extracted myself from his grasp with a bland smile and a nod
for the Mills-Amershams, who were just emerging from their pew.

But when I did go to his house, a little before three o'clock—
because lunch hadn't taken long, and Pip had disappeared to his
room straight afterwards to finish his homework, and because
Henry is not given to hyperbole, and his use of the word *miraculous*
was playing on my mind—when I went to his house, as I say, shortly
before three o'clock last Sunday afternoon, he kissed me. He did it
without preamble, the moment I entered, and he didn't even preface
it with "Hello!" or "Do come in!" let alone . . .

He seized my face with his hands and pounced on it with his mouth, and when I recoiled, the combined weight of our bodies slammed the front door shut, so that I found myself pressed between it and him. When I failed to kiss him back, he didn't stop, he only ground his lips the more furiously against mine, like a dog scrabbling at a door, desperate to be let in.

I didn't struggle. Once, as a child, playing hide-and-seek with my siblings, I trapped myself inside the old oak chest where spare blankets were stored. As long as I kept my eyes shut and recited the lyrics to "Hello, Hawaii, How Are You?" on a continuous loop, I was able to postpone Death by Panic Attack, indefinitely. I la-la-la-ed under my breath for about five minutes (it felt like five hours) until Deb came to my rescue.

Hello, Hawaii! How are you? / Let me talk to Honolulu Lou, / To ask her this, / "Give me a kiss" . . .

"I'm sorry," Henry panted, at last, red-faced and out of breath. He maintained his two-handed grip on my head, as if I was a trophy, and he was about to lift me to a delirious crowd. "I'm sorry. I should have told you first, but when I saw you standing there in all innocence, I couldn't stop myself. We're free, Kate! We're free and Nina is saved!"

"What?"

"Guy's dead!"

My handbag slipped from my shoulder and slumped to the floor. Somehow I got away from him; somehow, when my legs crumpled, the stairs were there, and I was able to sit down.

Henry produced a letter from his pocket, and he didn't just pass it to me, he knelt at my feet and pressed it into my hands, and avidly watched my lips as I read. Sometimes I would whisper a word or phrase out loud: "in Rossett Falls" . . . "his appendix" . . . "leaving from Halifax, Nova Scotia" . . . "the SS *St. Ursula*"—and he would echo it out loud, with greater force.

The letter was from Nina, of course. Guy had died very suddenly, in early February. She had decided to return to England, and would arrive in Liverpool on Saturday, March 16. She didn't want or expect anything of her father, but felt he ought to know.

. . .

WHEN I'VE PACKED THE FINAL plate from the dresser, I rattle the tea-caddy against my ear and grimace. Bother rationing! Tea is the only comfort going on these sleepless nights.

I put water in the kettle and strike a match to light the stove. The gas ring makes a comforting *whumph*, lifting the darkness with its faint blue glow.

I shouldn't, but I will: just a weak one; just half a cup.

. . .

I MADE MY WAY HOME from Henry's without losing my way or getting run over: a minor triumph in itself, given the daze I was in. Pip swung on the banisters while I was putting my coat away, keen to fill me in on the gorier aspects of the French Revolution. (Even the most brutal Schadenfreude has an air of respectability when it's history homework. I can't complain; I'm always wishing he would be more communicative.)

Suddenly he said, "Are you okay, Mum?"

"Why?"

"I don't know. You seem sort of vague. Where have you been?"

"I just went for a walk."

Goodness, I must have looked an absolute fright, for Pip to notice. I added that I did feel a little peaky, but that all I needed was a lie-down, and perhaps we could discuss guillotining later on, instead? He offered to run me a bath, which was nice, and presented me with a squashed, rather fuzzy, mint humbug, which wasn't quite as nice, but very touching, all the same. I couldn't bring myself to tell him that his father was dead. Once I've fathomed it myself—in a week, or two, or three—I will.

I wallowed in the soapy water for ages, staring at a strand of my own hair that was stuck to the side of the bath, and sliding it about with my toe to make it form various shapes: a Loch Ness monster; a camel with no legs; a head with a tall wig, like Marie Antoinette's. It seemed irrational to get upset about Guy's death, and almost equally irrational to get upset about Henry's kiss—so longed for, yet so strangely sordid—but I couldn't help myself on either count. I cried into my flannel, so that Pip wouldn't hear, and felt somewhat better afterwards.

Ron arrived the next day, and Sunday's events took on a dreamlike quality. Whilst I was lugging my brother's suitcase up to his room, and chatting about the latest (blessedly mundane) family news from Carlisle, and getting the supper on, it was easy to forget what had happened. A strange death and a strange kiss: these things had to be dwelt upon to be believed, and I didn't have time to brood. I reverted to thinking about Guy and Henry in the usual way: constantly but calmly, and at the back of my mind.

Ron, Pip, and I spent Monday evening chatting and listening to music on the wireless. Ron said that we seemed well and "very jolly," and he gave us presents: a football and a pair of goalkeeper's gloves for Pip, and the collected works of Virginia Woolf for me.

By Tuesday, I'd persuaded myself that absence was absence, whether by death or divorce, and that *The Kiss* was just *the kiss*. I decided it hadn't been so terrible: that it was more surprising than outrageous; that Henry hadn't been himself; that it wouldn't happen again.

That afternoon, after school, Ron and Pip had a kick-about in the garden. I huddled in my coat and watched them from the bench under the horse chestnut tree: two scrawny figures loping about on the lawn. You could tell at a glance that they were related, and that they weren't much cop at sports. I winced whenever the football cannoned into Ron's stomach, or smacked the side of Pip's head, but they seemed to find it hilarious. They also laughed when it careered into a patch of purple crocuses beside my bench.

"Hey!" I shouted, kneeling to inspect the damage. Most of the blooms were fine, but a dozen or so were bent or broken. I picked these and bunched them up, hiding the most damaged ones in the middle and binding them together with a scrap of twine from my pocket. They made a minute, but rather lovely, posy. Purple spring flowers always make me think of Teodora Woodrow, and I remembered that it was the twelfth of March that day: her twenty-fourth anniversary.

I touched the flowers to my nose. They didn't have their own fragrance, but they carried the scent of freshness and spring on their petals.

"You two?" I got to my feet with a tired sigh. "I'm going for a walk; I won't be long."

Ron was bent over, clutching a stitch in his side; Pip was tossing the ball from hand to hand while he waited for his uncle to recover. My brother looked round and waved, cheerily enough, but Pip called out, "Where are you going?"

"Just over the fields."

I waved again and turned, but I could feel his anxious gaze on my back as I walked away.

· · ·

"CROCUSES?" SAID HENRY.

It was difficult to believe that the flowers themselves had annoyed him, yet he'd seemed all right, up until I offered them. A bit polite, a bit wary, but all right.

I shivered in the March wind, and prayed he wouldn't invite me in. It had been a bad idea to come.

"I thought you might like them—"

"—for Teodora's anniversary. Yes, you said, but crocuses aren't... I always take purple hyacinths."

I shrugged, which was probably a bit mean. A man is allowed to be particular when it comes to honouring his murdered wife.

"I'm sorry," I said. "I didn't realise it mattered. Not to worry; it was only a thought."

Henry unfolded his arms, softening a little.

"It was a kind thought. *I'm* sorry. Come on in, out of the cold, and let's start again."

"No, no, I shan't stop."

Shirley barged between Henry's legs to come and greet me, and when my face broke into a smile for her, I realised that it hadn't done so for him. Our conversation had been entirely straight-faced, from the moment Henry opened the front door, to now. Shirley plonked her bony backside down on my feet, which I've come to understand as an expression of goodwill. She closed her eyes and lolled her tongue, as I bent to scratch her head.

"Take the flowers, anyway," I said, carefully maintaining my smile as I straightened up.

"Not unless you come in."

"No, thanks."

"Please, Kate?"

"I'd really rather not."

I needed an apology for Sunday first, and if Henry couldn't see that for himself, I wasn't going to point it out. He pretended not to notice the posy when I offered it, and I dropped my hand to my side, rather than insisting.

"Pip and I will be gone in a couple of weeks," I said. "I've found a buyer for the house."

Henry shook his head gently, and fixed his eyes on mine. He smiled, at last—the kind of smile that certain, melting dreams are made of—and kept on shaking his head. The way he looked put me in mind of Max de Winter in the novel *Rebecca*, especially that bit near the beginning where the narrator thinks he's asking her to be his secretary, and he says, "No, I'm asking you to marry me, you little fool." I thrilled like a young girl when I read that line for the first time, seven or eight years ago, but I can't say it moves me anymore.

"Is there any further news of Nina?" I asked, partly to change the subject and partly because I was interested.

The smile faded. "No. Only that she'll be arriving in Liverpool on Saturday, late morning, and I've decided I'm going to meet her off the boat. If God can give her a second chance, so can I."

Whenever God crops up in conversation, Henry's voice turns snappy, and his chin juts out. He and I might attend the same church, but we don't share the same intuitions about matters spiritual. This "second chance" that Nina is supposed to have been awarded, for example: What sort of God decides that the best way of mending one person's soul is to fatally rupture another person's appendix? For Henry, it's proof that "God moves in a mysterious way, his wonders to perform"; to me it's suggestive of an Almighty with a morbidly elaborate imagination.

I fidgeted with the keys in my pocket, and stroked Shirley again, and did whatever I could to avoid Henry's gaze.

"Why don't you come with me?" he said.

I did look at him then.

"What . . . ? To Liverpool? On Saturday?"

"Why not?"

"*Why not?*" I spread my arms wide, incredulous. "Henry, I don't know where to begin. I'm the last person in the world poor Nina will wish to see!"

"Never mind *poor Nina*—" her father snorted, but I beat the air with my hand, and turned to go.

I knew, in that moment, what I should have known long before: Henry and I will never understand one another.

. . .

ALL THIS HAPPENED THREE DAYS ago, and we haven't met since. Teodora's purple hyacinths were left by the wall that night, as usual, but Henry came and went without stopping.

. . .

TODAY—THE DAY AFTER MY LATEST sleepless night—is Saturday, and I make an early lunch with real eggs. Bearing in mind that they are currently rationed at one per person, per week, and that Pip and I (after much deliberation) recently declared Poached Egg on Buttered Toast the number one foodstuff of all time, this is a very bad moment to lose my appetite. Damn it! I break the unctuous orange yolk with my fork and take a bite—but it's no good; I end up donating it to the boys.

"You're having a l-lie down, this afternoon, whether you like it or n-n-not," my brother announces. He's very firm about it, just like Mum used to be when we were children, and that makes me smile.

"I can't. Pip's school shoes are about three sizes too small, and if I don't take him into town today—"

"L-leave that to me," Ron replies, unmoved. "You c-can't afford to get run-down; you've got a house-move to org . . . to organise. Off to bed with you!"

I fold my napkin slowly. Lying in the dim quiet of my bedroom, rather than jolting into Chester on the bus and queuing at Clarks:

it's an appealing thought. I start to protest, just because I feel I should, but Pip interrupts: "Oh, *Mum*! Why can't I go into town with Uncle Ron? I'm *always* going with you, and I've never been with him before."

On which unflattering basis, I give in. I issue firm instructions about the shoes (dark brown, not black; lace-ups, not buckles; make sure the sole is good and stout), before eking another half cup from the teapot and making my way upstairs.

If I'd caught the bus, I would likely have mortified Pip by dozing in my seat. Having got into bed, however, I feel wide awake. I listen as they wash up the lunch things, and fetch their coats from the understairs cupboard, and consult the bus timetable. (*The number 5!* I'm tempted to yell, *Ten minutes past the hour!* but they work it out on their own.) Minutes pass, and then there's a whispered, "Bye, Mum!" at my bedroom door, the front door shuts, their footsteps fade away down the drive, and I'm alone.

Sleep comes close, but it never quite catches me. My mind wheels freely from picture to picture: white dogs with sly eyes, ocean liners, ill-fitting shoes, willow-pattern plates, Japanese prisoner-of-war camps, Guy in an open coffin, poached eggs, purple hyacinths.

"Purple hyacinths." My voice is louder than I intend, and it jolts me awake. I stare at the ceiling for a while, my eyes open wide, before checking my wrist-watch. It's just gone half past one. Pulling my sweater back on, I hurry downstairs to the telephone. I speak to the operator, and agree to hold, and while I'm waiting I chew my nails.

"Pearson's Books?" a faraway voice enquires, at last.

"Deb, it's me."

"Kate! Is something wrong? Is Ron . . . ?"

"Ron's fine. Really, everything's perfectly fine."

I know why she sounds like that. A telephone call at an odd time, or an unanticipated knock on the door, or an official-looking letter: they all arrive like a kick in the stomach. It's the war's fault, of course; it's turned everyone into a nervous wreck.

"Honestly, don't worry. He and Pip are getting on like a house on fire; they've just gone into town together, on the bus. Listen, Deb, I'm sorry to bother you at work. Are you busy?"

"The shop's pretty busy, but I'm not: I've just stopped for a sandwich while Eileen holds the fort. Why? What's up?"

"I was hoping you could do me a favour. It's a silly thing, really— just a thought that came to me—so if this is a bad time . . ."

"Out with it."

"Do you remember the big hardback book I almost bought for Mum last Christmas? It was called *The Interpretation of Flowers* by Dora and Emily Pettit. I ended up deciding it was a bit twee for Mum, and got her those Agatha Christies instead."

"I remember."

"Do you still have it in stock?"

"Goodness, I'd have to check. I think so. Why? Oh, let me guess: the famous Henry Woodrow has given you a dozen red roses, and you need to refer to a book to find out what it could possibly mean?"

"Very funny. No. I want to know about purple hyacinths."

"Hyacinths?"

"Specifically purple ones. I know it's an odd thing to ask, but I can't explain now; I promise I'll give you the full story next week. Would you mind . . . ?

My sister sighs, but not with genuine annoyance.

"Wait there."

While she's gone, I look around at the half-emptied hall, and the white patch on the whitish wall where the mirror used to hang. The narrow terrace in Carlisle is much less spacious. It's hard to picture it clearly, having only seen it once, but I remember cheery yellow walls and a window box bursting with red geraniums. It's only ten minutes from the bookshop—and a heartbeat from Deb's house—so we'll be able to walk to work together.

Deb must have left the office door open, because I can hear the faint buzz of voices, and the rattle and *ping* of the till. I wish I could step into the sound, and be there now, instead of having to wait till next week.

There's a prolonged series of bumps and crackles, and finally Deb's voice is saying, "Right-o. I've got it. Are you still there?"

"I'm here."

"Purple hyacinths?"

"That's right."

She hums as she scans the index, and I revert to biting my nails.

"Here we are . . ." There's more humming, and the swish of turning pages. "Right! Ready?"

"Ready."

"It's pretty brief, actually. *The Purple Hyacinth symbolises remorse. A gift of this exquisite and fragrant bloom may be interpreted by the recipient as a plea for forgiveness.* And underneath there's a little drawing of two ladies in crinolines; presumably the droopy one with the hanky over her face is begging forgiveness of the one with the patronising smile and outstretched arms . . . That's it, I'm afraid."

I nod slowly, and keep on nodding, forgetting Deb can't see me.

"Kate? Are you still there?"

"Sorry! Yes, I am. Would you mind reading it out again?"

She does so, adding, "I'm dying to know why you're interested, but I suppose I'll have to curb my curiosity . . . for *now*."

I catch myself nodding again.

"Thanks, Deb, you've been an enormous help. You should get back to your sandwich."

"You are all right, aren't you?"

"Yes, yes."

We talk for a little longer—or rather, she says things and I respond distractedly, or not at all—and then she's gone, and I'm glancing at my watch, and it's a quarter to two already.

Ideally, I would take time to think—maybe that's all I need to correct the skewed angle of my thoughts—but I don't have time. Henry said that Nina would arrive in Liverpool late morning and so . . . and so, I've always been hopeless at mental calculations. They'll need time to collect her luggage, and perhaps to get some lunch, or, at the very least, a drink, and then they'll have to make their way to Lime Street to catch the train back to Chester, and then a bus or taxi from Chester Station to Cottenden. It's unlikely they'll be home just yet, but I can't be sure.

While these thoughts are flitting through my head, I pull my coat and shoes on and root around for pen and paper, so that I can leave a note for Ron and Pip. Bother! There's so much stuff piled up on the floor, or poking out of the half-packed boxes, but nothing to write with; not so much as a pencil stub.

Oh, forget it!

I leave the house and walk briskly down the drive, my cold hands curled inside my pockets. It's starting to rain.

Never mind about the note; it's not as if I intend to stay out long. I'll probably be home first, and even if I'm not, they won't worry; they'll assume I've gone for a walk.

. . .

JUST TO BE SURE, I ring the doorbell and rap with my knuckles, but nobody comes. Shirley's murderous rumble of a bark is distantly audible; it sounds as though Henry has shut her in the kitchen, which he always does when he goes out, as she has a habit of disembowelling sofa cushions when she's lonely. I know this because, on the rare occasions Henry has been away for more than a few hours, he has asked me to come over, to feed and walk her. This is also the reason I'm able to locate the spare front-door key, underneath the second-largest flowerpot.

I let myself in with a self-assured air, in case the net-curtain twitchers are at their posts, even though I don't feel self-assured, in the slightest. I've got one inner voice accusing me of lunacy, and demanding that I go home right away; another crying, *Hurry up! Hurry up! Hurry up!* non-stop; and a whole horde of others muttering under their breath, speculating on what I may or may not be about to discover, putting two and two together and making . . . goodness knows what; all sorts of horrors and impossibilities. I try not to listen to those. They make the hallway seem loud, although in reality, once the door swings shut behind me, it is velvety-quiet. Shirley has recognised my "Hello?" and contents herself with a half-hearted scratch at the kitchen door, and a whimpering sigh.

The desk in the sitting-room remains one of the most bizarre things I've ever seen. All those ornate dragons swirling over the dark wood, and the intricate carvings, and the odd-shaped drawers and slots and shelves and hinges and handles and knobs and keyholes. It looks less like a piece of furniture, and more like something that's masquerading as a piece of furniture in order to disguise its sinister intent. I'm not keen on the idea of touching it, let alone pulling it apart; I keep imagining built-in traps for the deterrence of thieves; cunning little blades that spring from nowhere to lop off probing fingers.

It's almost half past two, and there's no time for my usual silly whimsies. Where on earth do I start?

I try several drawers, but only uncover mundane things: packets of blank envelopes; tins of drawing pins and paperclips; butchers' bills. At first, I close each drawer carefully, after I've searched, but then I start forgetting which ones I've checked and which I haven't, so I leave them hanging. I feel as though I'm inside a dream—one of those infuriating nightmares where you know perfectly well what you need to do, and how, yet you're powerless to do it.

I force myself to pause and breathe. I try to picture Pip on that March afternoon, almost exactly three years ago, when I caught him red-handed at a game of German Spies.

Wasn't it *behind* a drawer? This one? No . . . this one. I pull on the tiny pearly handle and manage to extract it from the desk with a tug and a jiggle. Disregarding the possibility of a miniature mantrap, I reach inside and feel about. If my fingernails were longer it would be easier to get a grip, but . . . there . . . a click, and a grating noise, and the little ebony box slides out. There was a false base, which lifted, or slid . . . it *slid* . . . and here we are, at last. I've found it. The black velvet purse.

I have to sit down. I'm feeling distinctly strange, as if my leg bones have started to melt. If I'd forced myself to pause, in the first place, and think logically, I'd never have connected Teodora's flowers with my memory of the little black purse in Pip's hands. Something other than reason has been dictating my movements, ever since Deb told me the meaning of the purple hyacinths, and now—if I can only get my fumbling fingers to loosen the drawstring—now I'll find out whether that something is an idiotic presumption, or a mysterious kind of wisdom.

A length of fabric slithers onto my lap, first of all, as delicate as a shadow. It's a single silk stocking. I look at it for longer than I should—a part of me knows I must hurry; a part of me simply can't—before laying it beside me, on the sofa. There are two papers inside the purse, too: a newspaper clipping, and a letter written in blue ink and folded so tightly that it takes me ages (*Too long! Too long!* says the inner voice with the short fuse) to open it up without tearing the pages.

Dear Mr. Woodrow,

It seems stupid, me writing a letter to you. It's not like I
want you in my head, but there you are anyway

I turn to the end, in search of the signature: *George Tyler.*

I read the address at the top of the first sheet: *Strangeways Prison,*
Manchester, and the date, *February 4, 1923.*

Next I look at the newspaper clipping. The caption says, *Farm*
Lane Strangler Hanged, beneath a photograph of a fair-haired boy
with wide eyes. Someone has pencilled a date along the edge of the
page: February 6, 1923.

Finally, I read the letter through, from beginning to end. George
Tyler's handwriting is large and clear, but my hands are trembling so
much that I have to put the pages down and smooth them over my
lap, in order to make anything out.

As I come to the end and start again, my stomach hurts as much
as if a wound had opened up, and I press on the place where the
blood would be gushing, if it were real.

A key twists in the front door, and a pair of footsteps enters the
house. I shove the letter under my thigh and look up. That's the
sound of a hat dropping onto the hall table.

Henry is back.

He'll come into the sitting-room next. I know he will, because
he keeps his keys in a porcelain dish on top of the desk, and returns
them without fail, as soon as he comes in, no matter what's on his
mind. I haven't got time to cover my traces; there's too much to do:
drawers hanging out of the desk, the ebony box lying open on the
floor, the contents of the velvet purse spilling over the sofa.

Sure enough, the sitting-room door opens. I have my back to him
because that's how the sofa is arranged, and I can't bring myself to
turn round.

"Kate! Why on earth . . . ? But thank God you're here; I wanted you so dearly; I was just about to telephone. Nina wasn't on the ship! She—"

But then, I suppose, he notices the disorder, and works out what I've done; what I've seen; what I've read. He stops speaking, and the silence stretches on and on. In the end I turn round to make sure he's still there, and as I move, he moves. He comes round the sofa, picks up the coiled stocking, and, after a moment's hesitation, sits down beside me. His woollen coat smells of rain.

"Was it you?" I wonder, placing the letter back on my lap. I sound as though I've got a sore throat, although I haven't. It's impossible to look at Henry directly—I think, if I do, I'll forget how to speak altogether—but I'm aware of his broad outline, and the way he keeps running the stocking back and forth through his fingers.

"Was what me?" His tone is dull and uninquisitive; he knows what I'm asking.

"Teodora tried to leave you," I say. "She tried to take Nina. I think you must have followed her. I think you must have . . ."

Surely I'm making up a tale, the way I used to make up tales for Pip, the difference being that this one is too dark for bedtime. Henry—for all his fidgeting with the stocking—is attentive. Pip used to fidget too, when he was deeply involved in a story. I can picture him now, knotting the fringe on his candlewick bedspread, or twisting the buttons on his pyjama top.

"You killed her, and you let George Tyler hang for it."

All he has to do is deny it! Is that too much to ask? I wait and wait for the explosion of outrage; the wounded protest—*Kate, how could you? How could you think such a thing? You're talking about me! Me! Your friend, Henry!*—but there's nothing. He winds either end of the stocking around his hands, and stretches it. It is surprisingly robust, for something so dainty-looking. I think of Pip again. At least he's not alone. At least he's got Ron.

"Oh, Kate," says Henry.

Is that all?

I force myself to turn and face him. I tell myself that it's only Henry; only the same old Henry Woodrow—same firm mouth, same neat moustache, same sorrowful eyes—and the horror of it is that I'm right. I know this man better than I think; too well to feel wholly surprised when he slips the soft silk stocking around my neck, and twists, and pulls.

. . .

Strangeways Prison
Manchester

February 4, 1923

Dear Mr. Woodrow,

It seems stupid, me writing a letter to you. It's not like I want you in my head, but there you are anyway, night and day, standing at my elbow like a ghost, even though you're not dead. You're the least dead out of the three of us, what with Teo gone, and me where I am. Two days now, barring a miracle.

The chaplain comes to see me pretty often. He's nice; a real gent. He says I should write to my mother, and I've tried to, but I can't. I start picturing the details: her bent fingers fumbling to open the envelope, her short-sighted eyes trying to make out my scrawl, the kitchen chair she'll be sitting in, the blue flannel dressing-gown she'll be wearing. It takes all my courage away—not that I've got much courage to start with.

Anyway, it's you—not her—I want to share this place with. Did you know that the walls in the condemned cell are mint green, except here and there where the paint has chipped away, and the red bricks show through? Other men who have been here before me have written things on the walls, but the powers-that-be have scrubbed them off again. I can still make out the traces of their graffiti, but I can't make sense of any of it, which is sad, because what if they were trying to tell me something? Last night I wrote my name in pencil on a bit of wall near the floor. I wrote it as small as I could, where the shadows gather in the corners, but I don't suppose it'll last long. Someone will spot it, and wipe it away.

It stinks of bleach in here. I've always hated that smell, and so did Teodora. When she was waitressing, it was her job to get a sponge and a big bucket of bleach at the end of each night, and clean the urinals out back. It used to drive her mad. Once, when I asked her why, why, why she was going to marry you, she said, "I won't have to scrub these stinking pisspots when I'm in Cottenden, George—isn't that enough?" At least that much came true for her. I know (because she told me) that you were not a good husband, but your house was nice, and it smelled like roses.

It's awfully quiet in the condemned cell, so when you imagine it, make sure you include that. Quiet, but not silent: every now and then faint shouts and clangs drift over from other parts of the prison, depending on which doors they're locking and unlocking. Also, when you're alone, your own breathing can start to seem loud. This might be because it's the only noise going, or it might be an effect of all the hard, shiny surfaces (there are no muffling carpets or curtains or bookcases in here, Mr. Woodrow).

The food is not bad at all. Last night I had meat and onions in a rich gravy, but it was difficult to focus on enjoying it, as you will perhaps understand. The chaplain tells me not to be afraid of death. "It will be quick," he says. I don't tell him this to his face, because he's only doing his best, but he's wrong. There's nothing quick about this situation. My mind dies a million deaths an hour, in anticipation of the real thing. It's been going on for months now, and it feels like forever.

What would Teo say, Mr. Woodrow? You ought to have let her and the baby come away with me, like she wanted, but I suppose you realise that now. It must be a kind of hell for you, too—knowing what you've done, and sitting tight while another man swings for it. Sometimes, when I'm lying here on my pallet, scared to think, and scared to fall asleep, I feel a big wave of pity for you, Mr. Woodrow. It doesn't last long, but it's real—I'm not being funny. You wouldn't swap places with me for anything, I'm sure, but the feeling's mutual, if you want to know, and I'm glad I took this chance to tell you so.

Yours sincerely,
George Tyler

✻ 13 ✻

Nina

March 16, 1946

THE SUITCASE BUMPS AGAINST NINA'S LEFT LEG WITH EVERY stride. It's annoying, but she can't stop to adjust her grip on the handle; she must hurry. Someone is in pursuit, she's sure: whether it's an official from the ship, to tell her she's forgotten the rest of her luggage; or the American man with his religious tracts; or kind Mrs. Bell; or Dad. It doesn't matter where she ends up, just so long as she gets away from them all.

There are parts of Liverpool with which Nina is familiar. She knows the spots that exist for visitors: Lime Street Station, of course, and the half-built cathedral, and the Empire Theatre where she's been for concerts and Christmas pantomimes, and the Walker Art Gallery, where Miss Holtby once took Nina's upper-fourth art class to look at the Victorian paintings. That Liverpool, with its cascading flights of steps and neoclassical columns, is a world away from this one. She doesn't belong in the docklands; she's not even sure it's permissible to walk along this road.

The snow that followed the SS *St. Ursula* across the Atlantic has degraded to a cold drizzle, and the tarmac is a mishmash of dry patches and greasy puddles. A group of men emerges from a tall gateway across the way, and one of them calls out to her. At the same time a train thunders by on the overhead railway, making it impossible to tell what he's saying—it might be anything, from a well-meant pleasantry to an obscene threat—but the best thing is to lower her head and keep moving. As she picks up her pace a truck whizzes past from the Tate & Lyle sugar refinery, too close to the curb, and splashes rainwater up her legs. She's not going to cry though; she's past all that. Quite when she got past it, it's hard to say: maybe that first night at the farm, when Guy left her upstairs on her own; or the following morning when she saw her unloved face in Aunt Calla's dressing-table mirror; or when she realised she'd gone and lost Rose's unopened letter.

The dizzying cranes, the bomb-damaged warehouses, the ships under repair, the ships in steam, the clangs and booms from the wharves: everything here is colossal and inhuman. Or maybe it's not; maybe it's just that Nina can't cope with grandeur of scale anymore. All she wants is a tiny hiding place; a foxhole, where she can curl up, all alone, among the dangling tree-roots and the smell of soil. Come to think of it, with such modest ambitions, she might as well have stayed in Manitoba. She should have fled the farm on foot, and set up home with the coyotes.

The little suitcase slaps against her calf, and the sable coat flaps damply. It looked so luxurious, that first winter when Guy bought it, but now it's sleek with rain, and raddled. It used to be that when you stroked the sleeve your hand sunk into a downy warmth, but now there's no sinking into anything, and your palm comes away all briny and smudged. *It suited me then*, Nina thinks, *but it suits me better now.*

It wouldn't be so bad if Mrs. Bell—the elderly widow from the next-door cabin—were the one to catch up with her. Mrs. Bell has been very kind to Nina ever since Thursday's "near-accident," which nobody comes close to calling "near-suicide." It was an officer who inched up behind Nina, as she stood and swayed on the penultimate rail, and yanked her to safety, but it was Mrs. Bell who looked after her for the remainder of the voyage—placing endless cups of sweet tea on her bedside table, and gripping her arm like a vice on the rare occasions they ventured out on deck ("Blame my old age, dear, I'm not so steady on my legs as I used to be").

Something horrible squelches under Nina's shoe (it might be vomit, or even worse; she looks away too quickly to tell), so she deliberately walks through a puddle, in an effort to wash it off. The puddle is cold and grimy, and her shoes are not watertight.

She imagines a chauffeur-driven Daimler slowing down to match her pace, and Mrs. Bell winding down the window. *Mrs. Nicholson? Nina? What I need is a paid companion; what I need is you, dear . . .* It would be toasty-warm and fragrant in Mrs. Bell's car, as it would in Mrs. Bell's life more generally, and the duties would be light: chatting over pre-dinner glasses of Harveys Bristol Cream; dealing the cards for after-dinner Bezique; squirming under the weight of her employer's misplaced pity.

She frowns, shifts the suitcase to her other hand, and gives a minute shake of her head. The other night, Mrs. Bell had been cro-cheting in Nina's cabin while Nina tried to sleep. All at once the old lady had laid her yarn down on her lap and intoned, softly, "*The Lord on high is mightier than the noise of many waters, yea, than the mighty waves of the sea.*" Nina had kept her eyes closed and said nothing.

That quote has haunted her, ever since—not the bit about the Lord's mightiness so much as the description of the waters and the sea. She's even caught herself whispering it, like some lunatic. The following morning, when she was alone, she took the Gideon Bible from her bedside drawer and skim-read the psalms (she was pretty sure it was from a psalm) until she found it. Psalm 93, verse 4.

"*The mighty waves of the sea*," she mutters now, in time with her walking. "*The mighty waves of the sea.*" At least there's nobody close enough to hear, or to see her lips move.

The ocean breathes in Nina's ears night and day, sleeping and waking, and she's afraid it always will. It surges in an eternal frenzy of anticipation, while the balls of her feet shift and wobble on the spindly rail, and the wind toys with her body: a ruffling caress of her hair, here; a sly jab in the backs of the knees, there.

As she hurries along the docklands road, Nina shuts her eyes—a dangerous thing to do, with all these trucks and lorries hurtling past—but she only does it briefly, knowing it's no use. There's no shutting these thoughts out; they insist on their right to be heard. Just as she can no longer think of her mother without seeing a man's shadowy hands reaching round her neck, so she's unable to think of her own future life without seeing a pair of shoes tottering on the second to last rail, and the sea miles below, and the decision hardening in her brain. There will always be a part of her fainting with fear—and perverse desire—for the bleak, billowing expanse of her almost-grave.

She jumps when a car toots its horn, and clutches the little suitcase to her chest like a shield. It's all right, it's fine—the car accelerates and drives away without stopping—but it's a reminder that this is the main road into the city, and anyone coming from the ship is likely to pass this way. Nina glances over her shoulder and turns into the next side street.

The terraced houses on the left-hand side have been wiped out in the Blitz; the houses on the right are more or less intact, except for the odd boarded-up window. Two women in floral housecoats are talking over a low wall, and a gang of skinny kids is playing in the middle of the road, but no one takes any notice of Nina.

She walks and walks, taking turns at random, ducking past the running children, and the stray dogs, and the loiterers; barely noticing the red-brick houses she passes, the Irish pubs, the bookmakers, the pawnbrokers, the corner shops, the rattling bikes, the green buses and trams—on and on, trying hard not to think, until her feet are sore and she can't even tell which way the river lies. She gets lost, wilfully, and tells herself she doesn't care; that she was lost already; that nothing matters.

Which is all very well, but what does a lost soul actually do with herself, in practice? Nina considers the question. What if she were to lie down in the middle of the road with her arms outstretched? Fate could then decide whether to squash her flat with the Tate & Lyle truck, or have her scooped up by some unlikely saviour. She smiles faintly and decides she's not that defeated—not yet; it would be too embarrassing. Give her a few hours, and a bottle of cheap gin from the off-licence, and she might be persuaded.

For the time being, she can either carry straight on, or turn right into Bold Street, or turn left, up a flight of steps, to a church called Saint Luke's. She chooses the church. Her feet are tired, and she needs somewhere quiet where she can sit and think.

Even from the steps she catches the familiar bomb-site smell of damp plaster and charred wood, but it doesn't register; much of Liverpool smells the same. It's only when she reaches the doorway that she understands the building is a shell. There's nothing left, besides the Gothic Victorian walls: no stained-glass windows, no roof, no door, no pews. Nina sidles past the Danger of Falling Masonry sign, and wades down the central aisle through rubble and weeds. Jackdaws perch on fragments of ornate stone, but as she advances they flap up and away, through the open ceiling. The herring gull ignores her: he's too busy hopping about where the altar used to be, wrestling with a discarded chip wrapper.

Nina sits down with her back against a pillar. It's a hiding place of sorts, though there's no protection from the drizzle. There's a withered memorial wreath propped up against her pillar, and she tries to read the inscription, but the ink has run, and she can't make anything out.

At last she's free to rest her legs and close her eyes. She wonders what Dad is doing: whether or not he glimpsed her at the docks; what he's thinking if he did; what he's thinking if he didn't; whether he will collect her luggage and take it back to Cottenden.

What on earth possessed her to write to him, in the first place, before leaving Canada? Some deeply instilled, barely understood sense of duty, presumably, which insisted that her father must be her keeper again, now that her husband was dead-in-inverted-commas. She'd suspected it was a mistake, as soon as she'd posted the letter, and she'd known it for sure the moment she spotted his trilby hat amongst the hundreds of people milling about on the quay, and Mrs. Bell had said, "Can you see your father, dear?" and she'd heard herself say, "No."

It was easy enough to give him the slip. He'd been waiting at the gangplank nearest the bow of the ship, so she'd mingled with a group of passengers who were exiting via the one nearest the stern, shown her papers as briskly as possible, and resolved to abandon her luggage, apart from the small suitcase she'd taken with her on board. Mrs. Bell's voice had wailed, "Nina!" from somewhere on the upper deck, but she'd been too scared to turn round, even to wave. The American man was waddling up and down the dockside with a handful of tracts, and when he saw her he started forwards, crying, "Hey there!" but she'd elbowed her way through the crowds and broken into a run.

Nina tears at a clump of grass that's growing through a crack in the stone floor. Back at 7 Canal Road she could at least have a wash, a square meal, and a sleep, but then, she could get those things in prison, if she made up her mind to commit a felony, so it wasn't saying much. She won't go back to her father for anything; she would rather die.

—*Why?*

—*Because.*

—*No, go on. Why?*

—*Because everything about him is heavy as lead, that's why.*

It's a clumsy answer, but it will do. She knows what she means. When Nina thinks of her father, heaviness describes the sensation, precisely: the heaviness of his censure, of his sadness, of his secrets. She remembers the way his dark moods used to settle on her lungs and make it hard to breathe. God, even his love weighed a tonne— back in the olden days, when she had it.

Nina listens to the murmur of traffic outside the church and wonders about catching a bus, or tram, or train, and letting it whisk her off to . . . somewhere. Anywhere. After all, how *do* you go about beginning a new life? Who do you turn to for help? (Not for the first time she thinks, fleetingly, of Kate Nicholson, but that's an idiotic idea if ever there was one. Kate Nicholson, of all people . . .)

She opens the suitcase and feels for the wad of pounds sterling Guy had given her at Halifax. There wasn't much cash to spare, he'd admitted apologetically; everything they owned had been ploughed into the farm. Glumly, Nina counts her notes. There's enough here to tide her over for a week or two, but she must find a job, urgently; and a cheap place to stay, even more urgently; and something to eat and drink even more urgently than that . . .

There's a bar of chocolate tucked down the side of the suitcase. The chocolate, along with the pocket money and the fake death certificate, was her husband's idea of a parting gift. She'd been furious at the time ("As if I'm a child, to be pacified with treats!") and sworn never to touch it—but she wolfs it, now. So much for principles.

There's something else caught in the ripped lining of the suitcase. She feels around inside the hole and fishes out a pink envelope.

Nina stares for a moment. So *that's* where it was hiding. She slits the letter open with her thumb.

The war was at its peak the last time she saw Rose, in January '43. It was cold and dark at Buxton railway station, and Mrs. Allen had made a rabbit pie.

The letter begins *Dear Nina*, and it's nice to read those words in Rose's handwriting. They may be no more than a formality, of course—she's braced for that—but at least they have the ring of affection.

23A Hillier Street
Buxton
Derbyshire

December 2, 1945

Dear Nina,

I bet you weren't expecting to hear from me! If this letter reaches you (and it's a big "if" because I only have your old address, so I'm relying on your dad to be charitable and forward it), you might recognise my handwriting on the envelope and think, "Oh no! Not another harangue from yet another person who doesn't understand anything!" and chuck it on the fire. Actually, I wouldn't blame you if you did. I'm afraid I was rather hard on you the last time we met, and I shouldn't have let on to your dad about the guesthouse in Cheap Street. In my defence, Mum had made a superb rabbit pie in honour of your arrival, and I was upset about that, on

top of which, you and Guy were _very_ spoony that evening, and I felt such a gooseberry, standing around on
the station platform.

I still don't think it's a wonderful idea to run off
with other people's husbands, but I'm no longer in any
position to cast stones. I find myself, as the euphemism
goes, "in trouble," and it's a lonely place to be, and of the
various friends I've had over the years, you are the one I
long for the most. If that sounds faintly insulting ("one
Bad Woman seeks another Bad Woman for shared
confidences and self-recrimination"), it's not meant to.
Dear Nina, I know we've had our ups and downs over
the years, and sometimes I've hated you, and you've
probably hated me too, but at the same time I've always,
always loved you. Please believe that.

Peter is a married man, as well—he was in the
army, and we worked at the same anti-aircraft bat-
tery in Dorset, for a while—but the ending of my story
is even less respectable than yours, because Peter has
gone back to his wife and children. He has no idea I'm
pregnant, and I'm not going to tell him. As far as he's
concerned, we are two honourable people who resisted
our mutual attraction for five years, excepting only for
fifteen minutes in the back of a Ford supply truck at the
end of an extremely drunken VJ-day party. (Believe it
or not, it's true: aside from that, we didn't so much as
hold hands for _the entire duration of the war!_) Neither
of us mentioned the "incident" the following day—I'm
not sure how much he remembered—and a few days
later we parted, like the old friends we'd always been,
and he went off to Scotland to reunite with his beloved
wife and their two sons.

The baby is due early May, and you can imagine how Mum and Dad feel about it. I almost added, "I don't know what I'm going to do," because that's what people say when they feel this desperate, but actually I know <u>exactly</u> what I'm going to do. I'm going to stay here in Buxton, as dependant on my parents as if I were little again, only <u>then</u> I was free and loved, whereas <u>now</u> I am bowed beneath the weight of their unspeakable generosity, and my own utter awfulness.

What does it take to pass beyond the reach of forgiveness? One too many drinks and a moment of madness—that's all! Oh, they <u>say</u> they forgive me, but Mum has a way of tightening her lips whenever she speaks to me now, and Dad can hardly meet my eye. Sometimes I find myself wishing they'd beat me or something, because I could protest against that—fight back. They've never been cruel, though; just disappointed. Eternally, incurably, grindingly, horribly, crushingly, dully disappointed.

They've concocted a face-saving story, which goes, "Poor Rose married, on impulse, while she was away with the ATS, only to be widowed a week later when her husband was knocked off his bicycle." (There's a much, <u>much</u> more detailed version, which I won't bore you with.) Mum has even provided me with a brass wedding ring, and I'm not allowed to leave the house unless it's jammed onto the appropriate finger. Heaven knows whether the neighbours really believe this tragic tale, but they've been kind enough to pretend they do—so far. Let's hope nobody ever asks to see the marriage certificate! Frankly, I wouldn't put it past Mum to mock one up.

Peter and I were idiots, but when I think of every-thing that's happened over the last six years—when I think what Hitler has done to the Jews in Europe—it doesn't strike me as the worst crime in the world. I put that to Dad the other day (the Nuremberg trials had just begun, and I'd been reading the prosecutor's open-ing speech in the paper, and I suppose I had a rush of blood to the head)—but do you know what he said in reply? He said a sin was a sin, whichever way you look at it, and that I was on "a slippery slope"! Meaning what?? An unmarried mother today; a mass-murdering fascist dictator tomorrow?

Oh Nina, I wish we were kids again. You probably don't wish any such thing, but from where I'm sitting (at the kitchen table, where Mum is peeling potatoes, Dad is drinking a cup of tea, and the only person to have spoken within the last hour is me, when I looked up from writing this letter and said, "Hasn't it gone dark? Looks like it might snow!" and nobody made <u>any</u> response <u>at all</u>), childhood looks like the Garden of Eden. Do you ever think about your treehouse? I do. We were so happy, sitting up there with a stash of wormy apples, poring over your dad's atlas. (We probably thought we weren't happy, but we were.) I think of all the things we wanted to do with our lives, and the places we planned to go, and it makes me want to cry.

Could I see you sometime, Nina? It's probably a hopeless request: even if this letter reaches you, you're probably far away by now and busy. Perhaps you and Guy are married now, with a child of your own? Perhaps you'd rather put the past, including me, behind you. All these things are more than likely, but on the off-chance that you do read this, and you're not on the other side of the world or anything, and Guy (and the baby?!) can spare you ... well. You know where to find me.

I was going to sign off in our secret code, but I couldn't remember how it went, and then I actually did start to snivel, which led to Dad shoving his chair back and taking his tea in the other room, and Mum saying, "It's a bit late for tears!" in her new, hard voice. Oh God, Nina, they are being so good to me, and at the same time so bloody, bloody awful.

I wish you would come.

Fondest love,
Rose

   . . .

IT'S GOING DARK BY THE time Nina turns into steep, narrow Hillier Street and makes her way to 23A. Mrs. Allen opens the door. She's dressed to go out, in a navy-blue coat and a hat made of feathers, and her expression is politely blank, until she sees who it is, and after that it's merely blank.

"Nina."

The rain has grown heavier and windier, over the course of the day. Nina's hat blew off outside Buxton station and rolled along the gutter, and she was too tired to chase after it. As she walked through the familiar town, she avoided looking in shop windows for fear of her own reflection.

"Nina?" Rose calls excitedly from somewhere inside the house. Her father emerges from one of the downstairs rooms, also coated and hatted, and joins his wife at the door. He just about manages a nod of greeting, though it's little more than a twitch of his chin.

Neither of Rose's parents invite her inside, but they don't shut her out, either.

"Nina? Is it really you?"

Rose is coming down the stairs, one at a time, holding tightly to the banister. She squeezes past her parents and comes to stand in the doorway.

"Hello!" says Nina, looking up at her friend from street level.

"It *is* you!"

Rose places her hands on Nina's shoulders. She looks younger than twenty-six; too young to be so unmistakably pregnant. Her face has taken on the soft, smudgy look of a small child's, and her mouth, without lipstick, has a defenceless air. At the same time, she seems as weary as old age, in her shapeless woollen dress and carpet slippers.

"I read your letter today," says Nina.

"I posted it in early December."

"I know."

"It's now mid-March."

"I know."

They laugh in the old, secretive way that belongs to their treehouse days, and draw one another into a hug. Nina hasn't laughed like this for years; not since the two of them trained their telescope on the Athertons' bedroom window, and made bird noises to baffle Mr. Lawson.

"Come in, out of the rain."

Rose takes her by the hand and pulls her inside. Mr. and Mrs. Allen are forced to make way.

"Nothing has changed since I wrote to you," Rose whispers in Nina's ear, as she drags her down the hall to the kitchen. "Nothing!"

Nina is worried about her dirty shoes traipsing over the clean carpet, but it's impossible to resist Rose's impetus.

"Everything's changed for me," she whispers back. "We went to Canada, after the war, and—and Guy died—"

"Oh, Nina, Nina!"

Rose presses her hand. Their talk is rapid and sparse; they are like prisoners either side of a wire fence, snatching at an illicit opportunity to confer. The parents follow them into the kitchen.

Mr. Allen stands squarely in the doorway. "Now then," he begins, firmly.

"I needn't stay long..." Nina pleads.

"Nina's staying for a few nights," says Rose, firmly. "I'll put the camp-bed up in my room; neither of you need worry about a thing. You get off to your bridge party."

The parents exchange a sharp glance, and Nina understands what Rose meant when she wrote about her mother's mouth having tightened. It snaps shut like a trap now, which it hardly ever did in the old days; only when she was extremely cross.

Of course, the Allens lost their son, Michael, in '42. That, along with Rose's *trouble*, is enough, and more than enough, to explain it. Perhaps it's crossed their minds that a kinder God would have arranged things differently; would have preserved the son and discarded the daughter.

There's a large framed photograph of Michael in his Merchant Navy uniform, hanging in the hall, and three smaller photos on a shelf in here, alongside the egg-timers and recipe books: Michael as a gawky schoolboy; Michael as a young dairyman, with a newborn calf in his arms; Michael as a bridegroom, standing alongside his new wife, Lyn, of black-cherry-dress fame. There is nothing of Rose: no photographs, no magazines, no heaps of half-dried laundry, no hairbrushes snarled up with blonde hairs. It's a colder and more disciplined kitchen than it was when Nina last saw it, eight years ago. All the washing and drying-up has been done, and the damp cloths are folded neatly over the side of the draining-board. A pair of freshly polished shoes sits on a sheet of newspaper beside the sink. The clock on the wall has a noisy *tick-tock*; bossy as a metronome. The only unruly item in the room is the dented pan on the stove, which sizzles and gives off a smell of onions and dripping. Every now and then it spits and snaps, and a drop of oil splashes the wall-tiles.

"We need to get going!" says Mr. Allen angrily.

"We do!" his wife concurs. "Sid and Ethel hate to start late."

"Go, then!" Rose's hooded eyes look contemptuous, though they may be simply tired. She adds a shake of pepper to the onions, and gives them a stir, before sitting down heavily at the kitchen table. "*Go*! What are you worrying about? That Nina's bad example is going to corrupt me, or that mine is going to corrupt her?"

"Rose!" The parents protest as one.

"We're both hardened sinners, so you might as well leave us to it."

Mrs. Allen takes time to primp her feathered hat and straighten her gloves, as if to make it clear that she's only leaving because she chooses to do so, and not because her daughter so obviously wishes it. Mr. Allen gets upset, in a restrained way, because he can't find the good umbrella—*no, no, not that one, the sturdy, black one*—which is eventually located in the umbrella-stand, in the hall. ("Of all places," mutters Rose.) At long last, they go.

Neither Nina nor Rose speaks for a while, after the front door has slammed shut. They sit and look at one another, as the tension ebbs and their shoulders drop. Eventually they smile, and Rose gets up to put the kettle on.

"What can I do to help?" asks Nina.

"You could put some bread under the grill. Is fried onions on toast all right, for supper? I know it's a bit odd, but it's all I seem to want at the moment." She points accusingly at her bump. "Honestly, it's true. I've dreamt about onions and dripping for the last three nights in a row. I made them for breakfast yesterday, but Dad went up the wall; he said that having the kitchen stink of onions at eight o'clock in the morning was the last straw."

"They smell good to me."

"I like them a little bit burnt . . . ?"

"Me too."

Nina sets a couple of trays with knives, forks, and plates, while Rose makes mugs of tea and piles the onions on top of the toast. This time yesterday, Nina was poking at a shrimp cocktail while Mrs. Bell made small talk, and the religious American man eyed her up across the dining-room, and the ocean seethed outside the windows.

"It's good to see you, Rose."

Nina picks up one of the trays and follows her friend through to the sitting-room.

"Ditto. Switch the fire on, will you? I'll draw the curtains."

. . .

". . . ALTHOUGH IT WASN'T REALLY TILL Canada that things started to go wrong between us, and even then, I thought we'd come through it together."

"I don't see you as a farmer."

"Well, no. And then, one night in February, right out of the blue—"

"Guy died?"

"Yes, he . . . It was appendicitis."

"Gosh, that's unbelievable. Awful. After all those years in Bomber Command."

They slump side by side on the sofa, sated with talk. Rose has described her time in the ATS, the deaths of various mutual acquaintances ("Poor old Harold Lamb! You remember him? In an air-raid, of all things!"), her friendship with married Peter, and the pregnancy. In return, Nina has told—if not everything, then nearly everything. As much as she can risk. She hadn't foreseen how tempting it would be to tell the whole truth.

Sometimes the wind tosses the rain against the window with such violence that it sounds like a hooligan chucking fistfuls of stones. Nina thinks of Mr. and Mrs. Allen struggling to and from the bridge party beneath their sturdy black umbrella, and wonders whether her presence at 23A Hillier Street will make them anxious to come home all the sooner, or to stay away all the longer. She still finds it difficult to grasp the fact that she's a social outcast. One minute she was a pretty child, and adorable by definition; next she was a woman stepping out of line, and everyone hated her.

Not quite everyone.

Rose slides right down in her seat, until her outstretched feet are almost touching the glowing bars of the electric heater.

"That thing Guy said about your mother..."

Nina turns her head, and there's a long pause.

"You're remembering our séance, aren't you?"

"Yes."

They look at one another uneasily.

"Do you think there's any truth in it?"

"N-no..." Rose frowns. "Except... there was one time, years ago, when I was staying with my brother. We were chatting over breakfast, about this and that, and I referred to your mum having died in a road accident, and I remember... I don't exactly know what I remember... just the way Mike and Lyn glanced at one another, I suppose, as if they knew a different story. But when I asked why they'd looked like that, they said, 'Like what?'—you know how grown-ups are—and I never got to the bottom of it."

Nina nods and runs her fingers over her throat. It doesn't occur to her to say, *We're the grown-ups now.*

Rose laces her fingers and rests them on her bump. "I think you should telephone your dad. I'm not saying you should arrange to see him or anything, but you should let him know you're safe."

Nina sighs heavily as Rose goes on, "He might think... Goodness knows what he might think, especially if he discovers your luggage was on board. He might think you've chucked yourself into the sea, or something."

"Hmm."

If Nina were to stare at the electric heater for long enough, could she hypnotise herself? A good life would be one that kept her right here, on this spot, forever.

Rose struggles to her feet ("God, I'm like a beached whale!") and holds out her hands.

"Come on, get it over with, and then I'll make some more toast."

. . .

THE ALLENS' TELEPHONE IS ON the hall table, underneath the large picture of Michael in his uniform. Rose has turned the hall light on, but Nina turns it off again; she can see well enough by the glow from the sitting-room and kitchen. When the hall light is on, her reflection becomes visible in the glass of the photograph frame, and her features mingle weirdly with those of the dead young man.

It seems to take ages for the call to connect, and Nina's spirits are starting to lift—*at least I tried*—when the mechanism clicks and a voice says, "Yes? Who is this?"

"Dad, it's me."

There's no direct reply, only the burble of what sounds like several male voices in discussion. No particular word or phrase is audible to Nina, but the tone is serious; possibly worried. Who are these people? It doesn't sound like much of a party. And why on earth has her father invited people round? He hates any sort of "do"—or he always used to.

"Dad? Is that you? Are you there?"

The first voice resumes, loud and clear. "Am I speaking to Nina? Mrs. Nina Nicholson?"

"Yes, but . . . Who am I speaking to?"

Another bout of background conversation, and then the man clears his throat and says, "Ah, good evening, Mrs. Nicholson. This is Sergeant Murray. We've been wondering how to trace you."

The police officer tells his tale, and Nina listens.

Occasionally she murmurs, "Yes," or "No," or "I see." At one point she tries to sit down on the floor, but the telephone cord won't stretch that far, so she stands instead, with her back pressed to the wall.

Rose hovers, to begin with. "What's happened?" she mouths. "Is everything all right?" She doesn't receive a direct answer, but she must glean something, because after a while she backs off, in silence, to the sitting-room. Once or twice she reappears in the doorway, pinching and plucking at her lips, as the news unfolds across Nina's face.

. . .

NINA LIES ON THE CAMP-BED, staring at the white flowers on Rose's bedroom curtains. They stand out clearly against the blue background, even though it's dark, because of the street lamp right outside the Allens' house. One of the flowers, which repeats several times throughout the fabric, used to look like a friendly elephant, but now it resembles the face of the fat American man. Nina tries to see it as something else—these curtains are familiar, from summer holidays of old, so they should contain all sorts of patterns and possibilities—but she can't get rid of him.

Rose is tidying downstairs. Nina listens to the clink of cutlery, and the gush of water in the sink. Later on she hears Mr. and Mrs. Allen's latchkey in the door, and Rose hurrying to meet them, and the excitable hum of their voices. They are very much upset, of course—she can hear the tone of the parents' questions, and Rose's attempted answers—but they are also a family bonded (for the time being, anyway) by the illicit pleasure of Being Shocked.

Someone puts the kettle on. Someone else—Mrs. Allen—creeps upstairs and whispers through the bedroom door, "Shall I bring you some tea?" and Nina whispers back, "No, thank you." Mrs. Allen lingers on the landing for a moment, as if unsure what to do for the best.

An hour or so later, Rose tiptoes into the bedroom and starts to undress. "Nina?" she whispers, but Nina is curled up on her side by then, pretending to sleep.

It's not until the early hours, when the curtain flowers have lightened from beige to cream, that Nina, hearing Rose toss and turn, can bring herself to say, "Are you awake?"

"Yes," comes the reply, straightaway. "Bloody heartburn. Are you all right?"

Nina can't answer that. Rose's mattress squeaks as she levers herself up and out of bed. She takes a seat on the dressing-table stool and looks down on the camp-bed.

"You're cold," Nina observes, at eye level with her friend's bare ankles, and the shivering hem of her nightie.

Rose shrugs and says, "Will you have to go to Cottenden?"

"I suppose so. The funeral and everything . . ."

"I'll come with you."

"I can't ask that. In your—"

"Please don't say *in your condition*. Of course I'll come."

The air is heavy with questions. Rose deserves to know what happened—all she's had so far are eavesdroppings—but she's too tactful to ask. Nina turns onto her back and searches for the American man in the curtains. There he is.

"There was only one witness—other than the bloke who was actually driving the car. Do you know who it was? Have a guess."

"Who?"

"Kate Nicholson. She and Dad must have formed some sort of—friendship—I think, after Guy and I . . ."

A charged silence follows. It seems inevitable that one of them will ask, *What are you thinking?* but neither of them does.

Nina goes on, "Sergeant Murray said that the two of them—Dad and Mrs. Nicholson—were together at 7 Canal Road, but they had a falling out, and Dad stormed out of the house. She says she left shortly afterwards, and as she turned the corner near the humpback bridge she saw him step into the main road, right into the path of a speeding car."

"Oh, Nina."

"One second he was there; then there was an almighty bang, and he was gone. Except, of course, when she reached the junction, she could see that he wasn't *gone*, like some kind of neat magic trick; he was way down the road, in the hedge, and Sergeant Murray advised me not to request to view the remains, because they're not—" She pauses, out of breath, and her voice wobbles. "I wasn't *going* to request to view them. It hadn't even crossed my mind."

Rose leans down to touch Nina's hair. She's crying. "It's an awful road. There were always dead rabbits and hedgehogs and things. And there was that summer when Miss Riley's cat got run over."

Nina nods. She starts to say something, then stops, then starts again.

"Apparently he turned to face the car as he stepped into the road. That's what the driver told the police." Her voice, after its brief wobble, has gone flat. "He said Dad was staring straight at him, and that there was no expression on his face."

One of Rose's tears drops onto the pillow. Nina reaches her hand out from under the blanket and strokes her friend's ice-cold foot.

It's all too obvious where the conversation goes next. Nina will have to say, *Do you think it was my fault?* and Rose will have to reply,

Of course it wasn't your fault! and they will both think (though nei-ther of them will say): *Who knows?*

Nina gives Rose a gentle shove.

"Your teeth are chattering. Go to bed."

"I'm fine."

"Go! Please."

Rose wipes her face on her sleeve and stands up.

"Okay. But I'm right here if you need me."

"I know. Thank you."

Rose lies back down with a groan, and the bedsprings creak under her weight.

"Kate Nicholson asked Sergeant Murray to pass a message to me," Nina says, as if it's a mere afterthought.

"Oh?"

"Yes. Just in case he managed to trace me. She said that I mustn't blame myself, on any account; that Dad's . . . that his *problems* . . . went deep, and that they weren't caused by me."

"That was kind of her, I suppose?" says Rose.

"She is kind."

Nina turns her face to the blue-and-white curtains. *Kind, yes,* she tells her American man. *But is she also truthful?*

The blowsy white flowers repeat, over and again, and the man winks knowingly, over and again—and that's all she's getting for an answer.

EPILOGUE

Kate

June 8, 1947

MY FAMILY SAY I MUST BE A SAINT TO AGREE TO TRAVEL ALL the way down from Carlisle to Lincoln to meet Nina. That's not a wholehearted compliment, in case you're wondering: by *saint* they mean "pushover." Pip has already told me that he wants to visit RAF Charlwood—the ex-airbase where his father spent most of the war— so when I write back to Nina, I suggest this as a meeting-point, and she concurs by return of post.

"You're not taking my grandson to meet that woman," my mother declares. "That's the last thing he needs."

I've already given Pip the option to stay at home, but he insists on coming. We're going to have a half-term motoring holiday—just the two of us, plus the dog—including a brief stop at Charlwood, during which he's excused from making conversation with his father's other widow, so long as he manages a polite hello and goodbye.

Carlisle, Pearson's Books, Ron, and the rest will cope without us for a few days.

. . .

NINA IS SITTING ON A stretch of overgrown grass beside the boundary fence, squinting at the flat land and the enormous sky. It's a bright day, and she appears to have forgotten her sunglasses. A light coat and a straw sun hat are lying on the ground beside her.

The prospect of this meeting hasn't put me in the best of moods—I snapped at Pip on the drive down, because he got the map upside down and took us on an unwarranted detour to Market Rasen—but I soften when I see her. There's something about the hasty way she struggles to her feet, which makes me want to say, *Don't look so worried! It's fine; everything's fine.*

"Hello," she says, guardedly.

"Hello, Nina."

Pip mutters something under his breath, and wanders off to look at the abandoned airfield. We watch him dawdling along the fence, running his fingers over its diamond-shaped gaps, as a light wind hums through the steel wires and ruffles his hair. His eye is caught by an aeroplane carcass at the other end of the runway. Both its wings are missing and the black livery is patchy and rusting.

"Lancaster?" I ask, as if I didn't know, and Nina nods.

It's Shirley who sets us at our ease, by yanking on her lead and snuffling madly at Nina's bare toes.

"Hey!" I object. "You'll have my arm out of its socket!"

Nina bends to stroke her. "Hello there, you ugly old mug. I don't suppose you remember me." As she straightens, she tells me, "It was good of you to take her on. I couldn't have risked it, really; not with Evie around. Rose's baby, I mean."

Nina's face reddens as she stumbles on her words, and she tries to hide it by fussing over the dog again, but Shirley has lost interest. She's spotted the rows of Nissen huts behind us, and is throttling herself on the lead in a frenzy of curiosity.

"These were the WAAF quarters," says Nina, as we reach the nearest hut. She speaks with a faintly apologetic air, as if I'm well within my rights to be bored or offended by the sound of her voice.

"You lived in one of these? Goodness. It must have been a bit bleak in the winter."

"Oh, well. It was all right, really."

The hut is locked. Nina swings the padlock absently, so that it clangs against the door. I peer through one of the windows, framing my eyes with my hands, but it's too dark and cobwebbed to make much out. I think I see a metal stove and an overturned chair.

"Is Rose doing well? And the baby?"

"Yes, thanks. We like living in Lincoln, and we've both found part-time work, so between us we manage to earn our keep and look after Evie. It's not aways easy, but—"

She dismisses the rest of the sentence with a wave, as much as to say, *never mind all that.* Her worried gaze follows Pip's progress along the edge of the airfield, until she catches me watching her, and brightens, self-consciously.

"Thanks ever so much for coming all this way," she says. "There's something I need to tell you. It's . . ." She swallows. "Well, it's about Guy. Sometimes I feel I'll go mad, if I don't share it, and you of all people have the right to know. It didn't seem right to put it in a letter, or tell you over the telephone."

We strike out through the long grass, letting Shirley dictate the way. *Oh Nina,* I think, *there's nothing you can tell me about Guy that will surprise me.* I'd say it out loud, if it didn't sound so patronising; it's what I believe. How long did I know Guy? Thirty years? She was married to him for two. I bet she's going to tell me something conscience-cleansing, like *He never stopped loving you,* or *His dying words were of Pip.*

Shirley rolls on her back in a sort of ecstasy—she seems to like the long grass—and we stop to wait.

If Nina's presence is upsetting, to a degree, it's not because of the affair with Guy, it's because of the subtle resemblances to her father. By and large, I think, she is her mother's child. The shape of her face, the colour of her hair, the sense of humour that narrows her eyes: these are Teodora's, in as far as I can presume to judge, from one glimpse of a crumpled photograph. Henry lurks, nonetheless, when his daughter's face is tilted at a particular angle, or when she stiffens certain muscles in her jaw, or when she wrings her hands with embarrassment.

I hope we don't have to talk about Henry; or not much, anyway. Over the last few months I've rediscovered sleep, but I'm still haunted by nightmares, in which my furious teeth feel the spongy yield of his lower lip all over again, and my fingernails puncture his cheeks and pool with his blood. In my sleep I relive the weepy shout with which he shoves me aside and rushes from the house. Sometimes I dream I'm showing George Tyler's letter to the police, to the newspapers—to Nina—saying, *Look! Proof!* but I can't, because Henry took it with him. It must have whirled from his limp grasp when the car hit, and the blue ink could not have survived the rain.

Besides which, of course, the letter wasn't proof of anything.

Deb thinks Nina ought to be told, and sometimes I agree; sometimes I don't. I look at her now, smiling round at Pip as he runs to catch up, and try to imagine myself saying, *Nina? There are a couple of things you ought to know about your father . . .*

I won't do it. I can't, and if Deb demands to know why not, I'll say, *Because she's thinner and paler than she was, and she's got more than enough to grieve for, as it is.*

"Mum?"

Pip is scrupulous in addressing me, and me alone. Still, he looks pleased and bright.

"Look, Mum, I found this under the fence."

It's an aluminium cigarette-lighter similar—though not identical—to the one Guy used to use, before he switched to matches and a pipe.

It's stamped with the RAF eagle motif, and their motto: *Per ardua ad astra.*

"'Through adversity to the stars,'" Pip translates, a tad smugly. He does Latin at his new school. "Can I keep it?"

"I don't see why not."

I hand him Shirley's lead, and the two of them break into a run, heading for the lane that opens out beyond the empty WAAF huts. It's more like a tunnel than a lane, with the elm trees arching and meeting overhead. Their teeming leaves rustle in the wind, and splashes of sunlight break the green shadows along the pathway.

"That's Roman Lane," says Nina. "It goes all the way to Lincoln, if you fancy a walk? I could treat you both to tea at Annabelle's Café, and if you've got time you could come and say hello to Rose and Evie . . ."

I'm about to object, on the grounds that the car is parked here, but she adds, in a subdued voice, "Sometimes it's easier to talk, when you're walking. Do you know what I mean?"

Pip lets Shirley loose. It's good to see him running, and teasing her with sticks. Things have been better since the move to Carlisle, and especially since last Christmas, when he finally agreed to look at his father's farewell letter. I don't know what Guy wrote—Pip didn't tell, and I didn't ask—but whatever it was, it drew the poison.

"Pip seems . . . happy?" Nina suggests, cautiously.

"Things have been better for him, since his father died. Simpler." I touch Nina's arm by way of apology. "I don't mean to sound cold-hearted—it's awful, what happened—I'm just thinking of it from Pip's point of view."

"That's all right—but what do you mean?"

Pip is out of earshot, but I'm still careful to lower my voice.

"He told the boys at his new school that his father had been killed during the war. I kept quiet when I found out; I thought he'd be mortified if he knew I knew. But then, one afternoon, he invited his friend Tom round for tea, and referred to it quite openly, in front of me.

When my father's plane was shot down . . . He's put Guy's photograph up in his room—the one of him in uniform—and . . . oh, I don't know. Sometimes I think he's persuaded himself it's the truth. It's as if he's thinking, *A death is a death, and the cause is neither here nor there, especially when he <u>could</u> have been shot down, so easily, so many times.*"

"Whereas if Guy were still alive . . ." Nina waits, inviting me to finish the thought.

". . . then the self-deception might be harder to pull off. A death is a death, but desertion is something else altogether."

I'm not sure I'm making sense—I've never voiced these ideas before—but Nina is nodding intently.

"Is it easier for *you*, knowing that Guy is dead?" she wonders. "Tell me honestly; you won't hurt my feelings."

I consider the question. "Actually, yes. It *is* easier. When Guy left, the pain was all-consuming; it was like being infected by some hideous, unpredictable virus. Knowing he's dead . . . it's a sharper, cleaner wound. Something is finished. I don't have to wonder all the time what he's doing: whether he's happy; whether I'm glad or sad that he's gone; how much I hate him, how much I still love him . . . Oh dear, you look shocked. I'm not saying these things to hurt you."

"No, no . . ."

Pip is limping gamely towards us with a bead of blood rolling down his shin and Shirley at his heels.

"It's nothing," he announces airily, before we've had time to ask. "I tripped and fell quite hard, and there was quite a lot of blood, but I'll be fine."

He holds his leg out and lifts the hem of his shorts, so that I can inspect the damage.

"I reckon you'll live," I conclude, mussing his hair.

"Nasty, though," says Nina, in a much more flattering tone of concern. "Have you got a handkerchief, or anything? Here, take mine. We can pop into my flat, when we reach Lincoln, and dress it properly."

The handkerchief is plain white, with no unmanly frills. Pip accepts it with a gruff "Thanks," and ties it round his knee. A second later he's off again, darting through the wavy shadows like a fish in clear water.

"What was it you wanted to tell me?" I ask. "Here am I, rattling on; it's supposed to be you doing the talking."

Nina looks towards the trees, as if she's spotted something in the fields, although there's nothing but acres of rippling wheat.

"I feel silly now, bringing you all the way from Carlisle just to say that Guy still loved you. You and Pip, both."

We smile at one another quickly; a little bashfully.

"It's not silly, it's kind."

Nina seems deflated, all the same, and we're both stuck for words. The silence grows too deep, and carries on for too long. Eventually I think to ask about Evie (*Does she sleep well? Eat well? Does she have any words yet?*), and once we're done with Evie, we move on to other topics: the aftermath of war (of course); Henry's death (briefly); my job at the bookshop and Nina's job at a gentlemen's outfitters; the terrible winter we've emerged from ("That snow in January!" Nina exclaims. "It was like being back in Canada!"). We talk about the wildflowers along the lane and the birdsong that fills the trees. We're fairly certain we can hear chaffinches and song thrushes, and very certain about the wood pigeons.

Nina tugs at the cow parsley, ripping a lacy flower from its stalk.

"There's no such thing as a happy ending, is there?" she asks, suddenly. "Or rather, there are lots of so-called happy endings, all through life, but they're never *actually* conclusive. They're never the be-all and end-all they claim to be."

"How d'you mean?"

"Oh, I don't know. I feel like I've been waiting all my life for this great moment of resolution, where everything finally slots into place and I know what's what . . . The Kiss, The Wedding. Birth, Death,

Victory in Europe, the A-bomb . . . whatever it may be. These momentous events happen, and every time I think, *This is it, at last!* but then everything gets shuffled up again, like the pieces in a kaleidoscope, and nothing ever stays the same. Do you know what I mean?"

I study her, through the corner of my eye.

"You're settled for the moment though, with Rose and Evie?"

"Yes, *for the moment*. But Rose has met this chap at work. He's sweet, and I'm happy for her, but there's bound to come a day when she wants to marry, and then I'll have to move on, and it's just . . . it's wearying. When does it ever *end*?"

The lane is opening out now, as the trees dwindle and the towers of Lincoln Cathedral come into view. Pip crawls through the hedge with Shirley in tow, his hair full of leaves and bits of twigs, and takes hold of my hand with that unthinking, childish instinct he's beginning to lose.

"You're right," I tell Nina. "There's just no let-up. *Life will be the death of us*, to quote someone wittier than me."

"Who?"

"I don't know, but I can't have made it up myself. It's too true."

She laughs, as if I've said something comforting and wise, which I'm afraid I haven't, at all. It's perfectly idiotic to be flooded with hope on the basis of such passing things as a shared joke, and the prospect of tea in a café, and Pip's tuneless whistling, but I'm not sure either of us can help it. Perhaps it's for the best.

This time tomorrow we may be unhappy all over again—who knows?—but here we are for now, strolling in a friendly silence with our coats and hats over our arms, and the summer sunshine warm in our hair.

 READER'S GUIDE

1. How did the prologue set you up for the rest of the novel?

2. How do you think the backdrop of the Second World War motivates the actions of the main characters?

3. There are many strong settings in the novel: London, small English villages, an RAF airbase, and backcountry Canada. Did you have a favorite setting?

4. What did you think of the choice to alternate chapters and change POV? How did this influence the way the story was revealed?

5. Purple hyacinths populate the novel—what do you think they symbolize? Did their meaning evolve as you read?

6. The sable coat from the title is encountered by both women. What does it reveal about each character?

7. Over the course of the story, which character surprised you most? In what ways did your perception of the character change?

8. Letters appear throughout the novel—why do you think the author chose to include this form of writing?

9. What role do secrets play in this story? In your own life, what's the biggest secret you've ever uncovered?

10. Why do you think Kate's story is told in the first person, while Nina's is told in the third person?

11. The book leaves Nina and Kate in June 1947. How do you picture their futures?

12. Did you choose sides? If so, are you Team Nina or Team Kate?

❋ ACKNOWLEDGEMENTS ❋

AS ALWAYS, A SPECIAL THANK YOU TO MY AGENT IN THE UK, Joanna Swainson, who has been such a supportive friend over the years. Huge thanks as well to my US agent, Sarah Levitt, who is always a joy to work with.

Thank you to the whole Tin House family: first and foremost my inspirational editor, Masie Cochran, but also Win McCormack, Craig Popelars, Becky Kraemer, Beth Steidle, Nanci McCloskey, Dassi Zeidel, Allison Dubinsky, Alyssa Ogi, Elizabeth DeMeo, Jacqui Teruya, and Jae Nichelle.

Thank you to my pal and fellow writer, Kath Reed, for all her wise words and insights.

Much love and thanks to my family, especially Chris, Isabelle, Stephen, Mum, Dad and Sarah.

More Gothic Gems *by* Elizabeth Brooks

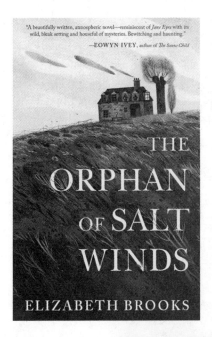

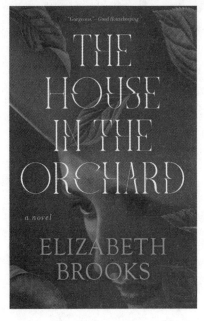

The Orphan of Salt Winds

ELIZABETH BROOKS'S GRIPPING DEBUT MIRRORS ITS marshy landscape—full of twists and turns and moored in a tangle of family secrets. A gothic, psychological mystery and atmospheric coming-of-age story, *The Orphan of Salt Winds* is the portrait of a woman haunted by the place she calls home.

"Reminiscent of *Jane Eyre* with its wild, bleak setting and houseful of mysteries. . . . Bewitching and haunting."
—EOWYN IVEY, author of *The Snow Child*

Available wherever books and ebooks are sold

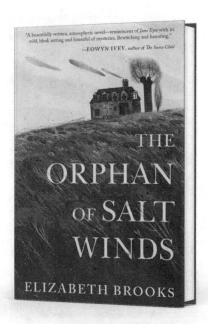

The Whispering House

IN *THE WHISPERING HOUSE*, ELIZABETH BROOKS WEAVES a simmering, propulsive tale of art, sisterhood, and all-consuming love: the ways it can lead us toward tenderness, nostalgia, and longing, as well as shocking acts of violence.

> "Eerie and addictive. . . . Like *Wuthering Heights*, *The Whispering House* is a melancholy novel, its characters filled with dark longings."
> —*THE NEW YORK TIMES BOOK REVIEW*

Available wherever books and ebooks are sold

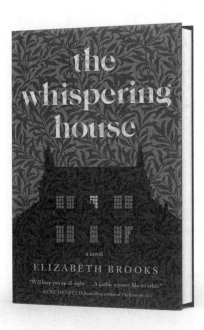

The House in the Orchard

WITH EACH PSYCHOLOGICALLY GRIPPING TURN, *The House in the Orchard* masterfully explores the blurred lines between truth and manipulation, asking us who we can trust, how to tell guilt from forgiveness, and whether we can ever really separate true love from destruction.

> "Reading this one feels like wandering darkened hallways with a candle flickering in a ghostly breeze.... A gorgeous historical novel."
> — *GOOD HOUSEKEEPING*

Available wherever books and ebooks are sold

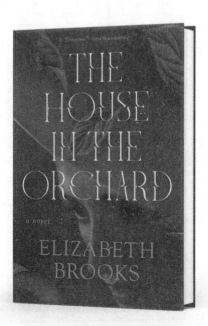

Elizabeth Brooks is the author of *The Orphan of Salt Winds*, *The Whispering House*, and *The House in the Orchard*. She is from Chester, England, graduated from Cambridge University, and resides on the Isle of Man with her husband and two children.